PRAISE FROM PREVIOUS WORK:

"If her first novel, *Hoot to Kill*, is any indication, Karen Dudley has a bright future ahead in the mystery genre."
—*Winnipeg Free Press*

"Karen Dudley's *Hoot to Kill* is a refreshing blend of murder, environmental infighting and owl lore. . . . the discerning reader will welcome Robyn, a bright and funny addition to Canadian crime fiction."
—Gail Bowen, author of *Verdict in Blood*

". . . feel-good, crack-paced, chuckly and informative . . . tongue-in-cheek flavour."
—*Quill & Quire*

"Dudley writes her characters with wit, realism and charm."
—*Canadian Bookseller*

"I'll look forward to more Devara . . ."
—*Prairie Fire*

"In this impressive debut novel, Dudley has created an ecological murder mystery that has a firm eye on popular culture."
—*Uptown*

Hoot to Kill, the first in the Robyn Devara series, is an Arthur Ellis Award for Best First Crime Novel nominee.

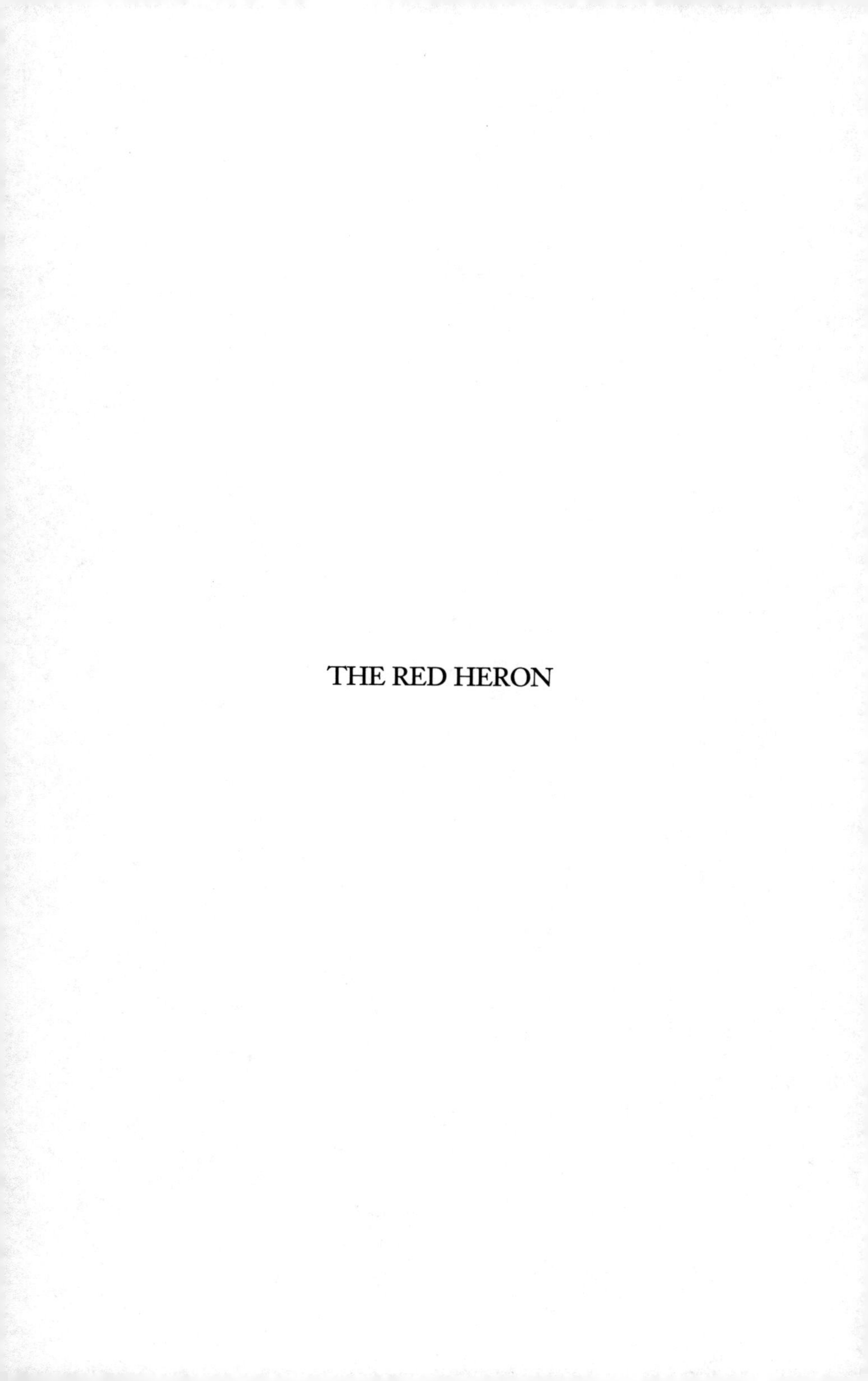

THE RED HERON

A ROBYN DEVARA MYSTERY

The Red Heron

BY KAREN DUDLEY

The Red Heron

published by Ravenstone
an imprint of Turnstone Press
607 – 100 Arthur Street
Artspace Building
Winnipeg, Manitoba
R3B 1H3 Canada
www.TurnstonePress.com

Turnstone Press gratefully acknowledges the assistance of the Canada Council for the Arts, the Manitoba Arts Council and the Government of Canada through the Book Publishing Industry Development Program for our publishing activities.

Canada

Cover design and artwork: Doowah Design

Interior design: Manuela Dias

This book was printed and bound in Canada by
Friesens for Turnstone Press.

Canadian Cataloguing in Publication Data

Dudley, Karen.

The red heron

ISBN 0-88801-240-3

I. Title.

PS8557.U279R44 1999 C813'.54 C99-920155-7
PR9199.3.D8317R44 1999

with love to my dad,
for Mary Poppins

and my mum,
for Old Possum's Book of Practical Cats

Table of Contents

ACKNOWLEDGMENTS

ALTHOUGH THIS IS a work of fiction, I have tried to write the science as accurately as possible. Because of this, some readers may be amazed at the depth of my knowledge. Ha! Perhaps instead they should be impressed by those helpful folk who are, first, experts in their field, and second, willing to talk with me about their work. Many thanks to Don Harron, Sheila Leggett, and Patricia Foo for information about environmental consulting; Neil Wandler and Gary Byrtus for telling me about pesticides and contaminated sites; and Joe Keenan for taking me on a truly fascinating tour of the Winnipeg RCMP Forensics Lab. The staff at the Calgary Public Library were, as usual, extremely helpful. Another big thank you and another box of doughnuts to the staff at Turnstone Press (yes, I'll bring coffee, too); Marijke Friesen for the great author photo; and Terry Gallagher for designing such a creepy cover. My editor Jennifer Glossop deserves many thanks (and a visit from the pond gnomes) for her criticism which was always fair, somtimes painful, but never harsh. The result was a much better book.

Thanks to budding editors Jack Smith (a.k.a. my dad), Carolyn Walton, and Kaye Due for their comments; and my mum who continues her career of marketing my books (and even managed to sell a copy of *Hoot to Kill* while walking the dogs). And finally, I am still and forever grateful to my husband Michael who keeps my finger away from the Delete key on those days when I hate everything I've written, and celebrates with me on the days when I don't.

"Man can hardly even recognize
the devils of his own creation."

—Albert Schweitzer

CHAPTER 1

IF YOU HAVE TO RECOVER FROM A BROKEN LEG, I can think of worse places to do it than at June's Bed and Breakfast. It's located four hours north of my home in Calgary, about a half hour east of Edmonton, in one of those enormous turn-of-the-century farmhouses, the kind with hardwood floors, Escher-like staircases, and time-darkened oak trim. The rooms are smallish but cheery with floral wallpaper, pastel throw rugs, and puffy quilts made especially for June by the residents of Holbrook's seniors' center.

There is a living room with deeply cushioned couches, a front porch that catches the morning sun, and even a cozy little parlor-cum-music-cum-Internet room. But the kitchen is the beating heart of the house. It's a large old-fashioned room. A brick fireplace warms the whitewashed walls, and cooking pans dangle from ceiling beams like a line of shiny copper bats. With several modern appliances, including a dishwasher, microwave, and two conventional ovens, June's kitchen embraces the best of both past and present, and is, at once, kitchen, dining room, living room, and den. Many are the evenings I've spent curled up with a good book in front of the fireplace, or seated at the table with June as she dispensed cinnamon rolls and advice with equal facility.

The whole house is filled with those special touches that breathe the word "home." And the gods knew I was in dire need of its comfort. I was suffering from a broken arm, a shattered leg, and a depression deeper than the Sarlak's pit. My temper was uncertain of late, a phrase that sounds so much more civilized than saying I was a grouchy bitch. But the truth is, it wasn't so much the grumpiness that was getting to me as it was the self-recrimination. It's not every day one's actions result in such painfully visible and, according to my doctor, lasting results. That I would forever walk with a limp was just one of the little reminders I had of Marten Valley.

Marten Valley. A small logging town in British Columbia. A town where I'd been sent to survey for spotted owls, and had found, in addition to the birds, blatant industry violations, a massive cover-up, and a murdered body. The final confrontation with the murderer was the reason I was currently masquerading as a gastropod.

In deference to my assorted casts and slug-like mobility, June had prepared a room for me on the ground floor. In older days, it had been a study for the man of the house. June had hauled out the monstrous desk many years before, but she had kept the shelves of books that lined the walls, added a couple of large wingback chairs and footstools, and dubbed it the library. After the kitchen, it was my favorite room of the house.

Ah, that kitchen. There's something about a place where wonderful food is prepared that draws the culinarily challenged in the same way as loons are drawn to water. As soon as I finished unpacking (i.e. unzipping my suitcase), I wedged my crutches under my armpits and swung down the hall, stopping briefly to wave to my co-workers from Woodrow Consultants. They were unloading their bags from the van. It was late morning, and as soon as they finished ditching their gear, they were heading out to the job site. I would be staying behind—and, despite the tantalizing smells coming from June's kitchen and the promise of an afternoon of friendly conversation, I was still sore about it.

"Are you hungry, Robyn?" June asked with a smile as I entered the kitchen.

"You need to ask? I didn't have time for breakfast before I left, and I could smell those cinnamon buns from Calgary."

She chuckled. "Well, I'm afraid you'll have to wait a few more minutes." She glanced over at the clock. "They'll be out in five."

"I think I can hold out till then," I said in a quavery voice.

"Silly thing!" June laughed and shooed me towards the table.

I sat down and reached across to the sideboard to snag the latest issue of *The Holbrook Times*.

"Another gnome-napping?" I asked, indicating the front-page photo. "Ye gods, don't these people have lives? With all the crap you have to bring on a vacation, why would anybody want to haul around a stupid *gnome*?" I snorted.

June turned and gave me a long look. "And just who peed in your cornflakes this morning?"

I flushed. "Sorry. Let's try that again." I tapped the picture of a garden gnome at the Louvre. "Gee, June, has there been another gnome-napping?"

"Yes, it's that season again," she replied. "Janice Parker's gnome just got back from Paris."

"Looks like he had a good time."

"Indeed. It seems he also went wine-tasting at all the best vineyards."

"No kidding? Maybe I should slap a cap on my head and a pipe in my mouth and go sit in somebody's garden."

"Tell me about it. Janice was rather envious."

The Holbrook gnome-nappings had started the previous summer when Gael Blackhall's garden figurine went missing. Gael ran the community theatre company so everybody had a good laugh when her gnome was returned a few weeks later with a small packet of photos showing him enjoying the Stratford-on-Avon Shakespeare festival. Carolyn Walton's gnome quickly followed suit, whooping it up under a tarp at the Edmonton Folk Festival. As soon as the tales of these gnome-nappings hit the newspapers—which they did primarily because Carolyn happened to be a local reporter—well over forty Holbrook gnomes had come down with a bad case of itchy feet.

Garden gnomes had jetsetted across three continents to places like Hong Kong, London, Athens—even the Serengeti plains. Gnomes had been photographed in front of border signs, national monuments, and historic buildings. One lucky little guy even had his snap taken on the French Riviera, complete with beachwear and a rather fetching pair of sunglasses.

"One of mine's missing," June said.

"What? A gnome?"

Her eyes sparkled. "Yes. I noticed he was gone last week."

"And you don't know who took him?"

She lifted her hands in the air. "Haven't a clue. I doubt whether it's anybody from Holbrook. Too many gnomes are taking trips for it to be strictly local. I think a lot of them are being borrowed by people in Edmonton. Anyway, I'm quite looking forward to seeing where the little fellow's been."

"Pretty sad when your garden gnome has more fun than you do."

"I'll say. You know, they've hung up a map of gnome destinations."

"Gnome. . . ?"

"Destinations."

"You're kidding."

"Oh no. There's a big world map in the town administration building. They've been marking all the destinations with red tacks. It's become quite a little tourist attraction in itself."

"That's weird, June," I said, shaking my head.

She shrugged off any responsibility for the matter. Then she served me up a mug of hot chocolate and a warm roll plump with raisins and dripping with sugary cinnamon syrup.

"Wow!" I exclaimed.

"I'm a little surprised the Woodrow crew wouldn't stay for a bite."

"I'm sure they wanted to," I mumbled around the hot roll, sucking in air to cool my gums. "But Ben was all fired up to go check out the site."

"Did they have lunches?"

"Yeah, but don't worry, as long as you lay out the rolls, they'll still devour the whole batch when they come back."

"Unless you beat them to it."

"There is that," I admitted.

June served herself a roll and settled across from me at the table.

Four years had passed since my best friend Megan brought me home to meet her mom, but in many ways it seemed like a lifetime ago. Though I had fledged long before, June sized me up that first weekend and immediately folded me under her maternal wing—an unfamiliar sensation for me, as my own mother is so enamored of my older brother Neil that I often wondered if the word "daughter" was even in her vocabulary.

Until Megan's move to Calgary to attend university, it had just been her and June living in the old farmhouse, but that summer they expanded their home to include me. June seemed to know without my saying what my family situation was. And she had, with the same perspicacity, recognized my need to be taken into hers. In the intervening years, we had become quite fond of each other, brought closer by Megan as well as by a shared love of birds, science, and classical music. Sometimes I thought that if I were any closer to the woman I would have imprinted on her.

"More hot chocolate?"

"Mmmm. Please."

As I held out my mug, June peered down at my leg cast.

"Ah. I see you've been autographed."

"And liberally."

"Let me see, Madame Curie, Jane Goodall . . . Gandhi. My, you do get around, don't you? Queen Elizabeth, too, and . . . oh dear, Sid Vicious?"

"Complete with hugs and kisses," I told her. "The jokers at the office found a marker and had themselves a fine old time."

June cocked her head to read another signature. "And what, may I ask, is a Prostetnic Vogon Jeltz?"

I rolled my eyes. "It's a he, and trust me, you really don't want to know. But I have a question for you."

"What's that?"

"Can you *please* tell me what Kelt wrote?" I rapped my leg cast significantly.

"Can't you read his handwriting?"

"I could if I could see it!"

Everybody else at the office had taken turns decorating my casts with fake signatures the day I'd gone in for a visit. I was wondering where Kaye had learned to forge Queen Elizabeth's signature so well when Kelt took over the marker.

He'd had it poised over my arm cast, ready to write, but then he stopped and grinned mischievously.

"Let's get your leg up on the chair," he'd said. And like an innocent, I'd helped him heave the cast up. That was when he flashed his twinkly peepers at me and started writing. On the *bottom* of my foot.

"Nobody will tell me what it says," I complained to June now. "They're getting quite a kick out of it, though. The curiosity is killing me!"

She put her mug down and bent over to take a look.

"Oh," she said, and started snickering.

"What? Is it rude? June, nobody will tell me what it says! I tried everybody at the office and they just looked and laughed. The *postman* won't even tell me."

"The postman?"

"I was desperate," I explained. "I tried looking in the mirror, but the angle's all wrong. I damn near put my back out. You're my last hope."

She smiled even wider and shook her head. "Far be it from me to let the cat out of the bag."

"Ju-une!"

She schooled her expression back to calm and serene, and passed me another cinnamon roll to plug my mouth. It worked. I am, much to my chagrin, easily bought.

Even if June was keeping quiet about the message on my cast, at least one cat had been let out of the bag today—and he hadn't been too damn happy about it, either. In fact, Guido the cat was supremely *un*impressed with the whole vacation idea. My pet had not been, as it turned out, the best of travelers. But June had thoughtfully saved him a tuna steak from last night's dinner, and after one brief, unbelieving look, Guido had nabbed the fish as if he'd never seen one before (which he hadn't; I didn't even know that tunas came in steaks), and beat a rapid retreat under the far end of the table. I could hear his purring over the thrumming of the rain on the window.

The early spring day was chilly, with the kind of cutting wind that lays icy fingers on your soul. For the first time since I'd heard about the brownfields redevelopment project, I didn't envy my co-workers. I stretched my leg out, warm and comfortable in June's chocolate- and cinnamon-scented kitchen, resigned at last to the fact of extended sick leave from my job as a field biologist. No, I really didn't envy my co-workers right at the moment. But that didn't stop me from thinking about their work.

"So tell me about your protest group," I prompted June during a break in our conversation. "Megan said you and your birding buddies started one up."

"As soon as we heard about this toxic-waste treatment facility."

"*Proposed* facility."

June snorted inelegantly. "It'll be approved by the powers that be, I have no doubts on that score—but ultimately it won't go through if we have anything to say about it."

"What are you planning on doing?"

"Well, we're trying to figure that out right now, but there's some conflict within the group about how to approach the whole issue."

"Conflict?"

"Yes, mostly between the birders and the hunters. Since it might damage Beaverhill Lake, a lot of the waterfowl hunters are with us on this—or at least they would be if it wasn't for a few anti-hunting types who don't think the hunters should be involved."

"That seems rather narrow-minded of them."

"And short-sighted," June agreed. "I don't think we can turn up our noses at their support. A few of these hunters carry a fair bit of clout, and if we can get Ducks Unlimited interested. . . ."

"Then you've got the wetland preservation people on board. Good idea. So what's the problem? The hunting thing?"

"In part. Personalities, too. Honestly, sometimes I just want to smack the lot of them! They seem to forget what the real issue is." She rolled her shoulders and shook off the tension. "Anyhow, I can't just sit by and let that toxic-waste facility go ahead, not without a fight. To tell you the truth, Robyn, I don't feel entirely comfortable with what Woodrow's doing here."

I sat up a little straighter. "But we're—they're—going to clean up the site."

"For what purpose? To put more toxic garbage in it. So in a few more years it can be just as polluted as it is now!"

"The standards are different now—"

"And most of the time industry monitors itself," she interrupted smoothly, her tone bitter. "I can't say I'm reassured by that."

"But the site has to be cleaned up. It's a mess."

"Oh, don't get me wrong, I want the place cleaned up—but I'm dead set against another industrial facility going in afterwards. Not with Beaverhill and those wetlands so close. And not after reading about all those other self-monitored plants that make a habit of dumping toxic waste into the rivers." She paused for a moment. "But most especially," she continued in a soft voice, "not after what happened to Eddie."

CHAPTER 2

THE AWKWARD SILENCE GENERATED BY JUNE'S last statement darkened the room like a flock of crows over a kill site. I was surprised—and more than a little dismayed—to learn about June's feelings. Oh, I had guessed right away that she'd be against the idea of a toxic-waste treatment plant, but I'd had no idea she was ambivalent about Woodrow's role in the process. It made sense in retrospect, but I was starting to regret my suggestion that the crew stay at the B & B.

June got up and cleared the dishes away, refusing to meet my eyes—which was probably just as well because my eyes weren't exactly keen on having drinks with hers at the moment. I'd never had occasion to disagree with June, at least not about anything serious, and I didn't want to start now. From what Megan had told me, June was slow to anger, but when she did, it burned long and hot. Not the sort of fire you wanted to light on the first day of a three-week vacation.

I squirmed on the bench, trying desperately to think up another topic of conversation. I wasn't very good at confrontations—or at changing the subject. Just as I was about to launch into a jolly description of the genital apparatus of sundry flea species, June glanced out the window and made a pleased sound.

"Here's Matt coming," she exclaimed, her tone one of distinct relief.

And I hadn't even started talking about fleas yet. The tension between us must have bothered her, too. So I snatched at the cue and smiled back at her.

"Matt, eh? I've been wondering if I'd get a chance to meet him. Meggie says he's a ringer for Sean Connery." I repeated the only good thing Megan had said about the man.

June's husband Eddie had died almost thirty years ago. She didn't talk about him much—almost never in my presence—and I wasn't even sure how he died, except that it had had something to do with the pesticide plant where he'd worked. But during all those long years since his death, she had, according to Megan, never even glanced at another man—until now. And my friend was not too thrilled about the new development.

I'd had the first inkling of Megan's feelings about the situation a week before I came to Holbrook. I'd been grumping around my apartment all day, achy, depressed, and bored. Finally I gave up. First I ordered a pizza from Stromboli's, then I rang Megan and invited her over to share it with me. She was only too happy to take me up on my offer, as her television had sputtered and died the previous week, and *Star Trek Next Generation* reruns were on. Megan and I shared a lust for Captain Jean Luc Picard.

We drooled first over Captain Picard, then over a Stromboli special—plump shrimp, fresh basil, and enough garlic to keep the vampires away until sometime in the next century. Megan was still pecking at the remains when I asked what turned out to be the wrong question.

"How's your mum doing these days?"

It seemed a natural—even innocent—question, but Megan's expression grew grim and a little furrow suddenly appeared between her eyebrows.

"What's the matter?" I demanded.

"She's got a boyfriend."

"June?" I said in surprise. "Gods, it must be years since—"

"Ever since Dad died," Megan said flatly.

"Well . . . um, that's great. . . . Isn't it?"

She shrugged.

"You don't like him."

She shrugged again.

"Megan, it doesn't take a rocket scientist to figure out there's something wrong. What's up?"

"I don't know exactly, but I don't trust him and she's besotted."

"Besotted."

It wasn't a word I'd normally use to describe the practical June.

"Oh, on the surface, he seems great," Megan said. "The man could play Sean Connery's brother. And he's on our side."

"What do you mean 'our side'?"

"He's an environmentalist. You've probably even heard of him. Matthew Lees?"

I searched my mind. "The journalist?" I ventured.

"None other."

I was impressed. Matt Lees's exposé articles on environmental crimes had ruffled more than a few corporate feathers in recent years.

"How did your mum meet Matt Lees?" I asked.

"Apparently he was down in Mexico for that NAFTA thing—"

"What NAFTA thing?"

Megan looked at me impatiently. "You know, the three NAFTA signatories agreeing to get together and reduce or ban a bunch of pesticides and other crap."

"Oh, right. I'd heard that they'd named PCBs. . . ."

"And now DDT, heptachlor, and mercury have all been officially targeted for phase-out or reduction."

I whistled. "I didn't hear that yet. DDT, eh? That's great! And heptachlor! You know, they're still making that stuff down in Mexico, and a lot of farmers down there still—"

"Do you want to hear about Matt or not?" Megan demanded.

"Sorry." I waved my hand for her to continue.

"Matt was down in Mexico when he got wind of the Reisinger project."

My heart sunk. "That waste treatment facility in Holbrook?" I asked in a small voice. "The one Woodrow's working on?"

Megan nodded. "Yeah, and don't bag out on me again. I *know* you want to be involved in it. Now quit interrupting, I'm telling a story here. After Mexico, the NAFTA pesticide commission was meeting in Montreal, so Matt decided to deke over to Alberta to check out the Reisinger story."

"That's a hell of a deke."

Megan shrugged. "Not if you're a journalist, I guess. And it will be the first toxic-waste treatment plant in western Canada. Besides, they used to manufacture heptachlor and chlordane at that old plant, and now that it's to be phased out and . . . well, I guess the whole thing makes a good story. Anyhow," she dragged the word out, "as I was saying, Matt came to town several months ago to find out more. He was boarding with Mum until it became obvious the attraction was mutual. Now he's renting a little house, supposedly so Mum's sterling reputation won't suffer."

"Really? That's sweet, Megan!"

I could tell from her expression that she thought it was anything but.

"Are . . . are you, uh, jealous of him?" I asked.

"Don't be ridiculous!" she snapped, then jumped up and started clearing the table.

Bemused, I sat and watched her, at a bit of a loss over what to say or ask. It may have been a somewhat tactless question, but it was an obvious one and, judging from Megan's vehement denial, perhaps a very pertinent one. Over the years, Megan and June had had the usual mother-daughter conflicts, but I'd never seen Megan quite this upset. On the other hand, nobody had tried to replace her father before.

"I'm sure he's not trying to replace your dad," I told her. "Your mum's been alone for a long time now and—"

"Robyn," Megan cut me off. "Spare me. I do not have a problem with my mum having a significant other. I have a problem with the man himself. I'd love for my mother to find somebody. Just not him."

"But what's wrong with him? He sounds great."

"Yeah, he *sounds* great, but there's something about him that's just . . . well, off."

"Like what?"

"Like, Mum can't get a hold of him sometimes and then when he turns up again, he never really says what he was doing."

I shrugged my incomprehension. "So? The guy's an investigative journalist. Of course he'd have to be a bit secretive—especially with the kinds of stuff that he writes about. What else?"

"Well, he never talks about his family. . . ."

I snorted. "Come on, Meggie, neither do I. Lots of people have family troubles, and most of the time, they don't want to talk about it."

"Well, Mum doesn't even know anything about him," Megan said stubbornly. "And she doesn't seem to care. That's weird."

"How do you know what she knows about him?" I demanded. "Does June tell you everything?"

"Of course not."

"Well, then. How many times have you met him? *When* did you meet him, for that matter? How long have they been seeing each other?"

"I didn't even *hear* about him till I met him, which was last weekend when I went home. They've been seeing each other for a couple of months now."

I digested this for a moment.

"Did it bother you that she waited so long to tell you?" I asked carefully.

Megan clattered the dishes in the sink. "Robyn, I know where you're going with this. Believe me, I've wondered if I'm just jealous, but I don't think I am—or at least I hope I'm not. I'd hate to think I was that selfish. But . . . just do me a favor."

"Sure."

"Check him out for me. When you go up to Holbrook next week. I'd really like to know what *you* think of him."

I've never been the most perceptive of people, so I knew Megan was desperate when she asked me to give Matt Lees the once-over. Now that I was in Holbrook and about to meet the man himself, I was determined to perceive whatever I could and try to set her mind at rest. As June opened the door for Matt, I quickly brushed the cinnamon bun crumbs off my shirt, smoothed down my curls, and prepared to carry out my mission.

Matt Lees didn't notice me right away. He strode in through the kitchen door, all his attention focused on a suddenly pink and flustered June. His hair was steely gray, still thick, with just a slight wave to it. He looked like he kept himself in good shape, but his best feature had to be his eyes. Warm and sparkly, they were the sort of eyes that smiled when the rest of the face did, which, judging from the crinkles, was often. Megan had been right about one thing, the man did bear a remarkable resemblance to Sean Connery. I had to award him points for that. Lucky June.

"Look!" He exclaimed to June, brandishing a white envelope. "Your gnome is back!"

"My gnome? Already?"

"Yeah. I just spotted him under the lilac bush. He was—oh!" Matt turned and saw me for the first time. "I'm sorry, I didn't see you there."

"Matt, I'd like you to meet Robyn," June took his arm and guided him over. "A good friend of Megan's—and mine," she smiled at me, all earlier tension gone.

"It's nice to meet you," Matt said with a wide smile. "June's told me so much about you." He offered his hand.

A good firm handshake. Two more points.

"Hey, Matt. It's good to meet you, too. I read your articles about the Swainson's hawks. They were very good."

"Well, thanks. Somebody had to do it."

"Saw a need and filled it, eh?"

Matt gave me a lopsided smile. "I guess so. I just got so damned mad, I had to do something. It was either write about it or sit around watching my blood pressure soar."

I knew the feeling. In 1996, some twenty thousand Swainson's hawks had died on their wintering grounds in Argentina. The culprit had been a pesticide called monocrotophos. Used primarily to rid alfalfa fields of grasshoppers, monocrotophos proved to be unsafe for birds at any of the rates recommended in agriculture. Too bad twenty percent of the world's Swainson's hawks had to die in order to discover *that* particular fact. But thanks to Matt Lees, that particular fact became public knowledge and monocrotophos had been removed from the Argentinian market. Score one point for the birds.

"I'm afraid that's how I get most of my stories," Matt said now with a grimace, "by getting so angry about the issues that I'm forced to write about them."

"So what's making you mad in Holbrook?"

"Reisinger's plans for a toxic-waste treatment facility," he answered without missing a beat. "With all the bird life around here, it's a really bad idea—"

"Now, Matt," June broke in, heading off further tensions, "Robyn's on vacation. I don't think we should be lighting a fire under *her* blood pressure—not until she's been here for at least twenty-four hours."

Matt smiled sheepishly at her. "You're right, I'm sorry. I tend to get a little carried away sometimes."

I waved away his apology. "That was nothing. You should hear my boss."

"Hmm. I've been hearing quite a bit about Woodrow Consultants since I've started looking into this business. Good reputation, that firm. Is Benjamin Woodrow as much of a character as everyone seems to think?"

I laughed. "Even more," I told him. "Don't worry, you'll have a chance to, um, experience him. He's been looking forward to meeting you ever since I told him you'd be here."

"I can't wait." He looked down at his hands then and blinked a bit in surprise at the envelope still clutched in his fingers. "Hey, I forgot about this." He handed the envelope to June. "Sorry I came bursting in like that before. I was so excited when I saw the gnome was back, I wanted to see where it had gone."

We all laughed and June tore open the flap, her eyes dancing with merriment.

"So where'd he go?" I asked.

"Well, let's see. . . ."

June removed a sheaf of photographs from the envelope.

"Oh my god!"

It wasn't an exclamation of pleasure.

She flipped quickly through the small pile of photos, her face getting paler by the picosecond. "Is this . . . is this a joke?!" Helplessly, she held the pictures out to Matt.

"What's wrong?" I demanded, straining to see over Matt's shoulders. "Where did he go?"

June was still holding the first photograph in her hand when Matt finished riffling through the pile. His expression had hardened to granite, but it wasn't until June sank down onto the chair beside me that I could finally see what had shocked them both.

It turned out, it wasn't so much where the garden gnome had gone, but who he had gone with. As in all the other gnome-napping photos, the cheerful little figurine had been carefully posed. But it hadn't been placed beside a monument or a border sign or a famous building. This gnome was beside a person. And whoever that person was, he was horribly, unquestionably dead.

CHAPTER 3

"DO YOU KNOW WHO HE IS?" I asked June.

She had pushed the photograph toward me, and I was looking without touching. I doubted whether whoever had left it had also had the courtesy to leave their fingerprints, but you never knew. I hoped it would be the case.

The picture was a Polaroid, so tracking down the killer wouldn't be as easy as checking the local photomat. And whoever took the picture was most definitely a killer. You couldn't fake something like this. Not that well.

The man's face was a warped ruin. His cheeks were sunken, his skin, devoid of any color, clung closely to his bone structure. His nose was pinched tight, slashing his face with a sharp line. But the eyes were the worst. The red of burst blood vessels was visible even in the Polaroid, and the eyeballs bulged from his face like bubbles of blown glass. However he had died, one thing was certain: it had not been a painless death.

The gnome—June's gnome—was one I recognized from previous visits. Megan had dubbed him Shaft because of his pea-green tunic, orange hose, and the odd fullness of his red cap, which I thought was just an imperfection, but Megan maintained was an afro. Though I'd never been a huge fan of lawn art, I'd always liked this particular specimen. Not any more. He was looking a little the worse for wear. Face cracked, one eye chipped out, he had been placed beside the body and seemed, in a macabre sort of way, to be watching the man's death with a demonic smirk. I shuddered and averted my eyes.

In answer to my question, June nodded once curtly, her lips pressed together so tightly I could see patches of white at the corners of her mouth.

"It's Richard DeSantis," Matt answered for her, his tone unbelieving. He stared at the photos for another minute, then shook himself. "Stay here. I'll call the police." He squeezed June's shoulder and went down the hall to the telephone.

"Richard . . . DeSantis?" I echoed. "DeSantis as in Grant DeSantis?"

June swallowed visibly. "Richard is—was—his stepson," she replied. "My god! Who would do something like this?"

I took a slow, deep breath. Grant DeSantis. Reisinger Industries' CEO. The man responsible for bringing a toxic-waste treatment facility into a town that hadn't yet decided whether it was being honored or victimized by the project. Or had it?

"He went missing two days ago," June said softly. "Nobody knew where he'd gone. He doesn't live in Holbrook. He was just here for a visit."

"And everybody thought he'd left without saying goodbye?" I guessed.

June nodded. "He told me he'd had a falling out with his stepfather—"

"You knew him?"

She blinked and looked down at her hands. "A little. I met him when he was here visiting last fall. I liked him, though I didn't know him well. He was very good at finding heron colonies. He even found one I'd never seen before, and I've been going out to Beaverhill Lake for years."

"He was a birdwatcher?"

"Oh yes, a very enthusiastic one at that. He was supposed to come out with our birding group last week to see if the herons were back, but he had a dreadful sinus infection and had to cancel out. And now. . . ." She trailed off and sighed heavily.

"I'm sorry, June." I patted her hand, feeling more than a little awkward at the role reversal. I'd never seen myself as the Florence Nightingale type.

She sat silently for a moment. "You'd have liked him, Robyn. He was quite an environmental activist. He was also supposed to get married next month to a young conservation worker down in Mexico. That makes it all the worse."

"Why did he have the same last name if he was a stepson?"

"Melanie remarried when Richard was quite young and Grant adopted him." June closed her eyes and shook her head slowly.

Matt came back into the room then, took one look at June, and put his arms around her.

"I'm sorry, babe," he murmured. "If I'd known what those photos were—"

June offered him a somewhat shaky smile. "That's okay, Matt. It wasn't your fault." She took a deep breath. "Is the RCMP sending somebody?"

In fact, the RCMP sent several somebodies, led by none other than Staff Sergeant Gary Ross. I'd met Gary a number of times during previous visits. Though I'm generally a law-abiding citizen, he never failed to intimidate me.

He was an imposing type, black of hair, big of muscles, and inscrutable of face. In actuality, I was better acquainted with his considerably more gregarious wife, Dana, but still the relationship between Gary and me had been cordial if not friendly up till now. So what had I done to merit the scowls he kept wafting my way? I was curious, but it didn't seem the time or place to ask. Mostly I was trying to stay out of the way. Guido the cat had made himself comfortable on my lap, so I sat quietly at the kitchen table, listening to June and Matt tell their stories.

"And you didn't notice the gnome before Matt came over? You didn't notice anybody in your yard?" Gary was asking June.

"No. I had a full house arriving today. I've been cleaning and baking since early this morning. About five I think."

Gary scribbled something in his notebook.

"You can't really see the spot from the house," Matt explained. "That lilac bush is so thick. It was only when I came up the walk that I saw it."

Gary asked a few more questions while a constable pulled on rubber gloves, and bagged the photos and the envelope they came in. Several other officers were busy in June's yard.

"I'm sorry we probably got fingerprints all over them," June apologized to the constable as she labeled the bags. "But we thought they'd be vacation pictures, not—that."

The constable gave June a reassuring smile. "We'll just get you to come down to the station in the next day or so and leave us a set of prints for comparison," she told her. "Don't be too concerned, I'd probably have done the same."

The RCMP were packing up to leave now, the photos and poor old Shaft encased in clear plastic and packed carefully in a box. But Gary didn't get up from the table right away. Instead he gazed at me for a long moment.

"What?" I demanded, uncomfortable under the scrutiny.

"Can I speak with you alone?"

Urk.

"Uh, sure."

"We'll go in the living room," June told me. "Come on, Matt."

Gary watched them leave the room. I watched Gary. And Guido the cat watched the ham that June had taken out of the freezer for dinner.

I suppressed the urge to ask what was wrong. I had the distinct feeling that he was going to tell me anyway, and I didn't want to seem nervous, though Gary's scrutiny was enough to get the pope searching his closets for skeletons.

He looked at me for another long moment, then sighed. "I know about what happened to you." He indicated my casts with his notebook. "I know about Marten Valley."

It wasn't what I was expecting.

"Uh—"

"I hope you're not planning to take an active role in *this* murder investigation."

Great. My reputation had preceded me.

"Gary—" I began.

"Because if you are," he interrupted, "think again. I read the reports of what happened there. And your name jumped out at me and your—how shall I put it—unofficial participation in the investigation."

"But—"

"So I'm telling you now, in a friendly kind of way, to keep your nose out of this."

"I wasn't planning on it, Gary," I told him. "I mean, I'm hardly mobile here."

"Nevertheless. I just wanted us to be clear on this."

"Don't worry," I assured him. "This is much-needed vacation time for me. I intend to stay well away from anything to do with murder."

I should have kept my mouth shut. The only thing I hate worse than eating my own cooking is eating my own words.

CHAPTER 4

THOUGH IT WAS LATE AFTERNOON, June and I were still lingering in the kitchen. She was whipping up a batch of cheese scones, and I'd been set to spinning lettuce for a salad—a task that was awkward but not impossible for someone with one functional arm. Matt had left earlier to finish up some work before joining us for dinner. My cat was hunkered down on the radiator, ostensibly watching the rain run in rivulets down the window pane, but at the same time keeping a careful eye on the ham that June had glazed with mustard and brown sugar, and decorated with whole cloves.

It hadn't taken us long to talk out the subject of Richard DeSantis's death. June was the only one who had known him, and she hadn't known him well. Until the RCMP found his body, there really wasn't much that could be done—or said. But talking about Richard DeSantis led to talking about Grant DeSantis, which in turn led to talking about Reisinger Industries and the Norsicol brownfields redevelopment.

Brownfields redevelopment. In layperson terms, brownfields are abandoned industrial or commercial properties. Most sites are quite a mess, environmentally speaking, as opposed to greenfields, which are pristine. The redevelopment part comes in with the idea that the site can be brought back to economic life if environmental and liability concerns are addressed. In other words, if it's cleaned up.

It's real cutting edge stuff, not to mention very lucrative work for environmental consultants. It is also the kind of work that allows you to escape the office, and pull on rubber boots and backpacks, and slop through streams and mud and other assorted (and sordid) messes. The kind of work that reminds me why I became an environmental consultant in the first place.

The brownfields contract that Woodrow had snagged was the old Norsicol pesticide manufacturing plant just north of gnome-infested Holbrook. A company called Reisinger Industries had commissioned the site assessment and remediation, since they were considering turning the plant into a toxic-waste treatment facility. Landing the job had been quite a coup for Woodrow Consultants.

Kaye and Benjamin Woodrow had formed the environmental consulting company two decades earlier, long before terms like "environmental impact assessment" had made it into the public consciousness. Over the years they'd built up a small but solid team of professionals. There was Lisa McDonald, the company's soils specialist and a fine botanist to boot, and Nalini Mohan, who specialized in reclamation and clean-up. Ben Woodrow was the expert in water resources and fisheries, while between the two of us, Kelt Roberson and I had the birds, mammals, and reptiles covered.

On the non-scientific end of Woodrow Consultants, there were Kaye Woodrow, Ben's wife and the person who brought in all the contracts; Ti-Marc Lafarge, who kept us all organized; and Arif Pasula, who wrote programs, plugged our resource data into the computer, and kept us all supplied with reading material from his extensive mystery collection. We were an efficient bunch, and most of the time, we got along quite well. I certainly appreciated the sense of belonging I got from working at Woodrow, despite Ben's propensity for calling us turnips whenever we disagreed with him. Turnips, according to Ben, are the lowest of the vegetables because they're yellow, mushy when heated, and they give you gas.

As I'd told Matt earlier, Benjamin Woodrow was a rather colorful character, who'd had an equally colorful career before forming a consulting firm with Kaye. As an enforcement officer for the Florida Game and Freshwater Fish Commission, he'd patroled the everglades where he had been shot at by alligator poachers and attacked by the less-than-grateful alligators themselves. As a Fish and Wildlife officer in Alberta, he'd staked out rivers and lakes, and had even gone undercover to bust a poaching ring. He'd broken up the operation, all right, and confiscated several tens of thousands of dollars' worth of animal parts, but he'd also managed to confiscate a bullet from the leader of the group, namely by getting it shot into his butt. He called the resulting scar his "war wound" and displayed it proudly and—if he happened to have a couple of beer in him—often. As a result of all this, Ben harbored few illusions about his fellow man, believing in many respects that the human race had stayed on the planet well beyond last call. And most of the time, he wished he was a bouncer.

"I've seen a report on the state of that old Norsicol site," I told June. "So I've been preparing myself for several of Ben's little diatribes on the numerous pros and scant cons of wiping out the human race. Perhaps you ought to do the same."

"Just how bad is the site?" she asked.

I grimaced and started tearing up pieces of lettuce for the salad. "Bad," I told her. "We'll know more in the next day or two, once they have a chance to check out the place."

"Hmm." June took out a mixing bowl and started measuring ingredients. "So what exactly is involved in cleaning up a site like this?"

"A lot of things," I said. "You start off with a site assessment, which is broken down into four phases. Phase I is a background and document review, Phase II is a sampling program, and Phases III and IV involve the actual remediation of the site."

June took a block of orange cheese from the fridge and starting grating it into a pile. "So Ben and the others are working on the second phase?"

"Yeah, and a bit of clean-up stuff, too. I think they're all relieved to press on with the job. I heard Ben had a lot of trouble with Phase I."

"The document review?"

"Yep. The old plant's documentation was spottier than a sandpiper, which made the historical survey something of a challenge."

"I can imagine. Norsicol never did seem to have their act together."

"Yeah, well, most of their documentation was missing, and when the plant shut down, whatever technical records were around went to China along with the furnaces, compressors, vats, and other equipment."

"China?" June turned away from her scone mixture to give me a quizzical look.

I nodded. "Yeah. The whole lot was sold to a company in Beijing which is, of course, now defunct."

June rolled out the dough and started slicing it into diamond shapes. "So what did Ben do for historical documents?" she asked, intrigued in spite of her feelings about the project.

"Apart from calling everybody a turnip?"

June grinned and scooped the scones onto a cookie sheet. "Yes, apart from that."

"Well, usually if an operating company's records are sketchy or missing, you can rely on the construction specs to give you an idea of what the site was like. Unfortunately in this case, the guys who managed the construction of the Norsicol plant had been bought out years ago and nobody seemed to know what had happened to the old records. Sometimes engineers make copies of all the drawings of every facility they work on. Which is great—if you can track down the engineers, which Ben couldn't. Failing that, you can look for somebody who used to work at the plant. You can actually learn a lot about potential problem areas from former employees." I tilted the salad bowl towards her. "How's this?"

"Perfect, thank you." She popped the cookie sheet in the oven and came over to sit across from me. "That makes sense," she said, "talking to former employees."

"Oh yes, it's a good idea, but again, only if you can sniff out a former employee."

"Which Ben could not," June guessed.

"Nope. Most of the engineers went international and he never did manage to find any old workers."

June stroked Guido thoughtfully. "No, so many are dead now, or moved away. Abe Kershaw was the last I knew of and he died over ten years ago. And, you know, Norsicol paid a lot of men under the table."

"That would explain the lack of employee records."

"So what happens now?" June asked.

"We'll—they'll—probably need to drill about twenty monitoring wells just to get an idea of what's happening with the groundwater. I know they've got a roughneck crew booked for three days to drill them, and Nalini's organized a backhoe."

"What do they need a backhoe for?"

"There's a big tank buried over by the west building and it's leaking like a sonofabee so we'll—they'll—have to dig it out. It's called a 'tank yank' in industry-speak."

"Is there just the one tank, then?"

"I doubt it. That's just the one we know about. Lisa will do a vegetation survey to see if there're any weird changes in the plant life that might indicate another hotspot. Then, of course, we'll—" I caught myself again, "*they*'ll have to sample the sumps and tanks in the other buildings."

June's expression darkened as I described the work to come.

"It sounds awful!" she said, appalled.

On one hand, I could sympathize with her feelings about the project. The Beaverhill wetlands were a mite too close to the proposed site for me to be entirely comfortable with the idea of a toxic-waste treatment facility (though it more than met provincial and federal guidelines). But I wasn't quite as cynical as June was about industry, and at least Reisinger was cleaning up the site. It *was* a bit of a trade-off, I admit, but in my field that was something you quickly came to terms with—either that, or you made like a rat on a sinking ship and found yourself another field.

"That plant sounds like it's in bad shape, worse than I'd thought," June was saying.

I nodded. The old plant was, in fact, worse than bad, but I didn't want to get June riled up about it any more than she was already. I felt like I was tiptoeing on birds' nests, as it was. The slap of the back door opening was a welcome interruption.

"Hi, Mrs. M! I'm home!" A voice sang out from the mud room beside the kitchen.

"Hi, Tracy!" June called back. "I've got some cocoa warming on the stove. And"—she bent over to take the scones out of the oven—"some hot scones."

"Awesome!"

"Tracy?" I prompted.

"My newest guest," June murmured. "Her parents are old friends. Tracy's got a horse stabled over at Red Golding's farm, so she'll be staying here for a couple of weeks. I don't think we should mention the photographs to her. Not right now."

I was nodding my agreement when Tracy bounced into the room. Roughly eighteen years old with long brown hair and bright eyes, Tracy was perkiness personified. Feeling suddenly old and decidedly decrepit, I tried not to wince.

"It's totally gross out there today, Mrs. M! I could barely ride! I hope it's not going to do this for the whole two weeks!" She turned and caught sight of me. "Oh!" She exclaimed and giggled. "Well, hi!"

"Hey, Tracy, I'm Robyn."

"Robyn! That's right! Mrs. M told me about you! You're like some kind of biologist, aren't you?"

I wondered if Tracy always spoke in exclamation marks. "That's right. At least I am when I'm not in assorted casts."

"Oh, bummer! I'd hate to be in a cast! I wouldn't be able to ride!"

"June tells me you've got a horse. . . ."

"Yeah," her voice softened in infatuation. "His name's Marius. He's a bay thoroughbred and he's *gorgeous*! I've been working since I was fourteen to save up enough money to buy him. And even then my mom had to help me. I'll be in debt to her till I'm like, *ancient*!"

I didn't want to ask Tracy what "ancient" meant to her. I had a sneaking suspicion it was anything over twenty-five. I shifted my leg uncomfortably on the bench and sat up straighter, trying not to feel like some hold-over from the Cretaceous.

"Marius is totally worth it, though," Tracy continued, beaming broadly. Then her face fell. "But I've got to go back in three weeks and find a summer job."

"To pay for horse upkeep?"

She giggled and nodded. "Yeah, he, like, totally eats up my bank account! And I have to save for school, too. I want to be a vet."

Big surprise.

"Tracy," June interrupted. "Why don't you get out of those wet clothes and come back down for some hot chocolate."

"Fab idea, Mrs. M! I'll be right back!"

With a huge grin to me, she bounced out of the kitchen. June met my eyes and we exchanged smiles.

"Enthusiastic," I commented.

June rolled her eyes good-naturedly and started arranging scones on a big serving platter. "You have no idea. She's only been here for three days, but I've already heard more about horses than I ever wanted to know. Matt says he's never seen a person so completely horse-crazy!"

"Matt again, eh?" I drawled. "What with the, uh, photos and everything, I didn't get much chance to talk to him, but he sure seems like a nice guy."

And so he did. At least that was my first impression. But I felt a little disloyal to Megan by saying so. Still, I hadn't detected anything "off" about the man and I started giving serious consideration to the possibility that her problem with him was firmly rooted in jealousy.

"I like him," June said.

"Meggie was right about him being a ringer for Sean Connery."

June dismissed that with a wave of her hand. "Megan's had a crush on Sean Connery ever since I let her stay up and watch those

James Bond movies. I wouldn't say that Matt looks like Sean Connery, but he is quite handsome. With a nice bum, too!"

"June!" I exclaimed, a bit shocked.

"Well, he does," she protested. "I don't see why I shouldn't notice something like that. I'm not dead yet."

I couldn't argue with that, and when Kelt came in a few minutes later, dripping wet with his shirt plastered close to his body, I was abruptly reminded that I was nowhere near ready for the morgue myself.

Kelt Roberson was Woodrow Consultants' most recent acquisition, a small mammals biologist who specialized in wildlife surveys and impact assessments. He was also, in my humble estimation, the greatest thing since Tim Horton's sour cream glazed doughnuts. And like the doughnuts themselves, my excellent opinion of him (some might label it lust) didn't appear to be doing me much good. He was friendly enough, I grant you, but it seemed to be the I-like-you-a-lot-I-wish-you-were-my-sister brand of friendliness rather than the I-want-you-bad sort that I was hoping for.

I stared at him for a minute, then cleared my throat. "Everybody else float away?" I asked, managing a light tone.

"Close," he replied just as the rest of the troop squelched into the mud room.

Ben and Nalini were drenched, and Cam didn't look much drier. With the weather the way it was, that was to be expected. But from the look of her, Lisa, in particular, had been getting up close and personal with Mother Nature. Her clothes were covered in gooey black mud, despite obvious attempts to scrape them clean, and her face was streaked and splattered. I must admit to being a wee bit envious, until I saw how blue her skin looked underneath the mess, and heard her teeth chattering like hailstones on a garden shed.

"What the hell happened to you?" I asked.

She grinned sheepishly. "Slipped and fell in the mud by the truck." She jerked her head toward the others. "All they did was laugh."

I clucked my tongue and tried for a sympathetic look. But Lisa was notoriously accident-prone, always spilling her coffee or knocking plants off her window ledge. She was short like me, but the similarities ended there. Her hair was honey blond with natural lighter streaks, straight and shining (unlike my own rat's nest of auburn curls). Her eyes were a few shades darker than my sherry-colored ones, which was a devastating combination with her blond hair. She was also a real sweetie, so I couldn't even be jealous of her. That didn't, however, stop me from routinely thanking the gods that she was currently involved with a very nice photographer. I had quite enough trouble with my love life without having to deal with that kind of competition.

The gods grinned down on Lisa in ways that I could only dream of—except, of course, when it came to accidents. Rumor had it that she'd been born in the back of a Greyhound bus after it had broken down between Calgary and Regina. Perhaps that explained why ceiling tiles fell on her desk, or why the photocopier worked perfectly for everyone else, but jammed as soon as she used it, or why the elevator always stuck whenever she was in it alone, or why ... well, you get the gist. She had broken fingers, toes, and her arm twice. Once she'd even broken her leg while standing at a bus stop. Of *course* she had fallen in the mud.

"Bummer," I said finally.

She must have caught the note of amusement in my voice. She wadded up her mud-soaked jacket and made as if to throw it at me. It slipped, of course, and hit Kelt in the side of the head.

"Aargh!"

"Oh, I'm sorry," Lisa exclaimed. But something in her voice indicated she was anything but, and I guessed that Kelt had been teasing her about falling.

The Woodrow gang peeled off as many clothes as decently possible, and with longing looks at the pile of warm scones, they retired smartly to their respective rooms to wash up and change.

Tracy had had a head start on the rest of them, so she was down first. June served her up a mug of hot chocolate and settled her at the table with a cheese scone. The scones were singing a siren song of crispy edges and melted morsels of sharp cheddar, but I'd eaten my body weight in cinnamon rolls earlier and was resolved to ignore them.

"Wow! Thanks, Mrs. M!"

"Did you have a nice ride apart from the rain?" June asked her.

"I always have a good ride on Marius," Tracy answered with a dreamy smile. She took another bite of her scone. "I looked for herons like you said, but I didn't see any."

"The herons are back already?" I was surprised.

"I saw a black-crowned night heron on Tuesday," June told me. "But I've not seen a blue heron yet this year. If you're up to it, maybe we can drive out to Beaverhill Lake and bird from the car."

"June, that's the best offer I've had in ages!"

"You've got to get a life, then, girl!"

"Tell me about it."

The prospect of a birding expedition excited me more than it ought to have done. I'd obviously been moping around my apartment for too long. Still, the wetlands around Beaverhill Lake *were* heron heaven.

In 1987, the area had been declared a Ramsar site, meaning it was recognized as a wetland of international importance. Shorebirds and other waterfowl used the area as a staging ground during spring and fall migrations, and both great blue and black-crowned night herons nested in colonies in the trees and thickets around the lake. In a given year, there were anywhere from a handful to several dozen colonies in and around the area. Ten years ago, Holbrook's town council decided to commemorate this fact by commissioning an eight-foot statue of a great blue heron. The statue, which was remarkably realistic (except for its size), had been placed in the town square where it looked down on flowerbeds that spelled out "Holbrook."

I was about to ask June when we could head out to Beaverhill when the Woodrow crew thumped down the stairs and into the kitchen. They looked like hungry baby birds whose mother was falling down on the job. June laid a platter of scones on the table and prudently stepped back.

"Hey, Cam, there's a chair over here," I beckoned my replacement over. He'd been standing in the doorway, a little hesitant among the boisterousness of the others.

June gave him a broad, kind smile and shooed him toward the chair. Cam grinned back shyly and flushed a little before sitting down. He was a tall, stork-like man, early to mid-fifties, with soulful brown eyes, a quiet smile, and a soft voice. He had turned out to be one of those ever-so-rare people who really look at you when you talk to them. The kind who wait to make sure you're done saying all you had to say before taking their turn. A gentle soul.

As I had been effectively benched for the field season, Kaye and Ben had had to hire a replacement for me—at least for the Reisinger job. Kelt's ornithological talents were pretty good, but with all the bird activity in the area, Ben needed an expert. We'd picked up Cam in Red Deer on our way to Holbrook. Being a fellow bird enthusiast, talk had inevitably led to acquaintances of the feathered persuasion. When I had asked him how many species he had on his list, he'd just smiled and shrugged.

"Oh, I don't keep a list," he'd replied in his quiet voice. "It doesn't matter to me how many species I see. I just like to watch them. I don't care if I go out and all I see are mallards. They're still beautiful."

A birder after my own heart. I'd found myself warming to him immediately—even though he, too, had refused to tell me what was written on the bottom of my foot.

I turned my attention to Cam now. "So what does the site look like?" I asked him.

He grimaced around his cheese scone.

"It's a mess!" Ben answered for him. "Some of those drains lead straight into the east field, there's some revolting-looking gunk oozing up from a couple of the sumps. And let me see . . . rusting, leaking tanks in the basement, and big patches outside where there's obviously been a build-up of sterilants."

I wrinkled my nose in disgust. "Sounds like you'll have to suit up for some of it."

"And use the scuba gear when we're doing those tanks," Kelt added.

"But . . . but this is like totally gross!" Tracy's eyes had widened as the list went on. "How come they got away with stuff like that? Aren't there laws or something?"

"Not thirty years ago," I explained. "And what laws there were back then, weren't really enforced. Especially not in a remote location like this."

"But isn't it like going to make it worse if they build a toxic-waste treatment plant there?" Tracy asked after a moment. "I mean, won't that just be more toxic stuff everywhere?"

"That's what I think," June said.

Ben shot an apologetic look at June. "It may not be that simple," he mildly. "You see, Tracy, the old plant is what they call an orphan site. Norsicol, the original company—the one that was responsible for this mess—doesn't exist any more, so the land reverts back to the government. It's their responsibility to clean it up, but with all the oil and gas activity in the province, there are hundreds of contaminated orphan sites lying around, and not a whole lot of money for cleaning them up."

"But they'll have to clean this one up now," Nalini interrupted. "Any place where contaminated material is moving off site *must* be cleaned up. It's the law. And from what we saw today, the stuff is moving through the soil and into the ditches. It is most definitely making tracks off site."

"True enough," Ben acknowledged, and turned his attention back to Tracy. "But if you're the government, and you have to fork out a big wad of cash to clean up a site, you're going to want to get some returns on it."

"Which is why they jumped at Reisinger's offer to assess the site, and why they'll probably approve the new facility," June said bitterly.

Ben shrugged. "It makes sense from their point of view, although I can't say I like it much myself. But it'll still have to go through an impact assessment process. And Elliot Shibley's the project manager. I've met with him a number of times now. He's no turnip; he'll do a good job."

June didn't look reassured.

"In the end, what else are you going to do with a site like that?" Ben continued. "If you leave it, then the contaminants will eventually leach their way over to the wetlands anyway."

"It all has to do with the extent of reclamation," Nalini explained to Tracy, who still looked a little confused. "If you're reclaiming land that's slated for a public park, say, then you pretty much have to clean everything up as much as possible. It could—and probably would—run into the millions of dollars. Maybe even more. There was a pesticide storage site near Denver that cost two *billion* dollars to clean up—and that was in the 1980s. But"—Nalini held up a finger—"if you're going to build another industrial complex on the site, then you don't have to worry so much. There'll still be some contamination when all is said and done, but it won't cost you nearly as much to clean up."

"And you get that ever-so-important return on your investment," I added.

"But that totally sucks!" Tracy exclaimed.

June patted her hand comfortingly. "I couldn't have said it better myself, dear."

Chapter 5

MATT ARRIVED FOR DINNER WITH FLOWERS, a big smile, and bottles of wine so decent my tongue tried to form words like "piquant" and "unpretentious." He kissed June and offered that firm handshake all round. He was a charmer, all right. If I'd been twenty-five years older, I'd have probably been swept off my hiking boots, too.

We all had strict orders about dinner conversation. June's protective instincts were humming and she didn't want Tracy upset by discussions about the gnome and its grisly package of pictures. I suspected she herself was more distressed about it than she was letting on, and I said as much to Ben when I pulled him aside before dinner. He frowned as I told him about the pictures, and scowled when I told him the identity of the body. But after he had made all the requisite appalled and concerned noises, he agreed that it was best to keep quiet about it for tonight. At least until the initial shock wore off. He'd tell the others tomorrow when they went out to the site.

June started laying out the dinner while the rest of us sat around the table like bright-eyed pine siskins waiting at an empty bird feeder. Kelt and Lisa jumped up to help her, but she waved them back down and motioned Matt to the seat beside Ben.

Ben was as eager as I had been to meet Matt. But while I planned to scope out the guy for Megan, Ben had been wanting to check him out for very different reasons. He'd heard through the grapevine that Matt could be relentless, even unprinicipled, in obtaining information for his articles. Especially the really nasty exposés. I wasn't sure whether Ben respected or disapproved of Matt's alleged unscrupulousness (though I could hazard a guess) but he hated not knowing the truth behind gossip of this sort. I suspected he also hated the fact that there may be a kindred spirit out there that he hadn't encountered yet. After the usual round of pleased-to-meet-yous had been exchanged, we environmental types quickly got down to business.

"June tells me the two of you have started up a protest group against the plant," I began.

Matt's smile lit up his eyes with a warm glow. "That's right, but June was really the driving force behind it."

"Are you against toxic-waste treatment facilities in general or just this one in particular?" Ben rumbled.

Matt pulled a face. "A bit of both, really. They're a necessary evil, much as I wish we could do without them altogether. What I do have a problem with are the people and regulations that govern these plants. I've seen a lot of violations during the course of my work—very few of which are ever punished. Regulations are all well and good, but they mean nothing if they're not enforced. I'm afraid I've become quite cynical about the whole thing."

Ben nodded, sensing a soul mate.

"As for this particular facility? Well, it seems naïve to think that Reisinger Industries will be any different—and the epitome of stupidity to locate such a thing so close to the staging grounds."

"What are staging grounds?" Tracy asked me in a whisper.

"They're places where birds stop to rest and eat during migration," I murmured. "They're pretty important. If their staging grounds are contaminated and birds can't find anywhere else to get food or rest, they won't complete their migration and they probably won't breed successfully."

Tracy pursed her mouth in a small "oh" and turned her attention back to the conversation.

"But *something* has to be done with the site," Nalini was saying.

Matt nodded in agreement. "Yes, I've been out there. I understand why the government is so eager to ram this thing through. In any other place, it could be a good solution."

"Elliot Shibley's a good man," Ben said. "Seems quite sensitive to environmental concerns."

"Yes, I've met him, too. I agree with you. But he's still got to dance when Reisinger claps its hands. And I tell you, I've got little faith in Reisinger's board of directors or the present government, and with the wetlands a mere twenty or so kilometers away...." He shook his head slowly. "Ultimately, that's the reason I'm against the facility."

"It's bad enough that chlordane and heptachlor used to be manufactured there," June added, plunking salad and rolls on the table. "We were lucky there were no major spills back then, but luck has an unsavory habit of running out."

"What are chlordane and hep, hepa....?" asked Tracy

"Heptachlor. They're pesticides, part of the organochlorine family," June explained. "Like DDT."

Tracy's face had paled. "Do you mean they used to make *DDT* at that plant?"

"Not DDT specifically, but two related pesticides that were every bit as bad."

"But I never knew it was, like, DDT! That stuff is so *deadly*!"

"Yes, I know, dear. And their breakdown products are often even worse. Heptachlor epoxide is a lot nastier than heptachlor. And chlordane is so bad that one pest-control operator still had residue from it on his hands two years after his last exposure to it."

"Years?"

"Years," June affirmed. "And it gets blown around and transported over long distances. They've even found traces of chlordane in the high Arctic, and nobody ever used it up there." She started serving up a heavenly smelling mushroom bisque that was totally at odds with the topic of conversation.

"I still find it hard to believe we used them on food crops," June added as an afterthought.

So did I. It wasn't that I was a fanatic anti-pesticide crusader—not even Rachel Carson, of *Silent Spring* fame, had been completely against chemical pesticides (though the popular media portrayed otherwise). Instead, she had believed that pesticides should be used discriminately and only after extensive investigations. It seemed sound reasoning to me. But even Rachel Carson didn't fully realize the basic problems associated with the use of chemical pesticides.

If you had to choose an ideal target organism for an insecticide, ironically enough it wouldn't be a bug. Insects reproduce often and in great numbers, which means their populations bounce back pretty quickly after a pesticide application. To make things worse, most insects are specially adapted to deal with poisons. As a result, each new generation is progressively more pesticide-resistent. All of which means that farmers have to spray more and more frequently, and chemists have to keep coming up with other, more toxic, compounds.

"So, like, what brainiac decided to spray that stuff on food?" Tracy was disgusted.

Matt shrugged. "Pests destroy food crops. You have to do something about it. And people have been fighting *that* battle for a very long time. The Sumerians liked to use elemental sulfur to control insects. That was around 2500 BC. In fifteenth-century Switzerland, cutworms were such a big problem that they were actually put on trial in the religious court in Berne."

"Really?" Tracy slanted Matt a suspicious look.

He grinned and held up his right hand. "I swear. They were found guilty and banished, too. As a method of pest control, I don't think it was terribly effective, but it shows how frustrated people can get."

"Is that why they invented DDT?"

"Partly. Also because the medical profession realized that diseases like malaria and yellow fever were carried by insects." Matt served himself some salad and passed the bowl to Tracy.

"But why spray them on food?" Tracy asked, eyeing the salad with distrust.

"Because they worked," Matt said simply. "They kill the pests. Of course, they kill a lot of other things at the same time—including us—but nobody realized that until later."

"They stopped using them on food crops in the early 1970s," Ben added comfortingly.

"Because people realized they were poisonous?"

"Not at first," he replied. "But if you sprayed them in too great a concentration, then the foliage died. And if it rained a day or so after spraying, the stuff would wash into the soil where the plants would take it up and incorporate it right into the fruits and veggies."

"And people, like, *ate* that stuff?" Tracy asked, still holding the salad bowl.

"Oh yes," Ben shrugged. "Nobody really knew how bad it was—not until much later. And, of course, they're still being used in developing countries."

"Even though everybody knows it can kill them?" Tracy was aghast.

Ben nodded. "I'm afraid so. Like Matt said, pests kill food crops. It's a fact of life, but it's a pretty frightening fact in countries where food is scarce. That's why pesticides like DDT, lindane, and dieldrin are still in use over there, despite how poisonous they are."

Ben regarded the bowl of soup in front of him. "You can try talking to farmers about long-term health effects, but the cold, hard truth of the matter is, when you live day to day, hand to mouth, it's pretty hard to worry about what might happen to you ten or twenty years from now."

We might have been better off talking about the pictures of Richard DeSantis. This rather depressing conversation continued through dinner, dessert, and well into the evening. Not surprising, given the company—get a bunch of environmentalists and environmental consultants in a room, and conversation was bound to take a downward spin. I felt especially sorry for Tracy, whose bright eyes grew wider and wider as she discovered there were many, considerably less pleasant, things in the world besides horses. Before twenty-four hours passed, she was to discover a few more.

CHAPTER 6

HARRISON FORD—ANOTHER OF MY SECRET and (sadly) unrequited loves—once remarked that his favorite time of the day was 6:00 a.m. I couldn't agree more. Especially when 6:00 a.m. found me out in the wetlands watching as tens of thousands of geese landed in a field beside me while the rising sun painted the grasses with a coppery gold wash. Of course, it would have been even better if Harrison Ford was being painted with a coppery gold wash, too, but if he was, it wasn't happening in my vicinity.

I hadn't spied any herons yet, but there were snow geese in both white and gray phases, white-cheeked Canada geese, and greater white-fronted geese, commonly known as specklebellies, whose black splotchy stomach markings were as individual as fingerprints. They all landed in a flurry of honking and tootling.

As well as geese, there were northern shovelers, with long, spoon-shaped bills, and small flocks of blue-winged teal, dotted here and there with the occasional rufous flash of a rarer cinnamon teal. Pintails paddled about in shallow ponds, their long needlepoint tails resembling the bowsprits of old-fashioned sailing ships. Chunky, little, male ruddy ducks bobbed their turquoise bills suggestively at the females, who scuttled away indignantly, far more interested in eating than dallying. The puddles and ponds of stagnant water lent their own brand of perfume to the air, a cool breeze played hairdresser in my curls, and I could hear the whistling flight of buffleheads above me. Heaven, The Upper

World, Asgard, Elysium—whatever you wanted to call it, I was in it.

June and I sat in her car, bundled against the dawn's chill, watching the avian army descend on the aquatic plains. Early spring birding can be remarkably easy. Although the warblers and other songbirds hadn't yet made their way this far north, the waterfowl and shorebirds were here in force. Nervous after their long migration, they're likely to lift off *en masse* if you so much as crack your door open, so it's actually better to watch them from the car. Better for me right now, too. I sighed in happiness, and June lowered her binoculars and looked over at me, answering my smile with a broad one of her own.

"Better?" she asked.

I sighed again, dramatically this time. "Like night and day. Thanks, June."

She patted my hand. "Meggie said you were crawling up the walls. I thought it would do you good to come out here. I know it's always helped me stay sane. Somehow, when I'm out here, my problems seem so small and insignificant."

We sat in contemplation, paying silent tribute to the land and its abundance.

"You know, I used to come out here after Eddie died," June continued softly after a while. "I'd bundle Meggie up—she was still so young then, I'd just wrap her in blankets and lay her on the back seat. I'd come out here and sit for hours. Just sit, watching the birds and listening to the sounds of the morning. It helped."

I covered her hand with my own. In the four years I had known her, June had never spoken of the time after Eddie's death. Not like this, anyhow. Oh, she'd told me a bit about Eddie, about his dreams, his sense of humor, and his deep love of family. But on the subject of her own feelings, she had been as silent as an owl. Once I had asked her how difficult it had been to pick up and carry on. Her kind, open face had pinched tight with old pain and she answered simply that it had been very hard. I never asked again.

"I guess I should have talked more with people," she said now.

"My doctor kept urging me to. Perhaps I was too proud. Too proud of my strength and independence. You see, my father died when I was nine, and my mother when I was seventeen. That's a terrible age to lose everybody. A terrible age to become independent. But I had no extended family and no choice in the matter, so I did it and congratulated myself for having done it."

She paused and poured herself a little more coffee. "I don't know if you can imagine what it was like. You've got brothers and parents and aunts and uncles. But to have no one. . . ." She shook her head slowly. "When Eddie came into my life, it was like dawn breaking way up north after six months of night. With him, I had a family again, even before Meggie came. And when he died, I thought my life had ended. For a while, I wanted it to.

"But instead I came out here to these wetlands. I remember sitting here with Meggie while the birds flew over us on their way south, and the leaves changed color and fluttered to the ground in one last dance. That's what it seemed like to me anyway, one last dance before dying. I think I found it appropriate in an odd way, that sense of life ending. It would have been strange if Eddie had died in the spring, when everything is so fresh and full of life and promise. Even so, I felt as dry and dead as those leaves, without even the joy of having a last dance."

She paused and sipped her coffee. I stayed quiet.

"I kept coming out—even in the winter—I watched the clouds sail over the fields. The snow formed new patterns every day, depending on how the winds blew. And when spring finally came, I watched the buds swelling with life and then I saw the birds come back. Simple things, really, all of them. But incredibly healing."

June stopped again for a long moment. "I guess that's why I'm dead set against this waste treatment facility," she said finally, her voice hardening a little. "It would break my heart if anything happened out here, if there was a spill, I mean. I'd never forgive myself if I didn't do everything in my power to keep that from happening. This place taught me so much and, in a strange way, I feel close to Eddie out here."

Talk about putting your problems in perspective. As June remembered the pain of her past self, I squirmed inwardly. Here I'd been wallowing in self-pity for over a month now, but what was a broken leg compared to the death of a husband? A missed job compared to the loss of family? I thought of my recent bouts of selfishness and bad temper, and was ashamed.

Long after June had fallen silent, we sat watching the birds and listening to the heartbeat of the morning.

CHAPTER 7

WE PULLED UP TO THE OLD NORSICOL PLANT about mid-morning. After our dinner conversation the previous night, June had a hankering to see for herself how bad the site was, and I . . . well, I wanted to see what I was missing.

There were two access roads, one from the north and another from the southeast, both of which led to a central paved area. We came in on the north road. A sagging chain-link fence blocked off access to the main site, but the gate had rusted out years ago, and we were able to pass through without any trouble.

As chemical factories go, the Norsicol plant had been a fairly small one—at least by today's standards. Three box-like buildings lined the east side of the site. A smaller structure, probably the plant manager's office, was situated on the western edge. Any paint which may have decorated the buildings had long since flaked away, leaving pock-marked cinderblocks and stained concrete. The tiny windows had been boarded up decades ago, the plywood now gray and splintery with age.

A jumbled network of pipelines ran from the three main buildings to a row of bulk storage tanks which, once painted a bright gleaming white, now sat bleeding rust onto the ground. I couldn't help wondering what little surprises lurked in the bottom of those puppies. A few pigeons (rock doves to us birders) perched along the tops of the tanks like overgrown rivets. Several stunted, scrubby poplars were trying to open up to the freshness of the spring season. They weren't having much luck. The place looked old, dingy, and very, very dirty.

"This is disgusting," June said, her nostrils flaring out.

"It's not attractive," I agreed. "Look, there're the vans. I wonder where— Hey Lisa!" I called out the window to a figure crouched down by a clump of vegetation.

Lisa looked up and smiled. "Hi, Robyn, June. What are you guys doing here?" She stood and brushed dirt from her pants, succeeding only in smearing it around.

"Thought we'd come by and pay you a visit," I answered. "We wanted to see the site."

"There's not much that's nice to see."

"Yeah, we noticed. You doing the vegetation survey?"

Lisa nodded. "Yup. Ben's over in the west field with the drill rig. The backhoe's not going to be here till tomorrow, so everybody else is over at that far storage tank. I think Nalini's going in to get a sample. There's some gunk sitting in the bottom of the fifth tank. Why don't you go over and have a look?" This to June. "See environmental consultants at work and all that."

June smiled at her. "We just might do that."

"I'll be your tour guide," I volunteered. "But I think we should stop by the drill rig first." I turned back to Lisa. "You need anything?"

"No, thanks anyhow, I just had a coffee and one of June's muffins—which were excellent, I might add." She grinned at June, then her smile faded. "I'm really sorry about that thing with your gnome," she said after a pause. "Ben told us about it this morning. That must have been nasty to see."

I glanced over at June to see how she would respond. I had convinced her the night before to tell Tracy about it. I understood June's reluctance to do so, but with a killer lurking about, it was safer to be informed. Tracy had been disturbed, of course, but when you're eighteen and crazy-obsessed with horses, things like a stranger's murder are pretty incomprehensible and far-removed from your sphere of existence. Besides, she hadn't seen the pictures.

June had, and it was June I was more concerned about. She'd been unusually quiet both the night before and earlier this morning, so I had very carefully stayed away from the subject while we'd been birding. Now, as Lisa expressed her concern, I was relieved to see that June appeared to have recovered from much of the shock. Apart from a grimness around the eyes, her demeanor was one of sadness more than anything else.

"Thanks, Lisa. I didn't know him well, but it wasn't a pleasant thing to see."

"I don't suppose anybody's found him yet?"

"Not that I know of." June spread her arm out to encompass the landscape. "And you can see for yourself what it's like around here. Undeveloped, for the most part. And big, very big. I know the RCMP have organized search teams, but it's quite possible they won't find him."

An errant puff of wind gusted by and Lisa shivered a bit. "Well, I hope at least they find the guy who did it. That whole business with the gnome and the pictures was *sick*!"

"It was indeed," June agreed and fell silent.

Time to move on.

We drove across the field to where Ben and Maurice stood by the drill rig. The type of drilling equipment normally used in this kind of project resembles an oil rig in everything but size. Truck-mounted, the rigs we use are smaller mining drills. They're manned by the same sort of roughneck types, though. And Maurice—a regular contractor of ours—was one of roughest. At least in appearance.

I'd never seen the man truly clean. His fingers seemed permanently stained, the fingernails always black with soil and grease. His hair was an SOS pad of rusty curls, his teeth stained amber from the cigarettes he chain-smoked. But despite his generally decrepit appearance, Maurice had an innate knowledge of drilling and a real feel for his equipment. Hydraulic drills are notorious for breaking down—they're worked pretty hard—but Maurice kept his equipment in top shape and, if it did break down, it didn't stay that way for long. He also had a kind heart, and a repertoire of off-color jokes that kept me chuckling for weeks after an encounter with him. I'd liked him the first time I'd worked with him.

They were just pulling the auger out of the hole when we pulled up. We stayed in the car, not wanting to get in the way till they had finished. Ben gave us a nod and a brief smile before turning his attention back to the work.

"What's that?" June asked as Ben wrestled a large pipe into the hole.

"A split spoon sampler," I told her. "It's essentially a pipe that falls in half. You drill a hole with the auger, then you put the sampler in and hammer it down with a hydraulic sledgehammer. That pushes the sampler into the soil."

We watched as the roughnecks suited action to my words.

"Then, when it's gone down far enough, you use the drill to bring it to the surface. Look, here it comes."

We got out of the car to get a better view as the sampler was pulled from the ground like a deep-rooted weed. Ben and Maurice grabbed the pipe and whacked it against the side of the drill rig. The sampler split in half, revealing a long, tubular mass of mud.

"Take a look at that," I pointed at the core sample. "You can see different layers and colors. That's the soil profile. Usually the darker layers are the ones that were on the surface at some point. The black is humus, a surface accumulation of... oh, sand, clay, decayed plant material, that kind of thing. And you see that grayish-reddish section? That's clay."

"Why is it red?"

"Iron oxides, probably. And that brown-yellow bit? That's sand. Now we'll wrap it up, take it in to a lab, and get the different layers sampled and analyzed for contaminants."

"Fascinating," June remarked, moving forward to get a better look.

"Hi, guys," Ben smiled at us. "How are you doing?" The question was directed at June.

I knew what Ben was really asking about, and I suspected June did, too, but she chose to misunderstand him. "We're just out for a gawp," she said.

He gave her a close look, then smiled, acknowledging her evasiveness. "Sounds good. You playing tour guide?" This to me.

I grinned back and nodded as Maurice joined us.

"Jeeezus H. Murphy!" he exclaimed to me. "I almost didn't recognize you. What the hell happened to you?"

"Hey, Maurice." I pulled a sour face. "I had a stupid accident."

He shook his head slowly, the requisite cigarette sending clouds of smoke billowing through his hair.

"I know, I know," I said before he could open his mouth again. "It was very stupid and I'd rather not talk about it."

His eyes smiled and he shrugged. "You betcha," he said. "Say, did you hear the one about the traveling field biologist and the rutting elk . . . ?"

"Ready to become an environmental consultant now?" Ben asked June as Maurice regaled me with his jokes.

"It's very interesting work, but I think I'll leave it up to you," June said with a chuckle. She peered down into the hole. "Is that water down there?"

Ben looked down, too. "Yep, water table's pretty high around here."

"So will this be one of your wells?"

"Monitoring wells? No, not here. I just needed to grab a soil sample. Surface sampling isn't really appropriate in a case like this, we've got to go deeper. That's why we bring in these characters. June, this is Maurice and . . . Robyn, I don't think you've met Sid before."

"Hey, Sid," I smiled a greeting at the man in question. He, too, boasted grimy hands and a dangling cigarette. I turned my attention to the hole in the ground. "You're not sinking a well here?"

"No, we've got one just over there," Ben gestured behind me. I turned around and spotted the pipe sticking up about one and a half feet.

"Haven't flagged it yet, though."

"Flagged?" June asked.

"To make sure I can find it again," Ben explained with a lopsided grin. "You'd think those pipes would jump out at you, but you'd be surprised how difficult they are to see if you're any kind of distance away from 'em. I remember my first field project, the turnip I was working with forgot to flag the wells and it took us the better part of a morning to find the little bast—uh, devils."

We chatted and joked for a while, but I kept an eye on my watch. Drill rigs were expensive to hire, and I didn't think Ben would appreciate us building up our collection of questionable jokes while the drill sat idle.

"Come on," I nudged June after a few minutes. "The tour must go on."

Maurice fired off a last joke involving Greek gods and orgies. We laughed, said our goodbyes, and headed back to the car.

"Want to see the rest of the gang?" I asked June.

"Yes. This is fascinating," she said.

I directed her toward the row of storage tanks where I could see Kelt and Cam hunkered down beside a pile of ropes. As we pulled up, Nalini stepped into view, sporting a bright yellow protective suit that covered her from head to toe.

"Good heavens!" June exlaimed when she saw her. "Is that really necessary?"

" 'Fraid so," I replied. "You never know what's in those old tanks, but ten to one it's not something you want to get on you. She'll have to wear scuba gear, as well."

"Are the chemicals that toxic?" June's tone was a mixture of concern, disgust, and admiration for Nalini.

I shook my head. "It's not really the chemicals, although they are very likely quite toxic, but it's the lack of oxygen that's more dangerous. The entryway at the top of the tank isn't big enough to mix oxygen—and really, given what's probably in that tank, you don't want any oxygen around or the whole thing's liable to explode."

"I had no idea your job was this risky."

I cocked a half-smile at her. "It's not always this dangerous," I assured her. "Come on, let's go see where they're at."

"Hey, guys," I greeted them. "How's it going?"

"Quite well," Cam said. "We've managed to collect a few samples already. So far, all these tanks have interior ladders."

"That makes life easier."

"Very much so."

"What are you two up to?" Kelt asked.

"I'm touring June around the site."

"Well, you've come at a good time," Kelt winked at June. "It's not usually this exciting. We're about to lower Nalini into yet another tank of hell."

"So I see."

"I feel like a sacrifical virgin," Nalini grinned. "Being tossed down to angry gods."

"Don't worry. We'll save you," Cam assured her in his soft voice. His dark eyes twinkled. He was clearly feeling more at ease with the Woodrow crew. It would be hard not to feel easy with them—they were a goofy bunch.

"I think we'll watch from over there," I decided, pointing past June's car. "We'll be able to see better. Good luck!" This last to Nalini, who smiled absently, intent on checking her suit.

By the time we went back far enough to see the top of the tank, Kelt, Cam, and Nalini were halfway up the ladder. Kelt carried the tripod, a heavy-duty affair, six feet long and very sturdy-looking.

"They'll set that up and attach the winch to it," I explained to June. "Then Nalini'll hook her safety harness to that. If there wasn't a ladder inside, then they'd have to lower her down with the winch."

We watched as Kelt and Cam opened the top hatch and set up the tripod. Nalini donned scuba gear and hooked up her safety harness. Cam double-checked it for her. She glanced around, caught sight of us, and flashed the thumbs-up signal before disappearing down the hatch. Kelt and Cam watched intently.

We stood quietly for a few minutes, waiting for Nalini to reappear.

"She'll go down, grab a sample or two, and come right back up." I patted June's shoulder. She was looking concerned about the whole process. "It'll be oka—"

Clang! Crash!

A shriek echoed in the tank. I jumped forward, nearly leaving my skin behind, my injured leg protesting the sharp movement.

"Shit!" Kelt swore, and he and Cam leapt to the tripod.

"Check the winch!"

"Grab that!"

"Quick!"

"Okay! Okay, here I've got it."

"Good. Ease it up. All right."

"Don't worry, we've got you," Kelt called down into the tank.

"What happened?" I yelled, feeling as pale as June looked. "Is Nalini all right?"

"She's fine," Kelt called back. "The ladder must have been corroded. It fell off and scared the beejeebers out of us all. It's okay, though, the harness is solid."

"And she didn't drop the samples," Cam said in admiration.

June took a shaky breath. I myself didn't take a breath till I saw Nalini's bright yellow form climb out of the tank.

"Guess the Tank God wanted to keep you," Kelt told her and they all burst out laughing in a release of nervous tension.

"I don't think I'd be very good at this job," June told me as we made our way back to the car. "I can't believe you miss it so much."

I shook my head and patted her on the shoulder. "It's not always this dangerous," I told her again.

CHAPTER 8

"I HAD COFFEE TODAY, YES I DID. I HAD COFFEE."

He was an elderly man, poorly dressed and balding, with smudged glasses and thick, slack lips. "I had coffee," he repeated.

I looked up from my own mug and smiled. "That's nice. Was it good?" I asked.

He nodded vigorously. "Oh, yeah, yeah it was good." He paused and his face lit up with the wide sweet smile of a child. "They got good coffee here, you know."

'Here' was Hank's Coffee House, where June had dropped me off after we'd left the site. It was early afternoon now, and the lunchtime crowd had eaten and left.

On appearance alone, Hank's would have been counted among the trendiest of cafes in a larger city. Coffee was served in cheery ceramic mugs, a selection of papers and magazines were scattered about, and the décor boasted the requisite beat-up wooden chairs and weathered plank floors. The only difference was that Hank's chairs had acquired their battered look from years of customers' backsides rather than from any special paint or finishing technique. And the floor looked like weathered planks because that's exactly what it was—planks of wood torn off an old barn some thirty or forty years ago.

Nobody knew why the place was named after Hank—Megan's friend Dana was the present owner and operator. Actually, nobody ever agreed on who Hank was or whether he had existed at all. But

Hank or no Hank, the Coffee House was practically an historic monument in Holbrook and it was always as busy as a birdbath during a drought. I usually made a point of dropping by whenever I was in town. Dana made excellent coffee, and equally tasty salads and cornbread.

In a given week, just about everyone could be counted on to show up for their dose of Ketracel Brown. I thought I'd seen everybody in town at one time or another, but the man standing in front of me now wasn't familiar.

"Dana, she makes good coffee, yes she does. She makes good coffee."

"She really does," I agreed. "Why don't you have a seat? I'm Robyn. What's your name?"

He perched carefully on the edge of the chair beside me. "My landlady, she calls me Rocky. That's what she calls me," he answered.

"Well, hey, Rocky. I haven't seen you around here before. Do you live in Holbrook?"

"Oh yes, I live in Holbrook. Yes, that's right. I live in Holbrook." His voice trailed off. "Do you live in Holbrook?"

I shook my head. "Nope, I'm just visiting. I live in Calgary."

"Oh, Calgary, I've been there, yes I have, I've been to Calgary. A long time ago. We went on the bus. It was a nice bus. That Greyhound, they have nice buses. Did you come on the bus?"

I shook my head. "No, a friend drove me down."

"Are you staying in the hotel? I stayed in the hotel once, a long time ago. I stayed in the hotel."

I shook my head again. "No, we're staying at June's Bed and Breakfast. Have you ever stayed there?"

He thought for a long minute. "I don't think so . . . ," he replied doubtfully, then his face brightened. "I had breakfast today, yes I did. I had breakfast."

"That's good," I told him. "It's important to have a good breakfast."

He bobbed his head up and down like a ruddy duck. "Yeah, I

had breakfast. But I'm hungry again. I think I'll go home and have some toast." He stood up abruptly. "Well, bye." He gave me a last cherubic smile before turning and walking away with single-minded intensity.

"See you later, Rocky," I called after him.

He didn't turn around.

I drained my mug and Dana sauntered over to give me a refill. She was a merry, vibrant woman prone to wide, often dramatic, gestures. Her eyes were as black as currants and her long wheat-blond hair was usually held back from her face by an intricate pattern of braids. It was in a criss-cross style today, I noted with a touch of jealousy. My own rebellious curls gleefully refused to be confined by either braid or clip, so I'd cut the little beggers off a few years before. Having short hair made a lot of sense in my line of work. Which wasn't to say that I liked it short. The truth was, in the dark hours of night I still envied people like Dana with long, obedient hair.

Dana and Megan had gone through high school together, but whereas Megan couldn't wait to leave Holbrook for bigger, better things, Dana had been quite content to stick around and settle for a simpler life—especially after she'd met and married Gary Ross. Career opportunities didn't exactly sprout on trees in Holbrook, but Dana had done rather well for herself. She'd started working at Hank's Coffee House five years ago, and had bought out the previous owner three years later.

"Hope he wasn't bothering you," she remarked, jerking her head towards the rapidly disappearing Rocky.

"Not a bit," I assured her. "Is he new to town? I don't think I've met him before."

Dana set the coffee pot down on the table and flopped into a chair.

"Nah, he's lived here forever, I think. He spent a lot of time down at the mental hospital in Ponoka. The story is that he used to be quite violent, you know—attacking people for no reason and stuff. Now they keep him medicated to the eyeballs." She frowned her disapproval at a spot on the table and began scrubbing at it with her apron.

"I think it's sad," she continued after a moment. "He's a nice old guy . . . and one of my best customers. He can put away coffee like nobody else I know! 'Cept maybe Megan when she's studying."

I grinned. During her finals, Megan and the campus Java Jive had kept each other in the black.

"You know, it's been a while since you were up for a visit," Dana remarked, looking up from the now-immaculate table. "Although, I can see what your excuse is just from looking at you. I don't mean to be nosy or anything, but what the hell happened to you?"

I sighed inwardly. I didn't really like talking about Marten Valley, but I was fairly well known here, and with almost half my body in plaster, people were bound to be asking why. Gary had obviously been keeping quiet about what he knew—even to his wife. Big surprise there. The man was so stoic, he could give a Vulcan a run for his money. But maybe if I spilled the whole story to Dana, she could just pass it along to the rest of the town with their afternoon coffees. Maybe then everyone's curiosity would be satisfied. Maybe afterwards she would even satisfy *my* curiosity and tell me what Kelt had written on the bottom of my foot. It was worth a shot. As she topped up my mug with a flourish, I started telling her about spotted owls.

I gave her the long version and she made all the appropriate noises at the appropriate times. When I finally wound down, we sat quietly for a few minutes. I wanted to think that Dana was stunned silent by my astonishing investigative skills. Yeah, right. She was probably trying to think of a polite way to tell me how stupid I had been. But I was wrong on both counts. When she did open her mouth again, it was clear that her thoughts were a lot closer to home.

"I, uh . . . I heard about June's gnome," she said. "And those pictures."

"Those pictures . . . ," I echoed, the images nudging their way back to the forefront of my brain.

"I never thought anything like this would happen in Holbrook!"

"I know what you mean." I paused for a second. "Think anybody in town is capable of murder?"

She looked at me, one eyebrow quirked up. "Playing Sherlock Holmes again?"

I shook my head. "Just curious."

"Hmmm." Dana poured herself a glass of water and leaned against the counter. "To answer your question, I have no idea. Richard DeSantis was an absolute sweetheart. You'd have liked him. He was a real environmental type."

"Yeah, June mentioned that."

"You know, he convinced me to get this cooperative-grown coffee. He said they didn't use chemicals on it, and that the coffee bushes they planted were good for the local birds."

I looked down at my mug. "It's great coffee."

Dana nodded. "I know. I'd never even heard about it till Richard brought it up. He used to come in here fairly regularly whenever he was around. He's been in town a bunch of times over the past year, or however long the DeSantises have been living here. He and his fiancée are—or were—working in Mexico."

"I heard he was engaged."

"Yeah," Dana traced patterns in the condensation on her glass. "Esme. I never met her, but he seemed real taken with her. Liked to flash her picture around. I wonder if she knows yet."

"What were they doing in Mexico?"

"Conservation-type stuff. Some education, too, I think. He had a real bee in his bonnet about pesticides. I think they're trying to get the farmers not to use them. But they were finding a lot of resistence because of the malaria. You know, Gary and I went to Mexico last year, and I didn't even know they had malaria down there."

"They don't in the cities or the resorts. It's different in the rural areas."

"Yeah, that's what Richard said, too. He said they went to one village and over half the kids were dying of malaria or yellow fever."

I stared bleakly into my coffee cup as Dana related the depressing story. This, then, was the flip side of the pesticide coin.

The one thing that many North American anti-pesticide crusaders often forget is that insects in developing countries are more vicious, persistent, and far, far more numerous than they are in the north. They also carry parasites for things like malaria, yellow fever, and elephantiasis. When chemical pesticides were in wide use, many of these diseases were almost wiped out. DDT, for example, proved to be an extremely effective killer of the *Anopheles* mosquitos which carry malaria. The scientist who came up with DDT was even given the Nobel prize in 1948. Then came Rachel Carson and her book *Silent Spring*, and suddenly the general public became aware of the unintended consequences of these chemical pesticides. Disruption of ecosystems, contamination of water sources, death or deformities of non-target organisms. The use of DDT and its ilk was banned or restricted.

But, as Matt had put it so succinctly the other night, chemical pesticides work even if they do affect non-target organisms. In India, for example, there are now about thirty million cases of malaria each year, as opposed to one hundred thousand when DDT was in use. Today, between one hundred and two hundred million cases arise annually worldwide. Of these, about two million are fatal, and most of those are children. Try telling some farmer whose child is dying of malaria that he shouldn't use DDT because it makes birds' eggshells thin, and you're likely to be brushed off much in the same way as one of the vector mosquitos.

"That's pretty grim," I said to Dana when she finished talking.

She nodded her agreement. "Yeah, and I think I have it rough sometimes. It sure puts life into perspective."

"Yeah." There seemed to be a lot of that going around lately.

We sipped in silence for a minute.

"If Richard DeSantis was an environmentalist, how did he feel about his stepfather's role in this toxic-waste treatment facility?" I asked.

Dana took a thoughtful slurp of her water. "I wouldn't think very good," she said finally. "But I'm guessing. He didn't discuss it with me. Actually, I don't think Richard was ever close to him."

"What makes you say that?"

"Just a feeling. The way he talked about him. I was under the impression that Grant hadn't cared much for Richard. Richard's mother, on the other hand, dotes—or doted, on her son. She must be devastated."

It was late afternoon before I got back to June's. Dana and I had had a lot of gossip to catch up on, most of it thankfully of a more cheerful variety than poisons and murder. We sipped away an entire pot of French Roast, talking about Megan's dorky bosses and our unruly cats, agreeing that both terms were redundant. Dana told me about the coffee shop biz and commiserated with me over my lack of love life. And most unfairly, she, too, laughed at Kelt's mysterious message on my cast, and then flatly refused to tell me what it said. Bag.

For the umpteenth time, I wondered what the hell he'd written. I had hoped at first that it was something sweet, maybe even (be still my heart!) a little mushy. But people were getting far too many jollies from it for that—unless, of course, the idea of me with a functional love life was amusing. Unheard of, perhaps, but funny? I didn't think so. If not that, then what? A joke? That was more likely. Probably something off-color, too. Maybe it was better if I didn't know. Maybe, I reflected, I should stop showing it to people.

June was busy in the kitchen by the time I hobbled in. She was making some fancy dish involving herbed chicken and phyllo pastry. It smelled divine. Apparently Guido the cat thought so, too. He was perched on top of a shelf watching her like a green-eyed eagle.

June didn't normally cook dinner for her guests; it was, after all a bed and *breakfast*. But after the excellent meal she'd prepared for us the night before, Cam had flattered and sweet-talked her into making a deal for dinner, too. I am the first to admit that June is a marvelous cook, but judging from the look on Cam's face whenever he spoke to her, his flattery wasn't entirely motivated by his stomach. I liked Cam—he seemed a truly nice guy. Too bad Matt had gotten there first.

"Did you get some lunch?" she asked me as I stumped in. Guido, his eyes fixed intently on the chicken, didn't even spare me a glance.

"Yeah, I had a salad at Hank's."

"Was Dana there today?"

"Yup, she and I had a nice long chat, too. She wanted to know all about Marten Valley."

"Hmm. I rather thought she might. I didn't say anything about it, you know. I thought I'd leave that up to you," June said, sprinkling a dash of something on the chicken. "I didn't know how much you'd want to tell people and—"

"What the hell?" I exclaimed.

June spun around and looked out the window to where I was pointing. Tracy had just ridden into the yard.

Her face was pale, tinged with green, and twisted with tears, but even more shocking was the condition of her beloved horse—wild-eyed, stumbling with exhaustion, and lathered in sweat.

"Good god!" June breathed and shot out the door.

I made my way to the step and watched wordlessly as Tracy slid from her horse.

"I found him, Mrs. M! I found him!" she sobbed as she collapsed in June's arms. "Oh god! He was just l-l-lying there! A black bird w-w-was pecking on his head," she choked. "I threw a rock at it, b-b-but it came back! He was just lying there! It was *eating* him, Mrs. M!"

June half-carried the hysterical girl into the kitchen and lowered her onto a chair. Tracy clung desperately to her, fingers white where they gripped June's blouse.

"I didn't know what to do! The bird w-w-was *eating* him! I couldn't make it s-s-stop!"

"Shhh. It's okay, honey, you're here now. It's okay." June stroked Tracy's hair as she whispered words of comfort. "It's okay now. Did you find Richard DeSantis, dear? Is that what happened?"

Tracy nodded against June's shoulder. She was shaking badly now, crying with deep, wrenching sobs, her eyes scrunched shut against what she'd seen. My heart went out to her. I knew from personal experience that closing your eyes didn't help.

Above Tracy's head, June's eyes met mine. She jerked her chin towards the hallway and I nodded.

There was a phone by the front door with emergency phone numbers written handily on the pad of paper beside it. I punched in the one for the local RCMP detachment.

"Hello, my name's Robyn Devara," I told the woman on the phone. "I'd like to report a body."

Déjà vu.

CHAPTER 9

TRACY HAD BEEN UTTERLY INCAPABLE OF GOING BACK out to show the police where she'd found the body, but she had described the area pretty thoroughly. It was June who led the RCMP officers there, and June who sported a distinct green tinge by the time she finally got back. From what I could gather, Richard DeSantis had been halfway to fertilizer.

The Woodrow crew had been appalled when they'd returned and heard the news. Kelt, especially, got very quiet, and I knew he was thinking about the last time he'd been involved with murder. I know I was. On the other hand, as Ben pointed out after dinner, we were jumping the gun a little bit in calling it a murder.

"It could have been an accident," he said.

Kelt frowned and shook his head. "But what about the gnome and those pictures?"

"I haven't forgotten about them," Ben said, "but it's possible the poor guy had an accident, and some psycho found him and figured it would be funny to pull a prank."

Lisa snorted. "That's pretty psychotic."

"Without question, but it doesn't make him or her a murderer. I wonder how the police are treating it."

I kept quiet throughout the ensuing debate, but from my experience, it seemed that the RCMP were treating it like a homicide. There were an awful lot of blue-black uniforms around, and we'd all been questioned rather thoroughly. There didn't seem to be any doubt in their minds that Richard DeSantis had met his death under suspicious circumstances.

Much later, after everybody else had gone to bed, there was a light tap at my door.

"Kelt!"

"Hi, Robyn."

"Is anything wrong?"

Besides, of course, the fact that we were both dressed.

He shook his head. "Just thought I'd see how you were doing."

"Oh. Well, come on in. Have a seat. You might have to move Guido." I motioned him over to the wingbacked chair that Guido had claimed for his own. The cat cracked an eye open, daring Kelt to move him.

Kelt perched on the edge of the chair and gave Guido a scratch under the chin. Then he looked up and inspected the room. "Nice digs."

I settled myself on the foot of my bed. "I know, it's one of my faves. Which one are you in?"

"Green and yellow quilt, goofy-looking stuffed elephant on the dresser, uh. . . ."

"Big lilac bush outside the window?"

"Yeah."

"That's the room I'm usually in. I *like* that goofy elephant. What do you think of June?"

Kelt continued to stroke Guido, but the corners of his mouth quirked up into a smile. "She's great. I can see Megan in her—or her in Megan, I suppose. She's a nice lady."

"And a damn good cook!" I added with an appreciative grin.

Kelt gazed over at me and smiled. "So how's it going?" His smile faded as he asked the question.

My own grin did a disappearing act. "Uh, okay I guess. Under the circumstances. How about you?"

Kelt made a face. "Can't say I'm thrilled about the circumstances."

"No," I agreed. "Though I think I feel more angry than anything. Tracy was devastated. The doctor had to sedate her, but even then the poor kid lay there shaking for the longest time. June just looked in on her. She's finally asleep."

"Do you really think he died from an accident?" Kelt asked.

I shook my head. "Do you?"

"No. I can't see anybody doing that. Playing a prank, I mean. And in spite of what Ben says, I don't think he believes it, either. Seems more like a message to someone."

"I know what you mean," I agreed. "But a message to who, and for what?"

Kelt looked at me for long minute, his green eyes troubled. "I can guess what you're thinking," he said softly.

"You've got to admit that it's a little suspicious, given who his stepfather is."

Kelt just sighed.

"It *could* have something to do with the plant," I insisted. "The DeSantises moved in less than a year ago, and June says they'd been living abroad for years before they came here. The people in Holbrook barely knew them to say hello to, let alone well enough to bump one of them off."

"You're assuming a pre-meditated murder, though, complete with motive. What if it was just some lunatic?"

An image of Rocky flashed in my mind. Hadn't Dana told me he had a history of violence? I brushed it away. Rocky was too medicated to kill a mosquito now.

"I suppose it's possible," I answered Kelt. "But you've got to wonder how often that happens outside of one of Arif's novels."

"Well, there's always the obvious. . . ."

"The evil stepfather?"

Kelt nodded. "Yeah, or the mother, I suppose. I seem to recall it was you who told me once that most murders were committed by family members."

"So I've heard." I paused for a moment. "But what about this gnome thing? That seems more like something a local person would do. Or at least someone familiar with the whole gnome-napping joke."

"So? The DeSantises have been around for a number of months. I'm sure they've heard all about the vacationing gnomes."

"Maybe." I was unconvinced. "But how does that fit in with your message theory?"

"It wasn't a theory, it was just a suggestion."

"And a very interesting one at that. I don't know, Kelt, I'm still suspicious about the waste treatment facility angle."

"You're not going to go and do a *Rear Window* on me now, are you?" Kelt tapped my leg cast significantly.

"Would that be a bad thing?"

He dropped his face into his hands.

I leaned forward. "Come on, Kelt, you can't tell me that you're not thinking the same thing. Family problems are one thing, and quite frankly, they're none of my business. I admit it! But if Richard DeSantis was killed because someone doesn't want his stepfather to start up a toxic-waste treatment facility, then what might that someone do to people who are cleaning up the site and making it possible? At the risk of sounding melodramatic, you guys could be in danger out there."

"More than you know," Kelt muttered.

"What are you talking about?"

Kelt hesitated a few seconds. "There might be a problem with the site," he answered reluctantly.

"What kind of problem?" I demanded, my tone sharp.

"We found a bunch of nails on the southeast access road yesterday."

"Sabotage?"

"Who knows at this point? Fortunately we'd stopped the van. There was a big puddle and Ben didn't want to drive through it till he knew how deep it was. I hopped out to check and that's when I saw the nails."

"What did Ben say?"

"Not much. As far as I know, nobody was thinking sabotage."

"Until now."

"Until now," he echoed in agreement.

Industrial sabotage was becoming more prevalent in Canada—primarily in Alberta. Over the past couple of years, there had been more than a hundred acts of sabotage at various oil and gas facilities in and around the Peace Country (which was turning out to be anything but peaceful). The perpetrators believed the gas wells and toxic sulfur dioxide emissions were poisoning the land, and claimed their activities were "legitimate self-defence against pollution."

Most of the sabotage was described as mischief, primarily minor damage to vehicles and property, but just the previous year, an oil executive had been shot and killed, and several oil and gas facilities had been bombed. There was no question that the war between industry and environment was escalating. A sobering thought to all who worked in the field—even those of us who were trying to clean things up.

"All the more reason to look into this murder," I said after a long moment. "We've got a possible saboteur out there. If Richard DeSantis was killed by a militant environmentalist, then our saboteur's not just puncturing tires."

"That's not the only reason you're wanting to get involved, is it?" Kelt's eyes caught mine.

I flushed and looked away. "You're right—although it is one of my main concerns. I'm strangely fond of the lot of you." I cleared my throat and paused, searching for the right words. "But it's Tracy," I said finally. "And her finding the body. It makes me see red. I'll never forget how I felt when I found a body, and I'm a biologist. I've seen a lot of dead things. I've *dissected* dead things. Tracy's just a kid. For somebody to leave a body out there where a kid could—and did—find it. . . ." I looked down at my hands.

"What can you do about it? You're not exactly mobile."

"I know, but I can nose around a little. Maybe go to Hank's tomorrow, and flap my ears around."

"No more than that?"

"Of course not."

"Okay. In that case, if you need any help, I can be your feet."

I lifted my head and gazed up at him. His eyes were sympathetic, his expression determined.

"Thanks." I smiled at him gratefully. "That really means a lot."

"Yeah, well, if you're going to tangle with murderers again, I'm going to make damn sure I'm around before he or she breaks your other leg."

"I'm not going to 'tangle with murderers'!" I protested.

"Uh huh."

"I'm not! It's more like an intellectual exercise. . . ."

"Right."

"I'm a biologist, Kelt. I'm *supposed* to be curious."

He shot me a disbelieving look. "Just as long as you remember that biology is the study of life, not death," he said tartly.

"But sometimes you have to study death in order to understand life," I tossed back.

Kelt blew out his breath in a long-suffering way.

Before he went back to his own room, he squeezed my shoulder and dropped a light kiss on my forehead. I stared after him, surprised and suddenly all too aware of how long it had been since anyone, besides Guido the cat, had kissed me. Sleep was a long time coming.

Chapter 10

"Oh. Hi!"

"Hey, Rocky, I wondered if you'd be here yet. How are you doing today?"

"I'm good. I had some coffee. Yes I did, I had some coffee."

"Already? You must get up early."

"Yeah, I get up early. Yes I do. I get up early and have breakfast. I had breakfast today. And then Dana she gave me a coffee. Yeah, she gave me a coffee. It was good."

"Great. I hope she'll give me one, too," I spoke loud enough so that Dana could hear. She laughed and made a show of rushing over with the coffee pot, obviously recognizing an emergency when she saw one.

June worked part-time at the tourism information desk of Holbrook's administration offices and she had dropped me off at Hank's on her way to work. She was going to check if I needed a ride back at lunchtime, but Holbrook was a small, friendly sort of place, and I was pretty sure that someone would run me back if I asked. Not that I planned on asking around just yet. I was determined to pick Dana's brains about Richard DeSantis. After I chatted with my new friend, of course.

"So Rocky, what are you up to today?" I asked. "Seeing as you've had your breakfast and coffee already."

"I dunno. I don't want to see Luke's ghost again. No, I don't want to see his ghost."

"Uh . . . you saw a ghost?"

"Yeah, I saw Luke's ghost. I saw his ghost this morning. After I got up."

"Who was Luke?"

"I worked with him over at the factory. Yes I did, I worked with him. He's dead now."

"Which factory is that?"

"Oh, they used to make chemicals at that factory. At the factory I used to work at. They made chemicals there."

"You worked at the old pesticide plant? Out by the wetlands?"

"Yeah, I worked at the plant, yeah. Before I was in the hospital. I was in the hospital, you know, they put me in the hospital. Now I'm out, but I have to take all my pills. Yes, I do, I have to take all my pills or they'll put me back. Look at all my pills." He pulled out a large rectangular case and popped the lid. Inside were rows of tiny compartments and enough pills to stock a small drugstore.

"You take all these, eh?"

"Oh yes, I don't want to go back to the hospital, no, I don't want to go back."

"I can understand that," I said. "So, Rocky, what kind of job did you have at the plant?"

"What kind of job?"

"Yeah, what did you do there?"

"Oh, I swept the floors and took out the garbage, I cleaned everything, yes I did, that was my job, to clean everything. Luke, he didn't clean, no he didn't clean like me. He mixed things up. I don't know what, but they were bad things. They made him sick. I never mixed up those things, no I never did that. Maybe I would've got sick, too. My dad, he got sick you know. Yes he did, he got sick from the plant just like Luke."

"Your dad worked there, too, huh?"

"Oh yeah, he worked at the plant. After the mine shut, he worked at the plant."

"The mine?"

Rocky nodded his head vigorously. "He worked at the coal

mine in Crowsnest Pass. Yes he did, he worked at the coal mine. I lived in Crowsnest Pass, too. Before my mother went to the hospital. They put her in the hospital just like me. They did, they put her in the hospital. I never saw her after that." His expression grew sorrowful.

"I'm sorry," I said, feeling inadequate.

"I never saw her any more. Then my dad, he came to work at the plant. Before he got sick, he came to work at the plant."

"And then you started working there, too?"

Rocky's face brightened. "Oh yes, I worked at the plant. Yes I did, I cleaned everything at the plant. I was a good worker."

"I'm sure you were. Do you remember much about the plant?" I asked gently. "Where things were stored and stuff like that?"

He shook his head. "I don't remember so good any more. No, I'm not so good at remembering." He paused. "I remember Luke, though, yes, I remember Luke. I don't know why he came back."

Rocky stood up abruptly. "I think I'll go home and have some toast now. Yes. I'll have some toast. Bye." With that he turned on his heel and strode out the door.

I blinked a little in surprise; his sudden exits were a little hard to get used to. Behind me, Dana chuckled.

"Close your mouth," she advised. "That's Rocky through and through. He'll talk your ear off for twenty minutes, then it's 'I've got to have some toast' and he's out of here like a shot."

"What was all that about a ghost?"

Dana shrugged and turned to the sink to rinse out a coffee pot. "Who knows? The guy's always seeing strange stuff. Kinda makes you wonder what they've got him on. He'll have forgotten all about it by tomorrow."

"Hmmm, I wonder if he'd remember anything about the plant if I showed him some photos, or even better, took him out there?"

Dana swung her head around and cast me a long look. "Why would you want to do that?"

"You know that Woodrow's doing the assessment?"

She nodded.

"Well, part of the process involves talking to people who used to work there. Especially for old sites like that one, there are a lot of places where toxic stuff may have gotten stored or dumped. Places that were never recorded in the written documents."

"Really?"

"Oh yeah. The first contract I ever worked on for Woodrow was a gas plant clean-up. It was a gross job, and a lot of the documentation was missing. Ben—my boss—tracked down some former employees at a couple of the local nursing homes. They were only too happy to talk to him, and because of it, we found several hotspots. Hadn't even suspected they were there."

"So you think Rocky might be able to help out now?" Her tone was doubtful.

"Who knows? Ben's been trying to find somebody who used to work at that plant. I guess they've all moved away or died or something. Rocky might not know much, but it'd be worth a try to ask him. As long as it doesn't upset him or anything. It sounds like he's had a pretty rough life. I don't want to be responsible for him seeing any more ghosts."

"Yeah, although I'd put that down to Richard DeSantis's death more than anything. Rocky got real spooked a couple of months ago when old Mrs. Kershaw died, and now with Richard dead and everyone talking about it, he's getting himself worked up again."

"I guess that's all over town now, isn't it? Richard DeSantis."

Dana nodded and gave the espresso machine a last polish. "It was before, what with June's gnome and all, and now that they've found his body. . . ." her voice trailed off meaningfully.

The timing had been right for the local weekly newspaper, and news of Tracy's discovery had been splashed across the front of this morning's *Holbrook Times*. There was one main article about the grisly find, a largish piece about the toxic-waste treatment facility, and a smaller one about the gnome and its packet of photos. But it was the big front-page photo more than anything else that arrested attention.

Richard DeSantis had shuffled off his mortal coil (or had it shuffled for him) in a remote, lonely-looking bit of wilderness. Pale-colored prairie stretched to the horizon of the picture, broken only by a stand of trees to one side, and a dark stain on the grasses where the body had rested. It was as if the man's death had seeped from his remains and spread out to mortify the ground around him. It was a pretty grim image even without the body.

"You think it was someone local?" I asked Dana now.

"From Holbrook? Why?"

I tried for a nonchalant shrug. "Just curious."

"As in, George?"

"Well, I heard about the protest group...."

"And you were wondering if anybody was worked up enough to do more than protest?"

"The thought had occurred to me," I admitted.

Dana snorted. "Not a chance. We're a very civilized group—a little hot under the collar, maybe, but civilized. June's the most militant, so you can imagine how likely it is that any of us would commit murder. She lets flies out of the house instead of swatting them, for god's sake! Besides, why would anybody like that kill Richard? If he had lived here, he would have joined our group, too. And if anyone was going to kill somebody over that plant, it would've been Grant DeSantis lying out there in that field, not his stepson."

And with a decisive flick of her towel, Dana changed the subject as if there was nothing more to be said on it.

I was still thinking about the murder when I tried to leave Hank's. I say 'tried' because I didn't quite succeed at first.

It was awkward humping about on crutches. Doors in particular were a problem. I'd discovered that the easiest way to get through one was to give it a good shove with my crutch and limp through quickly before it closed again. But when I shoved the door at Hank's, I heard a smack and a sharp cry. I elbowed the door open again and poked my head out. A woman stood on the front step, holding her forehead and crying great, racking sobs.

"Oh, gods. I'm sorry!" I tried to comfort her and keep my balance at the same time. "Are you okay? Please come in and sit down. Let me get you a coffee. I'm really sorry."

By this time, Dana had rushed over and taken the sobbing woman to a chair. I stood there feeling like an oaf.

The woman sank into the chair and cried as if her heart were broken. I felt lower by the second.

"I'm really sorry," I said again.

She shook her head and scrubbed at her face. "No . . . no, no. It is not your fault," she gulped. "I am okay. Really." She looked up and tried to smile at me through her tears.

Dana sucked in a sharp breath. "Esme?"

"Do . . . do I know you?" the woman asked, her voice rough with tears.

Dana shook her head. "No. I've seen your picture. I knew Richard."

"Richard!" Her eyes filled and she started to cry again.

Dana recovered herself. "Let me get you a coffee," she said.

I sat down beside Esme and patted her shoulder awkwardly. I was sure getting a lot of action with the Florence Nightingale routine, but I couldn't just stand by and do nothing. If this was the same Esme Dana had told me about before (and I was pretty sure it was), then the woman had lost her fiancé in the most horrible way imaginable. And I'd just smacked her in the head with a door. Way to go, Robyn.

Dana came back with a steaming mug and a box of Kleenex. A few more customers had come in and were casting inquisitive looks at our table, so Dana shot me a look that said "don't leave her alone." I gave her one back that said "I may have hit her with a door, but give me some credit." Dana nodded once and bustled over to serve her other customers. I stayed with Esme and offered the Kleenex box as she tried to get herself under control.

By the time she had calmed down to hiccups, her coffee was no longer steaming. I nudged the mug towards her.

"Have a drink. It'll make you feel better."

She took a sip and closed her eyes. Her eyelashes were wet, stuck together in spiky clumps. But even with red, puffy eyes and a growing bump on her forehead, she was stunningly beautiful. High cheekbones, glossy dark hair, and lovely skin the color of a latte. No wonder Richard DeSantis had flashed her picture around.

"I am sorry." She had opened her eyes and was looking at me.

"*You're* sorry?" I spluttered. "*I'm* the one who's sorry. Smacking that door into you like that!"

The bump on her head looked at me reproachfully and agreed, but Esme's eyes were full of apology.

"No. It was me. I was not paying attention. And then to cry like that—"

"Hey," I cut her off. "You had a good reason, and I'm very sorry about that, too. My name's Robyn Devara."

"I am Esmerelda de Los Angeles, but everybody calls me Esme."

"It's nice to meet you, Esme. Are you okay?" I wasn't asking about her bump.

She took a deep, shaky breath. "As okay as I can be for now. I don't think it has sunk in yet. There was a conference in Edmonton. I came with a delegation of conservation workers from my country. Richard had come with me, but he said he had some family business to take care of." More tears made tracks down her cheeks. "He would not tell me what it was. He said he wanted to talk to his stepfather first. And then I was so busy, and when he did not phone, I just assumed I had missed his calls. His mother phoned me yesterday." She gulped.

"Are you staying with the DeSantises?"

Esme nodded. "Yes. They are very kind. Melanie is trying to make everything easier for me, but she is—" she choked a bit "—very upset about Richard. It is . . . hard to be there sometimes. That is why I came to this cafe. I thought they needed some time alone."

"And then I smucked you with the door," I said morosely.

"It's okay." She felt her forehead gingerly. "It is just a little bump. I have had much worse. I am not very graceful sometimes."

"That makes two of us," I told her with a grin.

She tried to smile back at me, but her eyes stayed sad.

I cast about for another topic of conversation. "Uh, Dana—the woman who runs this coffee shop—she told me you were doing conservation work in Mexico."

Esme nodded. "Yes. I was born in a little town by the US border. I used to do a lot of work in South America, but my own people needed help so I came back."

"I've heard things are rough down there."

"Yes, the *maquiladoras* are a terrible problem."

"Maquil—?" I began.

"The *maquiladoras*. They are assembly plants, most of them owned by foreigners."

"Oh, right. I remember now."

"Yes. They come to Mexico because the labor is cheap and our environmental standards are very low. Most of the plants make very poisonous chemicals, and the owners do not care much what happens to the land or the workers. I have seen the children with deformities, and the birds that take one sip out of a ditch and fall down dead. I had to do something."

"I can understand that. I'm an environmental consultant. We try to clean up things like that here."

Esme's eyes brightened. "Ah. So you know what a mess we are dealing with."

"Sort of. I've read about some of those factories—the *maquiladoras*. They sound horrifying. We haven't got anything quite that bad up here."

"Yes, it is bad," she agreed. "Have you heard of a company named Dyncide?"

I shook my head. "I don't think so."

"They used to have a factory in my village. To make insecticides. Not any more. They closed a year ago, but they left their barrels and their chemicals behind. It is a terrible mess. The water has been poisoned so the poor people must collect rainwater. But large containers are very difficult to find so they use the old barrels to collect the water."

I sucked in my breath sharply. "That's suicide!"

Esme nodded. "Yes, but they do not know. Richard was trying to educate them, but it is difficult."

I looked at her with respect. "I admire you, what you're doing for your people."

But she shook her head a little as if to brush off my praise. "Richard thought the same way. That it was for the people. But I do it for me. These people—my people—they are so poor and there are many with sickness and tumors, but they still can laugh. I go to visit them and we are laughing and joking and telling funny stories. Sometimes I cannot believe it. But these people, they are what life is about. Richard knows this now, too. . . ." Her face fell. "Or, he knew it," she finished softly.

"I'm sorry."

She blinked away some tears and nodded her head. "Thank you, Robyn. And thank you for listening to me."

"It was a pleasure talking to you," I said.

She tried to smile but it trembled and died. "Thank you. And now I think I should go to see if Richard's mother needs me."

"I promise I'll stay away from the door until you leave," I said, coaxing a wobbly smile from her.

I figured it was the least I could do.

Chapter 11

JUNE WAS STILL OUT BY THE TIME I got back to the B & B. One of her neighbors had stopped in at Hank's for coffee and kindly offered me a ride back. As I mentioned before, Holbrook is a helpful sort of place. I parked myself in the living room and flipped through June's collection of compact discs. Mozart's *Missa Solemnis* was just getting underway when the doorbell rang and I was rudely reminded that not everybody in Holbrook had a heart of gold.

"Oh, so you're here again." The woman was unimpressed.

The feeling was mutual.

At first glance, she was a chirpy-looking type with wavy silver hair, dark, lively eyes, and skin that was all roses and cream. But the lines on her face were more familiar with frowns than smiles, her color had more to do with ill humour than good health, and if you looked closely at her eyes, you'd see that the sparkle you had mistaken for cheer was actually a gleam of pure malicious spite. Carole Miller had come calling.

She was a selfish, pompous woman with a pinched soul, a nose for scandal (real or imagined), and a slug of a son who had developed a weird and totally unwelcome crush on me several years earlier.

It had been dislike at first sight when I'd met Carole, and although I had known her only a few short years, everything I had seen or heard about her since had only strengthened my opinion.

June, who'd had to put up with the woman's acrimony for over twenty years now, disliked her intensely, although she was usually too good-natured to admit it. Megan actively despised Carole Miller and had once cheerfully observed to me that if she'd killed her when she'd first thought about it, she'd be out on parole by now.

"I'd hoped to find June in," Carole said to me with the disdainful sniff one usually reserves for dog shit or people who call during dinner to sell you long-distance phone service.

I peered around her to make sure her wormy son wasn't lurking around. Good. She was alone. Unpleasant enough, but not as bad as it could have been.

"Not home," I answered her quickly, and started to close the door.

Carole Miller stuck her foot in it. I briefly tossed around the idea of crushing her shoe, but decided against it for June's sake.

"Would you like to leave her a message?" I asked, looking down pointedly at the shoe wedged in the door.

"I want to know what's going on in this town," she announced. "I saw the police here the other day, and I heard all about June's gnome."

She made it sound as if June had offed Richard DeSantis herself.

"Why don't you just phone the RCMP and ask them yourself?" I was verging on rude now.

"I have. They were extremely unhelpful. What's being done to keep us safe? I'd like to know. How do we know we all won't be murdered in our beds? What's this town coming to, when the police can't even take the time to reassure innocent citizens?"

"I guess they have other things on their mind—like finding a murderer," I said. I might as well have saved my breath. Not to mention my sarcasm.

"You have to wonder what that boy was up to, getting himself murdered like that," she said sharply. "If anyone in that family was to be murdered I would have thought it would be *her* with her ever-so-superior attitude. Too good for the rest of us!"

"Are you talking about Richard DeSantis's mother?"

"Well, I wasn't talking about the *maid*." Her voice oozed derision at my stupidity.

I gritted my teeth. "What's wrong with his mother?" I asked.

Carole Miller sniffed again. "Melanie DeSantis is a bitch through and through, you just ask anyone. All expensive clothes and flashy jewelry. She wants to publish some fancy magazine here—something about western living, as if she'd know about *that*, living overseas in those countries for years and years. And she keeps firing her staff. My Howard worked for her and he said you wouldn't believe the screaming and yelling that went on in that office. She fired him! For no reason. A man like my son? You've never seen a harder worker. I told him it was just as well. Working for a bitch like that. Howard hasn't worked a single day since, and all because of her."

"Still, you've got to feel sorry for her," I remarked mildly. "Now that she's lost her son."

Carole Miller pursed her lips. "Of course." Her tone was clipped. "I'm sure it's a tragedy." She moved her foot out of the doorway. "You tell June I was by," she ordered. "She can phone me tonight."

"I'll be sure to do that," I told her with a false smile.

I closed the door, took a deep breath, and let it out slowly. I should feel sorry for her, I told myself. The woman was clearly unstable. Still, it was hard to remember that when she was right in your face.

The phone rang and I hobbled back down the hall to answer it.

"Hello?"

Nothing but silence.

"Hello?" A little testy this time.

Still nothing. I shrugged and hung up, turning my thoughts back to Carole Miller.

What was all that crap about Melanie DeSantis? Sour grapes because she'd fired Carole's useless son? Esme seemed to think Melanie was nice enough, and I was more inclined to believe her than Carole Miller. Still, there had been an odd note of sincerity in Carole's voice. I couldn't help but wonder what kind of person Melanie DeSantis was, and what, if anything, she had been doing to get people in Holbrook riled up.

June and I were hanging around in the kitchen again. She was spooning a batch of chocolate chip cookies onto baking sheets, and I was lounging at the kitchen table waiting for them to be done—and eating the raw dough whenever June wasn't looking. I'd concluded many years ago that the only way to eat chocolate chip cookies is either raw when nobody is watching, or warm with a glass of cold milk. I intended to do both. The Woodrow crew came in as I was pouring myself a glass of milk in anticipation of the first fragrant pans.

"Hey, guys," I called. "How was your day?"

Ben stepped into the kitchen first. "Well, I think we've got ourselves a saboteur," he announced in a calm voice.

June spun around and stared at him. "*What?*"

"What happened?" I demanded.

I'd worked directly with Ben on several projects before, so I'd been expecting a display of temper for some time now. Toxic waste. Improper disposal methods. Normally it was enough to blast him into orbit. His anger was rarely directed at us, but he did tend to beat his chest like a silverback at the more blatant examples of human incompetency and/or criminality. Which made his present restraint all the more unsettling.

Ben shucked his jacket and tossed it back into the mudroom. "Somebody slashed one of the tires on my van," he told us in that eerie matter-of-fact tone of voice.

"Oh my god!" June exclaimed.

"Did you see it happen?" I quickly scanned the crew to make sure they were all there. Everybody present and accounted for. I breathed a sigh of relief and sat back down at the table.

Ben was shaking his head. "No, though one of us must have come close. Only the one tire was slashed. He did a number on it, too. It's unsalvageable. I'm guessing something disturbed him before he could get to the others. Good thing, we had only the one spare."

"What were you guys doing?" I moved over to make room for Ben.

"Poking around inside the structures, checking out the drains and pipes," Ben answered accepting a cookie as June offered them around. "It must have happened then."

"That's terrible, Ben!" June's face was stricken. "Shouldn't you report it?"

"Already done. Unfortunately the RCMP are pretty helpless in a situation like this. They've promised to interview a bunch of people but. . . ." He gave an eloquent shrug. "We'll be watching our behinds now, that's for sure. I'm hoping this doesn't get out of hand—for us and whatever turnip is responsible."

"Why the concern for him?" June asked, puzzled.

"The site's a mess," Ben explained. "It's risky for us to be in some of those areas—at least without the proper protective gear. Whoever's doing this may not know how contaminated the place might be. It's dangerous. Even the soil's severely contaminated."

I looked at Lisa and raised one eyebrow.

She nodded unhappily. "Yeah, I knew we'd have to pull out the one tank on the east side, but it looks like we'll be yanking a few more. The soil's pretty discolored and it stinks, too, and you know those underground storage tanks are designed to last only about fifteen to twenty years, tops."

"Which puts the Norsicol ones in the definitely corroded category," I mused.

Lisa nodded.

"But the plant closed down almost twenty-five years ago," June was saying. "I know these pesticides are persistent, but shouldn't they have broken down by now?"

"Not necessarily," Lisa answered. "It's supposed to take about four to eight years, but really it's closer to twenty. And in Canada, you're looking at even longer."

"Why is that?"

Lisa and Kelt grabbed for the last cookie on the plate. She beat him to it by a fraction of a second and grinned in triumph before turning her attention back to June.

"Lots of reasons. Most of the tests were done in the US where soils are warmer and have more moisture, and where the growing season is a lot longer—all of which speed up the degradation process. Up here, the soils are colder, drier, and we have a short growing season, so the degradation process may be longer by twenty to twenty-five percent."

We sat and crunched cookies in silence for a long moment.

"What's the risk of groundwater contamination?" I asked.

The site was in much worse shape than anyone had thought. I found that my appetite had fledged, so I passed Kelt my uneaten cookie. I was just applying them directly to my thighs anyhow.

"It's hard to say," Ben replied. "The soil's fairly sandy, so the stuff could be percolating down. We'll have to monitor the wells, and find out how high the groundwater table is and how fast it's moving."

"Is Beaverhill in any danger?" June asked quickly.

"I don't know, June," Ben answered. "The area's got a pothole topography with moraine-type soil."

"Which means what, exactly?"

"Which means lots of clay with lenses, or areas, of sand. Clay's pretty impermeable to water. So the clay part is good. Low potential for contamination. But those sand lenses are a different matter. I just don't know yet. It's something we'll have to look at. Groundwater contamination may not be the biggest concern, though," Ben admitted.

"Oh?" June raised her eyebrows in inquiry.

"Beaverhill's a eutrophic lake—in other words, a big slough. But whatever you want to call it, it's got shallow, warm water and lots of shore vegetation. Most of the sediment on the bottom washes into the lake through erosion and runoff from the surrounding land basin. That's where we run into potential problems. The chemicals don't necessarily have to be in the groundwater to percolate through to the lake. If they're moving through the soil profile, then contaminated sediments could be washed into the lake. . . ."

"Then it's sayonara to the birdlife," Kelt finished.

"Actually," I remarked into the silence that followed this statement, "the birdlife may be able to help us—you—out with this."

"How do you mean?" Ben asked.

"This area is packed with blue herons," I explained.

Cam snapped his fingers. "That's right! I read about that guy's work. Down in the States."

"What guy in the States?" Ben demanded.

"There was a fellow down in Washington state who was using blue herons to study environmental contamination," I explained. "Mostly heavy metals and PCBs, but also DDT. Unfortunately, he died in a plane crash a few years ago and nobody's really continued with his work. His basic premise revolved around the fact that blue herons are fish-eaters—well, fish and other aquatic organisms—but the point is they're perched right at the top of the food chain."

"So high concentrations of contaminants in herons' eggshells and feces will reflect contamination in lesser species," Cam finished.

"Exactly," I agreed. "There are heron colonies all around Beaverhill. Cam could go and collect feces and eggshells, and send them out for analysis. It wouldn't even take very long."

"So we'd be able to tell whether this stuff is making its way into the food chain," Ben mused.

"And the herons may even be able to help you pinpoint the sources of contamination," I added.

"How?"

"Herons nest in centralized colonies," I told him. "And they forage for food within a given distance from these colonies. So. . . ." I passed it over to Cam with a flourish.

"So if we've got one colony that shows higher concentrations of contaminants than another, we've found ourselves a hotspot," he said.

Ben raised his eyebrows and regarded the two of us admiringly. "What a team," he said.

Cam and I grinned at each other and did a high five.

"How could they?" June broke in angrily. All eyes turned and looked at her. Her face was flushed pink and her eyes were like quartz.

"Excuse me?" Ben asked.

"How could they just bury these things and forget about them? I'd like to get my hands on whoever gave the go-ahead for that! Didn't anyone have a clue back then how dangerous these chemicals were?"

Ben gave her a sympathetic look. "Not really," he answered. "But they weren't completely ignorant of it, either."

Just then, Tracy came downstairs. Her face was still white and drawn, her subdued manner a mere ghost of her former bubbly self. We abandoned our depressing discussion and concentrated our talk on horses and other cheerier subjects.

There was a protest meeting against the waste treatment facility that night. June had invited me to go and Kelt had invited himself. In light of Richard DeSantis's murder, I thought it might be prudent of me to get a better handle on how the town felt about the Reisinger project. That was my reason for going. I wasn't sure why Kelt was tagging along.

June was chairing the meeting, so she sat with Matt and several other committee members on a raised platform at the front of the community center's main room. Kelt and I found seats towards the back. I struggled a bit with my crutches, and smiled an apology to the man beside me after I bumped him with my leg cast. More than a hundred people had turned out for the meeting, and the room felt crowded, the air warm and close. It was about to get a lot warmer.

The meeting started off harmlessly enough, with several of the committee members discussing the latest developments regarding the project. It took a good forty minutes to get through the agenda. Many in the group were unclear as to the steps involved in this kind of assessment and it took a good deal of explanation. I was happy to note that Woodrow's generally fine reputation was mentioned as a positive development. The subject of the DeSantis murder came up and everybody agreed on the importance of being considerate of the family despite how they all felt about Reisinger. So far, so good. But the problems started when the floor was opened up to suggestions for action.

"We can circulate another petition," an older woman suggested.

"Waste of time."

"They never pay attention to those things."

"What about more letters?" a dark-haired man called out. "We can target Reisinger, the province, the feds. If they get enough of 'em, they'll have to pay attention."

"Yeah, right," said a scornful voice.

I searched the crowd to see who the voice belonged to. There. Two rows in front of me. An older man, a farmer by the looks of his jacket. His hair was dirty blond streaked with gray and grease. He looked caustic and unpleasant, the kind of person who was never told that frowns use more muscles than smiles.

"Letters!" he jeered. "You'll never accomplish anything sitting on your butt."

"Larry's right. We've got to be more active than that!"

"Proactive rather than reactive."

The man beside me snorted audibly and stood up. I slanted a look at him. He was a short, pear-shaped type, fairly innocuous-looking with sandy hair and gold-rimmed glasses.

"It's too late for that," he said, pitching his voice so everyone could hear him. "The thing's a done deal."

"Ah Christ, Bert, not that conspiracy shit again!" A large, bearded man said in disgust.

"Shit, nothing! I know what—"

"Can we all just calm down, please!" June shouted as the noise level in the room started swell. "Everybody will get a chance to speak!"

More angry mutterings. I squirmed on my seat.

"But he's a goddamn conspiracy nut!" the bearded man insisted. "I don't have to listen to him."

"At least he doesn't get his thrills from shooting birds!" someone yelled.

A thin man jumped to his feet. "And just what the hell do you mean by that?"

"You heard me. I don't know why you're even here. What do you care about saving the wetlands? All you want to do is kill things—"

"*That's enough!*" June bellowed.

The crowd was shocked into silence.

"What do you mean by making accusations like that?" June demanded. The cords in her neck stood out like knotted ropes; her face was puce with anger. "We all have our reasons for being here—good reasons despite their differences. I will *not*—" she banged the table "—I will not have these holier-than-thou attitudes, not at any meeting I'm chairing. You all seem to forget we're on the same side. For god sakes, we're here to figure out a way to stop the damn plant, not to sling mud—and worse—at each other!" She stopped and took a deep breath. Her face was still pretty red. "I think we've had enough for tonight—"

"But, June, we haven't come up with a plan," the petition woman complained.

June gave her a hard look. "I know, Iris, but sitting around shouting at each other is not going to help us come up with one."

"And—"

"What I suggest we do," June interrupted her before another argument broke out. The crowded muttered and shifted. June waited until they were quiet again before she continued. "What I suggest we do, is have everybody write down his or her ideas. They'll be compiled and posted in the administration building. You can all have a look at them and then we can vote on them at the next meeting. At that point, we'll discuss any proposals that need further explanation—*quietly and in a civilized fashion*."

There were murmurs of agreement throughout the room. The temperature began to drop as tempers cooled. Then Larry the farmer stood up.

"And what if we *don't* agree with what you decide to do?" he demanded, his voice rough with frustration.

"You don't *have* to be part of the group," June snapped back. She took a deep breath and continued in a more reasonable voice. "It's your choice, Larry. This isn't my decision to make. We're a democracy. We go with what the majority decides."

Larry pressed his lips together and stared at June. She glared right back at him. After a moment he dropped his eyes.

"Okay," June said in a calmer voice, "we've got a pile of paper up here. Matt? Can you take care of that?"

He nodded. "Sure thing."

"Thanks." She turned back to the crowd. "If you've got a suggestion, then come on up and put it on paper. There're coffee and cookies in the other room, courtesy of Hank's Coffee House. We'll meet again in two weeks to vote on the proposals."

The meeting broke up noisily as half the group mobbed Matt while the other half made a beeline for the coffee. I found myself standing in the coffee line behind the man I'd jostled to get into my seat, the conspiracy nut.

"Sorry I bumped you like that before," I told him while we waited. "I didn't—*oof!*" I teetered off balance as somebody brushed past me.

He reached out to steady me. "That's okay," he said with a smile. "Still a little wobbly on the pegs, are you?"

"Yeah," I grinned back. "Are you really a conspiracy nut?"

He chuckled and lifted his shoulders in a good-natured shrug. "I've certainly got a reputation along those lines."

"No kidding?"

" 'Fraid not." He held out his hand. "My name's Bert Pine."

I balanced myself on one crutch so I could shake his paw. "Hey, Bert. Robyn Devara."

We chatted and waited for the line to move. Mostly small talk: where I was from, why I was in town, whether Oreos were better than Fig Newtons. We didn't get back to the topic of conspiracies until Kelt joined us and we retired to a quiet corner. I'd had no idea Kelt was a conspiracy buff himself, but once we started on the subject of hidden agendas, I might as well have been Claude Rains. Like had, quite obviously, recognized like.

"I never started out as a conspiracy freak," Bert was explaining to Kelt, who was nodding in sympathetic understanding. "But, you know, it's damn hard not to be when you find out what isn't being reported."

"And why," Kelt chimed in.

Bert clapped his shoulder. "Exactly! The Yellow Rain incident comes springing to mind."

"Uh, yellow rain?" I asked tentatively.

"It all had to do with biological weapons," Bert said. "And the good ol' US of A The whole mess started in 1981 when old Alexander Haig broke off talks with the Soviets because he said they were producing and stockpiling biological weapons. The US hadn't produced any chemical weapons of its own since the late sixties. Anyhow, Haig claimed that there'd been some toxic gas attacks in Laos, and that the Soviets were to blame for it. His report said it was like a cloud of yellow rain.

"According to this report, the poisons were mixed with some kind of sticky base like pollen, so it would stick to the victim's skin and penetrate more easily. Well, of course, Reagan and his bunch pushed to get Congress to renew funding to start making their own chemical weapons again. It took a few years, but by 1987, the States were a-churning out biological weapons again.

"And as for that yellow rain? Huh. What a crock! A fellow at Harvard did some research into it, comparing the Army's samples with samples that other scientists collected. Turns out Haig's toxic yellow rain was nothing more than bee shit!" Bert paused and sipped his coffee. "Didn't stop the biological weapons boys though."

"Bee shit?" I asked skeptically.

Kelt grinned at me. "Yeah, the local bees are pretty much confined to their nests in the winter. Come spring, they rise up in a mass cleansing flight to release all the wastes that built up over the winter."

"In a big ol' cloud of yellow rain," Bert finished.

I was sorry I asked.

"So you see," Bert continued, unperturbed by the look on my face, "when it comes to censored news and conspiracies, the 'why' is usually the key to the whole thing."

"It was the same with hemp," Kelt said.

"Outlawed in the States in 1937 because of a campaign launched by a certain newspaper magnate, who will remain nameless, who used his media empire to promote the idea that marijuana leads to unspeakable crimes and is dangerous to people's health. And all the while our Citizen Kane had his fat ass sitting on thousands of acres of timber land—in danger of competition from the growing hemp industry."

"And the petrochemical companies were involved, too," Kelt explained further. "They'd spent millions developing synthetic fibers and oils that could replace hemp products, and when they did, they jumped onto the anti-marijuana bandwagon."

"Unbelievable," Bert shook his head solemnly.

Kelt nodded his agreement.

This time, I hadn't even asked, but I was still sorry.

"And then, there was the business with Agent Orange. . . ."

"And don't forget the Nazi scientists illegally brought to work in American labs. . . ."

"And, of course, that Kuwaiti girl's testimony about Iraqi atrocities. . . ."

"And it turned out that she wasn't a refugee at all, but the daughter of the Kuwaiti ambassador to the United States. . . ."

I listened quietly as Kelt and Bert kept up in this vein for a while. Some of the conspiracies seemed straight out of the *X-Files*. I kept expecting little green men to enter into the equation at any moment, but when I asked about them, I was given a pitying look and told in no uncertain terms that they were gray, not green. So much for my contribution to the conversation. By the time June finished up and came looking for us, I was more than ready to leave.

Tap, tap.

I was just getting ready for bed when I heard the soft knock. I opened the door to the emerald eyes and smug, striped countenance of Guido the cat. Kelt had him in his arms.

"I found him slinking around the kitchen," he told me with a grin. "He was eyeballing the butter dish."

I sighed ruefully and cast an exasperated look at my cat. "Thanks, Kelt, you'd better toss him in here for tonight."

Kelt stepped into my room and settled Guido on the footstool. "There you go, son," he said, giving the cat a scratch behind the ears. Guido curled his toes in ecstasy. Given the same stimulus, I'd have probably done the same.

Kelt flopped down in the wingbacked chair.

"Gee, have a seat."

"Thanks, I did."

He reached over and started scratching Guido's ears again. If I were a Ferengi, I'd be damned jealous.

"Fun evening," I remarked after a moment.

Kelt quirked his mouth a little. "I guess. Remind me never to piss off June."

I widened my eyes in agreement. "No kidding. Meggie told me she could really fly off the handle. This was the first time I ever saw it, though—not that she didn't have good reason. That one guy was pretty inflammatory."

"Mmm. What did you think of Bert Pine?"

"The conspiracy nut?"

"He's not a nut!"

I gave Kelt the big sideways-look-with-raised-eyebrow. "Give me a break," I said. "The guy probably wears pointy ears in his spare time. Don't you think he was a little much?"

Kelt shook his head. "No, I don't. He's very plugged in to what's going on in the world."

"Yeah, but green—or, excuse me, gray—aliens?"

"Never know. I wonder what was wrong with the other guy—the inflammatory one."

"Maybe the aliens forgot to remove his anal probe."

Kelt grinned. "It's one explanation." He gave Guido one last scratch, then sat back in the chair. "So," he said, all seriousness now. "Enough about the protest meeting. How did the sleuthing go?"

"You mean, did I ferret out any militant environmentalists lurking around?"

"Yeah."

I shook my head. "Sorry. You saw them yourself. Just your average not-in-my-backyard folks. Dana told me that June was the most militant of the lot. She's got a temper, I grant you, but somehow I can't see her going out slashing tires and killing people."

"The two aren't necessarily related."

"I know. But they're not necessarily unrelated, either."

"Hmmm."

"I met his fianceé today," I said pensively. "Richard's fianceé."

"Oh?" Kelt gave me a searching look.

"Her name's Esme. She's really nice. I liked her. She told me about their work in Mexico. She and Richard have been trying to raise awareness about the *maquiladoras*."

"Ah." Kelt nodded in understanding.

"You've heard about them, then?"

"Yeah. Grim stuff."

"It is," I agreed. "Ever hear of a company called Dyncide?"

Kelt thought about it for a minute, then shook his head. "I don't think so. Why?"

"Esme asked me the same thing. They used to manufacture

insecticides in her home town. Polluted the hell out of the place, too. I guess she and Richard were trying to minimize the damage."

"The guy sounds like he was a pretty active environmentalist."

"Yeah."

"Still think his death is related to the Reisinger project?"

"Maybe. I haven't ruled out anything yet."

Kelt raised his eyebrows. "Not even the psycho?"

"Not even that."

"Any leads?"

"Not really. There is a guy who hangs around the coffee shop a lot. He's got some mental problems, but he's kept pretty medicated."

"Is he violent?"

"According to Dana, he was at one time, but I've met him and I can vouch for the medicated part. He's just a nice old guy."

"Hmmm, well, be careful."

"You too."

We talked a while longer about the site and our co-workers. Apparently Ben had already called everybody (including Cam) a turnip at one point or another, so essentially life was reassuringly normal despite the murder, sabotage, and the general disgusting state of the site.

But I hadn't forgotten last night's kiss, and all through our conversation, I wondered if Kelt would pucker up again—and how I would respond to it if he did. Tearing my clothes off and leaping on his unprotected body seemed like an attractive option. But when the conversation drew to a close, Kelt flashed a brief smile and left me alone in my room, unkissed and fully dressed.

Maybe he wasn't attracted to me. Maybe I was misreading the situation. The gods knew I'd done that often enough. I got under the covers and hugged my cat. In the world of birds, males grow brighter plumage when they want to mate. Life would be a lot easier, I thought morosely, if men would just do the same.

CHAPTER 12

"AND LAST YEAR I COUNTED seventy-eight blue herons nesting in that one stand of trees alone."

"That's incredible."

June nodded. "Yes, and there were four black-crowned night herons nesting on the eastern edge."

Cam looked up from his notes and scanned the now-empty trees enviously. I knew the feeling. However active the colony had been the previous year, it was tumbleweed time at the moment.

It was a typical early spring morning in rural Alberta. The kind of chilly morning where the sky is pale blue and endless, and small children suck in deep breaths and blow it all out in a long stream, pretending they're smoking cigarettes. The sun was up and shining brightly, doing its golden best to warm everything up, but the grass was still frosty in the shade and the puddles beside the road were crinkled with a thin coating of ice. Good thing we'd come prepared for the cool temperatures. I was bundled up in layers of sweaters. It felt more brisk than cold to me, though this was, in all probability, due to the fact that we had a fairly hefty thermos of coffee with us along with a trove of June's cinnamon buns.

The three of us were out by Beaverhill Lake—Cam to plot out the herons' nesting sites for sampling, June to point them out to him, and me to keep them both company and give myself another dose of the great outdoors. Part of me had been hoping that I might be able to lend Cam a hand in collecting samples, but one look at the squishy, muddy fields in between the road and the colonies put the kibosh on that. Probably just as well. I didn't want to risk covering up Kelt's mysterious little message with mud. At least not until I found somebody who would tell me what it said.

We had identified nine sampling sites that morning (including the one that Richard DeSantis had discovered), and we were now sitting beside the tenth. Even without June's eyewitness account, it was easy to tell that a big colony had nested here the year before. There were trees and bushes aplenty, and several dilapidated platforms of large sticks wedged in the crotches of the trees. Quite a few trees boasted more than one old nest—evidence of a congested community.

"I think I'll grab some samples from this one right now," Cam said with undisguised eagerness. "I'll be a while; perhaps you two should go on."

"How will you get back?" June asked.

He patted his jacket pocket. "I've got a cell phone. Ben or one of the others can swing by and pick me up at lunch."

He stuffed baggies in his pockets and checked to make sure he had his notebook. I waved as we pulled away, but Cam had already turned toward the deserted colony and was striding effortlessly across the uneven ground. I fought down an emerald surge of envy.

We may not have seen a heron today, but we'd spotted a variety of sandpipers poking their bills into the soft mud, and a couple of Wilson's phalaropes, spinning like tops in the water and snatching up the invertebrates that floated up in the whirlpools they created.

"I can certainly understand why you find this place so special," I told June as we drove off.

"I'd never live anywhere else," she said simply.

"Is that why you stayed in Holbrook after Eddie died?" I asked curiously. "I mean, wouldn't it have been easier in a larger city?"

"Maybe so," June answered. "Holbrook was pretty small back then, without many opportunities. But I love it here, and I had the support of many friends even if I didn't have family." She started up the car and we rumbled down the road.

Franhk!

I whipped my head around to locate the deep, harsh croaking. "June, look! A great blue heron!" I pointed out my open window.

June stomped on the brakes with both feet and we slid a few meters, coming to a crooked stop by the side of the dirt road. The heron was preening itself on a small grassy knoll a short distance away.

A farmer who had been following us for the last kilometer was quite obviously familiar with the vagaries of birders. Namely, that they brake frequently and often without much warning (June even had a bumper sticker to that effect). The man rolled his eyes in good-natured exasperation, flipped a friendly wave at June, and swung his pickup truck around the car.

We looked our fill at the heron, smiled at each other, and prepared to continue on our way.

"Last year, there was a colony of blue herons just over to the right in those trees." June told me. "I brought Matt out here last week, but," she chuckled a little, "I'm not sure he was too impressed."

"Not a birder, huh?"

"Not yet," she replied with a wicked gleam in her eye.

I laughed. "So, if he's not a birder, then what attracted you to him? I concede your point about the nice butt, but there're lots of nice butts out there."

June was silent for a long moment. "It's a little hard to explain," she said finally. "The day I met him, I felt there was a connection right off the bat." She shook herself a little self-consciously. "I don't know if it's chemistry or fate or what have you, but I tell you, Robyn, I haven't felt like that about anybody since Eddie died. And then we started talking about environmental issues and the project and just about every other thing under the sun."

"And you discovered your soul mate."

June lifted one shoulder in a shrug. "I don't know about that," she told me. "I think I'm a little past the stage for a soul mate. But a kindred spirit, definitely. One who's funny and kind and. . . ."

"Has a great butt," I smirked.

June grinned and whacked my leg. "I can see I won't be living that one down anytime soon."

"I promise not to tell Meggie," I told her solemnly.

"Cheeky thing."

"I am, I really am," I agreed and we laughed together.

"So, what's on for the rest of the day?" I asked.

"Well, I don't know about you, but I've got a hot date with my washing machine," June said.

"Hot date?"

"With a cold rinse," she added.

"Huh. Sounds like my love life," I said with a crooked smile. "Especially the part about the cold rinse."

June chuckled. "Oh, come on now. That Kelt of yours is quite handsome, and—" she tapped my hand meaningfully "—he seems quite taken with you."

"Taken?" I snorted. "Takin' his time, maybe. I'm beginning to think it's another one of those 'let's just be friends' things."

"Ah well, time will tell," June said sagely.

I grunted, unconvinced. Easy for her to say. She wasn't the one putting herself through the cold rinse cycle on a somewhat more-than-regular basis.

"But before I do laundry," June said, "perhaps we should go visit your co-workers. We're not that far from the plant, and we've got extra cinnamon buns. Do you think they might want them?"

"Want them? June, trust me on this one. When they clap their eyeballs on those cinnamon buns, they'll probably fall to their knees and start singing hymns."

We came in via the southeast access this time. I remembered what Kelt had said about nails on the road, and I hoped they'd been cleaned up. I kept a careful eye on the crumbling pavement, but somebody must have picked them up because we got to the site without a single punctured tire.

"Do you see anybody?" June asked me.

I scanned the area. "Uh, yeah, over there." I pointed to the left of the three main buildings. I could see the crew lying face down on the ground behind a low rise. What were they doing? They didn't know about the cinammon buns yet.

"What the hell. . . ?" I muttered.

We pulled up and I opened my door.

"That's a weird way of collecting soil samples," I started to say.

"*Get down!*"

I heard a pop and an odd whizzing sound above my head. I didn't need more prompting. I hit the ground. Hard. I yelped in pain.

"*Robyn!*" June shoved her door open and ran around the car.

"*June! Get down!*" Ben yelled.

There was another retort. June hesitated.

"Get down!" I hissed, tears of agony streaming down my face.

She did.

"Robyn! Are you hit?" Ben demanded, wriggling over towards us. Another shot hit the side of June's car and he froze.

"I'm okay," I assured him tightly. "I lost my balance and I hit too hard. Gods, Ben, is anybody hurt?"

"Not yet," his tone was grim. "He started shooting a couple of minutes before you pulled up. Are you sure you're okay?"

"I'll live."

"June?"

"I'm all right," she answered her voice shaking. "What . . . what are we supposed to do?"

"Hang tight for now. If they wanted to injure anybody, they could have done it by now. I think they're just trying to scare us."

"It's working," somebody said in a muffled voice. I thought it was Lisa but I didn't dare move my head to look. I had to force myself to breathe.

Every blade of grass stood out, distinct from all the others; every mote of dust glittered in the morning sunlight. The very air seemed to sparkle as if Nature herself was holding her breath.

Reality faded, then vanished, extinguished as effectively as the passenger pigeon. I lay on the ground, my throat aching with the effort of suppressing the scream I could feel inside me.

Suddenly a vehicle rumbled to life. I jumped and cried out as the movement twisted my leg. The landscape lost its preternatural clarity. Reality sputtered and resumed. From across the field, behind a thick stand of tangled brush and trees, I heard a truck pull away and drive off. I turned my head and looked at Ben.

"Not yet," he said, catching my look.

He waited for what seemed like an era before he slowly lifted his torso from the ground. He stopped and waited. Nothing. Carefully, he brought his knees up and rose to a crouch. Still nothing.

"I think he's gone now," he said unnecessarily. He stood all the way up and strode over to where I lay helpless on the ground. "Kelt, come and give me a hand!" he barked.

Between the two of them, they managed to hoist me to my feet.

"Now I know what an up-ended turtle feels like," I groaned. "Aah! Be careful." They settled me against the car and June gave me a hug. My leg throbbed with each pulse.

By the time I'd steadied myself, everybody was on their feet, pale and shaking with reaction.

"Oh my god!"

"Did you see him?"

"Are you okay?"

"I didn't see a thing!"

Ben checked everybody over before pulling his cell phone out of the van and punching in the RCMP's number.

June's laundry, I guessed, was going to have to wait.

CHAPTER 13

THE REST OF THE DAY WAS A WRITE-OFF. The RCMP had come out in force in response to Ben's terse phone call. A grim-faced Elliot Shibley had arrived soon after. At least I was assuming he was grim. I'd never met the man, but I was willing to bet he didn't always look like Steven Seagal in a tight spot.

We'd been questioned, then comforted, then questioned again. The site had been combed over for physical evidence, and several constables were still moving around behind the stand of trees where the sniper had hidden. A local towing company was preparing June's car to be hauled away. The sergeant told her they were going to retrieve the bullet, hopefully identify what kind of gun it had come from, and match it to any suspect's gun.

By the time Canada's Finest were finished, so were we. The afternoon was well past middle-aged and there wasn't much time or desire left to do anything else. It was a sober group that packed up and left the site. June and I hitched a ride back into town with one of the constables.

The pain in my leg was unremitting—at least until I got back to June's and got a handful of painkillers into me. June poured herself a stiff sherry. She was just putting the kettle on for me when the Woodrow crew trooped in. Ben disappeared almost immediately—to call Kaye, I guessed. Everybody else gathered around the kitchen table (and the sherry bottle).

"I've never been so scared in my life," Lisa declared, staring down at the amber drink in her glass. Her sunny disposition had dulled and darkened in the hours following the incident.

"When did you realize that somebody was shooting at you?" Cam asked. Ben had phoned him right after he'd called the RCMP.

"It took me a minute," Lisa said. "Gunfire doesn't sound like it does on TV. I never knew that. Ben figured it out right away, though."

"It's not the first time somebody's taken a shot at him," I remarked.

"No," Lisa agreed. "He really kept his head, too. Got us all down on the ground in no time." She took another healthy sip of her sherry. I found myself wishing I hadn't taken painkillers. A glass of sherry would have gone down very nicely right about now.

The incident had rattled me. I couldn't forget how helpless I'd felt lying there on the ground. If the sniper had been in earnest, I wouldn't have been able to do a thing about it. With these casts, I couldn't even crawl. I was feeling very, very vulnerable and I didn't like it one bit.

"I've been thinking," I broke into the conversation, which had continued without me. "What about the ladder in that tank? The one Nalini went into. Do you think it was sabotaged, too?"

Nalini started. The thought had obviously never occurred to her.

Kelt rubbed his chin, considering the question. "I didn't think about it till now. I don't know. It was pretty corroded."

I turned to Nalini. "Weren't the other ones corroded, too?"

"Yeah. Yeah, they were."

"But none of them broke."

"No."

"Perhaps we shouldn't go borrowing trouble," June suggested in the silence that followed.

"It's not really borrowing trouble," I protested. "And I don't mean to upset you." This to Nalini. "But before today's little incident, somebody dumped a box of nails on the access road and then slashed one of Ben's tires. If that ladder *was* sabotaged, then it's important that we know about it. There may be a few other surprises lurking around."

"It means we can't trust anything," Lisa broke in.

"A moot point now," Kelt said. "I don't know about anybody else, but I for one will be taking a long, hard look at every piece of equipment before I use it."

"We'll all be taking precautions," Ben agreed, joining the group at the table. June poured him a sherry. "Thanks, June. Teams of two for everything. Minimum. If it takes us longer to finish the work, then so be it. I'll bill Reisinger extra. I've already discussed it with Elliot. Reisinger doesn't want injuries any more than we do."

He paused and sipped his drink. "So. We'll check all the gear over tonight. Anything we take to the site gets brought back here at night and locked up. We'll inspect any equipment or infrastructure on site and take precautions even if it looks solid. We're about done with those outdoor storage tanks, yes?"

Nalini nodded. "But we've still got a few tanks and sumps to sample inside."

"Good enough. We'll wait on those till I've finished with the wells, then I'll supervise." Ben paused for a second, then turned his attention to me. "Robyn, I know you're technically on vacation, but I wonder if I could impose on you to meet with Grant DeSantis?"

I lifted my head up. "Me?"

"Yeah. He wants to hear about the precautions first-hand."

"Um. So soon after his stepson's murder?" I was incredulous.

Ben nodded once. "I know it sounds strange, but Elliot told me the man's in denial. The funeral's not till Friday. I guess he's burying himself in work until then."

"When does he want to meet?"

"First thing tomorrow morning."

"Okay."

He gave me a relieved smile. Ben hated meetings unless they involved doughnuts. Somehow I didn't think Grant DeSantis would be laying out the sour cream glazeds.

"Thanks, Robyn. I owe you. Now as for the rest of us, the RCMP have also promised to beef up their presence in the area—"

"Do you think that will be enough?" Cam asked.

"I do. The publicity alone will make it difficult for our friend to pull any more tricks. And with this shooting incident, the sabotage has gone beyond mischief. I think the RCMP will be taking it very seriously. I'm sure we'll be seeing a lot of them. I know it's nerve-wracking, but we've got to finish the job. The backhoe's coming first thing tomorrow, and Maurice and Sid will be around for most of the day. There'll be enough people milling around to keep our friend away. I think we'll be safe." He paused and drained his glass. "So, do we have any idea who our friend might be?"

We all looked at June. She flushed a bit and shook her head.

"I've been going over it in my mind and I'm stumped. Most of the members of the protest group are, well, getting on a bit in years."

"That doesn't eliminate them."

"It does if that ladder was sabotaged. I'm not sure *I* could get up there."

"But we don't know if it was or not."

"I know," she said, deflated. "I guess I don't really want to believe that somebody I know could be capable of this. The nails and the tire are one thing, but shooting at people?" She shook her head. "That's something entirely different."

"Does anybody in your group own a gun?" I asked.

"They've probably all got guns, Robyn. Quite a few of them are hunters, you know. They want to save the wetlands so they can still hunt ducks."

"But whoever was shooting us was using a rifle," Ben said. "Not a shotgun."

"I don't know what to tell you," June said unhappily.

"That's okay," Ben told her. "If they're the type to do something like this, then chances are they probably wouldn't have joined your peaceful little group. Cheer up. It was worse in the Everglades when the alligator poachers were shooting at me. Those guys weren't just trying to scare us. And then when I was undercover for Fish and Wildlife. . . ."

I excused myself after a while and limped down the hall to my room to lie down. Reaction had well and truly set in. I was exhausted. My leg and arm felt heavy and unresponsive, and my head was spinning from the painkillers I'd popped. Ben's stories were entertaining, but I had no stomach for them now—and I'd already seen his war wound. I turned on my clock radio and fiddled with the dial until I found CBC. They were playing Rachmaninoff's *Vespers*, a piece of music that I always find spiritually soothing. As I got into bed and pulled the covers up to my chin, I decided there wasn't much point in getting up for dinner. I was more than done with this day.

Chapter 14

My meeting with Grant DeSantis the following day was everything I thought it would be. Him doing most of the talking, me saying "yes" and "of course" and "we'll try our best," and no doughnuts. His office was straight out of *Fortune* magazine. Oak bookcases set against maple-colored walls. The big oak desk with a picture of the family placed just so beside the marble penstand. A hunter-green blotter completely bereft of doodles. It smelled of money in an understated way, the kind of coinage that spits scornfully on the elaborate accoutrements of other, more pretentious offices. I crutched in awkwardly, trying hard not to feel intimidated.

Grant DeSantis was tall and lean with salt and peppery hair and cool gray eyes—eyes that widened in shock when he saw me.

"I didn't think anybody had been hurt!"

"No. Nobody was," I hastened to reassure him. "This happened over a month ago. Didn't Ben warn you?"

His expression lightened and he cleared his throat. "Ah. Yes, I recall now. Thank you for coming in, Ms Devara."

"No problem." I scanned his face for signs of grief, but apart from some fairly serious bags under his eyes, there was very little evidence of it. He looked like your basic corporate type: well-groomed, clean-shaven, buffed fingernails. He wasn't actually sporting office togs that morning, but his whole demeanor reeked of business and professionalism, and you could almost see the psychic imprint of charcoal pinstripes on his body. I shook his hand and hesitated.

Ever since I woke up that morning, I'd been agonizing over whether I should express my condolences to him about his stepson's death. It was such a shocking and recent loss. Elliot had told Ben that DeSantis was in denial over it, but it seemed uncaring not to say anything at all. In the end, I settled for short and sympathetic.

"Thank you for meeting with me under the circumstances," I told him. "All of us at Woodrow were very sorry to hear about your stepson."

A shutter came down over his eyes. "Thank you," he said in a clipped tone. "Please sit down."

Wrong decision. I gave myself a mental kick. Robyn Devara, the walking social *faux pas*.

I was ill at ease now, but fortunately DeSantis didn't seem to want to make small talk. That was fine by me. I launched into a description of the precautions Ben and the others were taking, aware all the while that I was speaking too quickly and a little too loudly. But it was clear after a few minutes that Grant DeSantis was oblivious to both my nervousness and the specifics of what I was saying. In fact, rather than showing concern about the safety of the Woodrow crew, he seemed far more preoccupied with the potential damage to public relations. So much for caring.

"I assume that media relations are one of Woodrow's core competencies," he began after I'd said my piece.

Huh? "Of course," I replied smoothly, hoping that he would explain further.

"How does Ben Woodrow plan to manage the media?"

"Uh . . . well—"

"Because I'd like to get right on this, *before* it becomes a problem. Development must be marketed to the stakeholders, just as you would any other product. I'm sure I don't need to tell you that we've experienced some resistance to our plans for the site. I've been around a long while, I've worked on a lot of different projects. We need to minimize the damage this saboteur is doing—

especially after what happened yesterday. I don't want our new facility jeopardized in any way because of this. You know we still need final approval from the province. If we get enough bad press, that could be compromised."

"As far as I know, nobody from the media knows what's going on."

"That's not good enough. They will, take my word for it. We need to strategize. We need to develop a plan and implement it before they get wind of what's going on. I do *not* want any more negative publicity."

I wondered if he considered his stepson's murder negative publicity.

"Ben's asked us all to keep quiet about it," I offered.

"Good. That's a first step. If anybody tries to ask any questions, you have no comment. If they're persistent, refer them to me. Under no circumstances should any of you talk to members of the press. Some of them are quite skilled at misquoting and misleading. You're to leave them to me. I can give them the information they require. I've had experience with this kind of thing."

"Really." I remembered who I was speaking with and recovered myself. "Well, yes. That sounds reasonable. I'll let the crew know."

"Excellent." DeSantis stretched his mouth into a perfect, white smile. "I think we've caught this in time. With a little luck, we can keep it out of the papers."

"That would make our job easier," I told him.

He shook my hand, thanked me again for coming in, and asked me to give his regards to Ben. I made my way to the elevator and pressed the button. Grant DeSantis was pleasant enough despite the corporate babble, but there was a calculating coldness to him that raised a goosebump or two. But maybe I was being too judgmental. Maybe he wasn't himself. After all, his stepson had just been murdered. Still, I couldn't help wondering what other projects he'd worked on that had required this level of PR damage control.

"Ahhhh! Coffee! Doughnuts!" I exclaimed, catching sight of the Tim Horton's bags in June's car. "How did you know?"

June laughed and opened the car door for me. "I was guessing that Grant DeSantis probably wasn't a Tim Horton's patron. And after yesterday, I thought we needed a treat." She helped me settle in the front seat and handed me the bags. "Now, if you don't mind, we're going to go to my office. I need some things that I left on my desk, but I'll just be a second."

"Mmmmm. I don't mind," I replied around my doughnut. With a few sour cream glazed doughnuts in me, I would have agreed to swing by Carol Miller's place. As long as I could stay in the car, of course.

By the time we pulled up to the town's administration offices, I'd consumed one large coffee and two doughnuts. I'd contemplated a third one, but I was starting to notice the doughnut around my middle so I decided instead to drag myself out of the car and go have a look at Holbrook's latest tourist attraction. As I hobbled up the walk, June keeping slow pace with me, a middle-aged gentleman came out the double glass doors and saluted us briskly. He was quite a dapper-looking fellow with a carefully trimmed and combed beard, a small plaid bow tie, and a red wool cap set at a jaunty angle.

"Good morning, June," he greeted her with a wide smile, including me in the salutation.

"Everard! I haven't seen you in weeks."

He chuckled softly. "I'd heard the birds were back," he said cryptically.

June just laughed. "Oh, come on now, I'm not out birding *that* much!" She put her hand lightly on my shoulder. "Robyn, this is Everard McCloud, a very dear friend of mine. Everard, I'd like you to meet Robyn, a good friend of Megan's. I'm sure you've heard me speak of her." She gave him a mischievous wink. "Robyn's one of us, you know."

Everard shook my hand and gave me a friendly smile. "Ah, a fellow birdwatcher are you? Hello, Robyn, it's a pleasure. I hope you've been enjoying our birds."

I smiled back. "Hi, Everard, I have." I indicated my cast ruefully. "Though I'm restricted to birding from the car at the moment."

"Yes, I can see why," he replied and with exquisite (and all too rare) politeness did not ask me what I'd done to myself. "But that's the best way at this time of year. Are there many birds back yet? I haven't had a chance to get out."

I smiled back. "They're here in force. We saw all kinds of waterfowl and a great blue heron."

Everard was delighted. "I must remember to tell Vivian. She always loved the blue herons."

"How is she doing today?" June asked kindly.

"Oh." A cloud of grief passed over the man's cheerful countenance. Suddenly he didn't seem so dapper any more. "About the same, thanks. I'm just on my way to see her now."

"How are you holding up?"

"I can't complain much, but the house doesn't feel quite right without her."

June patted his arm. "I know. Listen. If you get too lonely, you come over. You've got a standing invitation for dinner."

"Oh, I wouldn't want to intrude. . . ."

"Nonsense!" She exclaimed, nipping his protest in the bud. "Friends are never an intrusion."

He smiled in gratitude. "Thank you, June. Perhaps I'll pop by."

"Anytime you feel up to it. It'll do you good to have a little evening out. And you tell Vivian I'll be coming to see her after lunch. I've got a book I think she'll enjoy."

"Thank you," he said warmly. He turned his attention to me. "It was nice meeting you, Robyn. I'm sure you'll have a wonderful vacation at June's."

I smiled back at him. "Thanks, I'm sure I will. And it was nice meeting you, too."

As he strode off, June watched after him and sighed a little. "It breaks my heart to see him like this," she said unhappily. "Vivian's been in the hospital for four months now."

"What's wrong with her?"

June's sad expression deepened. "Cancer," she said. "She's fifteen years younger than Everard and looks about thirty years older now. I don't think she'll ever get out of the hospital, but Everard keeps hoping. He goes to visit her every day, all dressed up, almost as if they were courting. And every day, he comes back looking a little more tired. It's a terrible thing to see hope dying day by day."

"He seems like a nice man."

"Oh, he's wonderful, very kind and warm. When Vivian was still able to get around, we'd often go birding together, just the three of us. It's been years now since we've been able to do that." June paused and shook her head. "Vivian got liver cancer, just like a lot of the other people who used to work at that plant. In some ways, I wish Norsicol was still around. They have a lot to answer for."

"Vivian worked at the plant, too?" I asked in surprise.

"Well, not really *at* the plant. She wasn't employed by Norsicol. The cafeteria services were subcontracted out. She worked there."

We went into the building then, and June left me by the map of gnome destinations.

"I'll just be a minute," she told me.

I nodded and hobbled up to the map. It took only a quick inspection to realize that Holbrook's gnomes were having a much better time than I was. Figures.

There were in excess of fifty bright red pins stuck in the map. I shook my head in disbelief (and not a little envy). Singapore, Vienna, Cairo. One not-so-lucky gnome had even been taken to Pittsburgh. That I could live without. I wondered if all the other gnomes made fun of him.

June was back within five minutes, carrying a small stack of papers and clippings. I glanced briefly at them. They were articles about the proposed facility. I'd been thinking about it myself, specifically about the contaminated site and the people who had worked there.

"How sick is Vivian now?" I asked when we were back in the car.

June shrugged a little. "Sick enough to be kept in the hospital, but not in a great deal of pain most of the time, thank heavens."

"Remember I told you that Ben's been trying to track down people who worked at the plant? Do you think Vivian might be able to help us?"

"Vivian?" June looked doubtful. "I don't know. She wouldn't have had anything to do with the plant operations. . . ."

"But maybe she noticed what was going on, or maybe she was told to avoid a certain area. It's worth a shot—as long as it's okay to ask her questions. If she's that sick, maybe I shouldn't bother her."

"Oh, I don't think she'd mind," June replied. "Vivian always did like company, and it might take her mind off things. When I go to see her this afternoon, I'll ask her if she's feeling up to having a visitor."

After June went off to visit her friend, I settled myself on the couch with one of Arif's mysteries. The heroine and her erstwhile husband had just been trapped in a pyramid by a suspicious cave-in when the phone rang. I set the book down, wedged my crutches under my arm and made my way down the hall to the phone.

"Coming, coming," I told it as it kept ringing.

"Hello?"

There was a long silence and then a *click*.

"Hello?"

Nothing.

"Damn," I cursed. It wasn't easy maneuvering on crutches and the phone had only rung six or seven times.

I was halfway back to the living room and the perils of Amelia Peabody when the phone rang again. I spun around and crutched my way quickly back down the hall before the phone rang a fourth time.

"Hello?"

Click.

"Little pukes," I thought sourly. Probably kids playing a prank. My younger brother Jack used to do the same thing until our father caught him at it and tanned his butt. Jack never played with phones again and, to this day, was not all that comfortable with them.

Well, I'd put a stop to this particular phone game right now and without the palm of my hand. I punched in Woodrow Consultants number. I'd just keep the line busy for a while—at least until the little reprobates decided to harass somebody else.

I needed to speak with somebody from the office, anyway. If the gods were smiling on me and Vivian agreed to see me, then I needed to bring the aerial photos of the site. I wasn't about to go rummaging around in Ben's stuff without his permission, and he wouldn't be back till this evening. So I did the next best thing. I phoned Kaye.

Kaye informed me that he had, indeed, brought the aerial photos with him. She also took the opportunity to do a little chastising.

"I thought you were there to rest." Her tone was severe.

"I am," I protested. "I just happened to find out about someone who used to work at the plant. She's a friend of June's."

"So why are you not leaving it for Ben to look into?"

"The person in question is pretty sick, Kaye. She's in the hospital. I'm not even sure yet that she'll see me, but I'm practically a member of June's family. If she's up to it and I go to talk to her, it's a little more friendly than a stranger, don't you think?"

"Hmmm."

I knew I'd won.

Kaye sighed. "Well, it's against my better judgment, dear, but I guess you're right. Root around in that old tan-colored case of Ben's, he's got all the paperwork and photos in there."

"Thanks, Kaye."

"One other thing," she said before I could ring off. "Ben told me about the tire and the nails and about what happened to that young man. I hope you're planning on staying out of it." Her tone told me that if I wasn't, I'd better change my plans pronto. "No playing Miss Marple this time." Kaye had been reading Arif's mystery collection, too.

"What is this?" I demanded. "One little incident, and I'm pegged for life."

"Having your leg and arm broken is hardly what I'd call a *little* incident, dear," Kaye said dryly.

I could almost see her hands placed squarely on her hips.

I huffed a sigh. "Okay, message received loud and clear."

I was in luck. Vivian was having a good day, and she'd agreed to see me later on that afternoon.

Vivian McCloud was a soft-spoken lady, as warm and friendly as her husband. She must have been quite lovely in her younger days. She wasn't exactly chopped tofu in her older days, either, though she was quite frail now and, as June had said, appeared much older than her years. But her hair had been neatly brushed and her blue eyes were bright and interested. We spent almost twenty minutes talking about birds before I broached the subject of the old pesticide plant.

"Yes," she said. "Everard was telling me they want to turn the old place into a toxic-waste treatment facility."

I nodded. "There's a lot of cleaning up to be done before that happens."

"That doesn't surprise me. Even back then, I wondered about that."

"Did you ever notice where they disposed of the contaminated stuff?"

"Oh heavens, yes. Back then, all the garbage was dumped in a big field on the east side of the three production buildings. Close to where those white storage tanks are. They dug a pit and everything went into it—kitchen waste, too. Then they'd cover it up with dirt every so often. I used to watch them when I was on my breaks. There were a few picnic tables set up outside for when the weather was nice, and you could see the field from the tables."

"I've got some photos of the plant site here. Would you mind taking a look at them? Maybe we can figure out where exactly this field was."

"Certainly."

Vivian was able to pinpoint the exact location of the field without any trouble. I knew it was one that Lisa and Nalini had already singled out for intensive testing.

"How about these spots?" I asked, indicating a couple of other areas in the photos where the soil was darker than anything in the surrounding areas. "Do you remember anything there?"

She shook her head uncertainly. "No, I don't. Oh, wait. This one here." She pointed to an area in the northwest corner of the site. "I think . . . yes, I think there may be something here. It's a little hard to orient myself." She turned the photo upside down. "But I think this is where I saw them that day."

"Them?"

"A few of the young men. I was sweet on one of them for a while. John . . . Boyer, yes, that was his name." She smiled and shook her head. "I haven't thought of him for years! Ah, I used to dream about him. And sometimes on my way home, I'd take a stroll through the yard, just to see if he was around."

"So you saw him and a few other fellows one day," I prompted, bringing her back to the point.

She smiled with just a hint of wistfulness. "Yes, I saw them working out there, right in this corner." She touched the photo again. "They were burying barrels."

"Barrels. You mean those big steel drums?"

She nodded.

"Any idea what was in them?"

"Nothing good," she remarked with asperity. "All the men were wearing gloves and those masks that surgeons wear. Of course, I recognized John even with the mask."

I circled the spot on the photo with a black grease pencil and turned my attention back to Vivian. Her eyes were far away.

"What happened to him?" I asked curiously.

She blinked and looked at me. "Oh, he went off to work with his brother up north. At a mine. Coal, I think it was. And by the time he left, I already had my eye on someone else."

We laughed softly together.

"That old plant was a nice place to work back then if you were a single girl. It seemed like all the young men worked there."

I imagined crews of young men drooling over young, pretty Vivian in the cafeteria. I was willing to bet that few of them brought lunches from home.

"I must have fallen in and out of love at least twice a month," she said, still smiling. "I think Grant was the worst though. I had a terrible crush on him. But he was a supervisor—though he was a bit young for it—and I was just a cafeteria worker."

"And that stopped him?" I asked incredulously.

She chuckled and patted my hand. "Things were a little different back then," she told me. "I was a farm girl, and he was from the city. Somewhere back east, if I remember correctly. Most of the young men didn't mind where you came from, but Grant DeSantis was a different breed. I remember he used to joke with some of the other city lads, calling the locals hillbillies," she chuckled. "Even thirty years ago, Holbrook had a lot of gnomes and suchlike. So you see, I was just another hillbilly to him. Back then, I used to think he was so sophisticated, but in hindsight, he was probably just a bit of a snob." She shook her head. "I dreamed about him for months, and he never even looked at me."

I smiled sympathetically, thinking of my own love life, then did a mental double-take.

"Uh, did you say his name was Grant DeSantis?"

Vivian looked at me, surprised. "What. . . ?"

"DeSantis? As in the guy in charge of the waste treatment facility that's coming in?"

Vivian looked confused. "I . . . I don't know," she said. "I don't think I ever heard who was in charge of that. I think Grant's last name was DeSantis but I could be wrong. I . . . I'm really not sure now. It's these dratted drugs, you see, they make my memory so fuzzy."

She seemed confused and upset, as if the transition from past to present had been too abrupt. I asked her what Holbrook had been like back when the plant was open, and she drifted off happily into her memories again. My mind, however, was racing ahead. If Vivian's memory was correct, then Grant DeSantis had both past and present connections to the site. Strange that nobody had mentioned it.

CHAPTER 15

"HEY, TI-MARC, IT'S ROBYN."

"Robyn, *comment ça va?*"

Ti-Marc was Woodrow's latest acquisition. A receptionist/office assistant with a strong French-Canadian accent and an even stronger flair for organization. He'd only been working for the firm for a month, but had already made himself indispensable.

"Not bad, how about yourself?"

"*Bien*, I'm always good. 'Ow's the vacation?"

"Oh, I've managed to find a bit of work to do. . . ."

"Work! Does Kaye know?"

I chuckled. "She knows and approves, so don't you start in on me."

"Me? I'm just the receptionist."

I snorted. "Yeah, right. Listen, Ti-Marc, I need you to check out that list of Norsicol's old personnel for me."

"The one that Ben put together?"

"Yeah, I'm looking for a guy by the name of Grant DeSantis." I spelled it out for him.

"You know those records are not complete, eh? 'E may not show up."

That was part of the problem with doing an historical document review for a company that no longer existed—the historical documents were often woefully lacking. Handy items like personnel or payroll records were rarely part of the package, so you had to go through the correspondence and any submissions, reports, or audits to find the names of old personnel. From what I'd heard, it had been a long and tedious job fraught with frustrated outbursts. I'd been glad then of my extended sick leave.

"Yeah, I know," I told Ti-Marc. "I think this guy was a supervisor, though."

"*Bon*, that might make it easier. You want to 'ang on? I'll see if I can find 'im fast."

"Sure. If it's not a quick find, you can call me back."

"Okay, *un instant*."

He was back in a couple of minutes. "Well, there was a G. Santir—spelled S-A-N-T-I-R. 'E was some kind of supervisor, I don't know what kind, but in 1971 and . . . *un minute* . . . 1972 'e was also in charge of safety it looks like. Is that your guy?"

"I don't know," I said doubtfully. "Are you sure the last name's Santir?"

"I can check the originals if you want."

"Would you please? I'd really appreciate it."

"*Pas de probleme*," he assured me. "I'll 'ave to call you back, though."

I gave him the number at June's and rang off.

Two hours and three more hang-up calls later, Ti-Marc phoned back. I was getting fed up with the prank phone calls, but I didn't want to miss Ti-Marc's call so I kept answering them.

I was a bit surprised to hear from back from Ti-Marc so quickly. On the surface, a few hours doesn't seem like a particularly quick response time, but when you think about the large filing cabinet of papers he had to go through to find what I wanted, well . . . as I mentioned before, he's efficiency personified.

"You may be right about this guy," he began without preamble.

"Oh?"

"I 'ad a look at the records. They're in pretty bad shape with stains and smudges, but it's possible the guy's name was DeSantis. I guess whoever typed the names up just took a guess."

I sighed a little, remembering the long line of more-than-dispensable temp workers before Ti-Marc came on board. One of whom had been responsible for typing up the list.

"How about a first name?" I asked.

"*Non.* Just a 'G'."

"Too bad. Look, thanks, Ti-Marc, I appreciate it."

"Is the guy important?" he asked.

"I'm not sure," I told him honestly. And I wasn't. So what if one of Reisinger's directors had been a supervisor at the old Norsicol plant? Sort of a pisser for Woodrow, of course. Ben had spent a lot of time and effort trying to track down old workers, and here was one perched right under his nose. Still, surely Grant DeSantis had some idea of what was involved in a site assessment. Why hadn't he mentioned that he'd worked at the old plant?

It was a question that Ben asked, too, albeit in different words.

"What the hell kind of *asshole* would forget to tell us something like that!?"

"Maybe he didn't think it was important," Nalini suggested.

He looked at her in disgust. "Don't be a turnip! He's not exactly new at this. He *must* have known that we'd be looking for former employees. Where the hell does he think we get this information from, anyhow? Jeez! This really gives me gas!"

Lisa, who was sitting next to Ben, eyed him a little nervously and inched her chair further away. As had become our custom, we were all sitting in June's kitchen, lingering over coffee and dessert. I'd reported my visit with Vivian, but I'd waited until after dinner to tell Ben about Grant DeSantis. And for precisely this reason. He was practically spluttering in indignation.

He swore a few more choice curses under his breath, then swung his attention over to June. "Could your friend be mistaken about this?" he demanded.

She considered the question for a moment. "Normally I'd say no, but with all the medication she's on these days, yes, it's very possible."

"You don't remember Grant DeSantis working there?"

June shook her head. "I never worked for Norsicol, Ben."

"It might not be him," I broke in. "What reason would he have to keep it a secret? If Vivian's right, then he was a supervisor, not a member of Norsicol's board of directors. So it's not as if we'd be holding him responsible for any of the mess. What other reason would he have to lie about it? Vivian wasn't sure of his last name, and Ti-Marc said it wasn't all that clear in the records, either. And even if the last name's right, we've only got a first initial. We might be barking up the wrong tree."

"How'd you like to find out for me?" Ben asked.

"What? You want me to meet with the guy again?" I asked, trying to keep the dismay out of my voice. I didn't care for meetings any more than Ben did. Especially doughnutless meetings with mackerel-like businessmen.

"No. Absolutely not. I need you to confirm it some other way. Then *I'll* bring it up with him. See if you can find some old newspapers or something in the library. Local papers are always writing crap about corporate golf tournaments and other PR events."

"It's a small library, Ben."

"I know, but it's worth a try. Maybe they've got some old company newsletters or some damn thing sitting around in storage. And uh—" he rubbed the side of his nose uncomfortably "—I, uh, I don't know if we really need to mention this to Kaye."

"I wouldn't dream of it," I assured him.

We cleared the table and retired to the softer chairs in the living room.

"Are you having problems with your phone?" I asked June, suddenly remembering the rash of hang-up calls.

"I don't think so," she answered. "Why?"

I leaned my crutches against the coffee table and lowered myself onto the couch. "The phone's been ringing all day, but when I get up to answer it, there's nobody there. It's a bit of pain in the ass. I'm not exactly Ms Mobility."

"Hmm. Yes, I see." June picked up Guido and settled him on

my lap. "I haven't noticed anything, but I'll ask Peggy tomorrow if there's a problem with the lines. It could just be kids."

"Yeah, that's what I thought, too." I shrugged it off and passed Lisa the video.

I had taken the initiative and rented a movie for the evening from the UNG video store. My colleagues had been getting a little grim these last few days, and even Lisa had lost a bit of her customary sparkle. It wasn't surprising, given the condition of the site. Not to mention the fact that we had been shot at the day before. We were all, I had decided that afternoon, in need of a good laugh.

UNG videos was a local independent. The name had puzzled me at first. A foreign film store? Asian action flicks, perhaps? Nope. It turned out the present owners were an environmentally aware couple who had taken over the space from a gun store and had, in one fell swoop, reduced, reused, and recycled the sign. They did have a fine selection of action flicks, but mostly the store was a B-movie buff's delight, boasting all the requisite *Plan 9's from Outer Space*, and *Brains That Wouldn't Die* as well as other, lesser-known works of trash. It was ideal for my purposes.

My plan, though not from outer space, seemed to work. I had selected a little-known zero-budget gem called *Mars Needs Women*, and we were all having great fun tearing it apart when the doorbell rang. It was Everard and he'd come with a present for me.

A little reluctant to leave the room just as the less-than-politically-correct Martians tried to kidnap a burlesque dancer (to the hooting derision of my co-workers), I nevertheless heaved Guido off my lap, shoved myself up, and humped out to the hallway. Everard was refusing June's invitation to come in for a cup of tea.

"No, no, I just stopped by for a minute," he protested as she tugged his arm in. "Vivian asked me to come by."

"Hi, Everard," I said.

"Hello, Robyn." He smiled at me. "Vivian really enjoyed her visit with you this afternoon."

"It was a pleasure spending time with her. She's a lovely lady."

"I've always thought so," Everard agreed, smiling a little sadly. He cleared his throat. "Well, the reason I came by is that Vivian remembered a scooter that she had. She used it to get around when she wasn't feeling so good. She had quite a few operations on her hip a few years back, you see. At any rate, she doesn't need it right now, and she thought you might be able to get around a little better if you had the use of it while you were visiting. She asked me to bring it over."

"Everard, that's sweet!" I exclaimed.

"You should be able to manage it with one hand. If you're going to be doing a lot of driving, you might have to recharge it. It's got enough juice now, though." He gestured towards his car. "I've got it broken down in the trunk, if June can lend me her strength."

"Of course I'll help, or better yet... Kelt?" June poked her head in the living room. "Can you give us a hand?"

The scooter was a bright candy-apple red with a small wire basket on the front. It probably did ten kilometers an hour at best, but I'd been confined to crutches for so long, those ten kilometers felt like the Indy 500.

"Everard, this is wonderful," I cried as I swung by the front porch again. "Thank you so much! Thank Vivian for me!"

By this time, everybody was on the front porch, laughing at my enthusiasm and at my left leg, which stuck out in front like a thick white lance. But I didn't care. I wasn't confined to crutches any more. I had freedom! I could go places myself! I was, perhaps not hell on wheels, but maybe ... yes, with Vivian's little red scooter, I was definitely heck on wheels.

It was late by the time we finished the movie and said our goodnights. I closed my door and turned the clock radio on low. But it was jazz hour so I turned it right back off again. Part of me was hoping that Kelt would continue his routine of tapping at my door for a late-night chat.

I'd briefly tossed around the idea of donning something slinky and sexy just in case he turned out to be a Martian with a need, but a quick rummage through the sleepwear in my suitcase had been enough to quash that notion. Extra large T-shirts, and more extra large T-shirts. Not exactly Victoria's Secret, I grant you, but probably a lot closer to the truth for the majority of women. Who knows? Maybe it was Victoria's *real* secret.

I pulled out a purple shirt that went down to my knees and began the process of peeling my off clothes. Then it happened. I caught sight of myself in the standing, full-length mirror.

Eep. Margaret Visser had, apparently, been right.

Visser once wrote that "Food shapes us and expresses us even more definitively than our furniture or houses or utensils do." From what I could see in the mirror, the food that was shaping me was June's cinnamon rolls. All I was missing was the cinnamon, but I had a hell of a handle on the roll part. I pinched a few inches experimentally. Perhaps I'd better declare a moratorium on the sweets.

Tap, tap.

I yanked on my purple T-shirt. Night of the Giant Living Eggplant.

I opened the door to what was becoming a familiar sight—Kelt standing in the doorway with Guido the cat in his arms.

"Let me guess," I said, disgusted. "The butter again?"

Kelt chuckled. "Nope, someone left the milk out."

I opened the door wider and gestured towards the bed.

"Put him down and have a seat," I invited.

Kelt unhooked Guido's claws from his shirt and settled in one of the wingbacked chairs. "Nice PJs," he commented.

I looked down at my shirt. Like everything else I owned, it was covered in cat hairs. "Uh, thanks." I paused for a moment. "No more sabotage today?" I asked.

"No. We've all got cricks in our necks from looking over our shoulders, though."

"I believe it. Sniper attacks aren't exactly covered in Bio 101.

I'm with Lisa on this one, I don't think I've ever been as scared as I was yesterday."

"Not even when this happened?" He indicated my casts.

"Well, maybe then," I amended. "How about you? How are you doing?"

"I had to sleep with the goofy elephant last night."

"Did it help?"

"Not much."

"Too bad."

"Yeah."

"You could always try Guido," I offered.

Or me, I added silently.

"Nah." Kelt gave me a tired grin. "I wouldn't want to deprive you."

I gazed back at him. His green eyes were clouded and he had serious bag action happening under them. "You seem pretty bummed," I observed.

Kelt shrugged off my concern. "Tired, partly. We've been covering a lot of ground in the last few days." He rubbed his eyes. "But I've also been mulling over what you found out today."

"I take it you're not talking about the buried drums."

"No, of course not, we all pretty much expected that. No, it's this Grant DeSantis thing."

"You mean why he didn't tell Ben about his connection to Norsicol?"

"You said yourself that Vivian might be mistaken. And even if she wasn't, maybe it's like Nalini said, maybe DeSantis didn't realize everything that was involved in a site assessment. Specifically the historical document review."

"Where did he think we were getting our background information, then?" I demanded.

Kelt shrugged again. "Maybe he never thought about it."

I slanted him a skeptical look. "Maybe he didn't want anyone to know he used to work there."

"Stop making him sound so shifty. Jeez, just because he didn't offer you a doughnut."

"He didn't even *have* any doughnuts to offer. But that's not why I'm suspicious of him."

"C'mon, Robyn. The guy probably didn't say anything about working for Norsicol, because he doesn't remember anything about the place. It hardly makes him a criminal. I have trouble remembering what I ate for dinner last night, let alone what I was doing twenty-five years ago."

"Yeah, but twenty-five years ago, you were probably putting frogs down girls' dresses."

"It was a toad."

"Nice. Okay, *if* Grant DeSantis was the guy we suspect he is and *if* he simply forgot—for some unfathomable reason—to tell us that he used to work at the plant, then why was his stepson killed?"

Kelt slapped his forehead. "Not this again!"

I smiled sweetly at him. "Just wondering."

"Well, cut it out. I'm too bagged tonight for wonderings." He yawned and scrubbed his face with his hands. "In fact, I should probably head off to bed."

"I'm sorry," I apologized, noticing again how worn he looked. "I didn't mean to go on about work and all that other stuff."

"That's okay," he crooked the corners of his mouth up into a sleepy grin and stood up. "I just wanted to make sure you weren't going to go charging after Grant DeSantis or anything." He bent down and brushed my cheek with his lips.

"Sweet dreams," he said with another yawn before letting himself out the door.

I don't know if you could call my dreams "sweet" that night, but hey, I had a lot of fun.

CHAPTER 16

I WOKE THE FOLLOWING DAY RESTED and with a renewed sense of purpose. It was still early when I hunted down a notebook and pen, and went out to hitch up my trusty steed. Ben had given me a job and I wanted to get it done as soon as possible. The more Ben knew about the site, the faster they could finish the work. And the safer they would all be. I planned on parking my butt at the library until the gods (or the research material) saw fit to inform me about Grant DeSantis. Had the man worked at the old Norsicol plant? I intended to find out.

But before I did that, I had to swing by his office first. I wasn't going back to ask Grant DeSantis any questions, and I certainly wasn't going back for the hospitality. I had to deliver the latest reports from the site. Ben had already sent them to Elliot Shibley, but now all of a sudden DeSantis wanted his very own copy. Elliot was out of town for a few days and his secretary had taken the opportunity for a holiday so the task had fallen to me to photocopy and deliver the reports.

I parked Vivian's scooter next to the eight-foot Blue Heron statue, copied the reports at the drugstore, stuffed them into my backpack, then crutched my way across the street to where Reisinger Industries had their offices. Talk about your poor man's Federal Express. I suspected Grant DeSantis's executive assistant thought so, too. She was too snooty to come and take the package from me, so I had to limp over to her desk, which was positioned right outside DeSantis's fancy office. That's where I heard the voices.

One male, one female, both raised in anger and both loud enough to leak past the closed door. I couldn't quite make out what they were saying, and I had a hunch the snooty assistant would frown on me putting my ear to the door.

"Can I help you?" the assistant asked brusquely.

"Yeah, I've got a package for Mr. DeSantis from Woodrow Consultants."

I inched a little closer to the door in the guise of taking my backpack off. The woman was speaking now. Her tone was full of bitter fury, though she'd lowered her voice. I strained to catch what she was saying, but . . . was she speaking English?

The assistant tapped one fingernail on the desk impatiently, so I pretended to rummage around in my backpack.

"I know it's here somewhere," I told her. No. The woman in Grant DeSantis's office wasn't speaking English—at least not entirely. Didn't seem to be affecting her ability to get her anger across, though.

I figured I couldn't keep the assistant tapping her manicure any longer, not without getting turfed out of the office. So I produced the package, feigned a smile, and gave her an insincere apology for taking so long. Then I pointed myself in the direction of the hallway. But before I could take a single step, the door to DeSantis's office smacked open and a woman came storming out.

Esme!

Grant DeSantis stood behind his desk. His face was purple with suppressed emotion.

"*Asesino!*" She turned and spat back at him. "*Y tú no cuidado!*"

What the hell?

Esme spun around again and gave a savage swipe to the tears that streamed down her cheeks. I was too shocked to get a word out, but I don't think Esme even noticed I was there. Her eyes passed right over me and rested only briefly on the assistant, who was staring at her like a sunstruck goose.

"*Asesino!*" Esme hissed again under her breath, and with that she strode across the room and slammed out the main door.

I swung my crutches forward and tried to follow her, but by the time I got to the elevators, she was long gone.

What the hell was that all about? I was under the impression that Esme got along well with Grant DeSantis. Not any longer, it would seem. And what had she called him? Asses-ino? Whatever it meant, it was nothing nice, judging from the tone of her voice.

My knowledge of Spanish didn't extend much past *quesadilla* and *enchilada*, but whatever Esme had called DeSantis, it hadn't sounded complimentary. As I drove the scooter over to the library, I resolved to have a look at a Spanish-English dictionary. I was more than a little curious about the word.

Like most small-town libraries, The Holbrook Municipal Library was a cramped building that nevertheless managed to house a pretty decent collection of fiction. I discovered a few mysteries I hadn't read yet, and I even found a Spanish dictionary, but I hadn't the faintest idea how spell the word I wanted to look up so it wasn't much use to me. The last of my luck started trickling away like a canteen with a leak when I asked the librarian about Norsicol newsletters.

"Newsletters from the old plant, eh?" The woman behind the desk sucked her teeth pensively.

"Have you ever heard of such a thing?"

"I think you might be out of luck on that one," she told me after a long moment of consideration. "I know there's nothing like that in the stacks and if they're over twenty years old. . . ."

"They would be."

She shook her head. "Then I seriously doubt we'd have them any more. We're bulging at the seams with materials as it is."

"Okay, it was a long shot anyway. How about old issues of the *Holbrook Times*?"

She smiled. "Now that we have. Going back to the mid-fifties at any rate. It's all on microfilm, though. Newsprint doesn't last long under fluorescent lights. You know how to use the index?"

I said yes and she took me back to where hundreds of microfilm boxes were stacked in chronological order. There was a binder of photocopied index cards and, for the dates I was concerned with, numerous references to Norsicol. I dug out my pen and notebook, and started jotting down numbers.

When I'd gone through several years' worth of cards, I skimmed off the appropriate microfilms, flicked on the film reader, and started scanning. Between the index cards and the microfilm itself, it took a few eye-straining hours to find what I was looking for. I was starting to develop an unhealthy fixation on Visine when a big headline flashed across the screen. I twisted the button to reverse the film.

"Well, hello there," I cooed to the screen.

The front page article was all about the winners of Norsicol's 1971 fall golf tournament. Must have been a slow news week. There was a picture of the proud players lined up and showing off their dental work and there, in the front row and just to the right, was my man. Looking quite a bit younger, of course, but it was unmistakably Grant DeSantis. So. DeSantis had, indeed, worked at the old plant. I scanned through the article but it didn't say much other than that DeSantis was part of the management team. Guess he was into buzzwords even back then.

I plugged my quarter into the machine to photocopy the picture and my eyes took a stroll through the rest of the page. "Plant Worker Injured." The headline cast out and neatly nabbed my attention. Unfortunately the accompanying article was superficial at best and downright inadequate at worst. It said just that there had been an accident and a worker (no name given) had been taken to Edmonton for treatment. No indication of where in the plant the accident had occurred or how serious it had been. However, if the injured worker had had to be taken to Edmonton, it must have been fairly bad. I scanned through the next few issues, straining my eyes for a while longer as I tried to find any follow-up articles. No luck. The accident and the anonymous worker were never mentioned again.

Deep in thought, I rewound the last reel of microfilm, then looked down at my watch. I blinked. Ye gods, I'd been at it for hours! All at once, I realized I was starving, my leg was throbbing, my hand was covered in ink from my leaking pen, and I had to pee. I turned off the light on the microfilm reader, found a clean spot on my hand, and rubbed my eyes. Any further research would have to wait until tomorrow.

I gathered my notes, crammed them into my pack, and swung myself first to the bathroom and then back through the stacks. But before I could leave the library, a sale table of books leapt from between the shelves and forced me over.

I rummaged around for a while and found a couple of dog-eared paperback thrillers, a slightly battered copy of *Budd's Flora*, and a book called *Spineless Wonders* which, instead of detailing my romantic history as I'd first suspected, appeared to be a fascinating and humorous account of invertebrates and the biologists who love them. A good haul for a buck twenty-five.

I'd just finished flipping through the last row of books, when I was suddenly accosted by a living, breathing spineless wonder.

"Hi, Robyn," Howard Miller whined.

Crap. If I hadn't been so preoccupied I might have seen him coming and ducked into the stacks.

"Howard." I nodded curtly.

He oozed up to me, clutching a copy of *Soldier of Fortune*, his stomach billowing over the waistband of his sagging jeans like a loaf of bread left to rise too long in its pan.

I've never been one to judge somebody based on appearance alone, but I have to admit the sight of Howard Miller gave me the creeps. It wasn't just his general state of sloth or his nervous habits, but more the way his tiny eyes constantly roamed over the more salient parts of my body. I always felt like I should shower after an encounter with him.

Four years ago, new to Holbrook and basking in the warmth and friendliness of Megan's family home, I'd actually tried to be nice to Howard. That was before I had an inkling of his personality. Megan had warned me off, but I figured everybody deserved a fair chance. Problem was, Howard mistook my friendly smiles and pleasant greetings for something I didn't even want to contemplate. In the three weeks I spent in Holbrook that summer, his persistence went swiftly from bothersome to irritating to creepy. In the end, I'd been forced to reject him quite firmly.

"I thought it might be you and I came over and it was you." Howard's eyes were fixed firmly on my chest. "I heard you were visiting June McVea again."

"Mmmhmm," I muttered, stuffing my books into my backpack as fast as I could with a single hand.

"What happened to you?"

"Accident."

"Wow. It must have been a pretty bad one. Is that why you're staying at June's?"

"Yeah."

He started chewing on a hangnail. He still hadn't lifted his eyes from my chest. I was fairly sure I knew what was coming next.

"Well, seeing as you're in town and everything. I was wondering if you wanted to go out sometime. You know, for coffee."

"Thanks, Howard, but I don't think so. Now if you'll excuse me, I have to get going."

"If you don't like coffee, we could do something else."

I shouldered my backpack and managed a tight smile. "Thanks anyways, but I'm pretty busy."

And with that I hobbled over to the front desk to pay for my books. As I left the library, I caught sight of Howard's reflection in the glass door. He was standing where I'd left him, hands crammed into his pockets, watching me leave.

I headed back to June's with my book-laden backpack stuffed in the basket of Vivian's scooter. With a bit of effort, I'd put Howard Miller out of my mind, concentrating instead on my discovery about Grant DeSantis. I was feeling pretty impressed with myself when I spied a familiar figure bent over a thick clump of overgrown rose bushes.

"Hey, Matt!" I called out.

He turned around and his face lit up when he saw me. "Robyn! How's it going?" He came up to the fence and leaned easily on the gate. "How are you feeling?"

"Better than the other day," I replied.

Matt's expression sobered. "Yes, just about anything would be better than having somebody shoot at you. How's June doing?"

I considered the question. "Mad," I said finally.

"Mad?"

"Furious, maybe. It really hit her sometime yesterday that whoever was taking potshots at us is probably somebody she knows. Yeah, I guess you could say she's furious."

"What were you and June doing out there, anyway?"

"We'd gone birding and June brought extra cinnamon buns. We decided to surprise the gang."

"And found yourselves surprised instead."

I grimaced. "You could say that."

"Any idea why it happened?"

"Uh, not really."

"Do you think somebody was trying to scare the crew off?"

"I hope not, but it's possible."

"Has anything else happened at the site since then? Or before then, for that matter?"

Matt's brown eyes were watching me with an intentness that suddenly made me very uncomfortable. All at once, I remembered Grant DeSantis and his obsession with media relations. Was Matt a little too interested in what was going on at the site?

I managed a nonchalant shrug. "I don't really know, Matt. I'm kind of out of the loop. And if you don't mind, I'd rather not talk about it any more. It wasn't a pleasant experience."

"Of course," Matt agreed so quickly I wondered if I'd misjudged him. "I'm sorry."

"'S okay."

"So, you were birding again, eh?" Matt said into the awkward silence. "I can see I'll have to dust off my binoculars one of these days."

"What?" I said. "June hasn't dragged you out yet?"

He grinned. "A couple of times," he admitted. "To show me some heron nests. There weren't any birds in them yet, though, so I'm not really sure what the point of it was."

I laughed. "To scout them out for the spring, of course. June's a pretty avid birdwatcher."

"I hear you're no slouch yourself."

"I like the little guys," I agreed before turning my eyes towards the house. "I thought there was an old woman living here."

It was Matt's turn to nod. "That's right. A Mrs. Kershaw. She died a few months ago. Her relatives are living overseas right now, and they asked June to rent out the house until they can come back and deal with it. It's a nice place, but it's packed with junk." He peeled off his gardening gloves. "You want to come in for a bit? I was just thinking of having a coffee."

"You got any cookies?" I asked hopefully. "I missed lunch."

"Oreos okay?"

"Cookies of the gods."

Matt laughed and held the gate open while I drove the scooter up the short walk. When I hobbled into the house, I could see that he hadn't been kidding about the junk. Whole mountain ranges of books perched on cabinets and cases, while rivers of loose papers spilled out across shelves and the floor. Knickknacks swamped every available space, and there was a riot of brightly colored throw rugs scattered across the floors.

"Wow," I exclaimed. "Holbrook's answer to the Augean stables?"

Matt chuckled. "I know. And I've even tidied things up a bit. It's a collector's dream in here. But the catch would be sorting through it all first."

"Hell of a catch."

Matt laughed again. "You have no idea—although the stuff I'm finding is pretty darn fascinating. When I shoveled out the bedroom, I found a stack of adventure magazines from the 1920s! In perfect condition, too. Some of them were still in brown paper bags."

"Amazing."

"Yeah, it's not all so interesting, though, you should see the stuff in the shed. Probably been sitting there for decades. I'm guessing three-quarters of it will have to hauled to that new waste facility—wherever they decide to build it. Come on, we'll sit in the kitchen. I spend most of my time there. It's considerably less chaotic."

I followed Matt down the narrow hallway into a small room bright with afternoon sunshine. There were piles of papers and notebooks, several different kinds of cameras and cases, and numerous newspaper clippings and magazine articles. The kitchen didn't seem any less cluttered to me, but obviously it all belonged to Matt, revealing, I suppose, that "mess" is defined by ownership.

But papers weren't the only items cluttering up the kitchen. I also caught a glimpse of bright purple. Something silky? Before I could identify it, Matt whisked it up and into a closet. I suppressed a grin. It had looked like a purple silk robe. Not the sort of thing a man would wear or, for that matter, anything I'd ever seen June in. That rich plum color *would* suit her complexion, though. Ah, love, that many-splendored thing.

As Matt set out mugs and sugar and a jumbo-sized package of Oreos, I set myself down on one of the kitchen chairs.

"Are cookies and coffee going to be enough?" Matt asked. "I could probably rustle you up a sandwich or something."

"No, no. That's fine, thanks. Although—" I paused for a second, remembering another problem I had "—you could do me another favor."

"What do you need?"

"I need to find out what's written on the bottom of my foot. Kelt wrote it and nobody will tell me what it says."

"On the bottom of your foot, eh?" Matt grinned. "Well, let's see. . . ." He bent down and had a look and . . . a laugh. Figures.

He looked up at me again, vastly amused. "And June wouldn't tell you what it says?"

"No."

I waited hopefully. And waited. And waited.

"You're not going to tell me, either, are you?"

He shook his head. "I'm sorry—"

"Yeah, right," I snorted my disbelief.

"I'll give you Oreos, though."

"Hmmm," I grunted noncommittally, not wanting to seem cheap and easy.

Matt took it as an agreement and starting rinsing out the coffee pot. "So where were you that you missed lunch?"

"Library," I told him. "I got seduced by a sale table, then a spineless wonder tried to seduce me."

"A spineless wonder?"

"Sorry. I was being a bit snotty. There's a guy who lives in town here. He's had a thing for me ever since I first visited."

"Not your type?"

I made a retching noise. "Not even close. He's a repulsive human being—"

"Is his name Howard Miller?"

I goggled at him. "How did you know?"

Matt filled the coffee pot with water and switched it on. "I've met him—and you're right, 'repulsive' is an apt description. June told me he'd been obsessed with you."

"I'm not sure you should be saying that in the past tense. When did you meet him?"

"A month ago, maybe. He contacted me about a story."

"A story for you to write?"

Matt nodded. "At least, he wanted me to write it. He seemed to think his ex-boss was involved in some shady accounting practices. He wanted me to investigate."

"So what did you do?"

Matt shrugged. "I told him I wasn't interested, but he showed up here one evening with proof. Or so he believed. He had some photocopies of documents, accounts ledgers . . . that kind of thing. He claimed his boss was playing Julia Child with the books. Funneling money out of the company."

"And was he?"

"She. He worked for Melanie DeSantis. And no, from what he showed me, there was no proof that she was doing anything shady. I'm afraid Howard didn't take it well when I told him so."

"I'm not surprised," I snorted. "What reason would Melanie DeSantis have to cook her books? Her husband must make a fair bit of change."

"You'd think so."

I shook my head in disbelief. "Wow. No wonder Howard was fired, if he was making accusations like that. His mother told me that Melanie DeSantis had canned him for no reason."

"I don't know anything about him being fired, but I sure wasn't going to get involved. As I said, there wasn't a shred of evidence that I could see, and the guy seemed a bit, well, erratic. Besides, I've got enough work on my plate."

"Looks like you keep pretty busy," I remarked, indicating the piles of paperwork.

"I'm researching the NAFTA pesticide bans," he explained, jiggling the filter on the coffee maker to get the last few drops in the carafe. "There's a fair amount of documentation to go through."

"Right. Megan told me you were involved in that."

"Well, I don't know if you could say I'm 'involved,' but I am working on a series of articles about it."

"It's about time they targeted some of that stuff for phase-out."

"Or reduction." He handed me my coffee and, like a true gentleman, passed me the entire bag of Oreos. "And the phase-out is only regional. It's still better than nothing, but I could wish it went a little further. And then, of course, there's the whole issue about banning. Sugar? Cream?"

"Both, please." I replied, scraping the icing off the chocolate biscuit with my teeth. "What do you mean?"

He fixed up his own mug and sat down at the table. "I mean that banning something sounds so definite, doesn't it? But even now in the United States, restricted use is still permitted for many of these so-called 'banned' substances."

"It sucks, I agree." I sipped my coffee. "But the thing that's always bugged me more are countries, like the US, that find the stuff too toxic to use at home, but perfect for selling to less developed countries."

"Tell me about it." Matt nodded his agreement. He rummaged in the bag of Oreos and pulled out a handful. "Oh, they put warning labels and application instructions on it so they can claim they're being responsible global citizens. But in reality, what Third World illiterate farmer is going to understand it?"

He popped another cookie in his mouth, got up, and riffled through a thick wad of papers on the side counter. "Get a load of this . . . 'Do not operate nozzle liquid pressure over 40 psi or with any fan nozzle smaller than 0.4 gpm or fan angle greater than 65 degrees such as type 6504. Do not use any can type nozzles smaller than 0.4 gpm nor whirl plate smaller than #46 such as type D-4-46.'"

He snorted. "I don't think *I* can even figure out what that means, and that's straight off a label for endrin—another of the Pesticide Action Network's Dirty Dozen that's officially 'banned' in North America."

"So an illiterate farmer. . . ."

"Probably hasn't got a hope in hell of understanding it," he finished.

"This is pretty damn depressing, Matt," I told him.

"I know," he agreed soberly. "That's why I'm writing about it." He passed the bag of cookies to me again.

As I drove off a while later, I reflected on my conversation with Matt. His concern for what we were doing to the planet was deep and abiding. So many people profess the same solicitude, expressing their concern about the sorry state of our environment over and over again—as they clean their homes with toxic chemicals, wipe up spilled juice with bleached paper towels, and drive their cars a few blocks to pick up a loaf of bread. When it came to the human race, I wasn't as cynical as Ben was (at least not yet), but I had to admit, it was nice to meet someone whose actions spoke as loudly as his words.

June, I decided, was a lucky woman.

CHAPTER 17

THE BURNING QUESTION WAS, DID JUNE KNOW IT? I had to ask myself this question after what Kelt had to tell me that night.

I'd been wondering off and on about his reasons for establishing this routine of nightly chats. I hoped it was the overwhelming attractiveness of my person (hey, I can dream), but I suspected it probably had more to do with a feeling of camaraderie resulting from our amateur sleuthing. We had, after all, been through this kind of thing together before. But whatever the reason, his heart or his gumshoes, he slouched there in front of my door with my cat slung over his shoulder.

"Bring him in. Have a seat."

Kelt plopped himself down on one of the wingback chairs and settled Guido on his lap.

"How'd it go today?" I asked him.

"Better. Lisa and I were sampling the runoff ditches. It was fun."

I pursed my lips in envy. "Had a good time slopping around, did you?"

Kelt grinned. "That, too. But Lisa's *hilarious!*"

"Uh, Lisa?"

"Yeah. This is the first time I've worked on a project with her. I thought I was going to wet my pants laughing. I'd never realized before how funny she is." He chuckled and shook his head. "She started singing these god-awful dead teenager songs—"

"Dead teenager songs?"

"Yes, she was trying to make them stick in my brain so they'd drive me crazy. I was forced to retaliate with TV commercial jingles."

"Commercial jingles."

"I had to do something," Kelt explained. "She almost got me with "Tell Laura I Love Her," but I managed to stick her with the Oscar Mayer wiener song." He laughed wickedly. "Anyhow, we had a great time. Even managed to forget about that saboteur for a while."

"Great." I pulled my lips into a smile.

And it was great, wasn't it? Didn't I want my co-workers to have fun on the job? To be able to forget about the sniper for a few hours? Of course it was, and I did. Besides, Lisa was in a romantic relationship. There was no need for jealousy. Still, if hearing Kelt rhapsodize about her was supposed to be music to my ears, it sounded to me like freeform jazz.

I realized that I'd been quiet for a little too long. I looked over at Kelt, but he'd fallen silent himself. His head was lowered and he was stroking Guido with unnecessary concentration. Was there more? I waited.

"Is . . . is June okay?" he asked finally.

I blinked. "What do you mean 'okay'?"

"Well, is she unhappy about something?"

"Kelt, what are you trying to say?"

He squirmed. "I'm not a nosy person."

"Are you going to tell me what's wrong?" I demanded.

"I just wanted you to know that I'm not nosy."

"Okay." I rolled my eyes. "You're not a nosy person. You're the antithesis of nosy. Apathy personified—"

"Hey!"

"I'm kidding. Now, what's bugging you?"

"It's just . . . I couldn't sleep last night." He broke off and bent over to pat Guido again. "I had really bad indigestion."

"And?" I asked, puzzled about what Kelt's stomach had to do with anything.

"And I went looking for a Rolaids. I didn't bring any."

"So?"

"So, my room is on the same floor as June's."

"So?" I demanded, irritated now.

"So, when I passed by June's room, I heard her crying."

"Crying."

He fidgeted again and refused to meet my eyes. "I wasn't *trying* to listen," he explained. "But it was hard to miss. She was crying pretty hard. Sobbing, even."

June sobbing?

I furrowed my brow. "She hasn't said anything to me," I mumbled. "And she sure seems happy. . . ."

"It sounded really bad," Kelt said. "I didn't really know what to do. I didn't think she'd appreciate me barging in and asking what was wrong."

"No." I shook my head. "Probably not. I don't know, Kelt. Maybe she had a fight with Matt. Or maybe it was the sniper attack. The gods know it took me forever to get to sleep after that. *You* had to sleep with the goofy elephant. Maybe June just had a delayed reaction to the whole thing."

"Maybe," Kelt still seemed troubled. He hadn't even smiled at the elephant reference. "I just thought I should tell you. It sounded as if her heart was breaking."

"Thanks. I'll keep my eyes open but I'm not sure what I can do."

Kelt didn't stay much longer after that and when he left, it was with a friendly smile and a brotherly pat on my shoulder.

Asexual reproduction was looking better all the time, I reflected as I got ready for bed. At the rate I was going, it was the only way I'd get any action. And by dividing and multiplying I'd lose weight, too. A win-win scenario. I pulled the covers over my head and fell asleep with the Oscar Mayer wiener song playing in my brain.

His fingers combed through my hair and continued down my neck to tickle my spine. I arched against him in ecstasy and he groaned. I was letting my fingers do their own walking, luxuriating in the ripple of his muscles beneath my hands. His green eyes were dark with passion. I could feel the scorching heat of his body hard against mine. That wasn't all I could feel. Thrusting member, prodigious manhood, throbbing python of love. The euphemisms flashed irreverently through my brain as his hands grasped my waist and pressed me closer to him. I felt his hands at the buttons of my shirt then shivered as the thin fabric slid from my shoulders.

"Kelt," I whispered.

He caressed me. Slowly and with infinite skill. "I love you." As he breathed the words, I caught a whiff of something faintly fishy.

Fishy? I extended my nose and surreptitiously sniffed his breath again. No, not really fishy, but a bit odd . . . sort of like . . . sort of like. . . .

"Have you been in the cat kibble again?" I murmured.

"Prroot?" he answered.

Wait a minute. . . .

"What the . . . ?"

"Mrrooowt?"

I cracked an eye open. Guido stretched across my pillow and yawned another stinky cat food-breath yawn right in my face.

"Arrgh!" I croaked in frustration.

I lay there for few minutes, desperately trying to recapture the shreds of my dream. Guido stretched again and proceeded to give himself a long and very intimate bath. I blew out my breath in a defeated sigh and kicked the covers off. It was with some effort that I refrained from kicking him off, too. Stupid cat. I was beginning to think the gods had purposely created him to screw around with my life whenever they weren't up for the job. I fluffed up my pillow and rolled over, turning my back on my cat. He was probably getting back at me for having him neutered.

Thump!

The sound was so muffled I wasn't sure I'd heard it at first. I flicked a glance at my bedside clock. Ten past one. I had only been asleep for an hour and a half, and the rest of the household had sounded pretty quiet even before I'd turned out my light. I listened intently, my ears ringing in the silence of the dream-filled house. Then I heard it again. A quiet thud by the front door. I waited a few more seconds, but the house remained silent.

I slipped out of bed and limped over to the door. Cracking it open carefully, I peered out into the front hall. Nobody there. I swung around, hobbled to the window, and peeked out the side of the curtains. The moon was a mere toenail clipping in the sky. By its silvery light I could see a bundled figure step off the front porch and slip down the path. Had someone tried to break in? No. There was something familiar. . . .

The figure looked back once at the house, and I recognized June's face in the dim light. I watched as she let herself quietly out the front gate, pushing it slowly so it didn't squeak. Once through, she set off down the street.

A strange time for a stroll, I mused, then shrugged. I had been a victim of insomnia myself all too often lately. And if what Kelt had told me was true, June was going through some form of emotional trauma. I wondered if it had anything to do with Matt. I didn't think they had been fighting but he was, as far as I knew, the first romantic encounter she'd had since Eddie's death. A new relationship was bound to bring back some painful memories. The kind that keep you tossing and turning all night.

I let the curtain fall and limped back to bed. Guido the cat was now sprawled across my pillow. I climbed under the covers, shoved him over, and composed myself for sleep. If June felt like going for a late-night stroll, it was no business of mine.

For the rest of the night, much to my disappointment, my dreams were amorphous rather than amorous. Stupid cat.

CHAPTER 18

I WOKE UP THE NEXT MORNING STILL WISHING I was an Oscar Mayer wiener. That rat bastard! Fortunately for Kelt, the Woodrow crew were already gone by the time I limped into the kitchen. June was rushing around, getting ready to do the same.

"I've got to go into the office for a spell," she explained as she set out muffins and scones on a serving plate. "I'll be back by lunch, so help yourself to some breakfast. How did you sleep?"

"Not too badly," I yawned, trying to wake up. "How about yourself?"

She waved off the question. "Oh, I had the light out by 10:30, and I slept like a log," she replied.

I paused in the middle of another yawn and regarded her with some surprise. As far as I knew, logs didn't go traipsing around in the dead of night.

"I'm off now, but I'll see you later," June tossed a smile my way, grabbed her car keys and headed out the door.

I poured Guido some kibble to get him out from under my feet, then scarfed down a couple of muffins and a big glass of juice. My brain was still sluggish with sleep and the wiener song, but it wasn't *that* slow. Where had June gone last night? And, even more importantly, why had she lied about it? I scrubbed my face with my hand and gave myself a mental shake. Talk about a nasty, suspicious mind. What did it matter? Maybe Kelt was right—maybe I was starting to see criminals everywhere.

Tracy stepped into the kitchen just as I drained my juice glass.

"Good morning," I greeted her.

She smiled wanly, a shadow of her former perky self. "Hi, is there any juice left?"

"Yup, and a plateful of muffins and scones. Jam's in the fridge if you want some. June's gone out till lunch. How're you doing?"

She lifted one shoulder in a shrug. "I'm okay." She didn't sound it.

I poured her a glass of juice. She thanked me with a small smile and settled at the table with her glass and a muffin. She looked so miserable, I had to say something.

"Tracy," I began awkwardly, "you might not know this, but the same thing happened to me a little over a month ago."

She looked at me in surprise. "You found. . . ."

"A body. Yeah, I did. It was awful."

Her eyes filled with tears, she tried to blink them away, then gave up and wiped her face on her sleeve. She seemed very young.

"I was in British Columbia doing some fieldwork. I was tromping through the forest, looking for spotted owls, and ended up finding way more than I bargained for. Believe me, I know exactly how you feel right now."

Tracy was silent for a long moment. "I . . . I was riding over to these trees," she said finally. "Mrs. M had been telling me about herons and how they like to build their nests in trees. I . . . I saw a whole bunch of sticks and stuff all crammed into a few trees. I thought. . . ." She took a deep breath. "I thought they were nests. I thought she'd like it if I found some herons for her. She's been totally nice to me. So . . . so I rode over. . . ." she trailed off.

"And you found Richard DeSantis instead," I finished for her.

She scrubbed her face and nodded. "I just . . . I just keep seeing him. . . ."

"I know. And I'm afraid there isn't anything you can do to make that go away. It sucks, but there it is. The only thing that's going to make it any better is time, and you pretty much just have to live through that a minute at a time. But I tell you, Tracy, it's a hell of a lot easier if you try to get back on track with your life."

"But—"

"Have you seen your horse since this happened?"

"N-no."

"Well, why don't you go and see him? Rub him down or brush him or whatever it is that you do with horses. You don't have to ride him necessarily, or maybe you can ride him around the barn. It doesn't really matter. What matters is that you need to get out and start thinking about something else or it'll drive you crazy. I know from personal experience."

She fiddled with her muffin for a minute, methodically breaking off pieces onto the plate, but not eating any of them.

Finally she looked up. "Mr. Golding's got a fenced field. Maybe I could take Marius and practice my gaits."

"That sounds fun," I said encouragingly. "What kinds of gaits does a horse do?"

As Tracy talked about her favorite subject, the tight look around her eyes began to ease. By the time she left, dressed in riding gear, she was, if not perky, at least a little happier looking.

Good deed done for the day, I trundled off to wash up and get dressed. I was just struggling into my socks (well, sock) when the doorbell rang.

"Hang on!" I called out and grabbed my crutches. I lurched down the front hall, tugged my shirt into place, and opened the door. Puzzled, I looked out at the empty porch. Nobody there. I swung around to peer into the mailbox. Maybe Canada Post had dropped a parcel off. Nope. Nothing there, either. Weird. I shrugged and went back in to finish dressing.

I heard the news at Hank's.

Actually, I saw the news before I heard it, though I didn't realize it at the time. I'd decided to give Vivian's little scooter a workout with a longer trip—specifically to Hank's for a mid-morning coffee and then onto the library to see what else I could discover about the accident at the Norsicol plant. On my way to the coffee shop, I drove past the Blue Heron statue that stood majestically in the town's square. Not so majestic this morning. There was garbage and what looked like smashed eggs all over the pavement, and the statue itself had been splashed with rusty red paint. I shook my head in disgust at the vandalism. The poor heron looked more red than blue now. It was going to cost a bundle to sandblast it. A couple of RCMP officers sat taking notes in their car in front of the statue. I hoped they'd managed to snag the kids responsible.

It never even occurred to me that the red I'd seen was not paint.

Hank's was doing a brisk business. Odd for this time of the morning. It didn't take long to find out why.

"Melanie DeSantis has been murdered," Dana announced as I crutched my way to the counter.

"*What?!*"

She nodded and grabbed a mug off the wall for me. "Some tourists found her this morning," she explained. "Someone slashed her throat in front of the Blue Heron."

"The statue?"

Dana nodded again and pushed the coffee towards me. I left it there untouched as I sank on the wooden stool and tried to come to grips with the news.

"But I saw the statue this morning. Are you saying that was *blood* all over it?"

"Yeah." Dana squeezed her lips into a tight line and whisked off to serve another customer.

I rubbed my face in disbelief. "What the hell's going on here?" I muttered to myself.

"Oh, hi."

I looked up from my untouched coffee. Rocky stood over me, a happy grin on his face. He was clasping a coffee mug to his chest.

"Hey, Rocky," I managed to rally. "Have a seat."

"Thanks." He plopped himself down on the stool beside me, and Dana topped up his mug on her way to the espresso machine.

"I had coffee today, yes I did, I had coffee."

"And it looks like you're going to have another one."

He smiled beatifically and brought his mug to his lips with both hands, holding it as a young child would. "It's good coffee here. Dana, she makes good coffee."

I nodded and brought my own mug up for a sip. The first one was difficult. The news had stuck in my throat like an oversized gobstopper.

"Here, this is for you," Rocky said.

I looked down at his hand holding out a dime to me.

"Oh, no," I protested. "You keep it."

"I want you to be happy," he said sincerely. "You should be happy."

"I am happy," I replied, managing a weak smile. It seemed to reassure him, though he kept his hand extended towards me. The dime gleamed dully in his palm. "You keep that," I said, folding his fingers gently over the coin, "buy yourself another coffee."

He smiled back at me. "I like coffee, yes I do, I like coffee a lot."

"So do I, Rocky," I agreed. The second sip was a little easier.

"I don't like Luke's ghost, though." A cloud passed over his face. "I don't know why he came back, Luke, I don't know why he came."

So Rocky was still on about the ghost. Not surprising. I searched his face. It had fallen into a despairing expression. He was obviously reacting badly to the news of yet another death. I patted his hand comfortingly.

"Don't worry about the ghost," I said in a reassuring tone. "Luke was your friend, wasn't he?"

"He was my friend, yes, Luke was my friend."

"Well, Rocky, friends don't hurt each other. He won't do anything to you, so you don't have to worry about it, okay?"

His face cleared. "Okay." He lifted his mug in both hands again and gulped his coffee. No wonder he went through so much of the stuff. "I'm going to go have some toast," he announced after draining his mug. "Yes, I'll go home and have some toast. Bye."

Rocky stood up, swayed a little on his feet, then bolted out the door, leaving me wondering just what effect all that caffeine was having on his system.

I wanted to press Dana for details about Melanie DeSantis's murder, but her customers kept her hopping like Michigan J. Frog without an audience. I waited for a while, but it didn't look as if things were going to calm down any time soon, so I tucked a couple of loonies under my mug, wedged my crutches into my armpits, and hobbled out to climb aboard my scooter.

I drove by the RCMP detachment office on my way to the library. The RCMP were busy, with several squad cars parked out front and a small crowd of people inside. As I rubbernecked my way past, another blue and white car pulled up. The officer helped an older man out of the passenger seat. Grant DeSantis. But a very different DeSantis from the one I'd met with the other day. His face was as white as his freshly pressed shirt, his tall form was stooped, and deep grooves lined his face with grief.

There would be no asking about the site now. No questions about where drums had been buried, or how rags had been disposed of. No questions about accidents or injured workers or why he hadn't told us about his old job. Grant DeSantis was a broken man.

Chapter 19

The library had a closed sign taped to the door, so I pointed my scooter back toward June's. By the time I wheeled up the walk and crutched my way onto the front porch, June was just pulling up in her car with a couple of strangers in tow. She introduced them to me as Fran and Vince Bartel, tourists from Ontario and her latest guests. My questions would have to wait.

After hands had been shaken and greetings had been exchanged, June hustled us all off the porch and into the front hall.

"Follow me and I'll show you where you can freshen up," June told the Bartels, leading the way upstairs. "I'm afraid I'll have to put you on the third floor, but there's a private bathroom and you should be quite comfortable. . . ."

I took myself into the kitchen and waited impatiently. It had seemed inappropriate to bring up the subject of murder in front of June's visitors. As it turned out, it might have been inappropriate, but not entirely out of place.

June stepped into the kitchen, closed the door, and threw me a questioning look. "You've heard about Melanie DeSantis?"

I nodded.

"These poor folks are the ones who found her."

"*What!?*"

"They were out to look at the heron statue, and they found her in the bushes."

"Ye gods!"

June nodded. "Yes, I know. They've had quite a shock, so I've invited them here to calm down a little. Where's Tracy?"

"Gone to visit her horse."

"Good, she doesn't need to deal with this right now. If Fran and Vince want to talk about it, that's okay, but I don't think we should bring it up."

I nodded. "Yeah, okay. What do you know about it?"

June shook her head. "Not much, I—"

"June?" A muffled voice called out from the hallway.

"We'll talk later," June murmured, then she opened the door. "Fran, Vince, come on into the kitchen. It's where everybody seems to end up around here. Why don't you have a seat and relax? I've got the kettle on for tea, and there are some blueberry muffins if you're hungry. I'm just going to nip upstairs and finish getting your room ready."

"Thank you, June," Fran smiled at her. "That would be just lovely."

I gestured the couple towards the table and hobbled over to sit with them.

Fran and Vince Bartel were on the far side of middle-aged. She was a plump, cheery type with a nattery personality. Her husband was a markedly quieter character, a short, cigar-shaped man with steel-colored hair and a pair of those black horn-rimmed glasses you see so frequently in bad high school science films. I half expected him to start lecturing about "Chemical Bonding and You," but even had he been so inclined, his wife didn't give him the chance.

"You've had a nasty accident," Fran chirped up, looking curiously at my cast.

"Yes," I agreed, without giving any more details. "I'm on the mend though. June's is a great place to recover."

"It is lovely," she agreed, and before she could draw another breath to ask me what I'd done to myself, I changed the subject.

"Whereabouts in Ontario are you from?"

"Thunder Bay," Fran answered.

"I grew up in the Ottawa Valley," I told her.

"Did you? I thought I recognized a bit of an accent." Fran was delighted. "Our Sally lives in Kanata, just outside of Ottawa."

"So what brings you to Alberta?"

"Oh, we wanted to see the Blue Heron," Fran explained. "We'd planned to come and see the Blue Heron, and then head to the Egg on the same day, isn't that right, dear?"

"Oh, yeah," Vince cleared his throat. "Yeah."

I looked at her uncomprehendingly. "The Egg?"

She nodded and smiled a little. "Yes, the big Easter Egg in Vegreville. I'm sure you've heard of it. You see, Vince and I are on a tour of all the big statues in Canada. The Gigantics, the book called them. We started with the Glooscap in Nova Scotia—I really liked him. I'd never heard of him before we read the book. Did you know, in Native mythology, Glooscap was supposed to have used Nova Scotia as his bed, and PEI as his pillow? Fascinating. Well, we started with him and we've seen, oh, I don't know how many others now, isn't that right, dear?"

"Oh yeah, yeah."

"Let me see, there was the Nickel, of course, in Sudbury, and there was quite a charming Moose in Moose Jaw. We also saw the Turtle in Turtleford, but he was badly in need of some paint." She sniffed a little disapprovingly. "And—"

"You've been traveling across Canada, just to look at giant statues?" I broke in.

She blinked at me in surprise. "Why, yes, Manitoba was by far the best province—they had a Viking and a Garter Snake, and even a Mosquito—but we still haven't been to the Peach in Penticton yet, or the Smoky the Bear in Revelstoke. They're all part of the plan though, isn't that right, dear?"

On cue, Vince nodded. "Oh yeah, yeah."

"But—" I began.

"It's not that unusual, you know," she explained "There's a book about them—the Gigantics, I think I already mentioned it. And we've seen other tourists at quite a few of the statues. There are a couple of young men—Mexican or perhaps South American, their skin was that lovely coffee color—we've met them a few times now, isn't that right, dear?"

His mouth full of blueberry muffin, Vince contented himself with a nod. His wife didn't seem to notice.

"They were very nice young men. They even took our picture in front of the Moose, or was it the Turtle? At any rate, they're touring the Gigantics, too, you see." She lowered her voice a little. "I think they were gay. They didn't say so, but they seemed very close. Ah well, they were a lovely couple and I guess a lot of young people are doing that these days, isn't that right, dear?"

"Oh yeah, yeah."

"We saw the Hat yesterday—in Medicine Hat, you know—and neither Vince nor I sleep much any more, so when we woke up at quarter to four, we decided to just get up and get on our way. That way, we could see the Blue Heron and the Egg on the same day. We were hoping to be in Penticton by Friday because some friends of ours there are having a little party and really we couldn't go without seeing the Blue Heron." Her face fell. "Although . . . now I rather wish we had."

"I'm sorry," I said softly. "It must have been a terrible shock."

"I couldn't believe it when we found her, poor dear," Fran said, her demeanor abruptly sober. "We're still trying to get over the shock, isn't that right, dear?"

Vince nodded slowly. "Yeah, yeah."

Fran dug around in the pocket of her sweater and came up with a crumpled Kleenex. She blotted her eyes. "The poor woman. Did you know her?" she asked June, who had just come back into the room.

June shook her head. "No, not really, they were fairly new to town."

"It makes you sick to think what some people are capable of these days," Fran snuffled, her voice trembling a little. Vince gave her shoulder an awkward pat. "I'll never forget the sight of her body lying there in the bushes. And why somebody would put one of those little gnomes there beside her"—she let out her breath in a sigh—"it's quite beyond me."

"Someone left a gnome beside her?" I asked, meeting June's concerned look with one of my own.

Fran was nodding. "Yes, right beside her legs. It was ghoulish." She shivered and pulled her cardigan more tightly around her shoulders. "I almost fainted when I saw it. You see, Vince had gone off to find a coffee shop so I decided to stretch my legs and take a peek at the Heron. I saw her feet sticking out of the hedge—except I didn't know at the time that it was a woman. I'm afraid I thought it was a drunk. We've got a couple in Thunder Bay, you know. The poor men drink themselves into a stupor and then pass out in the park.

"So that's what I thought it was—some poor soul drunk and asleep. Until I saw the gnome. I used to like those little gnomes." She rubbed her forehead. "But it had . . . blood all over it and . . . that's when I saw the blood on the Blue Heron. The sun wasn't very high yet, I'd noticed before that the Heron didn't seem very blue. I thought maybe it just needed painting . . . like the Turtle, you see. I tell you, I've never screamed in my life, but when I saw that blood. . . ." Her voice trailed off and she shivered again.

"Maybe Fran should have a little rest now," Vince said in a soft but firm voice.

June nodded her agreement. "I've fixed up a room for you. I think you should just spend the night here. The RCMP might have a few questions for you, but apart from that, it's been a bad morning for you both."

Fran smiled shakily. "Thank you, June, I don't know what we would've done without you."

"Come on, Frannie," Vince urged his wife up from her seat. "We'll go see the Egg tomorrow."

June escorted them out the kitchen door and to their room. I searched her face closely when she came back. She was pale and tired-looking.

"Are you okay?" I asked.

She shook her head and smoothed her hair with a distracted gesture. "What does it mean?" she said. "First Richard, and now Melanie."

"I don't know. But it seems like someone's got a hate-on for the DeSantises."

"I can't imagine what that poor man is going through."

"I don't suppose they've caught anyone yet?" It was more statement than question.

June shook her head again. "No. It's a dreadful thing. The Bartels have had quite a shock. There was a lot of blood, apparently."

"I know." I told June about seeing the statue. She swallowed hard and shook her head again.

"They think she was killed very early this morning," she said. "That's what Gary told me. He said her watch had stopped at ten to two. It must have been smashed when she . . . when she was killed."

"What was Melanie DeSantis doing out and about at two o'clock in the morning?"

"I have no idea."

"Well, didn't her husband report her missing this morning?"

June shrugged. "Not that I heard, but that doesn't mean much. I'll have to go back into the office later this afternoon. I'm sure I'll find out more then."

"In the meantime, maybe I'll give Ben a ring on his cell phone. Let him know what's happened."

The Woodrow crew were a sober bunch that evening. One murder could be dismissed as a random act, but two? Especially two from the same family. Had sabotage, in fact, escalated into murder? It was a profoundly disturbing thought. But any discussion of it had to wait until after dinner. June's murmured instructions were brief but to the point. As a result, dinner conversation revolved harmlessly around horses, giant statues, horses, field biology, and horses, with nary a whiff of murder or scandal. But once Tracy had retired with a horse book, and Fran and Vince had gone out for a soothing evening stroll, the conversation took an abrupt turn.

"I don't think there's any question the DeSantis family is a target," I began, stating what everybody else had been thinking. Matt had joined us for tea and dessert, so I was careful to keep any mention of sabotage out of the conversation.

"But for what? And why?" Kelt asked.

"Apart from the obvious?" Nalini asked.

"You mean the new facility?"

"It does vault to mind—"

"It's got to be Nueva Esperanza," Matt interrupted.

Seven pairs of curious eyes turned on him.

"Nueva Esperanza?" Ben asked, one eyebrow raised high.

Matt nodded and sighed heavily. "A small border town in Mexico, more a cluster of shacks, really. But the labor's cheap and the environmental standards are abysmal. A lot of the larger industrial corporations were pretty quick to figure out the benefits of moving their plants there."

"Familiar story," Ben rumbled and poured himself another cup of tea.

"Yes, but this one's got an ugly twist. Have any of you heard of Dyncide?"

I started and looked at Matt more closely. "I have," I said. "Somebody just asked me about it the other day. I don't know much more than the name, though."

"Well, Dyncide is part of a huge parent company called Goldor Industries, though it takes a lot of searching to discover that little fact. Goldor's been into chemicals since way back, and Dyncide had a manufacturing plant in Nueva Esperanza."

"I'm familiar with Goldor," Ben grunted. "They're a rather unpleasant bunch."

"So what happened in Nueva Esperanza?" I asked Matt.

"What didn't? To make a long and depressing story short, Dyncide went in, built their plant, and proceeded to contaminate the soil and the groundwater. Toxic wastes—including mutagenic solvents—were simply dumped in open ditches or holes. The plant was so close to the workers' homes that you could literally reach over the factory's fence and shake hands with someone in their backyard."

He paused and shook his head slowly. "Dyncide pulled out a year or so ago—"

"Without cleaning up?" Ben guessed.

"Without cleaning up," Matt affirmed. "There's so much xylene left in the soil even now that every time it rains the ditches fill with water whiter than this." He pointed to the jug of milk beside the teapot. "A lot of children are born with deformities. Some are even born with partial or missing brains."

"That's appalling!" June exclaimed, her eyes wide.

Matt patted her hand comfortingly. "I know. It's not something we westerners hear about much. Too depressing for us—and, of course, the people most affected are first, in Mexico, and second, very poor. I only discovered Dyncide's role myself last month."

"This is all terrible, Matt, but I don't see what it has to do with the DeSantises," June said.

"It has a great deal to do with them. You see, Grant DeSantis was one of Dyncide's executives."

Chapter 20

"He was curled up in my duffle bag." Kelt explained, settling my cat on my bed. "Now I've got hairy underwear."

"Sorry about that," I put my hands on my hips and glared at the unrepentant Guido.

Kelt shrugged easily. "No big deal."

"You want to come in and talk?" I offered.

"Yeah." He came in, folded himself into the chair, and sighed. "So. . . ."

I nodded. "So, indeed. What do you think?"

"I think if I was Grant DeSantis, I'd check my back for bull's-eyes."

"You think someone's after the family?"

"It sure seems that way. What's your take on Matt's theory?"

I pulled my mouth to one side. "I'm not sure. On the surface, a vendetta seems unlikely."

"Tell that to Salman Rushdie." Kelt waved off my response before I had a chance to open my mouth. "I know, I know," he said. "Different situation entirely. Still, you have to admit it as a possibility even if it's a remote one."

I snorted. " 'Remote' is an understatement. Think about it. If what Matt said was true, it was the poorer people who were most affected by the accident. How would they know about Grant DeSantis? Or, for that matter, where the DeSantises were living?

And where would a Mexican peasant find the money to come after them? I don't know, Kelt, there are a lot of questions."

"Not the least of which is, did Richard knew about his stepfather's connection to Dyncide?"

"Yes, I thought of that one, too."

"Didn't his fiancée ask you about Dyncide?"

"Yeah, she did."

"She knew what they had done in Mexico, and she was going to marry into the DeSantis family?"

I looked at Kelt. "I don't think she knew about the connection. In fact, I'm sure she didn't." I paused, remembering the last time I'd seen Esme. "That may have changed, though. She was ballistic last time I saw her. Slammed out of Grant DeSantis's office, yelling or cursing him out or something."

"What was she saying?"

"Something in Spanish, I think. Asses . . . ino? It sounded rude, but I have no idea what it means."

"Murderer."

I stared at him. "Excuse me?"

"It means 'murderer'."

"You speak Spanish?"

"And French and Portuguese. I can order beer and swear in German, too."

"Really? How talented of you. How did you get so multilingual?"

Kelt shrugged. "I grew up in Vancouver in an ethnically diverse neighborhood, and I picked up languages pretty easily as a kid. So I know that *asesino* means—"

"Assassin," I finished.

"Yep. Or murderer."

"Murderer." I pondered that for a very long moment. "But in what context? Richard? Or Dyncide?"

"That'd be your basic $64,000 question. Is she still in town?"

"I don't know, but I intend to find out." I fell silent again, thinking about Richard's stepfather.

If Richard had found out about Grant DeSantis's connection with Dyncide, how had he reacted? With anger? One would think so. Richard had seen first-hand the consequences of Dyncide's environmental offenses. Had he threatened his stepfather with exposure? A chilling thought for somebody as obsessed with public relations as Grant was. How chilling? Enough to forever silence the threat? Was that why Esme had called him a murderer?

"Who else do we have?" Kelt asked, interrupting my thoughts. "What about that guy? The one with all the meds."

"Rocky?"

"Yeah, you said he's medicated to the eyeballs, but if he has a history of violent tendencies. . . ."

I recalled Rocky's unsteady behavior and conceded the point. "I'll ask Dana if she knows anything specific about his past." I grimaced. "I like the old guy, though. I hope it isn't him."

"Okay," Kelt held up his fingers and began ticking off points. "We've got somebody out for revenge, your friend Rocky, Grant DeSantis himself—"

"And we can't rule out the sabotage connection at this point."

"I'm trying not to think about that."

"Sorry." I nibbled on my bottom lip. "Actually, I've pretty much ruled out the saboteur."

Kelt looked at me in surprise. "Really?"

"Mmmm. The MO doesn't fit."

"The *MO??*"

"It's an industry term," I smirked.

"Uh huh. Okay DCI Devara, what is it about the MO that doesn't fit?"

"The gun," I said without hesitation. "Melanie was stabbed and Richard was probably poisoned with something or other. A saboteur wouldn't go in for stuff like that when he's got a nice handy gun."

"Maybe he thought he'd try out all the standard murder weapons."

"Maybe, but it doesn't feel the same."

"Feel."

"Yeah. Haven't you heard of women's intuition? Besides, it all has to do with escalation. First he starts with the nails on the road, then the ladder and the tire, and then he shoots at us."

"But he doesn't kill any of us," Kelt finished, making the connection for himself.

"Richard was killed before the nails or any of that other stuff. If our saboteur is a murderer, then why aren't we dead?"

"Good point."

"Did you notice anything else at the site today?"

"No, and not for want of looking for it, either," Kelt replied with a shake of his head. "You know, Matt asked me the same question tonight, after you said goodnight to everyone."

"Really." I thought about that for a minute. "What else did he want to know?"

"If anything had happened besides the sniper attack. I managed to fob him off."

"Good thing. He's a little nosy about this, don't you think?"

"Mmm. Comes with being an investigative journalist, I guess. Still, I wasn't about to break Ben's rule about talking to reporters—even one like Matt Lees. Life's hard enough as it is with our sniper friend and a murderer still at large. I don't need Ben bitching out at me."

"That would be bad," I agreed.

Kelt covered a yawn. "I should probably get to bed," he said, "or I'll be useless tomorrow and I'll have Ben calling me a turnip all day."

He gave me a quick hug and kissed the top of my head. "Sleep well," he advised.

Despite the heartwarming encouragement, I somehow doubted I would. What I hadn't—couldn't—share with Kelt was that there was another possible explanation for these murders. An explanation that had everything to do with toxic chemicals and nothing to do with any industrial pollution in Mexico or sabotage at the site.

I seemed to be the only one who remembered what Ti-Marc had told me about Grant DeSantis's past. But maybe that was because I was the only one who knew the rest of the equation. Grant DeSantis, in addition to being part of the management team at the old Norsicol plant, had also been in charge of safety. Just for a single year, between 1971 and 1972. But that was long enough.

It was the same year that Eddie McVea had died.

Why had June been crying in her bedroom? Where she had walked to the night before? And, more importantly, why had she lied about it?

CHAPTER 21

JUNE A MURDERER? HOW COULD I even consider the possibility? She was like a second mother to me. In fact, given the status of my relationship with my own mother, June was more like a first mother to me. She was a kind, gentle soul—as Dana said, she let bugs out of the house instead of smacking them. The notion that she was a killer was almost beyond comprehension. Almost.

In the *Edmonton Journal* the next morning, along with a front-page article about Melanie DeSantis's untimely death, was a smaller article about her son's homicide. Homicide. Definitely not an accident. According to newspaper sources, Richard DeSantis had died from a massive ingestion of a still-unidentified poison. Not exactly the act of our gun-toting saboteur.

It had occurred to me sometime in the wee hours of the morning to wonder how June had known where to find Richard DeSantis's body. I knew that Tracy had described the general area to her, but the Holbrook region wasn't exactly a mecca of distinguishable landmarks. Had Tracy's description been enough, or had June been in possession of other information? I knew she'd gone out last fall to look at heron colonies with Richard. Had they gone out again this spring?

I had just a glimmer of the hell June had gone through since Eddie's death. But I knew she blamed his death on the chemicals at the plant. And the lack of safeguards—precautions that Grant DeSantis had been ostensibly in charge of implementing. Yet June had denied knowledge of DeSantis's position at the plant. In retrospect, it was difficult to believe.

After Eddie's death, June had made it her mission in life to find out every last detail about her husband's work and his workplace. She knew things about chlordane and heptachlor that I'd never even heard of. She had learned about the pesticides, their chemical composition, their effects on humans, wildlife, and the environment in general. She had examined in intimate detail each of Norsicol's safety regulations concerning them. Given that, it was hard to believe that she'd miss something as important as the name of Norsicol's safety supervisor.

Or had she? The other day, Ben asked her if she remembered DeSantis working at the plant. June replied that she'd never worked for Norsicol—a response which, I now realized, hadn't answered his question at all. Disturbing thought. I'd seen how angry she had been at the protest meeting. How high her passions could run. And that was just an unruly meeting. What would she be like with something more serious? How deep was her anger about Eddie's death? Deep enough for revenge?

All through breakfast, I forced myself to smile and chat with everybody, but even my Alphabits were spelling out words like "killer."

"Robyn!" June's voice cut through my thoughts.

I jumped guiltily as if she could read them. "Uh, sorry . . . I guess it's a little early for me yet. What did you say?"

"I was asking what you wanted to do today. With everything that's happened, I'll have to go into the office to do some damage control. Would you mind sticking around until the Bartels are up?"

I shook my head. "No, not at all. I'd planned to go over to Hank's later on and then to the library, but I can put it off until you're back. Go into the office. I'll just hang out and read or something."

"A good read sounds nice," Nalini sighed wistfully, gazing out the window. It was a dull morning, cool and dark with moisture-heavy clouds.

"We'll quit early today," Ben told her. "You all deserve a bit of a break. Beer's on me tonight, too."

That brightened the faces around the table like an early Christmas bonus. He certainly knew how to motivate his workers. I was all set to feel left out, but I should have known better. Ben also had a handle on how to motivate his non-workers.

"You too, Robyn," he said to me. "I appreciate your finding that cafeteria worker. And all that stuff about Grant DeSantis."

"Thanks, Ben." I smiled at him, feeling like part of the team again.

"Mrow." Guido the cat reached up and lovingly dug his claws into Ben's leg.

"Aah! Lay off, Guido. You wouldn't like beer," Ben winced as he disengaged Guido's claws from his jeans.

"Don't be so sure of that," Kelt warned.

"Mowph," said Guido in a tone that left no doubt as to his feelings on the subject.

Everybody laughed and breakfast broke up cheerfully. I managed to paste what I thought was a half-decent smile on my face, though Kelt looked at me a little strangely, so I'm not sure how successful it was.

"Are you sure you don't mind staying around?" June asked as she pulled on a dark green raincoat.

"Positive." I did my best to smile again.

"Thanks, Robyn," she patted my shoulder gratefully. "See you soon, I hope. If the Bartels get up before I get back, tell them there's quiche and muffins in the oven. If they want anything else, they can help themselves."

Tracy had taken my advice closely to heart and had already left to visit her horse again. I watched enviously as the Woodrow gang headed out into the blustery day, and speculatively while June headed off to Holbrook's administration offices.

June a killer. I shook my head in disbelief. Well, there were a few other possibilities to look into before I had to face that one. Once I had the house more or less to myself, I didn't waste any time punching in the DeSantis's phone number. A woman answered after the second ring.

"Can I speak to Esme please?"

"Esme?"

"Ah, yes, Esmerelda de Los Angeles. I understand she's staying with the DeSantises."

"Oh, I'm afraid she is gone. I understand she went back to Mexico two days ago."

"She did?" Before Richard's funeral? That didn't sound right. "Do you have a number where I can reach her?"

"No, I'm sorry."

"It's really important that I get hold of her."

"I can't help you. I'm sorry."

I replaced the receiver thoughtfully. Esme had left the country and left me with a few unanswered questions. And I already had a bellyful of those guys. I propped my leg up on another chair and settled in for a good think.

Was Grant DeSantis really capable of killing his stepson? I thought about his coldness, his apparent lack of grief. It was possible. But what about Melanie DeSantis? What exactly was her role in this scenario? Both Dana and Esme had told me she doted on Richard. Had, in fact, been devastated by his murder. If Grant DeSantis killed her beloved son, what then? A confrontation with Grant that ended in her death?

But what about June? I wanted to believe that she hadn't known about Grant DeSantis. About his possible role in Eddie's death. I wanted to believe it, but I didn't. And I felt like a slime mold because of it.

It was moving on toward ten o'clock before Fran and Vince finally appeared. Their grisly discovery must have really knocked the stuffing out of them.

I hadn't budged from the breakfast table except to shift a bit so Guido the cat could make himself comfortable on my lap. I'd been thinking furiously, but had come to exactly zero conclusions. By the time the Bartels finally stumbled downstairs, my brain was starting to overheat. I greeted them with a "good morning" that had more relief than cheer to it.

"Good morning," Fran returned my smile. "My, I can't believe we slept so late. We haven't slept in this much for years, have we, dear?"

"Oh, yeah, yeah," Vince waved a vague greeting my way and started searching single-mindedly—for a coffee pot, I assumed.

"Over there," I pointed it out to him. "I made a fresh batch about twenty minutes ago. Breakfast is in the oven. June had to go out."

They discovered coffee, quiche, and muffins, and started assembling their breakfasts, Fran nattering away the whole time, and Vince popping his two cents (and two words) in every now and again. Finally they settled down.

"Oh look, Vince," Fran exclaimed, picking up the newspaper from the side cupboard. "It's all about that poor woman."

She fell silent as she scanned the article. I'd already read it an hour ago. It was long but it didn't say much more than we had learned yesterday.

"They don't mention anything about that gnome," Fran said with a small shudder. "I dreamed about the dreadful little thing last night. All covered in blood." She shivered again.

"Now, Frannie," Vince gave her hand a little reassuring pat.

"Oh, I'm all right now," she told him. "It's just a little hard to get it out of my mind. You see, it looked so comical and so terrifying at the same time," she explained to me.

"Comical? Because it was a gnome?"

Fran nodded. "That and the missing tooth."

"Missing tooth?"

She nodded again vigorously. "Yes, it looked like it had a gap in its mouth. It was one of those heavy old concrete gnomes, so I suppose someone must have dropped it at some point—maybe even the person who put it there." She paused, suppressing another shudder. "Well, as I said, it looked as if it had a front tooth missing like that boy on the front of those *Mad* magazines that Sally used to read."

"Alfred E. Newman?"

She shrugged. "I suppose so. The gnome would've been funny if it hadn't been for ... well, you know." She paused and braced herself with another sip of coffee. "It's hard to get it out of my mind," she said again. Her eyes sought out the front-page picture of Melanie DeSantis. "I'm glad I didn't look farther into the hedge," she said fervently. "I'm glad that all I saw of the poor woman were her feet. It looks like she was quite lovely, doesn't it, dear?"

Vince turned the paper around and squinted at the picture. "Oh, yeah," he replied sadly. "Yeah."

I started off by asking Dana about Esme returning to Mexico, but Dana knew less about it than I did, so I slurped my coffee and bided my time for a few minutes. I had a lot of other questions besides that one, but I didn't want Dana to feel she'd been visited by the Spanish Inquisition. A more subtle approach was called for.

"So, what do you know about Melanie DeSantis?" I asked Dana casually as she filled my coffee cup again.

She shot me a sharp glance, then rolled her eyes. "I see Columbo lives," she remarked with a disapproving arch to her eyebrow.

So much for subtlety.

I pulled a glum look. "Come on, give me a break," I whined pathetically. "I'm laid up with all these damn casts. I've got to do *something*. And you won't tell me what Kelt wrote on my cast." I figured I'd go for the sympathy vote.

"So you're exercising your brain?"

"Well, I didn't hit my head." At least not *that* hard, I added silently.

"June said you were recuperating. . . ." I could tell by her tone that my whining was winning her over.

I grinned at her, sensing victory. "Come on, Dana," I urged, "I'm bored to tears. If I can flex my brain muscles on this, I'm sure

I'll get better faster. You know, healthy mind, healthy body and all that."

"That's what my yoga instructor's always saying," she mumbled half to herself.

"So tell me about Melanie DeSantis."

Dana let out a defeated sigh, snagged another mug off the wall, and poured herself some coffee. Leaning easily on the counter, she began to chew her lip thoughtfully.

"Not well-liked," she answered after a long moment. "She was lovely to anybody she considered her social equal, all friendly and charming. But she was less than lovely with everybody else, myself included."

"Class-conscious in a place like Holbrook?"

Dana pulled a face. "I know, pretty strange, eh? We're hardly Toronto or New York. But she always walked in here like she was bestowing the honor of her presence on the place. Man, I still remember the first time. Didn't want coffee and seemed to think I didn't know the proper way to make tea, like Canada was some backwater colony or something." Dana raised her voice to a haughty falsetto. " 'Do you have *anything* here I might be able to drink?' "

"Ouch."

"In a word. She got my back up right from the beginning, though once she realized that my apple cider was so good, she lightened up."

"Was she ever friendly?"

"Not really, except of course whenever she happened to bump into Barb Biedermann. Her dad's a doctor, so I guess Melanie figured Barb was a cut above the rest of us. Barb dresses pretty well, too, and so did Melanie—a bit gaudy maybe with the bright colors and the heavy jewelry—but classy stuff. You know, expensive. Did you know she started up a magazine? All about interior decorating and things like that. *Western Life*. She set up an office in their house."

I nodded. "Carole Miller told me about it. About the magazine, I mean."

Dana snorted inelegantly. "If you heard it from her, I bet you got an earful."

"Yeah, she said something about Melanie giving Howard the sack."

Dana grinned at me over the rim of her coffee cup, her dark eyes twinkling. "Who hasn't? I even fired him myself a couple of years ago. The guy's a worm. He hasn't tracked you down yet this time, has he?"

I made a face. "Just once, thank the gods. I'm trying to be more careful now."

"Good luck. He must have been a bloodhound in a previous life."

Dana paused and took another sip of her coffee. "Anyhow, I wouldn't blame Melanie for firing *him*, but she blew off a couple other people, too. Good people. Hard workers. I hear that she was pretty unbearable. Screaming at her employees and doing stuff to humiliate them in front of each other."

"Charming."

"Tell me about it," Dana agreed. "She'd only been in business here for eight or nine months, and already she had a reputation for being difficult to work for."

"Did she get any magazines out?"

"Three or four issues now, I think. It was supposed to be six."

"What was the problem?"

"Well, for one thing, every time she opened her wallet, the Queens cried out and cringed from the light."

"Cheap?"

"Like borscht. At least when it came to her business. That's why she had the office in the house even though there wasn't really enough room. She had them all working in the basement. She pinched pennies so hard the poor things cried for mercy. Unbelievable when you consider the money she has—or had, I should say. The employees used to joke that every time somebody said the word 'accounting,' she'd go off the deep end."

Interesting.

"Can you give me any names of people she fired?"

Dana tossed her braids over her shoulder and looked at me sternly. "A person doesn't kill somebody just because they got fired—at least not from a job they had for less than a year."

"I know, but it'll help me pin down Melanie DeSantis's character." Anything to take my mind off the problem with June.

"If you ask me, her death had very little to do with her and a lot to do with her husband."

"What do you mean?"

Dana looked around dramatically for eavesdroppers. I was the only person in the shop. Even so, she leaned forward and lowered her voice. "Gary told me last night that Grant DeSantis has been getting death threats!"

"You're kidding! What did they say?" I whispered back.

She shrugged. "Gary didn't go into too many details . . . something about a plant in Mexico."

"Mexico!" My brain perked up.

"Yeah. I guess Grant's been getting these death-threat things for a couple of years now."

"How did the RCMP find out about them?" I asked curiously.

Dana lifted one shoulder in a shrug. "I don't know. I think he told them himself."

"And now his wife and stepson have been murdered, so the police are looking into the connection," I mused.

"Yeah." Dana fell silent for a minute.

"Were there any witnesses to Melanie's murder? I mean, it *did* happen in the town square. You'd think somebody would have seen something."

"Nobody's come forward. Gary's working a ton of overtime, I don't think the investigation's going all that well. They still don't even know what killed Richard."

"Really." It was part statement, part question.

Dana took it as a question and shook her head. "Nope, apparently they ran some tests at the hospital lab, but they couldn't figure out what it was so they've sent the samples off to the RCMP forensics lab in Edmonton—and those guys are so backlogged, who knows when the results will come back."

"Hmmm." I fell silent for a minute. "There's just one more thing that's puzzling me," I said finally. "About the DeSantises."

Dana began putting out bread and sandwich fillings in preparation for the lunch crowd. "Shoot."

"Why are they here?"

"What do you mean?"

"I mean, why are they here now? The new facility hasn't been approved yet, but the DeSantis family moved here almost a year ago. Why?"

Dana started slicing tomatoes. "Same reason Elliot Shibley moved in. Reisinger bought the land and transferred some of their personnel here. They must be pretty sure of this project of theirs. But if you believe Bert Pine, it's all a big conspiracy."

"What? The project?"

"Yeah, you know, the government secretly approving the facility before anybody has a chance to get worked up about it."

I raised my eyebrows quizzically.

She grinned. "Hidden agendas? J.F.K.? Roswell? Marilyn?"

"Jeez, Dana, you sound like *The X-Files*."

Dana grinned. "Hey, it's my favorite show—and not just for David either. But Bert really takes this stuff seriously. I mean really, really seriously. He's a huge conspiracy nut."

"I know, I met him. Does he have anything to back him up on the toxic-waste facility theory?"

Dana shrugged noncommittally. "Depends on if you believe him or not. He says that his phone wires got crossed or something last summer just after the DeSantises moved here. According to him, he was talking to his wife when all of a sudden, he was on the hearing end of a conversation between Grant DeSantis and somebody named Paul."

"Paul," I repeated, unenlightened.

"Ormsby?"

"The provincial Minister of the Environment?"

Dana nodded. "None other. Bert says it was obvious from their conversation that the plant had already gotten the stamp of approval. There was something about a financial deal, too. A loan I think. That was, lemme see . . . ten, eleven months ago."

"But it *hasn't* been approved. Nobody's done an EIA. We're not even remotely at that stage yet."

Dana shrugged. "I'm just telling you what Bert said. He's been pretty worked up about the whole thing."

Just then a group of lunchgoers strolled in and started perusing the chalkboard menu.

"Anything else you want to know about, Columbo?" Dana asked with a low voice and sly smile.

"Funny. But since you mention it . . . what about Rocky?"

"Rocky? He's harmless!" She protested.

"I think so, too, but you told me he's got a history of violence."

"Years and years ago."

"What happened?"

"He attacked a girl."

"Attacked."

"Yeah," she agreed reluctantly. "With a knife. He wasn't getting any treatment back then. Everybody thought he was just a harmless idiot. But I guess he'd started to see stuff that wasn't there, and hear voices and sounds and things. I don't know if anybody paid much attention to him. Then one day he took a knife to this girl and cut her up. They paid attention then. She survived but she was pretty badly hurt. He spent years in the Ponoka Mental Hospital."

"Ye gods, Dana . . . a knife? Wasn't Melanie DeSantis killed with a knife?"

"Yeah. . . ."

"Look, I know. I like the guy too, I'd hate for it to be him. But who makes sure he takes his meds?"

"His landlady, Sue Barbeau. She used to be a nurse, so she looks after stuff like that. Robyn, it *can't* be Rocky! He seems like such a sweetheart. He won't kill mosquitoes even if they're sucking on him!"

The customers signaled their readiness to order and Dana hurried over. I sat there for a little longer. I wondered if Dana was a closet entomologist. Her criteria for judging people seemed to revolve around their reluctance to squish bugs. Not really what most would consider a glowing character reference.

Despite this, I felt a little better than when I'd arrived. June as a killer seemed an unlikely possibility when faced with the general murkiness of the DeSantis family themselves. Humiliated and fired employees, industrial pollution involving toxic chemicals, death threats due to the same, topped off with underhanded politics. There was a lot there to investigate.

And in another vein, I couldn't help thinking that Rocky, even on his medication, was still seeing things. The ghost of his friend Luke for one. Obviously, his pills were not one hundred percent effective.

CHAPTER 22

I LEFT HANK'S AND MOTORED OVER to the library. I wasn't too sure where to look for more information about the old accident. I'd had an idea the night before but if that didn't pan out, then I'd have to enlist some help. Fortunately, the gods, for some reason probably best left unknown, took pity on me. When I asked the librarian about back issues of APEGGA's newsletter, I expected her to shake her head much as she had done when I had asked about Norsicol newsletters the day before. Instead she smiled.

"Isn't this your lucky day!" she said.

"Oh?"

"One of our patrons cleaned out her attic last month and we've got boxes of donations sitting in the workroom. I know she had old APEGGA journals; her husband is a geophysicist and the worst pack-rat I've ever seen. Frankly, we can't use much of the stuff for the collection. I was going to put it out on the sale table but I just haven't had time to do it yet. You'd be surprised what people will buy for a quarter. Come on back and I'll show you the boxes. It may not be a complete set. Do you know which ones you're looking for?"

I didn't, but the librarian was nice enough to lift the boxes onto a table for me, and I was quite happy to root around in them. I found exactly what I'd been looking for in the last box.

APEGGA is short for the Association of Professional Engineers, Geologists, and Geophysicists of Alberta. My father is an engineer, so I was familiar with the organization. It's been around in one form or another since the 1920s. In 1972 they started publishing an informative little newsletter called *The Pegg*. It's filled with all sorts of numbers and facts interesting to engineers and earth scientists, including write-ups on industry accidents (which was interesting to a certain field biologist). The very first issue contained a piece about Norsicol. As I read about the accident, I could feel my blood pressure reaching for the sky. Norsicol, I quickly realized, should have had the pants sued off them.

According to the article, some fairly toxic byproducts of the chlordane-formulating process were being piped across the eastern part of the site in above-ground lines. I remembered seeing those lines when June and I had visited the site. Normally these pipes would be joined with a double valve, but in this particular case they'd been joined with a simple ball valve. The kind of valve that opens at the drop of a hat—or the pull of a pant leg.

A worker walking past the pipe had snagged the leg of his coveralls on the valve. When he pulled away, the valve opened, squirting a toxic soup of chemicals on his ankle. He was seriously ill in a matter of hours.

There was no question the valve had been below specifications even back then, but there had been a fire the previous month and the original double valve had had to be replaced. Too bad for the unnamed worker that Norsicol hadn't felt like waiting the two to three weeks it took to get a special valve in.

Under normal circumstances, APEGGA would have disciplined the maintenance engineer for approving a below-spec valve. But apparently Norsicol had laid off most of their engineers a few months before. A guy named Yves LaSalle was the person who had changed the valves—an engineer so junior he hadn't even worked the two years needed to get his professional stamp. Norsicol was therefore doubly guilty. They'd had a junior engineer working without supervision, and they had changed the valves without proper approvals. Because the fault lay with Norsicol, LaSalle had not been formally disciplined, but I was willing to bet my Captain Picard action figures that he still thought about the accident during the quiet, dark hours of night.

I was packing the old journals back into the boxes, so engrossed with the events of almost thirty years ago, that I failed to pay attention to the events of the here and now. And I was about to pay the price for that.

"Hi, Robyn," said a voice behind me.

I closed my eyes and sighed. I knew that voice.

"Howard."

"So there's sure been a lot of excitement around here," he said breathlessly. "Heh, with the murders and everything."

I shuddered a bit and tossed a few more journals in the box. "Mmhm."

"Heh. Guess that bitch finally got what was coming to her."

I tried packing faster.

"You know I worked for her. As an accountant."

Two boxes packed. Two more to go.

"She was a real bitch. So high and mighty and thinking she was better than everybody else. She used to make us work really late sometimes just so she could get it out on time, but she never put in any overtime. No way. Not her. She was too good for that." He snorted and laughed at the same time.

"I used to watch her through the window. She'd run out all painted up while we were left working. And she wasn't going out with her husband, either," he smirked greasily. "I think she was meeting that Lees reporter. The big shot."

"*Matt!?*" I exclaimed, startled into responding. "Why him?"

Howard shrugged and started chewing his fingernail. "He's new in town."

"That hardly means they were fooling around," I said, disgusted. I stuffed the books I wanted in my knapsack and slung it awkwardly over my shoulder.

"And he's covering up for her. I know what she was trying to do." His face had reddened in anger. "I'm a pretty good accountant, you know. I can tell when things aren't right. She was funneling money out of that company. I had proof of it, too. But when I took it to him, he told me I didn't have a case."

"Uh huh."

"He *lied* to me."

"And why would he do that, Howard?" I demanded, losing all patience. "Because of this alleged affair? Did you show this 'proof' to anybody else?"

Howard's eyes went shifty and he didn't respond to the question.

I curled my lip. "I see. And whoever else you showed it to didn't think you had any proof, either. Could it be that you didn't have as much evidence as you thought you did?"

"I think—"

"I sincerely doubt that," I broke in. I'd heard enough slander for one day. I often wondered why nobody had ever sued the pants off Howard for libel. Probably because the mental image was too repellent to dwell upon.

"And listen, Howard," I said, not bothering to hide my revulsion, "you'd better think twice about bad-mouthing Melanie DeSantis. The police are still looking for whoever killed her. They're probably very interested in talking to anybody who held a grudge against her."

Howard's eyes were shocked into moving up to my face. "But ... but, I never touched her," he whined.

"Excuse me."

I brought my crutch down hard an inch away from his foot. He jumped back.

"I wouldn't have done anything to her. Honest."

It was with a distinct sense of relief that I left him spluttering behind me.

I headed back to June's to dump my booty and grab some lunch. While I was there, the irritating pranks of the past couple of days escalated into something more serious.

It started out in the same way. I was in the kitchen, rooting around in the fridge for sandwich fillings, when the phone rang. I hobbled down the hall . . . for nothing. Another hang-up call. I returned the receiver to its cradle and wondered if June had gotten somebody to check her phone line.

It happened again two minutes later—just enough time for me to get back in the kitchen. Knowing it was probably a futile gesture, I limped down the hall and picked up the phone.

"Hello?"

Nothing. I can't say I was surprised. Pissed off, definitely, but not surprised. I slammed the phone down and turned around. I'd just made it back to the kitchen when the doorbell rang.

"Dammit!" I swore, swung myself back down the hall, and opened the door to nothing. Now I was really getting pissed off.

"Hello!" I shouted off the porch. "Is anybody here?" A black-capped chickadee chirped back at me. He was nice enough, but I somehow doubted he'd rung the bell. But if he hadn't, then who—

Crash!

"*What the hell?*" I spun around and lurched back into the house. It sounded like glass breaking.

And so it had been. Somebody had heaved a rock through June's kitchen window.

"Son of a bitch!" I cursed and hobbled over to the window, my crutches crunching down on the shards of glass littering the floor. Nobody in the yard.

Then I realized how visible I was. I ducked away from the window. What the hell was going on?

Moving as quickly as possible, I swung down the hall one more time and punched in June's office number. I told her what had happened in a few terse words.

"I'm on my way," she exclaimed and rang off.

I hung up the receiver thoughtfully now. The first flush of anger had burned away. I didn't spook easily but I had a strange chilly feeling in the pit of my stomach.

Who was doing this? Kids? I thought not. Kids didn't usually take practical jokes to this level. Who, then? The Norsicol plant saboteur crowned my list of top ten. With all the precautions and the RCMP presence at the site, maybe he'd decided to take his game elsewhere. It wasn't a secret that Ben *et al* were staying at June's. Was somebody trying to scare them off?

June arrived less than fifteen minutes later with a young RCMP constable in tow. Despite her examination of the broken window and a thorough search of the yard and its bushes, the constable really couldn't do much.

"I'm sorry," she told me. "There's nobody around now and we wouldn't be able to get prints from the rock." She shrugged, her short blond hair ruffling in the breeze blowing in through the broken window. "I've taken some samples of the glass in case we nab a suspect—"

"What good will a piece of the glass do?"

"Not much, probably," she admitted. "If he or she was standing close enough, then we might be able to get some tiny fragments from their clothes and match it to the sample. Refractive properties, color. . . ."

"But chances are he or she wasn't standing close enough."

"Right. Five feet max." She bounced the rock in her hand. "I doubt they got that close." She turned to June. "You've got an answering machine?"

"Yes."

"Then I would rely on that to screen your calls. At least it'll save you the hassle of trying to get to the phone." She looked meaningfully at my casts. "Or try dialing star and then sixty-nine, that'll give you the last number that called. Write it down and pass it along to us. We can take it from there. I'll make a report, of course—"

"Do you think there's a connection with the other sabotage?" I asked quickly.

Her face didn't give away anything. "Hard to say. We'll be looking into it, but it might just be a case of simple harassment. Unless you actually saw somebody. . . ."

I shook my head.

She shrugged again. "We'll keep an eye on the house."

Can't say I was reassured.

CHAPTER 23

MY GRANDPA DEVARA USED TO CALL ME a a stubborn little cuss, and as the years have gone by, I've had to admit his sagacity. At least about the stubborn part. To this day, I'm not sure I know exactly what a cuss is.

After June and I stuck cardboard and duct tape over the window and had a soothing cup of tea, my stubbornness began to rear its obstinate head. If somebody was trying to scare Woodrow off, well, too bad for them. I, for one, didn't scare that easily. Mischief, I could deal with. I could even cope with somebody shooting at me—as long as they weren't actually trying to hit me.

For the rest of that afternoon, I felt a bit like a warbler with a nest full of skreeling cowbird hatchlings. I flitted from one end of town to the other on Vivian's scooter. But instead of chasing down insects and worms, I was after leads and clues.

I didn't much care what the Millers thought about Melanie DeSantis, but Dana had dropped a few interesting hints about her, and a good sleuth investigates everything. Thanks to Dana and the Holbrook phone directory, I now had a list of names and addresses tucked in my coat pocket. It took the rest of the afternoon, several gossip sessions, numerous cups of coffee, and even more cookies to check them out.

I went to Nicola Stevens's place first. A production artist, she had been Melanie DeSantis's latest victim. She had quite a bit to say, but she kept pouring me coffee and passing me ginger snaps, so I sat there and let her say it. But when all was said and eaten, it pretty much boiled down to the fact that Melanie DeSantis was a bitch and impossible to work for. Dana had told me that much.

I didn't have much more luck with Evelyn Bowe, who had been one of the magazine's writers. She said the same sorts of things, though more politely. Ditto for George Lem, a soft-spoken graphic designer. I also didn't have any luck getting any of them to tell me what Kelt had written on my cast. Like everybody else, they got a good chuckle from it. And I got another bellyache from curdled curiosity.

It wasn't until I got to Averie Moppett's house that my luck started to change—though not with regards to Kelt's message. There were tea and lemon oatmeal cookies laid out at Averie's, which suited me just fine. Especially since she also proceeded to lay out exactly the sort of information I'd been looking for.

"She was *dreadful!*" Averie told me with feeling. "I'd never worked for anybody that bad before. And I swear to god I never will again."

"What was the problem?" I asked, my mouth full of lemon cookie.

She rolled her eyes. "What wasn't? I worked for her for five months, one week, and two days. By the end of it, I was throwing up every morning just at the thought of going in. I thought at first I might be pregnant, but nope. It was stress."

"That's pretty bad stress."

She nodded. "I'm very sorry that she's dead, of course—and in such a horrible way—but as my mom used to say, Melanie DeSantis would have tried the patience of a saint. She always insisted that all decisions important and otherwise had to pass by her, but she wasn't overly fond of spending time in the office." Averie threw up her arms in defeat. "What are you going to do? She didn't trust me or anybody else, for that matter."

"A control freak?"

Averie nodded. "She had a hard time relinquishing it. And because she wasn't around when decisions had to be made . . . well, deadlines didn't get met and then all hell would break loose. Of course it was never her fault, and it was up to the employees to fix things, no matter if it meant working overtime, which was, incidentally, unpaid, seeing as we were all technically on salary." She paused to pour herself another cup of tea.

"And then there were the 'accounting days'," Averie said after swallowing a healthy gulp of tea.

"Yeah, I heard about those. Sounds like she had a temper problem."

"That's putting it mildly," Averie snorted. "She wanted a business but didn't seem to want to put any money into it."

"Dana said she was cheap."

"In some respects she was." Averie paused to nibble on a cookie. "She had the most gorgeous clothes, you know. Worth much, much more than my yearly salary. She underpaid the lot of us and wouldn't fork out for a proper accountant, but she didn't mind spending money on herself. And her office!"

"Swanky?"

"Oh yeah. Antiques, Persian carpets, a very nice, very new, very expensive chair. It seemed like a waste of money for the amount of time she actually spent sitting in it. Us peons had to use crappy second-hand office furniture that she'd picked up at an auction in Edmonton."

"When was your last day?" I asked.

"Two days after they found Richard."

"Wow. That must have been difficult."

"It was. Melanie had been devastated. I felt a little guilty leaving under those circumstances, but . . ." She trailed off. "You know, I feel bad talking about her like this. I know I probably sound whiny—"

"Not at all," I hastened to reassure her.

"—but it's only been a week since I left, and I don't think I've worked it out of my system yet. I know she's dead and it's very tragic, but really the woman was poison to work for."

"Why did you stay so long?"

She sighed heavily. "I thought I could handle her. And I really liked the concept of a western life magazine. But ultimately she was bad for my health and it just wasn't worth that. I lasted a lot longer than some."

"Yeah, I heard Howard Miller worked for her for a while."

Averie shuddered. "Ugk! That guy makes my skin crawl."

I nodded.

"He didn't even last two months."

"Incompetent?"

Averie shook her head slowly. "No. He's actually a half-decent accountant. I should know, I took over doing the books."

"And the books were okay? No mistakes or problems?"

"No. They were spot on."

"So why was he fired?"

Averie threw up her hands. "God only knows. I sure don't. I was there the day she gave him his pink slip, though. You should have heard the yelling! I remember wishing I had a pair of those foam earplugs. She had him behind a closed door for a good long while. When he came out, he'd been fired. I had to escort him out of the office. He sure had a hate-on for her afterwards. And then she blacklisted him."

"Blacklisted!"

Averie nodded. "I overheard her. I guess Howard had applied for a job at a firm in Edmonton. I can't imagine he would have given Melanie as a reference, but for some reason she got a phone call from somebody at the firm asking about him. It sounded like somebody she knew."

"And she didn't give him a good reference," I guessed.

Averie opened her blue eyes wide. "Not even close," she said. "I heard her say a lot of terrible things, among them that Howard was a fuck-up."

"Ouch."

"Yeah. You know, the guy may have been a creepoid, but he didn't deserve that. It just goes to show you how nasty she could be."

We chatted a bit longer, then I finished my tea, brushed the crumbs off my lap, and said my goodbyes. It had been a long afternoon. I had a headache from all the refined sugar I'd ingested, and my back teeth were throwing a pool party from all the tea and coffee I'd drunk.

But, as I settled myself back on my scooter, my thoughts were on Howard Miller. Why had he been fired? Because he was repulsive? No. There were labour laws about that sort of thing. Why, then? Had he been stupid enough to accuse Melanie of embezzling? Certainly grounds for firing him if he had.

If I understood the sequence of events properly, Howard had found what he thought was evidence of embezzlement and had taken it to Matt, who turned down his request to investigate the matter. Howard then accused Melanie, who fired, then blacklisted him. All of which, I guessed, probably left Howard feeling angry and impotent. And soldiers of fortune wouldn't like feeling impotent.

Anger. Hate. Certainly two of the stronger emotions. Had Howard killed Richard to get at Melanie? By all accounts, the woman doted on her son. What better way to hurt her than through her son? Maybe Howard had killed him and then found it wasn't enough. Or maybe Howard had discovered he liked killing. That it made him feel powerful and potent. Scary thought.

I pulled up to June's house resolved to do everything in my power to avoid Howard Miller, even if I had to spend the rest of my vacation barricaded in my room.

"Wow!" Kelt was looking at me in admiration. "You got all those people to talk to you about this?"

I shrugged self-consciously. "Dana told them all about Marten Valley," I explained. "Specifically about how I 'caught' the murderer."

Kelt chuckled. "So now they think you're some kind of Scooby Doo?"

I pulled the corner of my mouth to one side. So far on this visit,

I'd been likened to Sherlock Holmes, Miss Marple, Columbo, and now Scooby Doo. There seemed to be a definite downward trend here. "Something like that," I told him.

Kelt and I were kicking back on the front porch, waiting for Nalini to finish showering and for Ben to finish his phone call to Kaye. Cam and June were safely ensconced in the kitchen, talking about herons, and I could see Lisa and Matt chatting in the living room, so I had taken the opportunity to tell Kelt about this afternoon's revelations.

"What do you think of it all?" he asked when I finished.

I shrugged. "I think Melanie DeSantis treated her employees like crap, but if anybody killed her because of it, my loonies would be on Howard Miller."

"Sounds like you don't like him much."

"He gives me the creeps," I told Kelt. "But it's not just personal dislike. If she canned him because he was making false accusations—"

"Which he thought were true."

"Indeed. He's an unwell individual. I honestly don't know how he would have reacted to that. He reads *Soldier of Fortune*, too."

"Not exactly *Starlog*."

I shook my head. "Nope. I looked at one once. Very pro-military, pro-guns. Way too much testosterone for me."

"Think he was getting tips?"

"Maybe, or just fantasizing."

"Okay, we'll count him in then," Kelt agreed. "At least that's one suspect I know you'll steer clear of."

I stuck my tongue out at him, but he was patting Guido and didn't see me do it.

"I find the vengeance angle quite intriguing," I said after a moment.

"Taking it more to heart now?"

I nodded slowly. "Yeah, ever since I heard about the death threats. And then, of course, there were the gnomes."

"Gnomes."

"The ones that were found with the bodies," I explained. "They were both damaged."

"Damaged."

"Chipped, actually."

Kelt threw up his hand. "So? They're gnomes. They sit in the garden and freeze and thaw and get hailed on. They're always crudded up in some way. My grandma's gnomes are a mess."

"Yeah, I know, but I think maybe in this instance they were deliberately defaced. June's gnome was missing an eye, and Fran Bartel told me this morning the gnome she saw by Melanie DeSantis was missing a tooth."

Kelt looked at me expectantly, so I explained further. "You know, an eye for an eye, a tooth for a tooth? Revenge?"

He considered that for a moment. "I don't know. Sounds pretty shaky to me. It could just be coincidence. Those garden gnomes can be fragile."

"Could be," I conceded. "But it still makes you wonder. All right then . . . what about Bert Pine?"

"The conspiracy guy? You're not serious."

"Why not?"

Kelt pulled his bottom lip thoughtfully. "I can't see what he'd have to do with this, unless he's a bit of a psycho."

"Dana said he's a big conspiracy freak."

"That hardly makes him psychotic. *I* read about government conspiracies, too, but it doesn't mean I'm going to go out and kill a bunch of people."

"You think his theory has merit?"

Kelt considered that. "It wouldn't be the first time the government's done some fancy footwork to further its own agenda," he said finally. "They're not stupid, they must have known that people were going to be protesting the facility. My guess is that they had a damn good idea how contaminated the site was, and they saw an easy solution to it in the form of Reisinger."

"Maybe so," I admitted. "It wouldn't surprise me. But do the murders fit in with that? Quite frankly, I don't think they do. If Bert

Pine, for example, was looking to murder somebody over this, you'd think it would be the minister or Grant DeSantis himself."

"Yeah, unless he was trying to pull a *Cape Fear* and get at the man through his family."

I arched one eyebrow at him. "You *are* a conspiracy nut! I was going to go have another chat with him. Maybe you should come with me."

Kelt nodded. "I'm not a conspiracy *nut*, and I don't think Bert Pine is a murderer, but yeah, I'll come with you. I'd like to hear about this conversation between DeSantis and Ormsby." He paused for a minute. "That was a good question you had: why the DeSantises have been living here for so long."

"It is puzzling me," I agreed. "I must admit, I'm pretty skeptical about the 'secret deal with the government' angle, but if that's all nonsense, then I can't see why the DeSantises were transferred here. Elliot Shibley could have handled everything—at least until the approvals came through."

"It's possible their move may have had more to do with Nueva Esperanza than with the waste treatment project."

"How so?"

"If Grant DeSantis has been getting death threats, Holbrook may have provided a nice quiet place for him to sit out the storm."

"But why Holbrook?" I asked him. "It's quiet, I grant you, but it's not exactly a retirement paradise. And if Melanie DeSantis was as class-conscious as Dana says she was, I can't imagine she would have welcomed a move here."

Kelt shrugged. "Maybe she didn't get a say in the matter. Maybe Reisinger already had their eye on the old Norsicol site."

"So they killed two birds with a single stone."

"Yeah." Kelt fell silent and rubbed his forehead pensively. "This stuff you told me about Rocky bears a second look."

I sighed a little. The guy had had such a tragic life, I hated to think he was in more trouble. "I'll have a word with his landlady tomorrow."

Kelt furrowed his brow. "I wish I could give you a hand," he said uncomfortably. "Short of faking a terrible illness I can't get out of work, but I'm really not happy about you tripping around after murderers."

"I'm not tripping, I'm just asking a few questions."

"Yeah, and somebody just heaved a rock through the window at you."

"It wasn't *at* me. I was in the front hall. And besides, the rock could have been thrown by kids."

"Well, be careful. I'd hate myself if anything happened to you."

I patted his shoulder comfortingly. It was nice to know he cared.

Chapter 24

THE BAR WAS FILLED WITH PEOPLE, SMOKE, and very loud country music, not necessarily in that order. I wasn't overly fond of country bars (or smoke or crowds of people for that matter), but it was the only place in town where you could dance, and the rest of the Woodrow crew were in the mood to kick up their heels. Fine for them, I thought grumpily, but two-stepping required two unfettered feet—something I was noticeably lacking at this time. I tried not to watch jealously as Kelt twirled Lisa expertly around the dance floor. For three dances in a row. He came back to the table flushed and sweating, so I snagged a free mug and poured him a beer.

He smacked his lips. "Ah! You read my mind!"

"Yeah. It was a quick read," I smirked. "Board book city."

My colleagues hooted with laughter, Kelt whacked me on the shoulder, and Ben bought me another beer.

It was my fourth drink of the evening, and I was starting to feel it. Never much of a drinker, I was your basic cheap date. One and a half beers and I was usually on the floor. That I had knocked back three already this evening was evidence of how badly I'd needed a good night out.

We joked and laughed and drank and generally had a fine time. Matt had opted out of the evening, saying he had too much work to do, and June had decided to stay home, too. Can't say I was unhappy with her decision. I wasn't good at pretence, and I found it exhausting to smile and talk with June as if there was nothing wrong. Cam had looked a little disappointed, though.

By 11:30, the music was cranked up to almost intolerable levels, and my head was definitely feeling the effects of too much alcohol. Ben, Cam, and Nalini were deeply involved in Ben's favorite debate about the value of wiping out all human life from the planet. A couple of farmers from the next table had entered gleefully into the fray. Kelt and Lisa had been swinging around the dance floor for almost an hour and I was feeling decidedly unhappy about it—and disgusted at myself for being so sensitive. Still, it was getting harder to smile around the lump in my throat each time they came back to the table. I looked away and comforted myself with another beer.

"You want to get some air?" Kelt shouted into my ear as they collapsed on their chairs again.

I nodded and he helped me gather up my crutches. I was glad my colleagues were having so much fun, but I was ready to leave. We signaled to Ben that we'd see him later, and squeezed our way out through the crowd. Along the way somebody tried out their Special K pinch. On my butt. Definitely time to leave.

We stepped into the cool silence of the night and I heaved a relieved sigh.

"Feel better?" Kelt asked.

I smiled at him. "Much."

He chuckled. "You were starting to look a bit pale."

"I was starting to feel pale," I told him. "I guess I don't get out much any more. Thanks, Kelt."

Kelt took a deep breath of night air and shook himself like a bathing bird. "I was ready to leave. Lisa danced the feet off me. She's going to have to find somebody else to swing her around now. I'm pooped."

"You didn't seem to be suffering too much," I said, trying not to sound bitchy.

"So, you want to head back to June's, or tool around a bit?"

"Let's take a stroll," I decided. "Or a wheel in my case. I could use some fresh air and a bit of quiet."

We went over to the side lot where I'd parked my little red scooter. As we rounded the corner, I saw a group of leather-clad bikers in the process of parking their motorcycles. Big motorcycles. Harley Davidsons with lots of black and chrome. Several bikers stood staring at my scooter in disbelief, their mouths hanging open, cigarettes dangling from bottom lips.

"That ain't no hog. That's a piglet!" one of them remarked finally and the others shouted with laughter. They were still cackling by the time I hobbled over and started stowing my crutches.

"Hey, baby, wanna ride on a *real* bike?"

I grinned and shook my head. Kelt was trying not to laugh. As I mounted up self-consciously, the bikers guffawed and hooted and slapped their knees before waving me off. Kelt was still smiling a block away.

We walked (and rode) in silence for a few blocks, simply enjoying the quiet, starry night. Ideal conditions for romance. Or not.

"What happened to Megan's father?" Kelt asked.

Not quite what I'd been hoping for. Story of my life.

"He died over twenty-five years ago," I answered after a moment. "It was quite sudden."

"That's sad."

I nodded. "Yeah, it was pretty rough on June. They were very much in love. It was hard on Megan, too, though she was too young to remember much about him. But growing up without a father...." My voice trailed off.

"I know the feeling," Kelt said softly.

I looked at him without surprise. Kelt never talked about his father. I'd expected something like this. "Your dad...." I began.

"Took off when I was eight."

"I didn't know that. I'm sorry."

Kelt was silent for a few steps. "I'd had a big fight with my sister," he said finally. "Sharel's four years younger than I am and we were always squabbling as kids. Anyway, we had this fight one day—nothing serious, just kid stuff—but when my dad came in to break it up, he really lost it and just screamed at us. The next day he was gone."

"And you thought he left because of you and your sister?" I guessed.

Kelt nodded curtly. "I did for a long time. Until I found out that my mom was starting to go blind. I guess my dad couldn't handle it."

"I'm sorry," I said squeezing his hand. "I had no idea."

Although it was too dark to see Kelt clearly, I felt him shrug.

"No, *I'm* sorry. I didn't mean for all that to come out."

"Hey, what are friends for?"

And we were that, if nothing else. But was there something between us besides friendship? All of a sudden, I found myself very tired of guessing.

"Kelt—" I began.

He turned abruptly. "Did you see that?"

"See what?"

"There's somebody skulking around over there. By that house."

"Where?"

"Over there." He pointed and I recognized Pam Swinton's house. She was a birding friend of June's and her yard was thick with trees and shrubs and birdhouses.

"I don't see any—" Then I spotted it. A furtive movement by the poplar trees. Someone was sneaking around in Pam's yard.

The dark figure stepped out of the shadows and I caught my breath in a gasp as I saw him more clearly. He was carrying something that looked suspiciously like—

"He's got a gnome!" I hissed under my breath.

"What?"

"He's carrying a gnome! Kelt, we've got to see what he's doing!"

"You stay here!" He ordered and slunk away toward the house.

"Screw that," I muttered under my breath and fumbled for my crutches. The scooter would be too noisy. I caught up with Kelt at the top of Pam's driveway. We hid in the shadow of a huge lilac bush by the fence.

"I don't see him any more," Kelt murmured.

Neither did I, but the moon had set and the light from the stars was faint at best. I scanned the yard carefully. There! A figure by the hedge—bending down with a pale envelope.

"Kelt, he's got pictures!" I breathed. "There's something in the hedge!"

The figure scuttled away from the house and hugged the murky shadows all the way down the driveway, right towards where we were hiding. Beside me, I could feel Kelt tensing for action. The figure moved closer and closer. . . .

"Get him!" I shrieked and shoved Kelt toward the moving shadow. With a startled *oof!*, Kelt crashed into the figure and the two men fell heavily to the ground. I stood gripping my crutches, ready to brain the mysterious skulker if he managed to wiggle away from Kelt. Not much chance of that. With surprise and tension on his side (not to mention the enthusiastic shove from me), Kelt quickly overcame the man and pinned him face down on the ground.

"*What the hell!?!*"

"What were you doing over there!" Kelt demanded roughly.

"I . . . I was putting the gnome back!"

"What gnome?"

"Pam's gnome. I took it on vacation. Who the *hell* are you?"

Vacation? Oops.

"Not so fast," Kelt barked. "Robyn?"

Quickly I crutched down Pam's driveway to the spot by the hedge where I'd seen the man set something down. Something being a gnome.

"Um. It's okay, Kelt," I called back. "There's just a gnome and some pictures here . . . just a sec . . . um . . . it, ah . . . it looks like the gnome went to Hawaii."

"*Hawaii?*" Kelt's voice rose incredulously.

"Uh, yeah. There's a beach and a bunch of hula girls and. . . ."

"You got me to jump this guy and all he did was take a gnome to *Hawaii?*"

I started to hobble back towards them. "How was I to know?" I demanded. "He looked so suspicious. You thought so yourself!"

"Yeah, but I wasn't planning on doing *this*!"

"Do you think you could let me up now?" the man asked plaintively.

Kelt jumped up with alacrity and made a fuss of helping the guy up and brushing him off.

"I'm really, really sorry about this," he said over and over again.

"I'm afraid we just saw you skulking around with a gnome and thought the worst," I added, coming up to the two of them. In the glow of a nearby streetlight, I recognized the man. "Randy?" I asked. "Is that you?"

"Who wants to know?" Now that Kelt had released his death grip, the man—Randy Hughes—was starting to realize how angry he should be.

"It's Robyn Devara, Megan McVea's friend."

"Robyn? What the hell are you doing jumping people?"

"We thought you might be a murderer," I fessed up. "We saw you with the gnome and—"

"You thought I was a *murderer?*"

"Well, yeah, with everything that's been happening lately—"

"What the *hell* are you talking about?"

It seemed that Randy (one of Megan's old flames and usually quite a nice guy) had been kayaking around Hawaii for the last month. Being a Holbrooker, of course he'd taken a gnome. And having been away until just this evening, he hadn't heard anything about murders or gnomes found by dead bodies.

I can't say he was terribly happy with us, but by the time I'd finished explaining the situation (with Kelt spilling out a long monologue of apology in the background) he'd at least understood our reasoning. With a last disgusted look (which I admit we deserved) he left us on the sidewalk and stalked off home.

It was pretty dark but I didn't need a streetlight to show me Kelt's expression.

"I'm sorry," I said again. "I thought. . . ."

"I *know* what you thought," he let out his breath explosively. "I may even have thought the same thing, but goddammit, Robyn, I wasn't planning on jumping the guy!"

He looked so pissed off that I had to suppress a sudden urge to laugh. Guido the cat had had the same expression on his face the time he'd fallen into a bathtub full of water. But my brief amusement withered and died as I thought about what kind of expression was probably on Randy's face right now. Some detectives we were turning out to be.

"I'm sorry," I repeated.

"I don't know what the hell got into you, Robyn," Kelt started berating me. "When I offered to be your feet, I didn't know you'd use me for kickboxing!"

I apologized again, but I don't think Kelt was listening. Now that the adrenaline was wearing off, I was secretly appalled at what I had done. I'd met Randy a few times in the last couple of years; he was a nice guy. I was fairly sure he wouldn't press charges. But what the hell had I been thinking? I tried telling myself that it *had* been a very tense moment. That Kelt's reaction was just a release of tension. Just the adrenaline draining away. It didn't make me feel any better.

Thoroughly chastened, I slouched back onto my scooter, my heart like an anvil in my chest. So much for quiet confidences. So much for romantic starlight. I'd obviously hit a snake in life's game of Snakes and Ladders. A very long snake. It's possible I wasn't right back at square one, but judging from Kelt's anger, I wasn't far from it. And I certainly wasn't anywhere near a ladder.

I was, it appeared, destined to remain single for a while longer. That it was my own damn fault in this case only made me feel worse.

CHAPTER 25

I WOKE LATER THAN USUAL THE NEXT MORNING, had a moment of silence for whatever died in my mouth the night before, then staggered to the bathroom. I considered brushing my teeth with Ajax, but June didn't have any so I had to settle for Crest. What had possessed me to drink four—no five!—beers the night before? I scrubbed my teeth twice, did the same to my face, and pulled the snags out of my hair. By the time I finished, I was feeling ready to face the challenges of the day.

There would be a few, I was sure of that. Kelt had been decidedly brusque after our close encounter with Randy the night before, and I didn't imagine he would have cooled down much even after a good night's sleep. I'd deal with him later. But the most difficult challenge of my day would come first—right after breakfast.

Tracy was the only one in the kitchen by the time I washed up and dressed.

"Good morning," I greeted her.

"Hi!" She grinned back, more her perky self than she'd been in days.

"How're you doing?"

"Better. Thanks for the advice."

"No sweat," I replied, sloshing some coffee into a mug. "Is June out?"

Tracy nodded. "Yeah, she's gone to visit a friend in the hospital.

She left you a couple of cinnamon buns for breakfast. They're on a plate in the cupboard."

"Hmmm." I poked experimentally at my middle. It seemed to have expanded significantly since I'd come. "Maybe I should just have some cereal or something."

Tracy giggled. "I know the feeling. I'd be like a total blimp if I ate these all the time!"

I looked at her slim eighteen-year-old body. "I don't think you have to worry," I told her with a hint of envy. "Besides, you'd never do that to your horse."

Tracy giggled again and I poured myself a bowl of something flaky. They were as boring as they looked—unless of course you loaded 'em up with brown sugar, but I guess that defeats the purpose. At any rate, I found myself wondering if all the songs were right and it was possible to live on love alone. It was certainly a lot more appealing than having to choke down these suckers every day. Then I remembered how angry Kelt had been the night before and I kept eating. If I tried living on love right now, I'd probably starve.

I wasn't about to let myself eat them, but I did have a use for those two enormous cinnamon buns. Once I'd finished my bowl of styro-flakes, I dug out the phone book, scribbled down an address, and popped the buns in a brown paper bag. I had an apology to make.

Randy Hughes lived a few blocks away from June in a smart little house that he'd inherited from his grandmother. Part of me wanted to put the buns on the step, ring the doorbell, and run like hell, but I had to admit my share of the guilt (perhaps even the lion's share) in last night's incident, and I owed it to Kelt and Randy to do this properly. Besides, I couldn't run with a cast.

"Hi." My smile was a little uncertain.

Randy regarded me for a long moment before sighing and opening the door wider to let me in.

"Hi, Robyn," he said with a rueful smile.

"A peace offering," I explained, extending the bag. "June's cinnamon buns."

His expression brightened visibly. "Now that just might save you," he replied. "I haven't had a chance to get groceries since I got back."

I winced at the reference to his vacation. "I'm *really* sorry about last night. . . ." I began.

He waved it off. "Forget it. I saw the paper this morning. It makes more sense now. Besides, there was no real harm done."

I let out my breath in a sigh. "Thanks, Randy. I thought Kelt was going to kill me."

"Who is this Kelt guy, anyhow? A football player?"

I winced again. "No, no. He's a work colleague."

"Huh. Did he jump you, too?"

Only in my dreams. Then I understood. "Oh . . . the casts. Nah, I had an accident in BC."

"You want to come in for coffee? I've got sugar but no milk."

I shook my head. "Thanks anyway, Randy, I should get going. I just wanted to apologize and bring you some buns."

"I appreciate that. Did, ah, did Megan come up with you this time?"

"No, I came by myself. Those lawyers keep her working hard."

"Oh," he said, sounding a little disappointed. I'd always suspected that he still carried a torch for my friend. "Tell her hi for me, then."

I smiled warmly. "I will. And I'm sorry again."

"It's okay, but maybe you should be a little less nosy next time." He smiled to take the sting out of the words.

"So I've been told," I muttered, tucking my crutches under my arms.

A thought struck me. "Hey, Ran."

He paused in the middle of closing the door.

I lifted my leg cast up on the step. "Can you do me a favor? Tell me what's written on the bottom of my foot."

He bent down and had a look. Then he straightened up and smiled broadly.

"I don't think so, Robyn," he told me, his eyes twinkling. "I'd say it's you who owes me a favor, not vice versa."

It was a bit slow going back, and I started to regret leaving Vivian's scooter parked in June's driveway. But I needed the exercise, so I gritted my teeth and focused on the sidewalk. As a result, I didn't see Rocky till he was almost on top of me. He stopped abruptly, rocking back on his heels.

"Oh hi," he said, but there was no sweet smile today. He looked upset.

"Hey, Rocky," I greeted him. "Everything okay?"

His thick lips started to shake. "Why did Luke come back?" he asked plaintively.

"You saw Luke again, huh?"

He nodded. "He was over by the store, yes he was. I saw him over by the store."

"Did you say anything to him?"

Rocky shook his head vigorously, almost unbalancing himself in the process.

"Are you scared of Luke?" I asked gently.

He hung his head and shrugged. "I just don't know why he came back. I don't know why."

"Well, a lot of upsetting things have been happening lately. Maybe you should stop thinking about Luke. Remember what I said about friends not hurting friends?"

Rocky nodded.

"Luke's not going to hurt you, I promise. Now, did you have coffee today?"

"Oh yes, yes I did. I had some coffee. Dana, she gave me some coffee."

"Good, maybe you should just go home and relax then. Maybe have some toast."

"I like toast. Yes I do, I like to have some toast."

"Do you want me to walk you home?" I inquired. It wasn't an entirely selfless offer. I'd been wanting to have a word with Rocky's landlady about his medication. No time like the present.

His face brightened. "I live on the next street. That's where I live."

"Well, why don't I come along with you and you can introduce me to your landlady?"

"Okay."

Sue Barbeau proved to be a fit-looking woman in her mid-forties. I recognized her from previous visits to Hank's Coffee House. She was either a regular there or Holbrook was as gossip-ridden as any small town. She had heard all about my escapades in BC and was more than willing to talk to a "real Joanne Kilbourne." Was I ever going to escape these crime-solver comparisons? At least I had moved up from Scooby Doo.

"Don't get too excited," I warned her. "Dana has been grossly exaggerating my talents."

"I think I'll go have some toast," Rocky interrupted us. "I'll have some toast now."

"Good idea," Sue said amiably. "Jeff got you another airplane book from the library this morning. I put it on the kitchen table for you."

"Oh good! Well, bye." He beamed, waved cheerfully to me, and disappeared down the hall.

"See you later, Rocky," I called after him, then turned to Sue and smiled. "He's a nice guy. Sure likes his coffee and toast."

Sue rolled her eyes and grinned. "He does at that. So what's on your mind, Robyn?"

"I'm a little concerned about Rocky," I began. "Has he told you about seeing ghosts?"

Sue sighed heavily and nodded. "Yes, I've heard all about Luke's ghost."

"He seems pretty worked up about the whole thing. I'll be frank with you. Dana told me about his medication and a bit about his history. I guess I'm wondering how effective his meds are."

"I know, I know," Sue said. "I've wondered about that, too. Especially after what happened to Melanie DeSantis. I'm well aware of Rocky's history. But the thing is, he had a full check-up six months ago and his medication was adjusted then. He'd been a little confused before that."

"Confused? About what?"

She shrugged. "Nothing terribly important. The day of the week, television shows, forgetting that he'd eaten meals."

"So you took him in to have his meds adjusted."

"Yes, he was just about due for his check-up, anyhow. And since then, he's been better than ever—apart from this business with Luke's ghost, that is."

I pondered that for a moment. "So it's unlikely he's having a problem with the medication. Was it a new kind?"

Sue shook her head. "Same stuff, just a slightly higher dosage. I've given a lot of thought to this, and I don't think it's the medication. And as long as he's on it, I seriously doubt whether he's capable of the kind of acts that are headlining the paper these days. And before you ask, yes, I make very sure he takes his pills."

"Then why does he keep seeing ghosts?"

Sue puffed out her cheeks in frustration. "My guess is that he's upset about the recent deaths and it's bringing back some bad memories."

"Did you know this Luke?"

"No. I moved here long after that plant shut down."

I sighed and rubbed my forehead. "Well, I guess the other possibility is that he's not seeing ghosts."

"What do you mean?"

"He might be seeing somebody who looks like Luke. But what if—and I'm just tossing this out here—what if this Luke came back to Holbrook? Not as a ghost, of course. But maybe Rocky's mistaken. Maybe Luke didn't die, maybe he just moved away, and now he's moved back. It could explain why Rocky keeps seeing him all of a sudden. Maybe he thinks the guy's a ghost so he never says anything to him and never realizes that Luke is really alive."

Sue looked surprised. "That never occurred to me," she said slowly. "I suppose it's possible, Rocky never says that Luke died, just that he got sick."

"The only problem I can see is that this Luke fellow would be thirty or so years older now. Do you think Rocky would recognize him?"

"It's possible," Sue conceded. "Rocky's got a good eye for faces. But. . . ." she trailed off thoughtfully.

I lifted one shoulder in a shrug. "It's a long shot, I grant you. But if there isn't a problem with the medication and he isn't hallucinating, I can't really think of another explanation. Besides a supernatural one, of course—and I think I'm too practical for that."

Sue smiled absently. "I haven't heard about any new arrivals in Holbrook," she said. "Especially not someone who used to live here. I suppose he might have moved to one of the farms or acreages, but I don't know how you'd find out such a thing. I haven't a clue what Luke's last name was and there's little use in asking Rocky. I've tried. He won't talk about Luke at all except to say he's seen his ghost."

I grinned at her. "Hey, Joanne Kilbourne. Remember?"

Sue chuckled. "Well, good luck to you. I'd really appreciate you solving this particular mystery. I'm quite fond of Rocky and I don't like to see him this upset."

"I'll let you know what I find out," I assured her.

I'd counted on asking June about the mysterious Luke, but by the time I finally grunted and sweated my way back to the house, she was out again. So I called on Ti-Marc's research skills instead. If Luke the ex-plant worker was back in town, I could kill at least three birds with one stone if I found him. I could set Rocky's mind at ease about the ghost. I could show that he wasn't hallucinating or having problems with his meds (and therefore could be removed from my list of suspects). But most importantly I could find another Norsicol worker for Ben. And for that alone, I wanted to talk to Luke. Not only so he could point out possible problem areas at the site, but also for anything he knew about Grant DeSantis and his inadequate safety regulations.

"Hey, Ti-Marc."

"Robyn! *C'est toi encore?*"

"Yeah. I need you to look up something else for me."

"And let me guess, you don't really want Kaye to know."

I smiled into the phone. "Well. . . ."

"*Bon*, what is it?"

"I'm trying to find out the last name of a plant worker named Luke."

"Luc? You only know the guy's first name?"

"Yeah, I'm afraid so. Look, I know it's a bit of a long shot, but I thought maybe you could check. I don't think it was a particularly common name back then. And it's probably Luke with a 'k-e', not a 'c'."

"*Anglais*, eh?"

"Yeah. At least I think so. Maybe you should check the French spelling too, just in case."

"*D'accord*," he agreed. "But I'm telling you not to 'old your breath, Robyn. 'E probably won't show up in the correspondence. We don't 'ave that many names. . . ."

"I know, I know. This is me breathing. Thanks, Ti-Marc."

"'Ow's it going up there?" he asked.

I screwed up my face in a grimace. "The site's gross. Disgusting, really. But I think they're all having a good time in spite of it."

He *tsk*ed. "Poor Robyn. Left out of all the fun, eh?"

I thought about last night and winced. "Oh, I wouldn't exactly say that," I told Ti-Marc ruefully.

As mobility was a bit of problem lately, and I was already sitting by the phone, I decided to get my other calls out of the way for the day.

First I rang up UNG Video and reserved *Godzilla Versus the Smog Monster* for tonight. It might help Kelt get over his bad mood, but if nothing else the rest of the crew would probably enjoy watching Godzilla battle it out with "a Horror Spawned From the Poisons of Pollution." Somehow, it seemed appropriate

Then I gave APEGGA a call. I might not have any luck tracking down Rocky's Luke, but I should be able to find out if Yves LaSalle was still a practicing engineer. And if the gods were really feeling kindly toward me, LaSalle would have squirreled away drawings of the Norsicol site.

I hadn't told Ben about the engineer yet. The accident hadn't involved a major spill, though I found it interesting that Norsicol had been cutting safety corners with such gleeful abandon. Mostly, I didn't want to get Ben excited about drawings that might not exist. Besides, Yves LaSalle could have gone international like so many others before him.

The gods turned out to be in a good mood, but they weren't about to hand anything to me on a silver platter. Yves LaSalle was, indeed, an active member of the association but the APEGGA receptionist adamantly refused to give out any useful information. Like his phone number or current place of employment.

"It's confidential," she informed me crisply.

"I'm not looking for him for personal reasons," I explained. "I'm calling on behalf of Woodrow Consultants. We're an environmental consulting firm and I need to talk to Mr. LaSalle about a site he worked on."

"I'm sorry," the woman said, at least sounding it. "About the best I can do is contact him and see if it's okay if we give out his phone number."

"That would be fine."

"It might take a few days, maybe even longer if he's in the field."

The gods were having second thoughts about their fit of benevolence.

"Whenever you can get it to me, that'll be fine," I told her. "We *are* working to a deadline, though."

"I'll see what I can do," she promised me.

The Internet, someone once said, can be a wonderful thing as long as you're not looking for anything in particular. I was, so of course I had to slog my way through numerous false hits (including one puzzling, but interesting, site about men in spandex cycling shorts) before finding what I was searching for.

I'd parked myself in June's little Internet parlor to search for information about Grant DeSantis. The man was a bit of a black hole. He was obsessed with media relations, had lied through omission about working at the Norsicol plant, and Esme had called him a murderer. But what else did I know about the man? He was about as emotional as an android and he didn't eat doughnuts (or, if he did, he wasn't into sharing). But what about his past career experience? Why *had* the DeSantis family moved to Holbrook before the Reisinger project had been given the green light? I couldn't dismiss that as easily as Kelt had. It took me the better part of the afternoon, but by the end of it, I had an inkling of what the answer might be.

With a bit of concerted searching, I managed to find a short bio of Grant DeSantis. It detailed his affiliation to Reisinger and Goldor and several of Goldor's subsidiaries and holding companies, among them Schaade Chemicals.

Schaade . . . I tapped my lip in thought. Now, where had I heard that name before? I typed it in as a search term and got more hits than Babe Ruth on steroids. None of them false.

Schaade Chemicals. Manufacturer of glues and other adhesives. Polluter of the environment. The story actually began several years earlier with the Bata Shoe company. In 1992, the Ontario Provincial Court ruled that Bata Industries and two of its directors were liable for environmental offenses. Bata had been knowingly storing chemical waste in drums and tanks which were corroding and uncontained. The company was fined and so were the two directors. The decision was a groundbreaker. For the first time in history, corporate directors were open to personal prosecution and liability with respect to environmental offences committed by the corporation.

A first time means a second time means a third time. The door had been opened and Schaade Chemicals was third in line. For years, the company had been accused of dumping and improper disposal of toxic wastes. And in 1995 they were finally found guilty of gross environmental offences. As per the Bata Decision, one of their directors had been found liable and fined an amount in the six-figure range. I went through fourteen articles until I found his name.

Grant DeSantis.

No wonder DeSantis was so concerned with negative publicity. Just how solid was he at Reisinger? It seemed to me that a man who had been involved with both Schaade *and* Dyncide might be teetering on the edge of early retirement. Add the threat of exposure, and what did you have?

Had DeSantis murdered his wife and stepson? The jury was still out on that one. Was he a weasel? It certainly appeared that way. Though, perhaps I shouldn't insult the family Mustelidae by saying so. A criminal, then. Yes, definitely that. At least when it came to environmental offences. Was that all?

The doorbell interrupted my thoughts. I grabbed my crutches and swung down the hallway, stiff from sitting at the computer for too long.

"There better be somebody there this time," I muttered to myself.

But when I opened the door and saw who was standing on the step, I wished conversely that it *had* been another prank.

Carol Miller. Again.

"Carol," I greeted her without a smile.

"Is June here?"

"No."

"I want to know when I'm getting my gnome back," she announced. "June knows all those police people."

"Your gnome."

"Yes, my gnome! They found it beside *her*."

Her.

"Melanie DeSantis?"

"Of course, Melanie DeSantis! I want to know when I'm getting my gnome back. Why do the police have to hang on to it anyhow? And what—"

"Why don't you just phone them and ask them yourself?" I cut her off.

"I have. They were extremely unhelpful. Nobody seems to care that my gnome was stolen. And not only that, *defaced!*" Her tone was outraged. "They poked his teeth right out, and that was a brand new gnome. It cost me over seventy dollars. Who's going to pay for it? I'd like to know." Her face was red with temper.

"I've got to go, the phone's ringing," I lied.

"When am I going to get my gnome back? And who's going to pay for it?"

"Sorry, I can't help you."

I shut the door and sagged against it. The woman was unhinged! It seemed to me that Rocky wasn't the only one around here in need of medication. Maybe Howard hadn't been murdering DeSantises. Maybe it had been his mother. She was certainly deranged enough to be capable of it. Where had *she* been when Richard and Melanie were being murdered?

Chapter 26

KELT'S TEMPER HAD COOLED OFF considerably since I'd shoved him so unceremoniously onto a total stranger. He didn't seem angry at all any more, but he was quiet and withdrawn that evening. In fact, the whole Woodrow crew seemed short-tempered and out of sorts.

"Could you *please* be a little more careful when you're taking your boots off," Nalini snapped to Kelt as they trooped in just before dinner. "You got mud all over my stuff yesterday."

"Sorry."

She sniffed. "It's a *new* pack."

"I said I was sorry."

"Uh, hey, guys," I called. "How's it going?"

"Good," said Kelt in a voice that implied it was anything but.

"I need a shower," Lisa muttered as she came into the kitchen. And she disappeared upstairs without so much as a smile. Cam followed suit, his eyes lowered.

Ben had a face as stony as one of those Easter Island heads. He must have blown up at somebody. It was enough to put anybody out of humour. But Ben was always getting pissed off about something or other. It was Kelt's shuttered expression that concerned me more. His green eyes looked at me and quite clearly closed me out. Ouch.

"Is everything okay?" I asked him in an undertone.

His expression unreadable. "Just fine."

So. I hadn't been forgiven yet. Well, maybe the Smog Monster would soften him up.

But it wasn't to be. Dinner was an unusually quiet affair and nobody, except me, seemed to appreciate the movie. Ben stared at the screen without cracking a smile. Lisa didn't even stay for the whole thing. And before the closing credits were finished rolling, Kelt said a quick goodnight and disappeared upstairs.

I sat in my room for a half-hour, waiting for Kelt to show up for our nightly chat. I wanted to tell him about Rocky and his hallucinations, and about Schaade Chemicals and the six-figure fine. I thought it made the case against DeSantis a little blacker. It also darkened the case against Howard Miller. Perhaps he'd been right all along. Maybe Melanie DeSantis had been funneling money out of her company—and straight into her husband's chequing account. If so, then Howard's anger at being fired and blacklisted was justified. And few things are more powerful than righteous anger.

It wasn't that I particularly wanted Rocky or DeSantis or Howard to be the killer (well, maybe Howard), but more that every failed hypothesis reminded me of the one I *didn't* want to think about.

The fact that the gnome discovered beside Melanie DeSantis's body had come from Carol Miller's yard made me think about where the first gnome had come from. If June was the killer, what better way to throw suspician off herself than to use her own gnome? Classic misdirection. And Carol's gnome? Well, I knew June despised the woman. Was this some way of getting back at Carol Miller for all those years of slander and hate mongering?

I punched my pillow around and continued to wait for Kelt. But the only one to come into my room was Guido, and he was more interested in cleaning his paws than in talking. I waited until the sounds of people getting ready for bed had quietened, then I hauled myself up the stairs. It was slow going, but I obviously had another apology to make.

I couldn't understand why Kelt was still so angry with me. It was a mistake! Didn't *he* ever make mistakes? It wasn't like Randy was going to sue.

I pulled myself up to the second floor and swung down the hall. Kelt's room was at the far end, by the oak wardrobe. I stood in front of the door for a long while, rehearsing what I was going to say. When I had it all straight in my mind, I pulled my shoulders back and tapped on the door. No answer. I tapped a little harder and door swung open. Not much, just a crack. But it was enough.

Through the crack I could see Kelt sitting on the side of his bed, his back to the door. Lisa was folded tightly in his arms.

I woke the next day with a song in my heart. A requiem, that is.

I stayed in bed until I heard the Woodrow crew leave. I wasn't ready to see Kelt just yet today. By the time I stumped into the kitchen, June had left, too. There was a note on the table telling me about some orange pecan muffins on the counter and a couple of x's and o's after her name. I didn't want to think about x's and o's at the moment.

I ate a quick breakfast, then fired up my scooter and headed over to Hank's for a chat with Dana. She was pretty good at cheering people up.

Unfortunately, she was too busy with a busload of tourists to do more than toss me a quick smile and fill my coffee cup. There was no sign of Rocky, either. I drank two cups of coffee, considered (and thought better of) eating a scone with cream, and leafed through an old issue of *Discover* magazine before I gave up waiting for Dana and left.

Still refusing to think about what I'd seen the night before, I took the scenic route back through the town square. Despite my Marten Valley-inspired reputation, I wasn't much of a gawking type when it came to accidents and other unpleasant occurrences (murder being the most unpleasant). In fact, I tried to stay away from them at all costs, but I had to admit to being curious about the scene of Melanie DeSantis's murder. A town square was not exactly the sort of secluded location generally favored by murderers. Why had she been killed in such a public place?

I slowed as I entered the square and took a long look around. The yellow tape that had roped off the giant heron statue had been taken down, and Melanie DeSantis's lifeblood had been scrubbed off both statue and pavement. The sun beamed down on the burgeoning leaves of the square's trees and bushes, filling the air with their fresh scent. It was hard to believe somebody had lost their life here just a few days ago.

I drove right up to the statue and scanned the edges of the square. The Blue Heron was perched in the middle of a central park-like area. It was surrounded by a cluster of red-osier dogwood with a manicured lawn and a flowerbed which spelled out Holbrook in yellow and purple pansies. There were paved roads on each side of the little park. Holbrook's town square hummed with activity as people went about their daily business.

Looking around, I wasn't surprised any more that there had been no witnesses to the deed. I'd never noticed the lack of residences in the square before. There were businesses, stores, and the administrative offices. Nary a house or apartment building to be seen. At 2:00 in the morning, the time Melanie DeSantis had been killed, the town square must have been as devoid of life as the ice planet Hoth.

I turned in the direction of the library but as I did, I noticed something odd. There was something wrong with the dogwood around the Heron. I got off the scooter and limped over to the bushes. Yes, here and here. I fingered the limp, brown leaves thoughtfully. The bushes themselves looked healthy with their green, lance-shaped leaves and bright crimson bark, but in this one area, the leaves were withered and dead.

Some form of phytotoxicity, I muttered to myself. From what? The brown was concentrated in one longish streak with spots on adjacent leaves. Strange. It was almost as if something had been thrown across the foliage. Something corrosive. Something definitely poisonous. Suddenly I remembered something Ben had said. I straightened as my mind made the connection, hobbled quickly back to my scooter, and started it up.

"Well, hi there, honey! I heard you were in town."

"Hey, Phil." I beamed a big smile at the man behind the counter.

Phil, owner and operator of Phil's Photomat, was short and chubby with a neatly trimmed white beard. Put a tunic on his back and a pipe in his mouth and he'd be a ringer for a garden gnome. I wondered if someday he might find himself bundled off to exotic locales.

We chatted a bit about inconsequential things before I got down to the purpose of my visit. In large centers like Edmonton and Calgary, the police have their own labs to develop and print photographic evidence from crime scenes. But it was different in small, rural-type locations. In Holbrook, the RCMP wouldn't have quick access to the lab in Edmonton. Instead they would have brought their film to be developed here, at Holbrook's only photomat.

I wasn't sure whether Phil could help me. I didn't know if the RCMP had already picked up their photos. And if they hadn't, I didn't know if Phil would let me have a look at them. I needn't have worried.

"Why sure, honey," he said when I'd explained what I was looking for. "Dana was telling me all about what happened to you in BC. Congratulations! Sounds like you could give old Ellery Queen a run for his money."

Dana was proving to be a handy, if unwitting, ally.

Phil lifted up the counter and motioned me through. I hobbled to the back room and sank down on a chair while he started sorting through envelopes of pictures.

"Hey, Phil," I said, suddenly remembering another problem I had. "Can you tell me what's written on the bottom of my foot?"

"What's that?" He looked up from his envelopes.

I rapped my leg cast. "My foot. Somebody wrote something on the bottom of my foot and I don't know what it says. Nobody'll tell me."

His eyes were bright with curiosity. "Let me take a look, then." He crouched down. "Oh! Hee hee."

"Well?"

He grinned up at me. "I don't think I should tell you, honey."

"Not you, too!" I tried for a pathetic look.

Phil straightened and, still chuckling, went back to his pictures. I seethed inwardly. That Kelt! One day he was going to pay for this.

"Here we are," Phil said interrupting my vengeful thoughts.

"You found them?"

"Yep. And don't go noising to Gary that I let you take a boo at these," Phil warned as he handed the pile to me. "These are just shots of the scene. If you'd wanted to see the other batch, I would have said no."

"Don't worry, Phil." I suppressed a shudder. "I have no desire to look at pictures of dead people. I just need to see what the area looked like."

"You chasing down a clue?"

I gave him a half-smile. "Maybe."

I examined the pictures of the first crime scene. The paramedics had taken away Richard DeSantis's body, but you could still see where it had been. The photos were black and white (for better resolution, Phil explained) but it was very clear that the vegetation under and around the body was dead and withered. I flipped through the pile until I got to the photographs of the second crime scene. It was just as I suspected—and feared.

I thanked Phil profusely, watched as he signed Roy Orbison on my arm cast, and promised to give Megan a hug for him. Then I drove over to the town's administration offices. There was a slight possibility that I was wrong about this, but a single question and answer confirmed my suspicions. I got back on my scooter and headed to the RCMP detachment office.

As I limped into the office, Staff Sergeant Gary Ross regarded me with a cool look that would have done Mr. Spock proud. I was trying to be brave, but he had one eyebrow slightly raised, which on Gary was like a murderous frown on anybody else. I gulped.

"Uh, hey, Gary. How's it going?" I began awkwardly.

"Robyn," he nodded. "What can I do for you?"

I could tell by the look on his face that he suspected I wasn't here for a friendly chat. I wasn't, so I didn't bother with the pleasantries.

"I think I know what was used to kill Richard DeSantis."

Gary's other eyebrow rose up. A scary thing to see. I fidgeted nervously.

"Oh?" he said after a lengthy pause. "And how would you have figured that out? I really hope you're not nosing around this thing. Dana told me all about Marten Valley."

Hmmm. So much for my ally. I'd thought Gary had been a little more reserved than usual.

"No, no," I hastened to assure him. "How could I?" I indicated my casts. "I'm recovering. It's just that I happened to notice a couple of things that you guys probably didn't notice, or if you did, you didn't put it together."

"There's sure been a lot of activity around here since you arrived."

Me? Surely he didn't mean to blame murder, sabotage, and harassment on me? I tried out the Bambi eyes on him and concentrated on sending innocent vibes his way.

Gary looked at me expressionlessly for a moment. "Okay," he sighed, "come on back and I'll take your statement."

We settled at a desk and he waited, pen poised over the paper. Like I said before, he wasn't exactly Mr. Talkative.

"It has to do with where Richard DeSantis was murdered," I said into the silence. "*The Journal* ran a picture of the scene and I noticed that the vegetation around where his body had been was dead, sort of brown and withered-looking."

"Mmmhmm."

"Uh, well, the thing is, you can see the same phytotoxic effects where Melanie DeSantis was killed."

Gary stopped writing and looked up. "Phytotoxic?" he inquired.

"Sorry," I apologized. "Trade jargon. I mean poisonous effects on plants. You can see it around the Blue Heron."

"There was none of that in the square. I helped gather the evidence."

I nodded. "I know two days ago, the dogwood was fine. Now there's a big streak where the foliage has turned brown. On the same side of the Blue Heron that Melanie DeSantis was found."

"And how do you explain that?"

"Pesticides," I replied.

"Pesticides?"

I nodded again. "Yeah, a concentrated solution of pesticides splashed on the foliage. It would probably take two or three days to show up, faster if the weather's warm. I think there was some sort of pesticide solution around when Richard died. It's possible he even ingested it—I know the toxicologist hasn't pinpointed a poison yet. Anyhow, I think the same stuff or something similar was present when Melanie DeSantis died, though I haven't a clue why. I checked with the town. They haven't sprayed herbicides in that area since last year."

Gary kept writing furiously for a minute after I'd run down.

"Any idea which pesticide we might be looking for?" he asked.

I paused for a moment. "I'm afraid I don't really know that much about individual pesticides. I'd guess there are probably a bunch of different ones that could do the same thing. You might want to check with Matt Lees. He'd know more about it than I do."

"Thank you, I'll do that."

He seemed to have thawed a bit, so I seized my courage, repressed the urge to ask him if he ever used the Vulcan nerve pinch in the line of duty, and took the plunge.

"Uh, Gary. Can you please tell me what's written on the bottom of my cast?"

He stared at me with that unreadable look.

I gave him an encouraging smile and lifted my foot.

Lips tight in a flat line, he bent down and flicked a glance at the bottom of my foot.

"I'm afraid not," he said shortly.

It had been a long shot, anyhow. At least he hadn't laughed.

I didn't have anything else to say and Gary wasn't exactly the friendly, chatty type. He thanked me for coming in, asked after June, and escorted me briskly out the door with further remonstrances against interfering in their investigation.

"There's been a lot of activity around here," he said again. "More than enough, if you ask me. I don't need you interfering and complicating things."

I said okay (what else could I say?) and limped down the front steps.

"Interfering, indeed," I snorted under my breath as I hitched up my crimson steed. I wasn't interfering with anybody.

Still, I couldn't help but be struck by the commonalities between the two murders. The vegetation under Richard DeSantis's body had been most definitely dead. And now the bushes around the heron statue were showing signs of poisoning. I didn't think it was a coincidence. It appeared that heron statues could be just as important indicators as their live counterparts were when it came to detecting pesticides.

CHAPTER 27

PESTICIDES AND GNOMES. Why were they both present at each murder scene? I could think of only one reason. Carole Miller's gnome had been a new one. So why was its tooth missing? Not from any weathering action. So. The gnomes were a definite message. An eye for an eye. Vengeance. Retribution. Punishment in kind. For Eddie? A strong possibility. Ben had told Tracy that strong concentrations of heptachlor and chlordane could kill the foliage of the plants they were sprayed on. But was that true of other pesticides? I didn't know.

Grant DeSantis had been receiving death threats because of Nuevo Esperanza, and Esme, I remembered now, told me she had come up to Canada with a delegation of Mexican conservation workers several days before the murders occurred. Even if Esme hadn't known about the DeSantis connection to Dyncide, it didn't mean that other conservation workers were ignorant of it. Which pesticides had Dyncide manufactured at their Mexican plant?

If the murders had been committed with pesticides and if those pesticides had been manufactured at the Dyncide plant, well, that would take the heat off June. But how could I find out? Matt? He probably would know the answer to my question, but I found myself a tad reluctant to approach him. He was just a little too curious about Woodrow and the Reisinger project for my comfort. There was one other person who might know. Someone who was plugged into the world. Bert Pine, the conspiracy guy.

I'd wanted to ask him about the conversation he'd overheard between DeSantis and the Minister of the Environment. Now, it appeared, I had a few other questions for him. And what about the sabotage at the site? It seemed to me that was something a conspiracy freak might know a lot about. Yes, talking to Bert Pine seemed more like a good idea the longer I thought about it.

After dinner, I decided to stop thinking about it and start doing it.

"You want some company?" Kelt offered as I struggled into my jacket.

I gave him an icy stare. "I don't think so."

He blinked. "Uh, okay. Where are you going?"

"Out."

Kelt took a step back.

"I'm going to see Bert Pine," I relented a bit.

"Don't you want me to come with you?"

"Thanks, but I'd rather go by myself. Excuse me." I grabbed my crutches and swung out the door, leaving a wide-eyed Kelt staring after me.

Well, what did he expect? He'd practically led me on with those kisses when all the time he'd really been interested in Lisa. I steamed about him all the way to Bert Pine's house, right up until I punched the doorbell. Then I recollected myself and pasted a friendlier expression on my face. Wouldn't do to scare off Bert Pine before I even opened my mouth.

Bert was surprised to see me standing on his porch, but he invited me in without hesitation and offered me a cup of herbal tea and a piece of carrot loaf. Made with wheat germ. Like this was supposed to be a big selling point. I refused with a polite smile. The way I was feeling right now, if it didn't have caffeine, refined sugar, or chocolate, then I wasn't interested in it.

I didn't feel much like small talk, either. As soon as Bert had settled on the couch with his cup of echinacea, I opened my mouth to come straight to the point. But my attention was arrested by what was on the far wall. A gun case?

"You're a hunter?" I blurted in surprise.

Bert twisted his head to follow my eyes. "Oh, the guns. Yes, ma'am, I am."

A man who drinks herbal tea and eats wheat germ loaves was a hunter?

"Just ducks," he said, reading my mind. "It's a helluva lot safer eating wild meat than stuff that's been raised in wire cages and pumped full of antibiotics."

"Yeah. I guess it would be."

"Is that why you came to see me? To ask about hunting?"

"Uh, no, I'm sorry. I was just a little surprised to see the gun case. No, I came to ask you about a conversation you overheard between Grant DeSantis—"

"Ah, I thought you might have heard about that."

"Yes, and I was wondering if you could tell me what happened."

Bert gave a little shrug. "It was the weirdest thing, but I guess it happens sometimes with these small-town phone lines. Dolores—my wife—was out at one of her birdwatching groups. She called to tell me she'd be a little late when all of a sudden the line clicked and I could hear two guys talking. They couldn't hear me—neither could Dolores, for that matter—and when I heard them mention Reisinger and one guy calling the other one Paul, well, it caught my attention."

"What exactly did they say?" I asked, fascinated.

"A bunch of stuff," Bert answered. "Nothing that you could point to and say 'Aha! Here's evidence of illegal dealing.' But it was more what they weren't saying than what they were, if that makes any sense.

"You see, when you take a long, hard look at this Reisinger project, certain facts can't help jumping out at you. Like how bad the site is. Even before you guys came into it, most folks had a pretty good idea the place was a mess. So why is Reisinger willing to take on that kind of liability?"

"Tax breaks and other financial incentives?" I suggested.

Bert nodded. "Without question, but the province hasn't

officially given their approval for the project yet. The kind of assessment and remediation plans Woodrow's working on don't come cheap, and Reisinger's footing the bill. Why? There's a lot of land base in Canada. Why doesn't Reisinger build their plant elsewhere?"

"Because they've already received unofficial approval for the plant," I took a stab at it. "The government wins PR points by getting the site cleaned up, and Reisinger wins because they don't have to fight to get approval on a pristine site. And they get financial incentives."

Bert nodded once curtly. "Paul Ormsby intimated as much during the conversation I overheard with DeSantis."

I thought about that for a minute. It made a lot of sense. "You know, they've been having trouble out at the site," I said carefully.

"Yeah, I read about it. Doesn't surprise me really—"

"Wait a minute. You read about it? Where?"

"Yesterday's *Edmonton Journal*. Didn't you see the article?"

"No."

"It was a pretty big piece. Hang on a sec." He turned and rummaged around in a pile of newspapers at the side of the couch. "Here, take a look for yourself." He handed it to me.

I read the headline, and my stomach took a nose-dive. Two words jumped out at me first—the name of the reporter. Matt Lees. I scanned the article, and my stomach crashed and burned. It was everything Grant DeSantis and his public relations had been trying to avoid. Instead of the three Rs, Matt had gone instead with the three Ss—sabotage, sniper, and speculation. It was all there on the front page. And how. When Ben read this, there'd be a fourth S—screaming.

But Ben already knew, I realized then, as the events of the last couple of days clicked together in my mind. The crew tense and snapping at each other. The absence of banter at the dinner table. Hoo boy! And I thought they'd just been getting tired. Ben must have gone nova! How had Matt found out about it all? Somebody must have talked.

"There's a lot of bad feeling toward industry in this province," Bert was saying.

With an effort, I brought my attention back to him.

"People are getting fed up with having their land and their livestock poisoned by companies that don't give two shits."

"People like you?" I asked, trying not to let my eyes flick over to the gun cabinet.

He gave me a steady look, aware of what I was getting at. "Not my style," he answered the unspoken question. "But I'm not surprised by it. I'm as frustrated as the next guy. But me, I fight in other ways. Your friend's protest group, for example. The simple fact that DeSantis has his grubby fingers in this project was enough to get me joining up."

"Oh?" I prompted.

"He's a prick through and through!"

I blinked, taken aback by his vehemence.

"The guy's a walking natural disaster. It was Matt Lees who put me onto him, oh, must be six months ago now, just after the Nueva Esperanza plant closed down. You do know about that, don't you?"

I nodded solemnly. "Yes, they manufactured pesticides, but I don't know what kinds."

"Huh. You know more than his stepson did, then. They made the drins—aldrin, dieldrin. Nasty stuff. Anyway, that's what started me off and, well, to make a long story short, I did a bit of my own snooping around. Found myself quite a few other examples of Grant DeSantis specials."

"Specials?"

Bert nodded, twisting his features into an expression of utter disgust. "Yeah, Dyncide's little projects have an alarming tendency to go wrong."

"Dyncide's active in other countries?"

Bert nodded again. "Oh yes, they've got plants in South America, Pakistan, and a couple in eastern Europe."

"And have there been problems at these other plants?" I asked.

"Problems!" Bert laughed humorlessly. "Accidents, outright violations, cover-ups. The list goes on."

"What was Grant DeSantis's involvement?"

Bert shrugged. "You name it, he had a finger in it. And most of the time, he was up to his hairy armpit in it. Some of the stuff was just plain criminal. Take the situation in East Germany, for example. Once the country reunified, there were tons of pesticides that lost their registrations—you know, crap that had been banned in the western half but not in the east. So with the reunification, all these pesticides were sitting on their butts with their expiry dates running out. Nobody seemed to know what the hell to do with them."

"Enter Grant DeSantis?" I guessed.

Bert touched his nose. "Right on the money," he answered. "Grant DeSantis, operating as a special consultant, advised several companies on how to deal with the mess. As a result of his advice, one German firm exported outdated and banned pesticides to Albania. Real nice stuff like mercury, dioxins, and lindane."

"How did they get that over the border?" I demanded.

"It was labeled humanitarian aid," Bert replied soberly. "By the time somebody opened it and found out what it really was, it was too late. With all the laws and restrictions on shipping the stuff, Albania can't send it back to Germany, so they're stuck with having to deal with it."

"That's revolting!" I exclaimed, appalled. "Grant DeSantis advised them to do that?"

"Yup. That'd be my guess. And still came out smelling like a rose. Dyncide—and Goldor Industries—protects their own."

I was silent for a moment, trying to absorb the extent of DeSantis's lack of conscience. It took a very long moment.

"In some ways these murders seems like poetic justice," Bert mused half to himself. "Grant DeSantis has a lot of blood on his hands. Indirectly, of course. But so many families have been devastated by the policies he's made or implemented. For his own family to be destroyed. . . ."

"Hardly seems fair to them, though," I interrupted a bit pointedly. It had clearly never occurred to Bert Pine that he might be a suspect in these very murders.

He waved off my comment. "I'm not unsympathetic," he told me. "I feel sorry for the wife, and Richard certainly didn't deserve an end like that."

"Have you told the protest group about this?"

Bert's mouth twisted to one side. "Of course. For all the good it did me."

"What do you mean?"

"Nobody really cares what happens in Albania or peasantville Mexico. It muddies the waters. And they don't want the protesting to get too personal, either. Figure it'll destroy their credibility or something. Trouble is, Elliot Shibley's a decent guy, and DeSantis is more a behind-the-scenes type. Most of the group don't seem to understand that those shadowy guys are the ones you have to keep the closest eye on. But when it comes right down to it, what do I know? I'm just the local conspiracy nut." His tone was bitter and resentful. Frustrated.

My eyes slid over to the gun case again.

A large Dairy Queen hot fudge sundae with double peanuts kept me company after I left Bert Pine's house. Almost, but not quite, as good as sex—at least to the best of my recollection, which seemed to be fading more each day. I settled at a quiet corner table and delved in. But after the first few mouthfuls of silky warm chocolate slipped down my throat, I stopped thinking about sex and starting pondering other, more serious, matters.

Was Bert Pine our saboteur? The man was certainly disillusioned enough to take matters into his own hands. And he had a whole caseful of guns. Our saboteur had used a rifle, which was not the gun of choice for a duck hunter, but I wouldn't know a rifle from a shotgun. It's quite possible Bert's gun cabinet boasted a few of each. So. Did that make him a murderer, too? I didn't think so, for the same reasons I'd explained to Kelt the other night.

Bert Pine had certainly been a wealth of information, but he'd left me with a wealth of questions, too. Where to begin, was one of them. Maybe I should just start with a clean slate. That's what all good sleuths seemed to do.

Very well. In most of Arif's mystery novels, the victim was killed for one of three reasons: money, sex, or revenge. I swirled my tongue around another mouthful of fudge sauce. Sex first, then. I kept eating my sundae, but I couldn't come up with a single reason why anybody would kill Richard over sex. And Melanie? Well, Howard said she'd been having an affair. But Howard had also said she'd been having it with Matt. Right.

Okay, what about money? Now there was a possibility.

Were the DeSantises, in fact, short of money? Possibly, after that whopping fine. Had Howard stumbled onto it? It seemed so, and he'd been fired and blacklisted for his trouble. Reason enough for murder? Yup. Did I have any proof? Not a shred.

I scraped the last molecules of sundae from the cardboard cup, licked my spoon, and considered, then thought better of, licking the cup. Then I sat back and kept thinking.

Revenge.

Ah, that was the real kicker. Howard and Grant, even Carol, were very likely suspects, but I couldn't get the damn gnomes out of my mind. An eye for an eye, a tooth for a tooth. A life for a life? Only two of my hypotheses fit into that scenario. One was unlikely. The other was June.

CHAPTER 28

WHEN I HEARD THE LIGHT TAP on my bedroom door early the next morning, I thought at first that it might be Kelt. Then I remembered about Lisa and my heart constricted. I didn't want to talk to Kelt. I pulled the covers over my head and squeezed my eyes shut. So much for my love life. Perhaps I'd just be one of those old ladies who lives in a big house with fifty cats.

Tap. Tap.

I groaned in protest but the thought of fifty Guidos had woken me up all the way, so I struggled out from under the covers and lurched to the door. June was standing there.

"Oh. Uh, goo' mornin'," I mumbled.

She smiled sympathetically as I scrubbed the sleep from my face. "Hi, Robyn. I thought you'd be awake."

I yawned. "I am, more or less. Wha's up?"

"What's up is I've got a hankering to go out to Beaverhill this morning. Want to come?"

"Yeah! Just lemme get myself together. What time is it?"

"Six ten. Why don't you wash up and I'll pack us some breakfast?"

"Great." I hobbled back to the bed and lowered myself down on the edge of the mattress. I was always up for an early-morning birding session, but all of a sudden I wasn't sure how I felt about going birding with June. Suspecting somebody of murder was liable to put a crimp in any conversation. I felt guilty and uncomfortable and generally like a cad, and found myself wishing I'd been more awake when she had made the offer.

I struggled into my clothes, pulled a brush through my curls, and stumped my way to the bathroom. I'd just make sure we kept the conversation to birds, I told myself as I washed the last remnants of sleep from my eyes. It wasn't like we'd have trouble filling a morning with bird talk. But I discovered, once we arrived at Beaverhill, that June had other plans.

The drive out to the site had been relatively quiet. I was trying to come to terms with consciousness, and June was either lost in her thoughts or respectful of my need to gather my own.

It was another sunny day, without the frostiness of the other morning. The songbirds had started arriving and the air was filled with twitterings and chirrupings. The robins had been back for a while now, but I could also identify the clipped *chebek* of a least flycatcher, the long, nasal *peeeer* of a peewee, and . . . I waited for a moment.

Tsee titi. Tsee titi.

Yes, there was a horned lark or two somewhere out there, as well. I smiled in delight. I once read that Mozart had been influenced by birdsong, and that if you listened closely to his melodies you could recognize the songs of specific bird species. I'd never tried this myself, but as June and I sat in the car with the windows rolled down to let in the music and the crisp morning air, I could see how a composer might be inspired by the feathered orchestra.

June had just handed me a much-needed cup of coffee when she made it clear that this was not an idle birding trip.

"So what's the trouble between you and Kelt?" she asked in a Borg-like tone that indicated evasion was futile.

I choked on my coffee. "Trouble?" I repeated after I'd mopped myself up.

June gave me a stern glance. "I know something's the matter. You two have been inseparable for the past week—until the day before yesterday."

"We're just friends, June."

She raised one eyebrow. "And Matt and I just hold hands," she said sarcastically. "Did something happen at the bar?"

I squirmed a bit, then sighed in defeat. "It's all my fault," I admitted to her. And I started telling her about the other night.

"We left the bar early," I began.

"That sounds promising."

I snorted. "I wish. We were on our way back to your house when we saw someone skulking around Pam Swinton's place."

"Skulking! Was someone trying to break in?"

"That's what I thought—actually I thought it might be a murderer leaving another gnome."

"Oh dear."

I nodded. "Yeah, I saw him leave a gnome and some pictures so when he slunk out of the yard . . . well . . . I, uh. . . ."

"What?"

"Umm. . . ."

"Robyn, what did you do?"

"I . . . I pushed Kelt on him." I said it in a rush.

"You what?!"

"I thought he was a murderer," I said defensively. "I got caught up in the moment, and I wanted Kelt to get him. But it turned out to be Randy Hughes. He'd taken one of Pam's gnomes—"

"To Hawaii."

I nodded morosely. "Yeah. Hawaii. With hula girls and stuff."

"Oh." June started chuckling. "Oh dear," she said trying (and not succeeding) to look concerned.

"It's not funny, June," I protested. "Kelt landed right on top of him!" Then I giggled. "They did a total face plant in the dirt."

June dissolved into laughter. I wasn't far behind.

"You . . . you should've seen Kelt's face!"

June covered her eyes and shook with mirth.

"Randy was . . . so . . . pissed!" I roared with laughter.

We chuckled and choked till our eyes streamed and our stomachs ached. When we finally calmed down, I felt better than I had in ages. I didn't tell June about Kelt and Lisa. I wasn't proud of the fact that I'd peeked into his room. And really. So what if Kelt and Lisa had a thing going? It wouldn't be the first time I'd been left on the sidelines. Maybe friendship would be enough. And Kelt and I *were* friends, I was sure of that. The incident with Randy would just turn out to be one of those things we'd laugh about over drinks.

Once again, my friend's mother—my second mother—had managed to put my life back into perspective for me. How could I even suspect June of something like murder? She was warmth and kindness and generosity personified. As we poured more coffee and unwrapped a couple of blueberry muffins, I firmly smothered any inner voice that might be telling me differently.

Guido the cat and I were sitting in the living room, warming ourselves in a bright patch of sunlight, and sipping tuna juice and tea (respectively) when the call from APEGGA came through. Yves LaSalle had given them permission to pass me his phone number. I punched it in as soon as I hung up.

"LaSalle here," he answered in a gruff voice.

I introduced myself and mentioned the Norsicol site. For a minute I thought we'd been disconnected.

"Hello?" I said into the silence. "Are you—"

"I'm here," he said and I could hear him take a deep breath. "Sorry about that. You took me by surprise." He cleared his throat. "The woman I spoke to from APEGGA didn't give me any details about why you were phoning. So someone's finally cleaning up that old site, eh? About time."

"Yeah, it's quite a mess."

"I'm not surprised. I suppose you're looking for drawings."

"That's right. Can you help us out?"

"It'll take me a while to dig them out for you but, yes, I kept drawings of every facility I worked on. Drives my wife crazy sometimes but you never know when they're going to come in handy. You in Calgary?"

"Not at the moment," I told him, "but we're based there. Mr. LaSalle—"

"Yves."

"Thanks. Yves, I also wanted to ask you about the accident."

I could hear him sigh. "Heard about that, did you?"

"Yeah, I read about it in *The Pegg*. I'm sorry to have to bring it up now."

"That's okay," he assured me. "You guys should probably be checking out those pipes, anyway. I left Norsicol shortly after the accident. I'd be willing to bet things got worse rather than better. They were well on their way to running that plant into the ground."

"Can you tell me about the accident?"

"It was a case of being too young and too insecure, I guess. Couldn't stand up to the maintenance supervisor. All he ever cared about was cutting costs, increasing production, and meeting schedules so he could keep cashing his fat bonus checks. Wanted the work done but wasn't willing to pay the overtime to make sure the job was done properly."

"So he pressured the engineers to cut corners on safety?"

"That's about the size of it. Most of the time they managed to stand up to him." He paused and his tone hardened. "But a couple of months before the accident, Norsicol realized that chlordane and heptachlor were on their way to being banned. They decided to cut back to a shoestring budget in order to maximize their profits. That included laying off all the senior engineers."

"You're kidding!"

"Wish I could say I was. I guess they wanted to squeeze what they could out of the plant before the ban forced them to shut down. Likewise, when that valve went, they didn't want to wait for a proper one to come in—every minute the plant didn't run meant the company lost dollars. And the company didn't like to lose money for any reason. Anyhow, the maintenance supervisor pressured me to replace it with a ball valve. The guy before him wasn't so bad but this fellow was a new guy—a real bulldozing type—and

I was too young and inexperienced to stand up to him. Hadn't even earned my stamp at that point. And as a result of that, somebody got hurt."

I waited, sensing he wasn't done yet.

"You know, it's one thing when someone gets hurt because of a real accident. Something that nobody thought about or caught in time. But in this case," he paused for another moment, "well, I *knew* that valve was a mistake but I didn't have the balls to stand by my decision. And somebody else ended up paying so I could learn that lesson. I almost gave up engineering because of it. Spent the next several years doing economic forecasts for the feds before I got into computers and mainframe systems engineering."

"Do you remember the name of the worker who was injured?"

"Oh, yes," Yves said gravely. "His name was Lieski. Luke Lieski."

"Luke Lieski," I repeated, scrawling the name on a scrap of paper. "Do you know if he ever recovered?"

"I'm afraid I don't. He went back home. To Ontario somewhere, I think. Is it important?"

"I don't think so," I told him.

"I've always felt terrible about it. Always felt I should've had more backbone. I should've stood up to that bastard supervisor."

"He sounds like a real piece of work," I remarked.

Yves LaSalle barked a humorless laugh. "That fellow worried more about his bonus checks than anything else."

"What was his name?" I asked, suspecting already.

"Grant DeSantis."

I sat up a little straighter. "Why does this not surprise me?" I muttered under my breath.

"Pardon me?"

"Uh, nothing," I told him. "Listen, I really appreciate your time on this, and I'm sorry I had to bring up that stuff about the accident."

"That's okay. It might help you out with the site. Who're you cleaning it up for, anyhow?"

I told him about Reisinger (minus Grant DeSantis's role) and briefly outlined their plans. Yves promised to dig out the drawings as soon as possible. I thanked him again, gave him Woodrow's phone number, and told him that Ben would be in touch.

When I hung up the phone I turned to find that June had stepped into the room and was now regarding me curiously.

"Luke Lieski?" she asked.

"Yeah, you know him?"

She nodded her head slowly, thoughtfully. "Of him. A long time ago. I haven't heard his name for years. I think he went drinking with Eddie sometimes. He and few of the other fellows from the plant."

"Any chance he's still around?"

She shook her head. "I don't think so."

"According to what I've found out, Luke Lieski was involved in an accident at the plant."

June crinkled her brow in thought. "I seem to recall something about that." She paused for a long moment before shaking her head again. "No, I'm sorry. I can't really remember anything else." She shrugged apologetically. "I'm afraid I had other things on my mind at the time," she said with a just a whisper of sadness.

I looked at her sympathetically, all suspicions momentarily forgotten.

"Wherever did you get Luke's name?" June asked curiously after a moment. "I barely remember the man myself."

"It started with Rocky," I told her and explained about Rocky's ghost sightings.

"That poor soul," June remarked sympathetically when I'd finished. "It's hard to imagine what his reality must be like. Do you really think he's seeing ghosts?"

"I think it's more likely he's seen someone who looks like Luke, or the man himself."

"So you're wondering if Luke's come back."

I nodded.

"Rocky could just be confused," she warned. "Don't put too much stock in what he says."

"He seems pretty convinced."

"Yes, well, he was pretty convinced that Sue was trying to poison him a few months ago."

"*Poison?*"

June nodded solemnly. "Yes, as close as Sue could tell, he saw her cleaning the bathroom—she uses baking soda to clean her sinks just like I do—at any rate, he saw her cleaning the sink, then he saw her take out the same box of soda when she made cookies. She tried explaining till she was blue in the face about cleaning with natural products, but it just didn't get through. He was telling anyone who'd listen that she was trying to poison him with cleaning chemicals."

I thought that over for a few seconds. "Hmmm. And here I thought I'd impress Ben and pull another plant worker out of the hat."

June patted my hand comfortingly. "You could try calling directory assistance, of course, but I wouldn't hold my breath if I was you."

I did and I didn't, and it was just as well. There was no listing, new or old, for anyone with the last name Lieski. So that, I thought to myself, was that.

"Any more trouble today?" I asked Ben. A stupid question. He had a face like a cumulonimbus cloud.

"Yeah, some asshole dumped oatmeal down the wells."

"What?! All of them?"

"Just a couple so far. He took the flags and tried to saw the pipes off. You can see cut marks on them. When he couldn't get them off, he decided just to screw up the wells."

"Are they salvageable?" I asked doubtfully.

"Not a chance. It's a sticky, gluey mess. Bastard knew what he was doing."

"Will you have to drill more holes?"

Ben blew out a frustrated sigh. "Yeah, he screwed up a whole section. Maurice's going to come out again for an extra day. You can be damn sure I'll be putting locking caps on this time."

"Ben, I'm sorry."

"If I find the turnip who's responsible, I'll wring his bloody neck."

It was a sober group that had filed into the kitchen that evening. Four days had passed since the sniper attack at the site. Four days of peace and quiet with nary a hint of sabotage. The RCMP had been diligent in maintaining a presence on and around the site, and Matt's article had sparked so much interest that the old plant had been inundated with an entire alphabet of media. CBC, ITV, the A Channel. You name it, they were there. With all the activity, we'd thought—and hoped—the sabotage had ended. It appeared we'd been wrong.

"Any trouble here today?" Ben turned the question back to me.

I shook my head. "Not that I know of. I've been out and about all day."

Ben grunted, still seething about the wells.

Dinner was a subdued affair. June had told me earlier that she'd apologized to Ben about Matt's article. I'm sure Ben appreciated the apology, but I didn't think it was coincidence that Matt was conspicuously absent from dinner that night. Just as well, really. Apology or not, Ben would have gone for the jugular.

Over red peppers stuffed with a spicy mixture of nuts and rice, I told Ben about Yves LaSalle, Grant DeSantis, and Luke Lieski. He wasn't surprised to hear about DeSantis's role in the accident, but he wasn't as quick to dismiss the possibility of Luke's return as June had been.

"Getting those drawings is a real bonus. But it would be a tremendous help for us to find an ex-employee who actually did the gruntwork at the plant," he said eagerly. "Especially if he knew about some kind of accident."

"Sounds as if he was personally involved in the accident, though," I said. "And if he got sick from it, the chances are good that he's not around to tell anybody anything. You know how toxic that stuff was. A lot of the other workers died from cancers related to the plant."

"And if he did come back, nobody seems to know about it," Kelt observed.

"Except Robyn's friend Rocky," Nalini answered.

"And he's probably just confused again," I finished.

"Nevertheless," Ben said. "It's worth trying to find out. I leave it in your capable hands, Robyn. Find me this worker, if you can."

CHAPTER 29

THE NEXT MORNING ON PAGE A7 of *The Edmonton Journal* there was a small piece about Richard DeSantis. Apparently my guess had been correct. According to the article, he had died of a massive ingestion of pesticide. Heptachlor, to be precise. Death had occurred in minutes.

In minutes. I thought about that for a while. It must have been a pretty strong solution. But if it had been so concentrated, then why hadn't he smelled it? According to anything I'd ever read, pesticides were pretty foul-smelling substances. It was possible he had committed suicide with it, but there were better ways to go, and from what I'd heard of him, he wasn't exactly the suicidal type.

Except for Guido the cat, I was alone in the house again. The Woodrow crew had headed out to the site earlier to grid out the runoff ditches, and June had gone into the office. How had Richard DeSantis managed to swallow a massive amount of heptachlor without realizing it? Did heptachlor smell bad? I could think of one way to find out. Hopefully the Internet gods were feeling kindly today. I sat down at June's computer and sacrificed a coffee and a cinnamon roll to them.

It worked. According to the United States's National Toxicology Program website, heptachlor and other pesticides were formulated by first dissolving them in petroleum-based solvents like xylene, and then adding emulsifiers so the whole mess could be mixed with water. And xylene, being a petroleum derivative, was, as

I'd suspected, highly odorous. Technical heptachlor, on the other hand, was another story entirely. Almost 95–99% pure, even a tiny amount of technical heptachlor would send a grown man into convulsions. A teaspoon would kill him. If Richard DeSantis had ingested technical heptachlor, that explained why he'd died so quickly—and why he hadn't smelled it. Technical heptachlor has a very mild, camphor-like odor.

Suddenly I remembered what June had said about Richard. Back before Tracy stumbled across his body. According to June, Richard had been an avid birder. So keen, in fact, that he was supposed to have taken the local birding group out to see the heron colony he had discovered last fall. But he'd had to cancel out because of a sinus infection.

I leaned back in the chair thoughtfully. Assuming Richard was still recovering, he might not have been able to detect a faint mothball-like smell. Had the murderer known that Richard's nose was stuffed up? Could he or she have mixed technical heptachlor in with something that Richard would eat or drink? A thermos of coffee perhaps?

I tilted back further, balancing the chair on two legs. Is that what happened to Melanie DeSantis? Had the murderer tried the same trick? I remembered the pattern of brown on the dogwood—almost as if something had been splashed across it. Women were more sensitive to smell than men were. Had Melanie detected a strange odor? As far as I knew, she hadn't had a sinus infection. Maybe she smelled something suspicious and tossed the mixture onto the bushes, thus forcing her killer to take other measures.

I brought my chair down with a thump, narrowly missing Guido's tail. He flattened his ears against his head and shot me a reproachful look.

"Sorry, Guido." I reached down to soothe him, but he shook me off and stalked over to a chair by the bookcase, where he proceeded to wash every trace of my touch from his fur. I turned my attention back to my problem.

I might have figured out the how of the matter, but the why

still eluded me. Was June a killer? I honestly didn't know. Her behavior had been decidedly odd lately. And I'd never known her to tell a lie—until the morning after Melanie DeSantis's murder. But what about Rocky and his hallucinations? What about Grant DeSantis and all his environmental crimes? What about Howard and his hatred of Melanie DeSantis?

What about the heptachlor, my inner voice piped up. I'd noticed before that it had a particularly loathsome habit of pointing out, and dwelling on, the unlikely, the unpleasant, and the unthinkable. But it was impossible to ignore.

The heptachlor. If the murders were linked to Nuevo Esperanza, why had the two victims been killed with heptachlor? The Dyncide plant had manufactured aldrin and dieldrin—two completely different pesticides. And Rocky wouldn't know what heptachlor was if it were spread on his toast. No, I might have suspected him of slashing Melanie DeSantis's throat, but the fact that heptachlor was present at the scene changed everything. The same thing could be said for my suspicions about Howard Miller. Somehow I doubted that Soldiers of Fortune ran around spiking drinks with insecticides. Too subtle.

I fiddled with the pencils on the desk. June had known that Richard DeSantis had a sinus infection. She had known where to find his body. She knew all about heptachlor, and its effects and properties. And Grant DeSantis had been in charge of maintenance and safety at the Norsicol plant when Eddie had fallen sick and died. Added together, the facts made me very uneasy, but it was this last that was so very damning. Was my friend's mother out for revenge?

Inadvertently my fingers tightened on the pencil I was playing with. It popped out of my grasp and went skittering onto the floor.

"Crap."

I bent down to pick it up. As I did, three things happened simultaneously. The window shattered. The bookcase exploded.

And, worst of all, my cat screamed.

CHAPTER 30

"GUIDO!" I SHRIEKED, THROWING MYSELF across the room. Blood and splinters of wood splattered June's books and stained the floor. Oh gods. Somebody had shot my cat!

I lurched across the floor and collapsed beside him.

"Guido!"

He cried, one agonized meow after another. He struggled to move, his left hind leg dragging uselessly behind him. His fur was wet and spiky with blood. I tried to look at his wound, but he hissed and swiped at me. My hand came away with four deep red lines. I didn't even feel it. His ears were plastered against his head.

And he kept crying.

"Guido, I have to see it," I pleaded. Tears were streaming down my face.

Somebody had shot my cat.

He hissed again. His eyes were slits in his head. Pale splinters stuck out of his leg like stiff guard hairs. Was it bone or wood? I couldn't tell. I touched his fur gently, searching for a bullet hole, but he pulled away and I couldn't get a good look.

"Please, Guido," I begged.

He squirmed away from me and squawked as his leg collapsed again.

Somebody had shot my cat.

"It'll be okay," I chanted over and over again. As if the words would make the reality.

He hissed and cried out again.

Savagely I grabbed my wits together. June! I had to phone June. I tried to stand, to walk to the phone, but the blood under my feet was slippery and I was off-balance because of the casts.

I swore as my foot slid underneath me.

I tried again but slipped before I got to a crouch.

"Goddamit!"

Guido cried out again.

I gave up and scrambled frantically over to the desk, half-crawling, half-pulling myself across the carpet. Shaking with shock. Cursing my damn casts. Leaving a streaky trail of Guido's blood behind me.

I got to the desk and gave the phone cord a savage yank. It crashed to the floor and I pulled it toward me. Somehow I punched in June's number.

"June!" It was all I could manage.

"Robyn! What's wrong?"

"It's Guido!" I started crying again. "Somebody shot him! He's bleeding, June! He's got stuff sticking out of his leg. Somebody shot him."

"I'm coming home right now. Try to keep him quiet. Don't move him, okay? I'll call Alva on my cell phone."

"Hurry."

"I've left already."

I hung up the phone and struggled back to my cat.

He lay on his side, panting.

Chapter 31

"He'll be fine," Dr. Alva Kimmins told me again for the third time.

I could have listened to her say those words all afternoon.

"The bullet must have hit the bookcase. It missed him, but the splinters from the bookcase didn't. I've got them all out now and he's resting."

"Those splinters were wood? Not bone?"

"Not bone," she assured me. "Nothing was broken except the skin. Some of the splinters were pretty deep in the muscle tissue, but he'll be okay with plenty of rest."

"Is he awake?"

"Not really. He's still pretty groggy from the anaesthetic."

"Can I see him?"

She looked at my puffy red eyes and the bloodstains on my shirt. Her expression softened. "Just for a moment," she told me and led me to the back room.

There was a row of gleaming chrome cages but Guido appeared to be the only patient. I crutched over to his cage and put my nose against the bars.

"Hey, baby," I whispered softly. "How're you doing?"

He lay on his side, breathing steadily, and watching the world through wide eyes and enlarged pupils. His left leg was bandaged neatly. I could see bare skin around the edges of it. Dr. Kimmins had had to shave him.

I poked my finger through the bars and stroked his head.

"What a pair we'll be," I told him. "Both of us with gimpy legs."

He didn't respond.

"We'll keep him for a couple more hours," Dr. Kimmins said. "Then if everything's okay, he can go home with you."

"Thank you so much," I told her fervently.

"Yes, thanks for seeing us right away, Alva," June said, stepping up beside me. She gave me a comforting hug. "Come on, Robyn. We need to go and have a little talk with the RCMP."

Indeed we did. Now that I knew Guido was going to be all right, the fist around my heart could loosen a bit. Now I could allow myself to get angry. Somebody had shot my cat. Whoever it was, was damn well going to pay for it.

Kelt came to my room that night, looking a little unsure of his welcome. I motioned him to the chair, too exhausted to play games.

Guido was home from the vet's now. Comfortably ensconced between pillows, he was sleeping off the effects of anaesthetic and shock, but my throat still threatened to close up every time I remembered how close he had come to the Great Tuna Packing Plant in the Sky.

It had been a rifle. The RCMP constable told us that much. Somebody had shot through the window and hit the bookcase. It was just Guido's bad luck that he'd been sitting in the chair beside the shelf. Had somebody been trying to shoot me? It didn't appear that way. I had been sitting at the desk which was beside, rather than across from, the window.

"Another scare tactic, then?" I'd asked.

Probably, the constable agreed. And since the gun involved was a rifle, it was likely that whoever had shot at us a few days ago had also taken a potshot at the house. Not a warming thought.

"How are you doing?" Kelt asked, his voice soft and sympathetic.

"I'm okay. I just. . . ." My eyes filled up and I looked away.

"I know," Kelt said.

"I thought he was dead."

"I know," he said again.

A few tears trickled down my cheek. If a person's body was supposed to be 97% water, I was down to about 80% by now. I dashed the tears away and sat there in silence for a few long moments, feeling uncomfortable. I didn't want to talk about it any more. I was just glad that my cat was okay. When the RCMP caught whoever shot him, well, then I'd have plenty more to say about it.

"Robyn, is there something wrong? I mean, besides Guido. You've seemed upset the past couple of days."

That was the last thing I wanted to discuss.

"Things are just pretty tense around here," I evaded. "What the hell's going on with you guys? Ben looks like he wants to rip somebody's head off."

Kelt puffed out his cheeks and sighed. "It was Matt's article."

"The article? But Ben's been through this sort of thing before and—"

"It was Lisa who talked to Matt."

That brought me up short. "Lisa?"

"Uh huh. She's young. She doesn't have a whole lot of experience with journalists. I don't think she realized what was happening."

I thought about it for a moment. "Just a chat with a friend, eh?"

"Yeah. Some friend. I've never seen anybody reamed out like that. Ben was purple, Lisa was in tears. It was ugly. I thought he was going to fire her."

"Really?"

"Mmmm. She was pretty upset."

I remembered that evening. The entire crew snapping at each other. Lisa encircled in Kelt's arms. Had Kelt just been comforting her? It was too new a thought to discuss with him.

There were other things Kelt and I could discuss, but I found myself feeling reticent about those, too. Once the upset over Guido had calmed, I'd had time to think about what I'd discovered today.

The use of heptachlor was damning, especially when added to Yves LaSalle's story about Grant DeSantis. If DeSantis had been so directly responsible for Luke Lieski's accident, then what role had he played in Eddie McVea's illness? I didn't know many of the details surrounding Eddie's death, but I knew that he'd died suddenly because of something at the Norsicol plant. That didn't sound like chronic exposure to me. And if Eddie had died from acute exposure and Grant DeSantis had played a part in it.... Well, it sure made me wonder about things that I didn't want to think about, let alone share with Kelt—even if he *didn't* have a thing going with Lisa.

I had always been a loner. Perhaps I should take a tip from Rudyard Kipling's cat. All places didn't necessarily have to be alike to me, but maybe it would be better if I kept walking by myself for a while.

The conversation sputtered and died. Kelt didn't linger.

I was still asleep when I heard the sound of Kelt murmuring my name and felt his gentle touch on my shoulder. I burrowed deeper under the covers, intent on relishing the dream. Just because I didn't want to confide in the guy didn't mean I couldn't indulge in a little harmless lust at his expense.

"C'mon, Robyn, I know you're awake."

I cracked an eye open. Not a dream after all. Kelt knelt beside my bed, shaking my shoulder.

"Wha's wrong?" I groaned softly.

"I need to talk to you. Are you awake?"

It was his tone of voice more than anything that brought me to wakefulness. I lifted my head from the pillow, unwelcome thoughts of mouth bunnies and pillow scars flashing through my mind. The last thing I wanted Kelt to see was me doing my impression of Dr. Evil.

"Robyn?"

I rolled over and regarded Kelt through sleep-puffed eyes. "What's the matter?" I demanded a little testily.

"Are you awake now?"

I stretched and sat up, and looked at the clock. Ten to five. Definitely on the early side for me.

"Yeah, yeah, I think so," I told him, scrubbing the sleep from my face.

Kelt looked as if he hadn't slept all night. He sported whole luggage cars beneath his eyes and his face looked pale.

"What's wrong?" I asked again, concerned this time. I bolted upright. "Is Guido okay?" Frightened now.

"He's fine," Kelt assured me quickly. "He's right beside you."

"Oh." I buried my hand in Guido's fur and sank back against the pillow with relief. "What's wrong then?"

Kelt took a deep breath and let it out slowly. "I'm worried about June," he said in the soft tone that people use in a sleeping household.

"June." It took a few seconds for my brain to click on track. "Why? Was she crying again last night?"

He nodded. "But there's more this time."

I sat silently, waiting for him to continue. I waited a long moment.

"I heard her crying again," he said finally. "I was trying to make up my mind whether I should go and see if I could do anything when I heard her leave her room and go downstairs. I don't know why it sounded weird. I mean, it's her house—she has every right to mooch around at night if she wants to—but it did. Sound strange, I mean. Especially after her crying like that. Anyhow, when I heard her creep outside, I uh, I, well. . . ." He broke off, flushing. "I got up and followed her," he finished quickly.

"What?" I squeaked.

"I thought maybe there was something wrong. Maybe something I could help with," he whispered defensively. "I was worried."

"Where did she go?" I asked, afraid of the answer.

Kelt shifted uncomfortably. "That's why I wanted to talk to you before anybody got up this morning," he said. "Robyn, June went over to the DeSantis house last night."

"She *what?*"

He nodded miserably. "She didn't go in or anything; she just stood outside the house for the longest time. It was weird. I felt like a worm watching her. After a while, a car drove up the street and she bolted like a jackrabbit."

I ran fingers through my tangled curls and sighed heavily.

"Robyn, what's going on?"

I flashed him wide Bambi eyes. "Why are you asking me?" I demanded, trying for moral outrage. It was pretty feeble.

Kelt reached out and touched my cheek gently. I dropped my gaze.

"I know something's been bothering you," he said softly. "I know you well enough now to figure that one out. And in light of what I saw last night, I can't help wondering whether it has anything to do with June."

I looked up and held his eyes for a long moment. For months now, I'd fantasized about having my wicked way with Kelt, boring my friends (well, Megan) and even my subconscious with what Freud would have termed my id impulses (I guess Freud didn't get out much, either). But in all my lusting happily ever after, I'd never seriously considered what the reality would be—and I wasn't talking about the wicked id impulsive part.

Kelt was an exceptionally nice guy, the kind of guy who wouldn't be content with just a physical relationship, the kind of guy who wanted a lot more. "More" meaning something along the lines of a soul mate to grow old with. And when I was being honest with myself, that's what I wanted, too. Trouble was, I was finding it hard (not to mention a little scary) to open myself up like that. I'd never been terribly adept at it in the first place and, in recent years, there hadn't been anybody to bother trying it on. Megan kept telling me that it's like riding a bike, but I never graduated past tricycles, so I wasn't reassured.

But the situation with June had me tied up in a knot more complex than anything Gordius could have devised. And now this! I bit my lip. It was getting too big for me. Were my suspicions justified? Or was I insane? Loner I may be, but it's possible I needed somebody else's opinion.

I looked at Kelt waiting patiently, kindly. I couldn't find a better somebody else even if I held a contest.

I gathered up my cowering courage and smiled weakly. "You're right, Kelt," I admitted. "A few things have been bugging me. They have to do with June, and what you just told me has made it twenty times worse. I'm sorry I didn't confide in you before but June—" I broke off, hearing footsteps coming down the stairs. The sounds of people up and stirring had been filtering down for a while now.

"We don't have time to go into it now," I told him, unsure even in my own mind if I was chickening out or not. "But I promise I'll tell you tonight."

I had a nasty feeling that Kelt could see right through me, but he smiled back, gave me a pat on the shoulder, and let himself out of my room.

Chapter 32

THOUGH THE WEATHERMAN HAD PROMISED sun and heat, it was a cool drizzly morning by the time I finally heaved myself and my assorted casts out of bed again. I kissed Guido behind his ear and scratched him under the chin, but he just cracked an eye open, grunted, and went back to his nap. At least his leg wasn't preventing him from sleeping. Dr. Kimmins had said that he should get lots of rest. It wasn't often that the thing you enjoyed the most was also the best thing for you. Not to mention the thing you did best.

I lingered over breakfast but the damp had seeped into my leg and it throbbed with a dull ache, making me irritable and snappy. Or maybe I was short-tempered because somebody had shot my cat. Or maybe it was because I suspected my best friend's mother of murder.

Whatever the reason for my mood, my leg did hurt, so I downed some painkillers and poured myself another cup of coffee. By this time, June had moved Guido to a well-padded basket by the window. He looked comfortable and was watching a fat robin test the ground for worms. I kissed the top of his head. June seemed quiet this morning, and I could guess why. I looked for a trace of her night-time activities on her face, but apart from a couple of bags under her eyes, she didn't appear any different from the June I'd known for the last four years.

What had she been doing lurking in front of the DeSantis

house last night? And what would she have done if that car hadn't driven by? As the questions flew and buzzed and stung my mind, I sat, hand propping my chin up. I found myself looking at her hands, strong from years of pounding dough, digging gardens, and running a household by herself. Was June strong enough to murder someone? Did she hate enough to kill?

That morning I finally admitted to myself that I did need to share my suspicions with someone. If only to get another opinion. If only to see if I was crazy. Well, Kelt had already volunteered a sympathetic ear. And the truth was, even the Cat that Walked by Himself had come out of the Wild Woods to sit by the fire every once in a while. Perhaps it was time I learned to trust somebody besides myself.

"...so when you told me where she went last night, everything just seemed to fall into place," I finished miserably.

Kelt and I sat on a park bench a few blocks from June's place. The weatherman had prophesied correctly and the clouds had scooted off earlier that afternoon, giving way to blue skies and sunshine and a lovely evening that was completely at odds with my spirits. Kelt and I—ostensibly out for ice cream—had spent the last forty minutes talking about June. I thought it would help to talk about it. I thought I would feel better. No such luck. I felt as though I'd just betrayed something very dear and very special, and the words were dusty spider webs in my mouth.

It didn't help that Kelt now shared my misgivings. I had hoped that he'd leap to his feet and tell me I was crazy, or that he'd come up with some innocent explanation for it all. But when I told him about Eddie and Grant, his expression darkened. When I told him about June's first nocturnal stroll, he turned positively black.

"Why didn't you tell me this before?" he asked when I'd finally run down.

I lifted one shoulder in a half-hearted shrug. "How could I?

I've told you what she means to me. I was ashamed to even think it. Kelt, you've been living in June's house for over a week now. You can see for yourself what she's like. Generous, kind, caring. I kept thinking I was insane even to consider it."

He put his arm around me. "What changed your mind?"

I leaned against his shoulder, needing his warmth. "It was everything all added together," I told him. "And after what you saw the other night. . . ." I trailed off.

Kelt waited for a moment. "You were wondering if she was planning to go after Grant DeSantis, too," he finished finally.

I nodded, unable to speak.

We sat in silence for a while, Kelt's arm rested lightly around my shoulder. It helped a little, I suppose, but not nearly enough. I had no idea what to do next. I couldn't—wouldn't—go to Gary with what were, after all, only suspicions.

"We need more proof," Kelt said finally, his thoughts obviously steaming down the same piece of track as my own.

"Any suggestions?"

"Well, the knife that was used to murder Melanie DeSantis would do," he said practically, "Or bloody clothes, but I doubt we'd find either. A short drive and a quick toss into one of the sloughs around here would have taken care of them."

I shivered a bit and huddled closer to him. A knife? Bloody clothes? Of June's?

"Pesticides would probably be the easier thing to go after," Kelt continued.

"Pesticides?"

"Yes, don't forget Richard DeSantis was killed by a massive dose of heptachlor. It's not usually something one has lying around."

"Are you suggesting we search June's house for heptachlor?"

"It might not confirm the suspicions we have about her, but it would certainly strengthen them. She's completely against chemical pesticides. . . ."

"So if she's got some hanging around her house. . . ."

"You'd have to wonder why."

I thought it over for a while, supremely uncomfortable with the idea. It seemed like such an invasion of June's privacy, but I couldn't see another way to handle this. I wasn't about to turn her over to the police, based on some unsubstantiated suspicions.

"I can look tomorrow morning," I said finally, my voice sounding as unhappy as my spirit. I looked up at Kelt. "I don't feel very good about this."

He hugged me hard. "I know. Me either. Just be careful, Robyn. I know how you feel about June. Don't do anything stupid because of it."

The hug was very nice, but I was still far, far from happy.

And when we got back to June's and Lisa told me that Megan had phoned and would I phone her back, I felt even worse. Right now Megan was the last person I wanted to talk to. I forced myself to call her anyway. It was the least I could do.

"Hey, Meggie," I tried to inject a note of cheeriness in my voice. I don't think I was successful, but Megan didn't appear to notice.

"Robyn! What's going on up there?"

"What do you mean?" I asked evasively, the guilt rising up like burning acid in my throat.

"I hear you've gone and jumped Kelt."

Oh, that. I breathed a silent sight of relief. Now *that* I could talk to her about.

"Who have you been talking to?" I asked, drawing it out.

"Is it true?"

"Well, it was more like he jumped—"

"You?" She squeaked. "He finally jumped you?"

"Ah, no. He jumped Randy Hughes."

"What? What are you talking about?"

"He had a little help from me. Kelt, that is. And, believe me, it's not nearly as exciting as you think. I was going to call you tonight." It was a little lie, but I couldn't really explain why thoughts of Kelt had been relegated to the back seat, while other, distinctly less pleasant, thoughts had taken over the steering wheel.

I filled Megan in about myself, Kelt, and Randy with suitably descriptive details. Megan almost choked with laughter.

"Only you," she gasped. "Only you would do something like that."

"I don't know why you're laughing so hard," I complained. "I've probably ruined my love life—not that it was anything to brag about in the first place."

"I'm sorry." Megan giggled. "Was Kelt very angry?"

"Uh, yeah. I think you could safely say that. He seems to have forgiven me now, but he still flinches every time I get too close."

Megan giggled again. "How's Ran?"

"Very understanding, thank all the gods. Especially after I brought him a peace offering of your mom's cinnamon buns. He was asking about you."

"That's nice." Megan paused for a long moment and when she spoke again, it was clear her mind was not on Randy Hughes.

"Have . . . have you met Matt yet?" she asked.

The real reason for this conversation.

"Yeah, Meggie. I have."

"And?"

I sighed. "And, I'm not sure. He loves your mum, that's pretty obvious."

"But?"

"But, well, he seems a bit unscrupulous. He weaseled some information out of Lisa and wrote an article for the *Edmonton Journal* about sabotage at the site. Ben was . . . not happy."

She pounced on it. "So you *do* think there's something wrong with him!"

"I don't know if I'd say that," I cautioned her. "He was only doing his job. And he doesn't know us from a hole in the ground, so why should he care about betraying confidences?"

"You'd think the fact that you're my best friend might have twigged something."

"Well, as I said, I'm not sure how I feel about him. He's very intelligent, funny, good-looking. And he *does* seem quite devoted to your mum. Apart from the incident with Lisa, I think he's probably okay."

"I guess that's something." But from the tone of her voice, she didn't think it was much.

The line was quiet for a moment.

"Hey, I saw Phil the other day," I said into the silence. "He sends a hug."

I proceeded to fill up my end of the conversation with snippets of news about Megan's hometown friends, carefully downplaying any information about murders and sleuthing. In turn, Megan told me about the cases she was helping with, her cat, The Bob, who had discovered the joys of mousing (and the even greater joys of leaving tiny decapitated bodies on the back step for Megan to step on), and Arif, who had taken Megan out for a movie and falafel.

I didn't mention Guido's injury, and I'd already asked June to keep it quiet. Megan had a heart of marshmallow when it came to animals. More than once, I'd seen her dissolve into tears while watching nature documentaries. She could read or hear about people killing or injuring other people. It bothered her, but she could handle it. But when it came to animals being injured, my hard-nosed lawyer friend fell to pieces. The news about Guido was better given in person, preferably with the cat himself purring beside her.

I listened to her news with half an ear, interjecting "uh huh"s and "you're kidding"s in the appropriate places. All I could think of was what Megan would say to me when she found out what else I'd been up to. What kind of person rummages through someone else's belongings. What kind of person does that to somebody they love?

I'd find out the next day.

CHAPTER 33

AND SO I FOUND MYSELF STANDING in the middle of June's basement, searching for evidence of her guilt. Kelt had wanted to stay behind and help, but there were only four more days scheduled at the site, and there was still a lot of work to be done. Besides, if someone had to invade June's privacy, I wanted it to be me.

I started at the bottom. And not because I felt I belonged there (although I did), but because my father had always kept any toxic compounds stored on shelves in the dark, cool air of our basement. It seemed logical that others would do the same.

I poked and peered and shoved boxes around as best I could with my left arm, but the only items of interest I saw were neatly stacked jars of jewel-colored pickled beets, garlic dills, and saskatoon berry preserves. Interesting to my stomach, which had been too roiled up to do much justice to breakfast, but meaningless in terms of murder and pesticides. June's basement was as tidy (and as pesticide-free) as one could wish. I took heart from the fact and shifted my search upstairs.

Some of the narrow staircases were pretty hard to negotiate, and it took me most of the morning to get through the house and the garden shed. By the time I reached the attic, I was feeling encouraged. Maybe we had this all wrong. Maybe June was innocent. Maybe. . . .

I opened the door of the attic and stopped short.

"Ye gods!" I exclaimed softly. "It's going to take me all day to get through this stuff!"

It has always been a theory of mine that even the tidiest of people need at least one place in which to cut loose. I, for example, had my desk, and my kitchen, and my living room sometimes, and . . . well, okay, I never claimed to be tidy. But June was; her house was always immaculate. And now I knew why.

A servant's living space in days long past, June's attic was a long, narrow room with sloped ceilings and a single, tiny, inadequate window. But it was what was in the attic that prompted my exclamation. There were boxes and small trunks dumped in unstable-looking piles; old lamps, their fraying cords draped over dusty shades; and stacks of wire racks and rods whose purpose I could only guess at.

In the far corner, an antique dressmaker's mannequin stood naked with a definite list to one side. Hundreds of old magazines, once piled neatly on a shelf, had slid and spilled across each other and down onto the floor below. Books, their spines dry and cracked, had been crammed onto the remaining shelves or perched on sundry boxes and trunks. Had I been a child, the possibilities of such a room would have made my eyes sparkle. As an adult, looking for evidence of murder, it made me want to cry in frustration. How the hell was I going to get through this stuff before June arrived home for lunch?

There are times in my life when it seems as though the gods are laughing at me, times when they appear to be going out of their way to make my life more difficult. And then, every once in a while, something goes right. Maybe the gods decided I'd had enough for a while. Maybe they figured I needed a break (on the other hand, maybe *they* needed a break and were kicking back in some divine lunchroom, sucking back mugs of ambrosia). At any rate, as I stood there contemplating the mess in the attic, the phone rang.

I waited for the answering machine to pick it up, then swore when I remembered I hadn't turned it on today. I was going to let it ring and just do the *69 thing afterwards (I had enough on my mind without dealing with hang-up calls), but it rang so insistently I finally slid down the stairs on my butt and answered it. Good thing, too. It was June.

"Robyn, you sound out of breath."

"Uh, I was just out on the porch," I lied quickly, feeling like a slime mold.

"Sorry to make you run like that, but something's come up and I'll have to be here all afternoon. I'm sorry. We'll have to go out to Beaverhill another day."

"That's okay, June," I said, trying not to sound relieved. I'd forgotten that we were supposed to go birding this afternoon. "I'll be fine on my own for the afternoon."

"Have you got a book to read or something?"

"Or something." I forced an rather unconvincing yawn. "I might just have a nap."

June chuckled tiredly. "Lucky you."

"Uh, do you want me to do anything about dinner?" I asked, suddenly smacked upside the head with a strong sense of conscience.

"If you could pop the lasagnas in the oven at about 4:30, that would be wonderful," June said. "Matt's taking me out for dinner and a movie tonight, so I'm afraid you're all on your own. In fact, I'll probably head out straight from the office if you don't mind being abandoned."

"I'll be fine," I told her again. "I can throw a dinner together for everybody."

"I wouldn't do that to you," June answered. The "or to them" was unspoken. June was all too familiar with my lack of culinary skills (and all too polite to mention it). "Everything's pretty much ready. There're a couple of baguettes on the counter and a caesar salad in the fridge. All you have to do is put the dressing on it. I didn't have a chance to get anything made for dessert, though. . . ."

"June, your lasagna is plenty. Even better than Stromboli's. I'm sure we'll manage without dessert."

"High praise indeed!" June laughed again.

"Well, you have a good time tonight," I told her, meaning it. "And don't worry about us—I'll send them all out for ice cream if they start whining for dessert."

June chuckled and I rang off. With June away for the afternoon and out for the evening, I'd have plenty of time to go through the junk in her attic. Plenty of time to search for evidence of her guilt. I didn't have to wonder why that didn't make me feel better.

As it turned out, I didn't need that much time. The attic was, as attics usually are, very dusty. All I had to do, I realized when I got back upstairs, was look in any boxes or trunks that were free of dust. Those would be the ones that had been opened recently. I got to work.

There were several dust-free boxes that were also light enough for me to manage with one arm, but where I half-expected to find pesticides or some other evidence for the abrupt ending of a life, what I found instead were the vestiges of a life that might have been.

Yellowed photos, their edges curling, showing Eddie with his arm around June, Eddie leaning against a picnic table and laughing, Eddie swinging a very young Megan over his head. There were programs from local plays, their print faded now; a well-worn handknit sweater the color of ripe cranberries; and pressed between the pages of an old book there were dried flowers. Roses I think. At one time white, now aged and yellowed like the photos of times long past.

As I stood there surrounded by June's memories, I recalled the Far Side cartoon in which an amoeba has just been accused of being the lowest life-form on earth—and I realized that Gary Larson had been wrong. There was a life-form that was even lower than a protozoa, and the next time I looked in a mirror, I'd be seeing it.

CHAPTER 34

THERE WASN'T ANY HEPTACHLOR in June's house. Ditto for bloodied clothes or suspicious-looking knives. I made very sure of it. Yes, she had been up in the attic recently, but not for any criminal purpose. It was understandable, I realized, given her budding relationship with Matt, that she might want to revisit her past. And perhaps lay it to rest.

But as I carefully boxed everything back up the way I'd found it and closed the attic door with an audible click, the miserable little voice inside my head wanted to know if, in doing so, June had laid anything—or anybody—else to rest.

Already feeling like a heel, I was about to have strong words with the little voice, when I remembered the shed. Not the shed in June's backyard. No, the one I was remembering was behind the house that Matt was renting. Old Mrs. Kershaw's house.

According to Matt there were all sorts of things stored in the Kershaws' shed. Gross things. Toxic things. And June had been asked by the Kershaw family to take care of the house until they could deal with it.

"So what exactly is in the shed?" Kelt voiced the question for me now.

I'd pulled him into my room as soon as he'd returned. Kelt had taken one look at my expression and folded me gently into his arms. I told him about my day.

"I don't know and I feel horrible, Kelt," I told him earnestly.

"I've got a lot of questions about this whole pesticide thing."

"Like?"

"Like I can't see June stockpiling the stuff. How was she to know that Grant DeSantis would come back to Holbrook one day? Did she have a batch of the stuff on hand just in case? I just don't see it."

"Maybe she found some sitting in that woman's shed, Mrs.... ?"

"Kershaw."

"Yeah, maybe Mrs. Kershaw had some old heptachlor lying around in that shed. Didn't you tell me that her relatives asked June to rent out the place?"

I nodded.

"Well, June could have gone over to check the place out, maybe clean it up a bit. And in the process she found the heptachlor."

I frowned and shook my head slowly. "I don't know about that either, Kelt. Megan told me about a big toxic waste drive they had seven or eight years ago. They were especially asking people to bring in old stashes of chlordane and heptachlor. She remembered because everybody was making such a big deal about it. I guess they figured people had it sitting around from when the plant was operating."

"So maybe she forgot to bring it in," Kelt said with a shrug. "It happens. Hell, I don't even know what's in my fridge half the time, let alone my storage room. Maybe Mrs. Kershaw didn't remember it was in there."

"But even if that were true, where did this heptachlor come from? Originally, I mean."

"The old plant," he answered promptly.

"Maybe," I nodded. "But Richard DeSantis died from ingesting heptachlor, not heptachlor—"

"Epoxide," Kelt finished, making the connection for himself.

"Exactly. If heptachlor had been sitting around for decades, how much degradation would have taken place? If the stuff that killed Richard came from the old plant, then why hadn't it broken down?"

Kelt thought about it for a moment. "Didn't Lisa say that heptachlor is pretty stable?"

"Yeah, but over that length of time? And if it was stored in a shed or even one of these old basements, it would've been exposed to extreme temperatures."

"Which would help break it down," Kelt mused. "So why was Richard killed with heptachlor and not heptachlor epoxide?"

"My question exactly."

"Maybe it was a new batch?"

"If so, then where would June or old Mrs. Kershaw have gotten something like that? It's been banned for years now. You can't just pick it up at your local garden center."

I paused for a moment and took a deep breath, trying to calm myself down. "It's possible he was killed with technical heptachlor," I told Kelt. "In its pure form it doesn't have much of an odor, so that would make the most sense—but there's nothing on the Internet about whether technical heptachlor degrades or not. And I don't know who I can ask about it. If I ask Lisa, she'll want to know why. If I ask Ben, he's liable to send me back to Calgary on the next Greyhound."

Kelt looked troubled. "I see what you mean," he said finally. "But this might be a non-issue if there's nothing in the shed. Maybe we should put all our questions on hold until I see what's out there."

"You're going to look in the shed tonight?"

Kelt nodded. "You said that June and Matt were out for the evening. Everybody else was talking about going to a movie. They're re-running *Aliens*. I've already seen it a bazillion times so I'll beg off."

"So will I," I decided on the spot. "I want to hear about what you find as soon as possible."

We had to put up with several knowing glances from Lisa and Nalini, but Ben and Cam seemed oblivious to the undertones. They all went off cheerfully discussing unstoppable aliens with acid blood and what would happen if said aliens ever got to earth. By the time they faded out of earshot, they were deep into a discussion of whether the planet would be better off with alien instead of human inhabitants. Two guesses who started that debate.

I'd jumped at my fair share of aliens exploding through chests, and covered my eyes as enough monsters ripped apart bodies, but I was more scared watching Kelt slink off into the twilight than I was watching any Hollywood gore.

I'd already bitten my nails to the quick, so I rummaged around in my knapsack, found a pack of gum, and started in on that. It was going to be a long hour. As it turned out, I didn't have to wait that long for something to happen.

Twenty minutes after Kelt left, the phone rang. Half expecting it to be the police calling to say they'd picked up a burglar at Matt's house, I answered tentatively. It was the police but they weren't calling about Kelt.

"Robyn. Gary Ross here."

"Hey, Gary," I gulped, thankful he didn't have a Vulcan's ability to mind-meld.

"Is Ben Woodrow there? I've got some news for him."

"No, I'm sorry, he's gone off to a flick. Do you want me to pass him a message?"

"Yes, if you wouldn't mind," Gary said. "Tell him we've got a suspect in custody. It looks as if he might be the one who's been sabotaging your site."

"You found the saboteur?"

"We think so."

"That's great. How did you find him?"

"We got prints from one of the well pipes that was cut. And now we've got a match."

"He left *prints*? Don't they teach them about that sort of thing in Crimes 101?"

"You'd be surprised how stupid some criminals are." He snorted. "You know, sometimes they come to the jail to visit their friends. And when they sign in, they'll use their real names even though there's an outstanding warrant on them."

"Oh. I guess they get to have a nice long visit, then."

"And we're always glad to oblige. Look, Robyn. We've got this man in custody now but the problem is, he doesn't seem to know anything about what's been going on at June's place."

"He didn't shoot my cat?"

"Doesn't look like it. We may be dealing with something—and somebody else."

I digested this for a minute.

"Who's your suspect?" I asked. "It's not Bert Pine, is it?"

"*Bert?*" Gary was incredulous. "Why would you think— No, wait, I don't want to know. It's not Bert Pine, but that's all I can tell you right now. I just wanted to warn you to keep being careful. If our fellow here didn't shoot out that window, then whoever did is still about. Don't take any chances."

"I won't," I told him. "Thanks for calling."

I hung up the phone and unwrapped another piece of gum. The saboteur had been caught. Ben would be happy to hear that news. I was relieved for my colleagues' sake, glad they could relax their vigilance a bit. But if the saboteur hadn't shot Guido, then who had? And why? I looked at my watch. And where the hell was Kelt? How long did it take to check a shed?

I sat down, pushed myself up, and sat down again. I picked up the book I was reading, but couldn't even get through one paragraph. I tossed it back on the coffee table and snagged one of June's gardening magazines instead. But I really didn't give a rat's ass about hybrid roses at the moment, so I put it back on the coffee table, too. I poked through a pile of magazines until I found the old APEGGA journal buried under *Fine Cooking*. Maybe I could distract myself with something work-related.

I flipped through the journal's pages, not really paying much attention to it. More concerned with the audible *tick tick* of June's living room clock. Kelt had been gone for over thirty-five minutes now. I tapped my fingers on my cast, realized what I was doing, and made myself stop. I turned the last page of the journal.

IN MEMORIUM.

The words were spelled out in old-fashioned gothic type. Underneath was the name Luke Lieski. So. Rocky's friend Luke had died after all.

I skimmed the page. The accompanying article was brief, most of it details of the accident which killed him and how it could have been avoided. There were a few sentences describing him as a hard worker, cheerful, and always willing to help out a buddy. He grew up in Ontario, and loved dogs and country music. The paragraph concluded with the standard phrases, "Luke will be sadly missed by mother Kathleen, father Paul, and twin brother Matthew."

I raised my eyes and stared blindly out the living room window.

Twin brother Matthew.

Matthew Lieski.

Matt Lieski.

Matt Lees.

And the bottom dropped out of my world.

CHAPTER 35

I WAS STILL GAPING LIKE A ZOMBIE when the second-last person I wanted to see walked in the front door.

"What's wrong with you?" June demanded, peering at my face in the dim hall light.

"What are you doing here?" I asked at the same time. "I thought you were on a date."

"I was tired," she explained, "and I didn't feel like seeing an alien movie so. . . ."

Then it hit me like a diving peregrine.

"Where's Matt?"

"Matt?"

"Yes, June, where's Matt? I need to know."

"He's probably gone home. Robyn, what's wrong?"

"June," I reached out and laid my hand gently on her shoulder, "he's the one. Matt is the murderer."

"*What?*"

"I don't have time to explain it now," I said, already halfway out the door. "Phone the cops. Tell them to get over to Matt's house!"

"But—"

"I've got to go, June. Kelt's there!"

I hobbled down the front steps and fell onto the seat of Vivian's scooter. It wasn't fast, but it was a hell of a lot faster than I could clock on foot. The trip seemed to take forever.

This whole situation had been about the old pesticide plant in the first place. I'd been on the right track, but I'd had the wrong train. This hadn't been about Eddie at all. Eddie hadn't been the only one to die because of conditions at the plant. I knew that. I slammed my cast down on the handlebars. I'd known it for years. But I hadn't known that one of them had been Matthew Lees's twin brother. Nobody had.

Until now. Now when everything finally seemed to fit. Rocky's "ghost," which wasn't a ghost at all. The pile of cameras in Matt's kitchen. There had been a Polaroid in that pile, and I hadn't given it a second thought—hell, I hadn't even given it a first thought. I'd just assumed that it was something he used for his work. And Matt "finding" the photos of the gnome. How convenient. Convenient, too, that we all, including Matt, handled them and got our fingerprints all over them. So that any prints of his would be disregarded.

And what about Matt himself? It never occurred to me to delve into the reason he'd come to Holbrook, of all places. A possible toxic-waste treatment facility wasn't that big a story, not internationally speaking—and not when compared to the NAFTA pesticide commission story he was supposed to be working on. The NAFTA pesticide commission. Of course! Meggie had told me that Matt had been down to Mexico recently to cover that story. And Mexico, in addition to hosting meetings of the commission, also boasted the last chlordane and heptachlor manufacturing plant in the world. Matt hadn't needed to find an old stash of heptachlor. He'd had access to a nice fresh batch of it in Mexico.

Bert Pine told us that Grant DeSantis had spent the last few decades wreaking environmental havoc all over the Third World. And there was another bit of evidence if I needed any. Matt said that he'd only recently found out about DeSantis's activities in Mexico. But according to Bert, Matt had told *him* about it months ago. Matt must have been following DeSantis's career for years, waiting for the right moment, the right place to carry out his revenge. And where better than in Holbrook? Where his twin brother had met his death? The idea had a certain appropriateness to it that would appeal to someone like Matt.

"Come on, dammit!" I urged my little scooter. It didn't help. I wished earnestly for one of the Harleys I'd seen the other night. "Come on, little piglet," I gritted my teeth in frustration. "Don't you want to be a hog someday?"

Just as I uttered the words, I heard a deep rumble. I looked down at the scooter in surprise. Had ever-so-fickle gods finally decided to take action? But the sounds were coming, not from under me, but over to the right? No . . . behind me! The rumbling grew louder and suddenly I was engulfed by it.

The bikers descended on my sorry scooter like a murder of crows. But instead of cawing and screaming, they laughed, gunned their engines, and honked their horns in a blast of camaraderie.

"Hey, guys!" I yelled with the half-formed idea of enlisting their help.

But the growling bikes easily overpowered my voice. I twisted my neck, trying to catch somebody's eye. If I could just get one of them to come with me. . . .

No such luck. They were too intent on their fun. Hooting and waving, they rode in circles around me, scraggly hair whipping behind them. A few seconds later, they left me choking on their dust with the echo of their laughter in my ears. I swore under my breath. The gods had a twisted sense of humor.

Or not, I realized as I pulled up to Matt's house.

The noise of the passing bikers had masked the sounds of my arrival. I shut the motor off and coasted to a stop in front of the fence. I held my breath and listened. Silence. I waited another few seconds before I let myself breathe again. The gate was ajar, so I eased my crutches off slowly and quietly, and limped over to push it open.

Scrrreeek!

I froze, unable to crouch down because of my cast. I waited for a long moment, but the night remained still. I took a deep breath and ducked through the gate.

The yard was quiet. It was just early dusk, but not even the flute-like call of a thrush broke the stillness. The front porch light was out and the living room was dark. Maybe Matt hadn't gone home. Maybe he'd decided to go see *Aliens*. Maybe . . . not. There was his car, parked on the far side of the fence. Over by the shed.

I limped across the lawn to the house. It was quiet, too, I noted. I kept to the shadows and crept closer. I prayed to the gods that Matt wouldn't look outside.

Then, I heard a sound. Not too loud. Like a grunt, or maybe some kind of animal. A dog in the garbage? Not daring to breathe, I slipped around the corner of the house.

The door to the shed was open, the doorway a black emptiness. A few meters away, Kelt lay unmoving, sprawled awkwardly half on the gravel driveway, half on the lawn. My first instinct was to rush over, but before I could take a single step, I saw it. A darkness under his head. A inky puddle that stained the gravel beneath him. And it was spreading.

I hugged the shadows closer, willing my body to become one with them, and pressing myself closer to the house and deeper into the overgrown rose bushes. I didn't even feel the thorns.

There was a gap in the kitchen window blinds. Stretching up, I peered through and saw Matt buttoning up his shirt. He looked normal, his expression was calm, his actions unhurried. Like someone changing their clothes after being out. I yanked my head down before he spotted me. Then I looked back at Kelt. But was Matt responsible for this? Had he hurt Kelt? Maybe Kelt had tripped in the darkness. I lifted my face to the window again.

Matt was busy at the sink now. Washing dishes? He had rubber gloves on. No.

He was mixing something.

I swore under my breath.

Dropping my crutches in the rose bush, I half-ran, half-limped over to where Kelt lay, still motionless.

"Kelt!" I hissed. "Come on, you've got to get up!"

No response.

I grabbed the sleeve of his jacket and shook him. Still nothing.

"*Shit, shit, shit,*" I swore again. I'd never manage to get him away by myself. Not with these damn casts on me. But maybe . . . I looked back at the rose bush. If I could get Kelt in there, perhaps Matt would think he'd regained consciousness and taken off. Maybe he wouldn't bother checking around. It was worth a try.

I bent over and, with my single good arm, I took a firm grip on Kelt's jacket. I managed to drag him a few inches, but goddamit, it was slow and—

Click.

The back porch light came on and with a sinking feeling I suddenly knew how a deer feels when it's caught in a car's headlights.

Good thing I wasn't a deer.

I dropped Kelt and lurched back into the rose bushes. The kitchen door opened and Matt stepped out. I scrunched myself deeper into the thorns.

He had a blanket draped over his arm and he was carrying a water bottle. I didn't need two guesses to figure out what was in it. And any lingering doubts I might have had about him fluttered away when I heard him whistling. It was a merry little tune, sprightly and happy. The sort of thing you might whistle when you're out gardening on a day off. And when I heard Matt whistle like that and saw him casually flip Kelt over onto the blanket and start rolling, I didn't need to see anything else because all I saw was red.

"You bastard!" I gritted and stepped out from the shadows.

He jumped and swung around, but before he had a chance to do more than look at me, I brought my right arm up and crashed the cast down on his head. He dropped like a stone.

About *damn* time that cast came in handy.

I didn't even bother checking Matt. I knew I'd hit him pretty hard. I'd cracked the plaster on my cast. Instead I half crouched, half fell by Kelt's side. He *had* to be okay!

"Are you all right?" I demanded roughly. Urgently.

He groaned and the fist gripping my heart loosened a little.

"Gods, Kelt," I murmured, starting to shake as reaction set in.

He looked up at me a little cross-eyed and gave me a wobbly smile. "Figures my guardian angel has crutches," he said before his eyes rolled up in his head and he passed out.

Chapter 36

JUNE GOT THERE A FEW MINUTES LATER, but by then I had myself under control. She ran up, distressed and out of breath, and stopped dead as her eyes took in the scene.

"Did you phone the RCMP?" I asked.

Her eyes were huge in her face. "No . . . I . . . I didn't know. . . . Robyn, what happened?"

"He tried to kill Kelt," I said dully. "Don't touch that water bottle."

She stared at it as if it were poisonous. And so it was.

"But—"

Just then Matt groaned. June sank to her knees beside him.

"Matt," she murmured brokenly. "What did . . . ? Why?"

I closed my eyes at the pain in her voice.

"June," he groaned and clutched his head.

"Why?" she asked again.

"Why?" He echoed. "Because he killed my brother. Grant DeSantis killed my brother. Can't you understand that, June?"

"I don't understand anything. What brother?"

"Luke. My twin brother Luke. They said it was an accident, but it was no accident. He knew the valve wasn't safe. He didn't care! All he cared about was money. He didn't care that Luke got sick. He didn't care that the poisons in Luke's body exceeded the maximum residue levels by millions of parts—"

"Matt—"

"He didn't watch his brother—his twin!—die vomiting and convulsing while the toxins destroyed his central nervous system. He didn't care, June!"

"I'm so sorry about your brother, Matt. I... I know what you've gone through—"

"How can you know?" He asked bitterly. "Just because your husband died? What's a husband compared to a twin? I was part of something," he choked. "One half of something wonderful. And Grant DeSantis took it away from me for money. For *money!*"

"But killing people? What did that solve, Matt? Why Richard? Why Melanie?"

Matt looked at June in pity. "Why them?" he repeated. "Luke died a month after Norsicol sent him home. He was covered in rashes, vomiting, convulsing, crying. Nobody could do a thing for him except watch him die. My mother never got over that. She died of a broken heart two months later. And my father spent the rest of his days in a mental hospital. He died screaming. He didn't even know who I was. I swore I would make DeSantis pay for that.

"Why them? Because killing Grant DeSantis would have been too easy. I wanted him to suffer the way my father suffered. To lose a son and then a wife."

"And the old plant? Did you try to sabotage the project, too? Was it you who shot at us? Shot at *Robyn*?"

He looked at her then, puzzled. "I never shot at anybody," he said. "What do I care about that project? It was Grant DeSantis I was after. I've been waiting for him for over twenty years. He destroyed my family. It was only just that I destroy his."

Bert Pine said that Grant DeSantis had devastated families. He said that one day it was bound to come back to haunt him. And so it had, in a way DeSantis had probably never dreamed of, but was in the end poetic justice. Just as Bert had predicted.

With some difficulty, I hoisted myself up from Kelt's side and limped to the house. Matt didn't seem inclined to go anywhere. Apparently he'd done what he had to do and didn't much care what happened to him now. There was a phone in the kitchen. I punched in the number, said my piece, and went back outside to wait. June was still slumped beside Matt when I heard the sirens coming.

I'd returned to my vigil beside Kelt, but when the paramedics arrived on the scene I had been politely but firmly pushed away. Off to one side, several RCMP officers surrounded Matt. As far as I could tell, he wasn't trying to deny anything.

I hobbled awkwardly across the grass and collapsed in an old lawn chair. My leg ached with a vengeance and my arm gave a tight twinge everytime I moved it. A junior paramedic descended on me. Now that the excitement was over, I realized that I'd been waiting for Matt in the middle of a wild rose bush. My body felt like a hundred sharp-clawed cats had scampered over me and whatever the hell the paramedic was trying to dab on me was making it worse.

"I'm okay," I said irritably, trying to push the gauze away from me.

He gave up, and handed a bottle and a pad of gauze to June. "Here, you see what you can do with her."

June accepted the bottle and cloth, and knelt in front of me.

June.

I'd been so relieved to find Kelt alive and more or less in one piece that I hadn't truly considered what all this would mean to her.

"June, I'm so sorry," I blurted out, forgetting to defend myself against the gauze. "I didn't even . . . aaaahh!"

"Shhh," she cut me off and dabbed expertly at the cuts and scrapes on my cheek. "Don't worry about that now, Robyn. Everything will be okay."

I should have been the one to say that. My eyes filled with tears. She deserved so much better than this. I've always known the gods could be a capricious bunch, but in this moment, looking at June's kind face etched deeply with the knowledge of betrayal, I hated them.

CHAPTER 37

IT WAS TESTAMENT TO JUNE'S RESILIENCE and spirit that she didn't feel the same. I said as much to Kelt, who lay under the feather quilt on his bed at June's Bed & Breakfast, nursing assorted lumps and bumps and a rather nasty concussion. Guido the cat had nuzzled his way under the covers to form a large purring lump on Kelt's chest.

"Poor June," Kelt let out his breath in a sigh.

I nodded my agreement.

"I guess your friend Rocky wasn't hallucinating after all."

I shook my head. "No, he recognized Matt all right, but he never knew Luke had a twin. I'm not sure he understands it even now."

Rocky was, in fact, quite confused about the whole situation. Even after Sue Barbeau tried to explain it to him, he remained convinced that Matt was Luke. At least he didn't think Matt was a ghost any more.

"So your theory about the gnomes was right. An eye for an eye. . . ."

"A wife for a wife, a son for a son." I plucked at my broken cast absently. I'd have to get the sucker re-plastered soon. At least I hadn't done any more damage to my arm.

"And that's why Matt used heptachlor."

I nodded. "Except when he tried to slip it to Melanie, she smelled it in the coffee and tossed it. I guess the knife was his Plan B."

I paced silently a while longer.

In a situation like this, you expect things to be black and white. Most of the books and movies and television shows I'd read or seen agree on this one basic premise. Guilty or innocent, good or evil, black or white. Never shades of gray. Matt Lees—or Lieski—had murdered innocent people, yet would I—or anybody else—have stayed sane, given the same situation? A brother dying an agonizing death. A mother dead of grief. A father losing himself in the horror of it all. I wanted to think that, under the same circumstances, I could rise above it, could avoid the vengefulness that had destroyed Matt's sanity and left two people dead. But in my heart I wasn't entirely sure I was that strong. Matt's was a very dark shade of gray, but gray nevertheless.

If I couldn't entirely blame him for his motive, I could still damn him for his treatment of June. He'd used her as a source of information and an alibi. It was through June that Matt had discovered Richard DeSantis's love of herons. It was through June that Matt had learned of the heron colony that Richard had discovered. I could just imagine him chatting up Richard, getting him talking about the colony, asking him to show Matt where it was. Never suspecting it would be the last place he'd ever see. And it was through June that Matt had built his alibi for Melanie DeSantis's death.

Not only had Matt gone out of his way to cultivate June's affections, but according to Dana, who'd had it from Gary, Matt had apparently done the same thing with Melanie DeSantis. I'd been shocked when I heard and my heart ached anew for June.

My first thought about the bright purple silk robe in Matt's living room—that June would never have worn such a color—had been dead right, though I'd ignored the feeling because I'd hoped the robe had belonged to June—along with everything its presence in Matt's kitchen meant. I'd been so happy for her it had blinded me to the obvious. Ever since I'd known her, June had always favored dark, understated colors. Melanie DeSantis, on the other hand, had worn bright, even gaudy, shades. Apparently the affair had begun at a conference in Toronto over a year ago, after Grant

DeSantis had all but forced his wife to siphon funds from her company to help pay his liability fines. And Matt had been there, sympathetic, kind, sexy. Melanie hadn't stood a chance.

Howard Miller had discovered the embezzlement, had guessed about the affair. He'd even tried to tell me about it. But who ever listens to worms? You just avoid them on the sidewalk whenever it rains. I should have remembered that worms form the solid base for the pyramid of life. As repulsive as I found him personally, I should have listened to Howard. He'd told me Matt had lied to him.

"Do you think he really cared for June?" Kelt asked the question I'd been asking myself ever since I'd found out about Matt and Melanie.

I flung out my arm angrily. "I don't know, Kelt. He *used* her! From what Gary said, everything Matt did with June seemed to have a single motivation—to kill Melanie DeSantis. The night of her murder, he arranged to meet June and then he arranged to meet Melanie later."

"Why?"

"For an alibi," I told him. "He phoned June up earlier that evening, saying he was lonely for her—if you remember, he hadn't come visiting that night. So June went over to keep him company. But Matt knew she couldn't stay the night because she had guests—us—at the B & B, so he walked her home afterwards. And that was when he scampered off to his little prearranged tryst with Melanie."

"So, how does that give him an alibi?"

"He set Melanie's watch back and then smashed it to make it look as if she'd been killed when he and June were together. Apparently, he was quite proud of his ingenuity." I ground my teeth together. "It doesn't sound like somebody who was in love to me."

And I had wondered why June had gone walking so late that night, thinking she was out for some dark purpose instead of going to see her lover. I sucked in my breath angrily, thinking of how Matt had used her. June would be in for a bad time when the papers got a hold of this.

But if June felt betrayed now, I couldn't imagine what Melanie

DeSantis's last moments had been like. Meeting a man she believed loved her. Laughing, kissing, being offered a cup of coffee. Smelling something strange in it—

"What about the gnomes?" Kelt interrupted my thoughts.

"What?"

"The gnomes. Why did he use them?"

"Who knows?" I curled my lip. "Maybe he wanted the publicity. He admitted to purposefully defacing them. I guess he wanted DeSantis to know it was a retribution thing."

Part of the reason I was so upset was that I couldn't forgive myself. I'd liked the man. Enjoyed talking to him. Admired him. I'd even thought June was a lucky woman for having attracted him. So much for my intuition.

"Hey. You okay?" Kelt interrupted my thoughts.

I blew out my breath in a long sigh. "Yeah," I said dejectedly after a moment.

"Need a hug?"

I quirked one corner of my mouth up. "Yeah," I said again. Cheerier this time.

"Well then, stop limping around and set your butt down here," he said, patting the bed beside him.

I set my butt down there and immediately felt better. Kelt gave good comfort. Was that what he'd been doing with Lisa? Comforting her after Ben's explosion? Maybe.

Hopefully.

"Kelt?" I asked after a long moment.

"Mmmm?"

"Why were you so mad at me after—"

"You shoved me onto your friend Randy?"

"Um, yeah. I felt terrible, you know. I don't know what possessed me—"

"It's all right." He interrupted me, then heaved a sigh like a hurricane. "If anything, I owe you an apology."

"Me?" I was startled enough to lift my head up from his chest. "Why me?"

He patted my head back down. "I really overreacted that night," he said slowly, as if searching for the right words. "I mean, I hadn't planned on jumping the guy—at least I don't think so—but, who knows? It was pretty tense."

"Kelt—"

"And it turned out he'd just taken the damn gnome to Hawaii." He paused and shook his head. "The next day, I felt terrible about chewing you out so badly, but I didn't know how to tell you that. And there you were apologizing all over yourself. I'm really sorry, Robyn. You didn't deserve that."

I was still leaning against him in a semi-hug. Kelt did not seem particularly inclined to move and I sure wasn't going to bring attention to the fact that my shoulder was playing footsies with his shoulder. But after a while, I did pull away. He was starting to nod off. Maybe, while he was in a weakened state....

"*What* did you write on the bottom of my foot?" I demanded, planting my fist firmly on my hip.

His lips twitched and he began laughing.

"Kelt," I said in a reasonable tone of voice, "these casts are very, very heavy. I'll sit on you if you don't tell me."

Hey, I figured it was a win-win scenario.

"Okay, okay." He held up his hands to ward me off.

Rats.

"It was in the nature of an experiment," he explained.

"An experiment? What—"

He held up his hand again. "It says," he paused dramatically, " 'If curiosity killed the cat, what will it do to the Robyn?'"

"What? That's it? *That's* what everybody's been laughing about for the past two weeks?"

He grinned again.

I scowled at him.

"I don't think that's very funny," I said huffily.

Still grinning, he shrugged, then hissed as the movement pulled bruised muscles. "I think curiosity just about killed the Kelt this time around," he groaned.

"Well, despite the peace of mind you cost me with your little experiment, I'm just as glad it didn't."

I stood up then, gave Guido a pat, and tucked the covers around them both. Rat bastard. I'd have to plan my revenge carefully.

"Pleasant dreams," I said and turned out the light.

Though most of my questions had been answered (some rather forcefully), there was still one very loose end.

The man who had been sabotaging the site turned out to be a Larry Bakker. I didn't recognize the name so I didn't make the connection until I saw his picture in the paper. Larry. The jeering farmer at June's protest meeting. The one June had all but kicked out of the group. In retrospect, I wasn't surprised that he'd taken matters into his own hands. But he hadn't been the one harassing me—or the one who had shot my cat. So who did that leave? Sherlock Holmes once said that "when you have eliminated the impossible, whatever remains, no matter how improbable, must be the truth." Mr. Spock said so too. There was only one other probable reason for what had been happening.

When I thought back to each incident, it struck me that I had been alone in the house every time. There had been no further incidents since Guido had been shot, but I hadn't been alone in the house since then, either. Somebody was harassing me. Not June. Not the other Woodrow employees. Me. There was only one person I could think of who would do something like that.

I pulled up to his house later that afternoon. I hoped his mother would be out, but frankly I didn't much care if she was sitting on the front lawn. I'd say what needed to be said regardless of who was listening.

"Robyn!" Howard greeted me with a oily smile.

His eyes dropped immediately to my chest, then blinked in disappointment as they took in the thick, shapeless jacket I'd borrowed from Kelt for the occasion.

"Howard. We need to talk." I didn't waste time on preliminaries.

"Oh, uh, sure," he said hesitantly, sensing perhaps on some level what was coming. "Come in."

He held the door open and I stumped into the house.

"Do you want to sit down?"

"No. What I have to say isn't going to take that long."

He was wary now, looking at me with a wobbly, nervous smile.

"I know what you've been doing," I said.

He jumped guiltily and flushed. His face was shiny with sweat. "I—"

"Don't bother," I said icily. "It's sick, Howard. Harassing somebody like that? It's also against the law. Goddamit! You even shot my cat!" My anger threatened to erupt. I clamped down on it ruthlessly.

"What!" He started again, looking shocked this time. "I never . . . I mean, I didn't mean—"

"I don't give a shit what you meant. You shot my cat, Howard. He bled all over the floor. He's limping around now because of you!"

His fleshy features quivered as his face started to cave in on itself.

"I . . . I'm really sorry," he blubbered. "I didn't mean to hurt your cat. I like cats. I just wanted to scare you a bit. You're so mean to me. All I wanted was to be friends with you."

To be *friends* with me?

"Look, Howard. You're not well. You're never going to have friends if you pull this kind of crap!"

"But I don't know what to do!"

Great. Now I was supposed to be a counsellor.

"Get away from your mother." I gave him the only advice I could think of. The only advice he needed. "Go to school somewhere. Move away. I don't care. Just do something to get away from her."

"But she needs me—"

"She needs counselling, and so do you. Get it. Fast."

He snuffled and wiped his nose messily on his sleeve. Revolted, I looked away.

"Are . . . are you going to press charges?"

"What do you think? Your Soldier of Fortune shit scared the hell out of me. You hurt my cat. What do you think I should do about it?"

Flustered, he hung his head.

"I'm really sorry," he said, his voice small, lacking its customary greasiness.

"You should be," I snapped.

I took a deep breath and held it. He'd hurt Guido, and I wasn't about to forgive him for that. But my sympathy had started to kick in. Howard could be a repulsive human being at times, but he was also emotionally and socially stunted. Was it his fault he'd been twisted by his poisonous mother? I let my breath trickle out slowly, taking most of my anger with it.

"Take my advice," I told Howard in a more kindly tone. "Ditch the Soldier of Fortune crap. Get out of here, get some counselling, and get your *own* life."

CHAPTER 38

WE WENT OUT TO BEAVERHILL LAKE AGAIN, June, Cam, and I. It was good to get out into the fresh air.

The funerals for Richard and Melanie DeSantis had taken place the day before. Though I hadn't known either one, I'd gone for the simple reason that June had asked me to. She wanted to attend, she said, because she'd liked Richard. It didn't take much to guess that there were other, far more complicated reasons besides that one, but I didn't press her and she didn't share any others.

I did wonder if she would express her sympathies to Grant DeSantis. But we went and sat in the back row, and when the minister pronounced his final blessing she nudged me and we slipped out. I wasn't really surprised. Although DeSantis's hunched form was the very image of pathos, I could understand why June couldn't bring herself to speak to him. Her face had looked gray and pinched for the rest of that day. I was hoping that a trip to Beaverhill would bring some color back to her cheeks.

Even in the wake of media attention from both sabotage and murder, plans for the toxic-waste treatment facility forged ahead—at least the remediation part of the project was going forward. Still no word on whether Reisinger would get the requisite approvals to build their new facility. Larry Bakker was also much in the news. It seemed that over the years he'd had numerous gas wells sunk on his land, and his cattle had suffered for them. Reduced milk production, strange behavior, neurological damage. The thought of a toxic-waste treatment facility had been the straw that broke his back. He'd apologized to Ben and, oddly enough, to Reisinger as well. The company was currently re-evaluating the situation.

The question of whether the waste facility would go ahead or not still loomed, but for the time being, Beaverhill Lake was safe and things like toxic waste seemed far away. The sky blushed a deep rose, and the breeze off the lake was soft and warm. There were ducks of every imaginable kind, loud flocks of geese, and a cheeky bobolink perched on the barbed wire fence to our right. A string of trumpeter swans made their stately way across the lake, and we stood in the blind on the shore and watched them.

"It's so beautiful out here," Cam said.

June smiled gently—the first smile I'd seen on her face since Matt had been arrested. "I love it," she said simply, and I wondered if the wetlands were again working their healing magic on her. I hoped so.

"I bet fall migration is something to see," Cam said.

June turned to him. "It's wonderful," she said.

"Is the bed and breakfast all booked up for fall?"

Now it was my turn to grin, though I hid it behind my binoculars.

"I'm pretty sure I've got room for you," June told him.

Cam turned to look at the swans again, but not before I saw the smile on *his* face.

With or without Cam, it would be a long while before June recovered from this, I realized all over again a few days later as I packed up to go. Ben, Lisa, and Nalini had already left the day before and we had waved Cam off this morning.

Megan had demanded and received time off work. She had planned on staying with her mother for a few days but June had insisted she was fine, and she wouldn't hear of Megan wasting her holiday moping around Holbrook. She then practically forced her into booking a hotel in Jasper for a few days, saying that Megan obviously needed a holiday, if the bags under her eyes were any indication, and wouldn't the mountain air be nice and refreshing. Megan took the hint and offered to run Kelt and me back to Calgary before she headed into the mountains.

I was glad she had. I certainly couldn't manage a car right now and Kelt's concussion had put the nix on his driving.

June was in my room, helping me stuff things in my bag. Guido the cat was burrowed deeply under the blankets on my bed, staring out suspiciously at the activity.

June looked bad. Her face was still pale, and her eyes had lost some of their life. Even her hair looked dull. I stopped and put my hand on her shoulder.

"Are you going to be okay?" I asked her in a low voice.

She looked up at me and smiled. A valiant effort. "I've been through worse," she said quietly. "I'll get past it."

"I could stay on if it would help."

She cut me off with a smile and a shake of her head. "I'll be fine, Robyn. The birders are coming in force in a couple of days. And, besides, you'll be starting physio soon. You need to look after yourself."

"If you need me, I'll stay. It won't kill me to wait another week for physio."

June smiled again. "I know, and thank you for that, but I'll be all right."

I still couldn't believe that I had suspected her of such horrible acts—especially after she confided in me the reason for her late-night tears. Apparently, entering into a relationship with another man after so many years had brought back a lot of the hurt and sense of abandonment she had felt at Eddie's death. It had been, she said softly, something of a surprise to discover that she hadn't worked through it all years ago. I didn't tell her that I already knew about her crying at night, and I certainly didn't breathe a word about the spin I had put on it.

There had been an explanation for her late-night jaunt to the

DeSantis house, too. She hadn't known about DeSantis's connection with the Norsicol plant. Yes, he'd been in charge of safety and maintenance when Eddie had died, but it had taken June well over a year to recover from her grief enough to start questioning her husband's death. By that time, Grant DeSantis had been long gone, replaced by a steady stream of transient, often unscrupulous supervisors. And then I came along and started shoving my nose into things. June had gone out that night to think. About Eddie. About DeSantis. About the murders of his wife and son, and about the ashy taste of retribution. Given her thoughts, it was natural that she would have ended up in front of his house.

Both innocent explanations. Both fitting in with June's personality far better than anything I had come up with. It was obvious, despite my recent collaboration with Kelt, that I still had a great deal to learn about trust.

"All set, Robyn?" Megan poked her head in the door.

"Just about." I stuffed the last shirt in the bag and June zipped it up for me. I turned to her.

"June—" I began, not really knowing what to say.

She hugged me hard. "I'll see you soon."

We walked out to the car. Everybody else was already loaded in. Megan helped June settle Guido's cat carrier in the back seat. Guido yowled a few times to let me know he didn't much like road trips. He'd probably keep it up all the way home.

His leg was coming along nicely, and unlike me, he wouldn't have a limp when all was healed and done. An anonymous benefactor had paid the vet's bill, or so Dr. Kimmins had informed me. I had a good idea who this mysterious person was and I was pleased that he'd thought of it without my asking. Pleased, but not quite ready to forgive and forget.

I'd had a quiet word with Gary about the harassment situation, and on his advice, I'd filed a complaint against Howard. The prank phone calls, even the rock through the window was one thing, but shooting a rifle at June's house (and my cat!) bumped it up to an entirely different level. An unacceptable level. Howard Miller needed psychiatric care, and the only way to ensure he got it was to press charges. In the end, it might be the best thing that ever happened to him.

I turned now and hugged June again.

"Thank you, Robyn," she whispered.

I didn't know what exactly she was thanking me for, but I hugged her back as tightly as I could.

We drove off waving and honking the horn. As we pulled away, I noticed an oddly shaped bundle in the back. Something small and chubby and wrapped in a blanket. I smiled wryly. Apparently one of June's gnomes was going to Jasper. I smiled a little wider as I thought about it. Thought about the little guy posing by the Jasper Park Lodge or perhaps rappeling down Maligne Canyon. It would make June laugh, I decided. And remembering the forlorn figure waving us off, I knew she needed a good laugh.

"You okay?" Kelt asked quietly, reaching over and catching up my hand.

I looked over at him. His green eyes were warm and understanding. And honest. That above all else. There would never be dark secrets here. No betrayals. With Kelt, what you saw was pretty much what you got. I liked what I saw. A lot. And when I got these damn casts off, I intended to do something about it.

For now, I contented myself with squeezing his hand.

"I'm okay," I told him.

AUTHOR'S NOTE

THE RED HERON is a blend of fact and fiction. The characters are, of course, fictitious as is the town of Holbrook, but Beaverhill Lake is a real place (and an absolute must-see for readers of the bird-watching persuasion). Fortunately, Beaverhill Lake is not in any danger from a contaminated industrial site. Norsicol is purely a product of my imagination; I wish I could say the pesticides were, as well.

The effects of chemical pesticides are well documented. However, in recent years, we've become rather complacent about pesticides, perhaps because so many of the more notorious ones have been banned or strictly regulated. That doesn't mean we're not using them anymore. In 1993, 1.1 billion pounds of active pesticide ingredients were used in the United States alone. That's roughly four pounds per person in a single year—a profoundly scary thought when you realize the toxic dosage for a human may be as low as one *millionth* of a pound.

Why we're still using these chemicals is a complicated question. For those wishing to explore this further, I refer you to Mark L. Winston's excellent book, *Nature Wars*. According to Winston, our pest-management battles have escalated into a war on nature. I would take this further and say that much of our way of life seems to be part of that conflict—with Robyn, and her real-life counterparts, as the Red Cross. But, as in any war, the sides are not always clearly drawn. I hope *The Red Heron* is a reflection of this.